The Science Fiction Tarot

ANTHOLOGY

Edited by Brandon Butler

The Science Fiction Tarot:
Luminous Symbols of All the Tomorrows to Come

Cover Illustration and Book Design by Louis Rivera © 2023
All Interior Illustrations by Marco Marin © 2023

All stories in this anthology are original publications with the following exceptions:

"Rocket Man" originally appeared in Interzone, February 2020

"Master Brahms" originally appeared in Apex, November 2018

"Soul Candy" originally appeared in The Pitkin Review, Fall 2016

"As Able the Air" originally appeared in Writers of the Future, Volume #36, April 2020

Published by Brandon Butler in association with TDotSpec Inc.

TDOTSPEC

ACKNOWLEDGEMENTS

This anthology was the result of the best people putting in their best. So many individuals gave over time, money and effort in order to make this happen (including you!), and none of what's here would exist if not for them.

First and foremost of those involved would absolutely be Andy Dibble, the man who put the 'Science Fiction' in 'The Science Fiction Tarot'. His efforts were critical in refining the concept, spreading the word and raising interest and there could be no better partner in working on this than with him.

Illustration and cover work was done by Marco Marin and Louis Rivera. You'll see Marco shine throughout this volume before every story, and his ongoing work throughout the months kept enthusiasm high for what we were doing. Meanwhile Louis kept aesthetics at the highest level as we created the card rewards for the project, as well as handing over one killer cover design.

Our submissions editors worked tirelessly on this volume. Don Miasek, Steven Kim and Andy put in a consistent and tremendous amount of work against an extremely high volume of submissions, and hats absolutely go off to Michelle, Evan, Shivani, Wayne, Nujhat, Martin and David as well. If not for every one of them, we would have made precisely zero deadlines.

Copyediting was done by the incredible work of Justin Dill, Julia Wong, Andy, and Lloyd Penny, the current editor-in-chief of Amazing Stories. Each of these individuals came in as the project was nearing its completion stages and made sure we didn't fall one step back. Thanks so much guys; every moment you spent on this was appreciated.

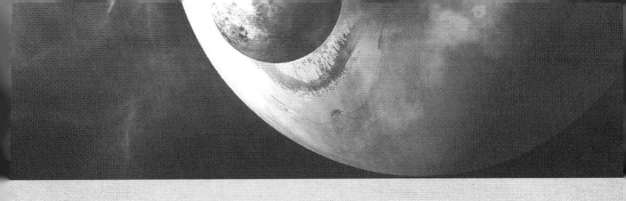

I'd also like to call out the many names of people who helped out in the advertising phase of this. Whether it was putting out advertisements, tweeting our progress or putting together launch parties. Thanks to Kristina, Michelle and Don for heading out and distributing cards cleverly designed by Peter Reynolds. And thanks so much to our Kickstarter backers, and those who chose to boost our signal when we were getting the word out -- people such as Polar Borealis's Graeme Cameron, Bad Dream Entertainment's Brett Reistroffer, Dreamforge Magazine's Scot Noel and Third Flatiron's Julianne Rew. And let's not forget Angelique Fawns and Stuart Conover over at The Horror Tree for lending an ear to our project during the submissions period.

And, of course, my esteemed thanks to old friends who are second to none, Steven Saville and Ken Liu for giving a shout over the many social medias. Here's to both of you and this crazy business we call writing.

Last but the opposite of least of all, thanks are to be had to TDotSpec main editor David F. Schultz and the Toronto Science Fiction Fantasy Writing Group and community. All this was made in many ways by tapping in to David's expertise on the trials and tribulations of honest work, and company of speculative authors and screenwriters and just plain readers he's founded is second to none.

Drop by sometime, if you're in the town. There's no telling what you'll find.

The Science Fiction Tarot Team

Lead Editor
Brandon Butler

Managing Editors
Andy Dibble
David F. Shultz

Illustrations
Marco Marin

Cover & Book Design
Louis Rivera

Submissions Editors
David F. Shultz   Don Miasek   Evan Hale
Martin Munks   Nujhat Tabassum   Shivani Kamdar
Steven Kim   Wayne Cusack   Y. M Pang

Copy Editors
Andy Dibble
Julia Wang
Justin Dill
Lloyd Penney

Advertising & Volunteer Work
Don Miasek
Peter G. Reynolds
Y. M Pang
Kristina Dudumas

Kickstarter Contributors

Alistair Kennedy   Bryan Dawe   Caitlin Colbert

Caitlin Jane Hughes   Campbell Royales   Cathy Green

Cerise Cauthron   Chris Griffin   Cora

Dave Foster   David F. Schultz   Davin Butt

Don   Douglas   Emile Jones

Gee Bedsole   George   gesina

Giusy Rippa   Heather McGuire   Jeannie

Jocelyn Tuohy   Jonah Moses   Juli Rew

Kasey Sergeant   Kristina Dudumas   Kyana

Kyle   Larissa Fernandes Santos   Laura Elmendorf

Lisa   Marco Marin   Marcus Evenstar

Marty Hoefkes   Matthew Midgley   Michael Feir

Michael Nikitin   Morgan Koler   Nicholas Stephenson

Nicole Lalumiere-Weaving   Nikki Lam   Paul Hart

Rahul Bhagat   Raine Anakanu   Randal Heide

Rio Murphy   Robert Brown   Sarah Miskiman

Scot M Noel   Spencer Guthro   Shereen Deal

shimacruel   Steve Krespel   Suemedha Sood

Suzanne Barcza   Tai Rui Tong   Tara Smith-Blass

The Creative Fun by Backerkit   Valarie Andrews

Vitaly Gann   Wyatt Lamoureaux   Y.M Pang

INTRODUCTION
Brandon Butler

Honestly? I don't know anything about Tarot.

Or, at least I didn't. Everything began on a Zoom call. At a time when everything that was anything happened on Zoom. I only vaguely remember the moment: someone mentioned that they'd started reading Tarot. Or maybe they said they wanted to read Tarot, or knew someone who did. I reached over my desk and jotted down a note: 'A Tarot Deck for a New Generation', and conversation continued.

Two years later, here we are.

So, 'what is this anyway?', you might ask. Is it the same as a regular tarot deck? Does it represent the original cards? Can you use them to read the future?

Well, no, not really, and… maybe? We'll see. A traditional tarot is split into what we call major and minor arcana. Major Arcana are 22 archetypical cards that represent or symbolize some aspect of life. 'The Wheel of Fortune' depicts destiny and luck. 'Death' represents change. 'Strength' represents… what it says on the tin.

We've gone ahead and created our own major arcana, choosing stories on 22 subjects to represent Science Fiction. 'Utopia', 'Time Travel', 'The Space Whale', and other subjects that may or may not be associated with Star Trek IV.

As for the minor arcana, that runs more like a regular set of cards: 4 suits, cards 1-10 plus 4 'court cards' each. Our anthology doesn't delve into that end of the deck, but we did roughly outline what that might look like, coming up with the suits of Aliens, Robots, Blasters and Cruisers. We even drew up a set of illustrations for some of their court cards, which you can find at the end of this book.

And that's our concept. Authors were encouraged to come up with their own card ideas, although we provided our own suggestions where necessary. And we received nearly five hundred submissions from around the world: Canada, the US, the UK, Czechia, France, Ireland, Estonia, Italy, Japan, Pakistan, India, Indonesia, and Australia, just to name a few.

It's been an incredible experience and privilege for all of the editors, authors and volunteers to put this work into your hands. Thanks for giving it a read.

So, ready? All right: let's shuffle that deck, and see what future the stars foretell.

—Brandon

Contents

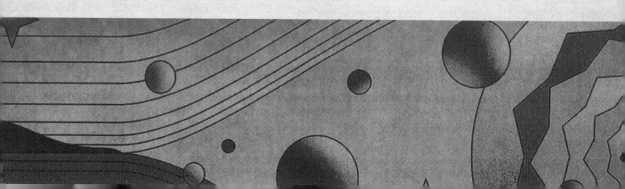

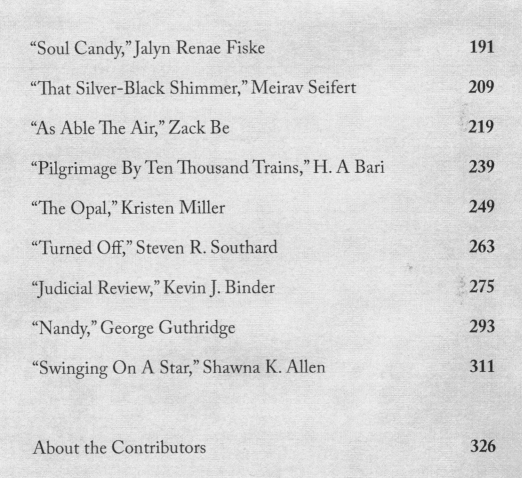

~0~
ALTERNATE HISTORY

ROCKET MAN
Louis Evans

Each night I dream of Moscow, bombsight nose cone dreams.

These dreams have no plot and no logic. The city is a plum, a windswept field, a stag's heart. It is an emerald, a green onion, an open mouth.

And me? I am a secant. An abscess. A segment of an orange. Coal-furnace tongs. A flaw.

In the instant before I wake, sweating, heaving, I am the first gasp of the inferno.

§

Top Secret
STRATEGIC MISSILE EVALUATION COMMITTEE

TO: Hon. Trevor Gardner, Assistant Secretary, U.S. Air Force Brig. Gen. Bernard Schriever, Assistant for Development Planning, U.S. Air Force

FROM: John von Neumann
Simon Ramo
Dean Woolbridge

Gentlemen:

This Committee was established to evaluate long-range nuclear weapons delivery systems, chiefly but not exclusively long-range missile systems, and to determine if any such system might contribute to the defense of the United States against her enemies and ensure her success in the event of a nuclear conflict.

The primary obstacle for any such weapons systems is the turbulence zone of the Earth's upper atmosphere. This zone was poorly understood until the past decade, but it is now generally accepted that no known automatic guidance system, whether mechanical or electrical, will function effectively at altitudes above sixty miles.

The research of this committee has been unable to discover any promising prospects for such an unmanned guidance system. An unmanned long-range nuclear missile cannot be constructed.
We propose, therefore, the development of a manned long-range nuclear strike rocket, which—

§

The simplest principle for guidance is the law of inertia.
  Otherwise things grow more complicated.

§

—with this attack profile, survival for the rocket's pilot will be impossible. However, given the experience with Japanese kamikazes in the Second World War, it is clear that a suitable cohort of pilots, properly trained and indoctrinated, may be relied upon to carry out such a mission. Our recommendation—

§

There is nothing for anyone to do on a rocket base in peacetime, and for rocket men there is less than nothing. We sit and we wait for the end of the world.

  If the red phone rings—it is white, bleach white, bone white, but the name persists—then we will all climb out of our beds and get into rows and go to our deaths. Otherwise we sit and wait.

  The Air Force knows that this is not the best past-time for men who must remain in peak condition in the event that they are called upon to climb into rockets, navigate those rockets into the stratosphere, and then steer them hurtling downwards into large Communist metropolises in order to scourge them with nuclear fire. So the Air Force occupies our time with daily drills and loyalty questionnaires and exercise and regular meals and outdated movies and mandatory pickup basketball games. In this way Uncle Sam lays claim to twelve of our twenty-four hours.

  However, it turns out that twelve hours a day is plenty of time to go crazy in.

  Capt. Johnson spends six of his remaining twelve hours in the gym. He is able to lift a large table or a small safe over his head and toss it as easily as I can toss a basketball. He is aided in this pursuit by an illicit stream of anabolic steroids, which a corrupt corporal smuggles to him.

Capt. O'Connell, Johnson's bunkmate, has developed a recreational addiction to the amphetamines that the Air Force makes available to us, in the unlikely event that we get a little drowsy while flying a nuclear missile for twenty minutes to the end of the world. When he is under the influence of this substance, he enjoys wood-carving. He can turn an old spoon or fallen branch into a duck faster than you can believe. He only ever carves ducks.

Capt. Wilson is a fanatical masturbator. Though a certain volume of pornography is available through the base's black market, the only aid upon which Capt. Wilson relies is his stash of back issues of Life Magazine. The state that Capt. Wilson leaves these issues in beggars the imagination.

And me?

§

A checklist is a sequence of necessities. It is a collection of many questions and one answer: go. Or no go. It is the moon, ten minutes before new: a world of darkness and a thin terminator of light.

Here is one checklist:

```
T - 10:00   FUEL CELL REACTION VALVES - LATCH
T - 8:30    2ND COOL LOOP PUMP - OFF (verify)
T - 4:10    REENTRY VEHICLE ENGINE LIGHTS - ON
T - 2:15    MISSILE LAUNCH OPERATIONS COMM CHECK
T - 0:45    GYRO DISPLAY COUPLER ALIGN -
            R=90+AZ, P=90, Y=0
T - 0:09    IGNITION COMMAND
T - 0:00    LIFTOFF
```

```
Here is another checklist:

1. Are you now, or have you ever been, a member of the Communist
   party?
   ☐ Yes ☐ No

2. Are you now, or have you ever been, a member of any group
   dedicated to pacifism, nonviolence, or denuclearization?
```

```
   □ Yes □ No

3. Do you have any family members who presently live in the USSR
   or any other Communist state?
   □ Yes □ No

4. Do you have any friends who presently live in the USSR or any
   other Communist state?
   □ Yes □ No

5. Do you have any ancestral connection to any place, city, or
   region presently located within the USSR or any other Communist
   state?
   □ Yes □ No

6. Have you ever visited the USSR or any other Communist state for
   any purpose?
   □ Yes □ No

7. Do you for any reason hold warm feelings toward any person,
   place, or thing that is or has ever been within the USSR or any
   other Communist state?
   □ Yes □ No
```

And so on.

Everyone knows what a checklist is supposed to say. Everyone knows what a checklist is supposed to do.

And yet, unbeknownst to all, at the heart of every checklist is a lacuna, an absence. A small silent question, implicit and unanswered. A space for free will.

§

On a rocket base, everyone goes crazy, rocket men most of all. Except for me.

I don't go crazy. I don't go crazy for a single, simple reason. I have a mission, a secret mission.

Nobody has given it to me and thus nobody can take it away.

My mission is this: I am going to miss.

§

The air is a beautiful thing. I have loved it for a long time, since well before my pilot days. I flew kites as a child, kites and balsa-wood models with wind-up propellers and paper airplanes. I loved the paper airplanes most of all.

With paper airplanes if you crease the wings in secret and throw them just right, they will pause at the peak of their path and just float. And then they begin to turn.

The way a nuclear missile can miss is nothing like this.

§

I will not hit Moscow and I refuse to miss only to crash into Leningrad or Stockholm or even the Russian hinterland. The warhead has altitude fuses and pressure fuses and if I land anywhere it will detonate. I will not take the risk. I will not trade many lives for few. I will trade many lives for one.

I am going to miss because I am going to skip.

The air is a beautiful thing, and from space it is just like the surface of a pond. The nose cone, pointed up, is a smooth stone.

I skipped my allotted portion of stones as a child, and if they send me out to end the world, I will skip one more, just one. I will turn belly-up and burn my rockets at the wrong moment, and I will skip right through the thin ribbons of aurora and out into the black.

Then I will die, of course.

§

This is my mission and it keeps me sane while I am awake.

It does not seem to do much for the dreams. Every night I dream of Moscow, plotless overpressure bombsight dreams.

Well. Almost every night.

§

I wake in the middle of the night from nameless dreams to the sound of sirens.

"Oh." I think. "This is it." I dress. I am hurried to my rocket. The drills are always orderly but this is pure distillate of chaos. Screaming men hurtle past me. I do not know their faces.

I board the rocket. I strap down. I run through the checklist. Launch control has a voice thick with tears.

The launch is like doing a belly flop from a skyscraper right onto the pavement below. The launch is like forgetting to breathe.

"This is it," I think. Pitch. Yaw. Roll.

Up and out. The turbulence of the ionosphere comes upon me. The rocket turns itself off. I turn it on again.

I can only see the barest slit of sky through the windows, above the controls. A curling ribbon of aurora drifts by and is lost.

It is very cold. My fingers go numb; so do my toes. That's good. Better to freeze than to suffocate. And both are better than burning. I am ready to miss.

I am ready to miss and so I do, performing the maneuver flawlessly. As though I had drilled on it for months and years in public, not merely in the shadow theater of the mind. I am ready to miss and so I roll, belly-up, and I fire the rockets, and I burn. And there I go, skipping out into the black.

I have not really prepared for this part, the suffocating over several hours. I try to think of the Muscovites I have saved, but I find the images do little for me. It is too easy for the mind's eye to drift over the earth, to the targets of my fellow U.S. rocket men, Leningrad and Stalingrad and Kiev, to the Russian missiles that will undoubtedly be landing on New York and Washington and Los Angeles, to—

So I don't think about it and instead try to whistle, a quiet little tuneless tune to draw down my last breaths.

It's about then that I hear the voices.

"Get him the hell out of there," they say, and then the hatch on my capsule opens and outside are a collection of officers wearing a collection of frowns. I have made myself very unpopular.

I am allowed to see my advocate before the court martial. He explains that this simulated attack, this loyalty pop quiz, is a new innovation, cooked up by the CIA to ferret out a suspected Russian mole. He explains to me that I am that mole.

"No," I say. "I just wanted to miss."

We do not reach a meeting of the minds on this point.

My advocate argues his theory of the case and I argue mine, but neither of us make much headway. I am found guilty of treason and cowardice and sentenced to death by firing squad.

They offer me a last cigarette but I decline. Rocket men don't smoke and so I had to quit long ago.

I am standing before a brick wall. I am blindfolded.

I am taking one calm, easy breath after another.

When a gun fires it sounds like the end of the world. And when it hits you, it is.

Then I wake up.

§

The simplest principle for guidance is the law of inertia.

§

What really happens is nothing happens. I am a rocket man for a long time and then I'm out. The world doesn't end and neither does the program. There are new rocket men after me and they go crazy in new and fashionable ways.

Me, I leave the air force and I start driving a truck. Sometimes I think about how I'm headed on a thousand-mile cruise mission, me in the capsule and my heavy craft behind me, but mostly I don't think about that. I get a trucker tan and a trucker paunch and a trucker hat.

Also I start writing. Short stories, poems. I keep a tape recorder and a typewriter in the passenger seat. When I'm driving I say what I'm thinking, and at night I type up the good bits. I submit to magazines in Los Angeles and San Francisco and Boston and Portland and St. Louis. The replies miss me over and over, mail following me across the country in the U.S. Postal Service's red-white-and-blue truck-missiles. Skipping across the map like stones on a pond. They are rejections.

A year, two, three. I was told that the dreams would stop but they don't. So one day I get out the notebook and I start writing. "Every night I dream of Moscow, bombsight nose cone dreams…"

And so on.

This story I submit to a prestigious New York magazine and what the hell they want it. The contract finds me within days; the mail is right on target.

Out comes my little story and, what do you know, it makes a splash. When we went up in the training rockets, we would come down in the sea, splash, and so I know about splashes. It is not about the prose, not really. The country is ready to have an argument about the rocket men, and so my story is the word that gets the whole room talking.

I am visited in a truck stop diner by two of Mr. Hoover's FBI men. They do not accept my offer of french fries and instead tell me that Uncle Sam is not that happy with the story I wrote and my decision to publish it like a gutless Commie spy rather than burning it with my lighter. I say tough tits. It turns out the FBI have nothing on me and so they leave.

Then I get a series of calls from editors, agents, publishers, journalists. They are not as able to travel as Mr. Hoover's boys, but they are just as eager to get a hold of me. "Can you write—" "Do you have—" "An interview with—"

A few years back Andy Warhol said that in the future everyone would be famous for fifteen minutes, and where does a rocket man live but the future?

I do newspaper interviews and radio shows and I go on television. The FBI men sit in the audience and they stare, but they don't say anything about me and so I don't say anything about them. I talk about becoming a rocket man. I talk about the dreams. Everything else is classified. I write more stories and they sell, but only the ones about rocket men get talked about. That's fine.

Eventually I have a book coming out. For this I am expected to travel around the country making appearances and promoting its release. Apparently some authors are picky about this sort of travel—cheap, frequent, unpleasant—but I am a trucker; this is very ordinary. More unusual is appearing in bookstores. More unusual is standing up to speak and finding that five or ten or thirty people are listening, in silence, that some of them are actually taking notes. Such regard is disconcerting.

In this way the eventual hecklers come as a relief. They wear air force patches or American flag hats and they interrupt. They call me a traitor and a spy and a coward. They shout and rage and have to be removed by bookstore employees, a contest that does not always favor the bookstore. I find their presence, their hatred, bracing.

Until one day a man stands up as I am reading an excerpt and says "fuck you!" and I realize it is Capt. O'Connell, of the amphetamines and wooden ducks.

I fall silent. He stares at me. I never understand a man's intentions in his eyes.

His hand dips into his jacket and then whips out. My lips are forming the word "gun." They should be forming the word "duck."

Capt. O'Connell, it turns out, can throw a carved wooden duck with remarkable speed and accuracy. It glides over the audience and hurtles towards my forehead. I wonder if that wooden duck thinks about my cranium the way I once thought about Moscow.

In the moment of impact there is behind my eyes a flash of light.

Then I wake up.

§

In a supercritical mass, fission, once begun, will proceed at an increasing rate.

§

Night after night I dream of Moscow, burning, and day by day I eat, I work, I lie, I hide my mission and then, one lunch, tin spoon halfway between plate and mouth, I snap. I am placing my spoon neatly down on my tray. I am stepping onto the chair, up onto the table. My boots are scattering trays and plates. People are beginning to rise, confused, disgruntled.

I stand in the middle of the table and I say, "I am a rocket man, and I am going to miss." Everyone is talking over me and so I shout it.

The silence when they understand my meaning is the silence of the shadows the bomb left on the walls of Hiroshima and Nagasaki. Nobody speaks or moves. Spoons and forks pause halfway through their trajectories and they hang for an endless instant. Everyone is looking up at me and I am looking down at them from the top of a parabolic arc.

Then Capt. Wilson climbs up onto his table. "I will also miss," he says. And Capt. Johnson, and O'Connell, and Janowicz, and Hiller, and—

Pandemonium in the mess hall. Someone, I think it is me, begins chanting: "Miss. Miss. Miss! Miss!" And the tide sweeps across the room and crashes off one wall and another, forcing the word out of every throat, the enlisted men pounding on the tables, flipping them, howling.

Eventually the military police arrive, square men in white helmets, batons at the ready. "Miss! Miss! Miss!" and we do not resist as they take us into custody.

It is my first time in the stockade, but in my heart there plays the ultrasonic song of the uncaged bird, because from lockup they will not summon me to the rocket, no matter what happens. MP sergeants and CIA spooks and generals and shrinks come to berate us, interrogate us, browbeat us, and we sit on our benches, two to a cell, and chant: "Miss. Miss. Miss."

This goes on for days, but then, there is nothing to do on a rocket base anyway. Capt. Johnson performs clap pushups by the hundreds and when the lights go out it happens that Capt. Wilson no longer requires the erotic ministrations of his beloved Life magazine in order to achieve, as it were, seminal liftoff. Good for him.

It is clear that the generals and so forth would prefer to come up with something truly medieval and do it to all of us, but on the other hand, there are only so many rocket men in America, and if a few dozen of them were taken out of circulation, Comrade Brezhnev might start feeling his oats. So we are at an impasse.

And then the news reaches us: we are not alone. At the other USAF rocket bases the same thing has happened—and, impossibly, miraculously, the wave has also spread to the USSR. I do not know the Russian word for "miss," but I suppose I will have to learn.

So suddenly the boot is on the other foot. We are now wheedled, cajoled, enticed. It does not matter. We are obdurate in our demands. "Miss. Miss. Miss."

The Americans and the Soviets meet about the problem. They keep us from meeting. The separation does not daunt us; what would we say to each other? Only this: "Miss. Miss. Miss."

Resolution is fast and clean and pure. A treaty is signed. An amnesty is issued. The rocket men disappear and so do their rockets. On the day they let us out of the stockade, we march past the skeleton of my rocket. They have cracked open its skull and taken its teeth and bones away for scrap.

As a result of the amnesty, I end up with an honorable discharge, and then I am immediately recruited into another department of the air force. There is a new interest in the civilian uses of rocketry. Telecommunications, science, navigation. Automatic satellites can function perfectly well in deep space, but only manned rockets can put them there. My skills are too valuable to cast aside.

Soon enough I'm going up every other week. I have a partner, a Lt. Nicholson. I fly the rocket; he operates the claw arm that throws the satellites into space. In college I drove a moving van at the beginnings and ends of semesters; it is a lot like that.

One mission we're up there and we've finished deploying a baker's dozen satellites and we're ready to come back home. "Ready to come back home," I say, into my microphone. Then my hands move over the controls. Pitch, yaw, roll, burn. I have done this countless times.

It is perhaps a minute or two or three before anyone realizes it is the wrong maneuver. There are voices in my headphones—ground control, and Lt. Nicholson. "Your angle's wrong—Captain, what's happening—what the hell—"

My hands know what they are doing.

They are trying to skip.

Now we're plunging downwards, nose up, headed into the elastic bosom of the stratosphere, headed towards a bounce that will send us out into deep space. There are zero more days of food and zero more days of water and perhaps another twenty-four hours of air. Lt. Nicholson is shaking my shoulders, and I want to give him the yoke, but he is not flight certified.

"You're going to miss!" he is screaming in my ear.

Down we go and the ribbons of aurora shimmer past us like the hair of a lover as they rise from your bed. Down we go, belly into the thing, and just when I see our altitude level and begin to climb, something inside me snaps back. I bring the nose straight down and we fall into the sky, into the turbulence zone that shakes our tin can like a baby god's rattle, into the plain and beautiful blue, and splashing down into the Gulf of Mexico.

For a stunt like this they will take away your pilot's license and they do. I walk around on the good earth and don't step foot in even a flight simulator. There's not a lot of money in my pocket and nowhere on the globe I am needed.

So of course I end up in Moscow.

The city is nothing like my dreams. It is just a place. I ride the metro through the darkness, a subcutaneous circle around the city. Taking orders from my travel book, I go to Gorky Park and watch an East German punk band shred the stage. At night I drink in expat bars. With the treaty there are more of us here than ever before.

Still it's ultimately a Russian woman I go home with, Yelena. One night, two. A week. She is a writer. Satirical poems and one-woman plays. We eat cheap pierogies and truly atrocious hot dogs from the first Howard Johnson's to open in Red Square. Eventually we sleep together.

Yelena is the first woman I've been with since the rocket base. When we make love I do not think of solid and liquid fuel, of booster stages, of thrust and yaw, of reentry. I am grateful for that.

Afterwards it's the middle of the night and I roll over in bed and there is an impossible brightness on the horizon, too bright for the eyes to bear, and I think, oh my God they did it anyway, hundreds of arrowhead bombers so much slower than my rocket but still with the same bitter fruit inside brighter than can be dreamed or borne and I wait for the overpressure and the light to take me to pieces—

Then I realize: it's just the sunrise.

And then: I wake up.

§

What happens, what really, truly happens, is—
    Every night I dream of Moscow.
    And over time, the dreams change.

~I~
THE CLONE

MASTER BRAHMS
Storm Humbert

"**K**night to E5," I said. "Takes pawn."

"Bishop, E5," Brahms said. "Takes knight."

My board was dwindling quickly, and my anger at such a one-sided defeat was increased whenever I looked up into Brahms' smug, synth face—my face.

"Master Brahms," Jill said from the hall.

As the house A.I., she always projected her voice as if just around a corner or down a hall, and it gave the illusion that a real person waited barely out of sight. Her words had the musical rise and fall of a lilt without the mispronunciations—an Irish girl speaking the King's. I often felt the desire to touch her upon hearing. The fact that I could not somehow made it sweeter, like the sour smell at the heart of good perfume.

Brahms and I looked toward the doorway, as if she spoke to each of us alone, then shared a grin at the all-too-common occurrence. I imagined a small sadness in his, however—a momentary reminder that he was a synth. I was as sad for him as he was for himself.

"Yes, Jill," we said in unison. We shot mirrored glances at each other, mixtures of confusion and annoyance.

"If you, in all of your capacities, could come to the solarium, there is something that requires your attention," Jill said.

In all of your capacities was Jill's gentle way of saying "you and all of your clones" without reminding any present that they were such. It was a deft way of referring to them, and I was glad she'd come up with it.

Dr. Welkie always said that the key to synth happiness was allowing the illusion of originality as much as possible.

It was in this knowledge that I'd taken such pains—from private wings of the manor to identical wardrobes and much more—to insulate my synths from this realization at all times. The illusion was so complete that I myself had felt the emptiness of doubt from time to time—the feeling that everything I remembered, wanted, loved, or hated was false, a duplicate program that rendered me something less than a person—but it was worth it. I loved my synths as much as I loved myself, after all.

Brahms and I nodded to each other and stood to leave.

"Jill, you can clean the board," Brahms said. "We're done."

"The hell we are," I said.

"Checkmate in six." He loomed behind his chair, inviting me to inspect the board, even though he knew I couldn't divine the sequence.

"Six, you say?"

He nodded.

"Then sit, let's play it out."

He shrugged and obliged, which was good because I was almost angry enough at his arrogance to have ordered him. Synths were fully sovereign individuals under the law, with one exception: they had no rights or legal personage when it came to a conflict with their original—in this case, me. Though I would never have actually done such a thing, of course.

So, we played the next six moves and were on our way to the solarium. I walked in front to avoid Brahms's shit-eating grin. When we arrived, the door was locked.

"Jill, open," I said.

"Denied, Master Brahms."

"What?"

"I am awaiting the rest of the party," she said.

Her politeness was sometimes an obstacle. Minutes passed in impatient silence, but eventually, four other Brahmses filed in through the door from the east wing. Brahms and I shot them what I assume were identical looks to the effect of "what took you so long?"

"Sorry," the front Brahms said. "We were finishing a set of doubles."

"I take it Brahms won," my chess partner said.

"The bastard always does," said another.

I rolled my eyes. Clearly our wit knew no bounds.

"Was Brahms with you?" I said. We were still one short.

"No, we figured he was with you."

"He's probably already in there reading."

That's where I'd have been if left alone. Odd numbers did tend to leave one of us out of many activities. Sometimes I wished I'd opted for eight, or even ten, of us, but other times I enjoyed being the odd man out—having some Brahms time. I assumed they all felt likewise.

"Jill, open," I said again.

"Of course, sir."

The doors opened, and we filed into the solarium. It was my favorite place on the property, and I assumed the others' as well. It was high ceilinged with large bay windows under Romanesque arches that faced west to make evening and twilight reading as it should be. Even in house shoes or slippers, one's feet clicked against the marble tile, and the clicks rang up and up, as if trying to escape through the ceiling. The air was fresh, thin, and drafty, as it should be in all truly old buildings, and bookcases lined the walls, flanked above and below by the thin metal tracks of sliding ladders used to reach the top shelves. And in the middle of it all, on the other side of the antique reading chair, lay Brahms, sprawled across the floor in a pool of his own blood.

Some of me ran to him while the rest stood frozen by my side. There was nothing to be done, we all knew, but I appreciated those who rushed to his aid. They were brave and strong and reminded the rest of us that we were as well, just not right then. The skull was mostly ruined in the back and top, and he lay as if tipped from the chair still sitting. I did not move to look at his face—my face—not because I feared its destruction, but because I feared its survival. I did not want to peer into my own dead eyes.

He'd been reading one of our favorites, *A Tale of Two Cities*, and it lay curled mostly under him, still open. My mind in those moments was indescribable—to look at one's own dead body, to know that's how I'd look if I died in that place and in so grizzly a fashion.

"Jill," Brahms whispered. "What happened?"

"Master Brahms killed Master Brahms," she said.

Suicide. The realization took something out of me—poured out some deep truth now shown for a lie. If the strength and courage of these others was within me, so too was the capacity for this sort of self-destruction.

"When did this happen?" Brahms said.

"Some time ago, sir."

"What? Why weren't we called right away?" another said.

"Master Brahms instructed me to wait."

"Where is his gun, Jill, and how did he get one?" a Brahms kneeling by the body asked.

"I do not know where Master Brahms acquired the firearm," Jill said, "but he took it with him when he left."

I thought I might be sick. As hollow as the prospect of suicide was, this was far darker. Brutality almost two-fold as grotesque because in the murder of a clone lay a trace of suicide as well. Had I been less shocked, I might have looked around and tried to observe which of us seemed already aware of our depravity. But all I could do was breathe and ponder the fact that even though I knew it was not my finger that had pulled the trigger, I was the killer and the killer was I.

"Who did this?" my chess partner bellowed. "Which one of you was it?"

"As if the culprit's just going to come out with it," I said. My tone still held a trace of venom from losing at chess. I was, at my core, a sore loser. We all were. "Jill, who killed Master Brahms?"

"Master Brahms killed—"

"Which Master Brahms killed Master Brahms?" one of the others cut in with an added glance at me as if I were stupid.

"There is only one Master Brahms," Jill said, oddly robotic.

We all glanced at each other.

Then, one of the Brahmses beside me stepped to the front, put his hands on the reading chair Brahms had apparently been sitting in when he'd been shot, and said, "Jill, as Prime Master Brahms, I order you to forego politeness and identify which of my synths here present killed the one lying dead."

"There is no Prime Master Brahms," Jill said in her more robotic tone again. "There is only Master Brahms."

Brahms was crushed. I could see the light in his eyes turn inward. He examined himself as if he were an alien thing to be understood anew. It was a painful confusion written on my face that was not my face. It was as if he stood in a lone light beam on the darkling plain, the void encroaching from all sides.

"I'm sorry to do this," I said to the poor fellow by the chair. "Jill, this is Brahms-dash-original, and I order you to forego politeness and identify which of my synthetics has killed the one lying dead."

"There is only Master Brahms," Jill replied, still in her less female more robotic voice.

Each Brahms appealed to her as the original, each believed it to be true, and each met the same retort. I felt as if I were watching the scene from outside myself. I couldn't make sense of where I was or what I was doing—that there was an "I" at all. The room and all the Brahmses inside appeared to me as shimmers, wiggles, and flittings of reality at the periphery of my vision that may have been real or imagined. Voices came as if underwater, and I felt as though I might fall to pieces—simply stop being—but then my voice from another's mouth brought the world crashing back.

"Jill, have you been compromised?" a Brahms said as he walked away from the door toward the center of the room. "Have any of your primary action functions or operation capabilities been altered recently?"

"Yes, by Master Brahms."

He nodded and smiled as if trying to charm Jill through her camera.

"And I don't suppose you could ignore some of Master Brahms's instructions? Be a lamb and unlock that door?"

"I'm sorry, sir," she said like a polite lady turning down a dance at a party, "but I must follow Master Brahms's instructions."

"As I suspected," he said. "Thank you, Jill. That will be all."

"My pleasure. Ring if you need anything."

Compromised? Yes. I felt myself again. Of course Jill had been compromised. How else could she have failed to acknowledge me as the original? My skin felt like my own again. In fact, the news seemed to have cheered the whole room.

"What now?" I said.

"Well, first we should determine who is the original," one Brahms said.

"Why?" my chess partner said. "What will that get us?"

"Well—"

"And even if it would get us something, how do you propose we do it?" He paused to let the room ponder, then resumed: "Without Jill to identify, we're left with the rippling pattern of the veins on the underside of each eye, and this is not only hard to identify with a certainty—though I have faith in all of us—but is impossible to check on oneself, which leaves room for lying."

I wanted to find out as much as the other Brahmses, to prove to myself that I was, in fact, the real Brahms, but an anxiety held my tongue. For the first time I could remember, I feared how such a test would go. I believed I was myself, but I did not know it for a fact. Plus, Brahms was right; it could neither be done, nor would it help.

"What's your genius idea then?" I said.

Brahms smiled. "Nothing. I suggest we do nothing."

"What?"

"Whichever of us did this had a reason," Brahms said. "He killed Brahms, left his body, and hijacked Jill to call a meeting and lock the door." He paused as he had above the chessboard, inviting examination. When nobody said anything, he sighed like an exasperated teacher with a dim student. "He wants something. We don't know what that something is, so we'll do nothing. Eventually, the culprit will try to push the game. He has to."

Nobody could see a flaw in the plan, so we seized upon doing nothing. We did nothing six-fold. We attacked doing nothing with vigor. We did nothing as nobody had ever done nothing before, but it did not last long. I was not a man built for nothing, and neither were my synths. I'd had myself duplicated mostly to make sure I would never be bored.

"We don't have it in us and he knows it," Brahms said after some hours.

"Who'd have thunk a man with the same mind as us would know our limits," I said. "A revolutionary idea."

"Quite," my chess partner said, unimpressed by my sarcasm.

"Well, not identical minds," another said.

"The differences are negligible—"

"What does it matter?" said a Brahms still by the body. "Is this quibble going to help us figure things out?"

"Do we even know what we're trying to figure out?" I said. "Are we after why he killed Brahms or why he's called us all here like this?"

"One would lead to the other," Brahms said.

"Not necessarily," said another. "In fact, taken on their own, not likely."

"Well, it seems that figuring out why we're here is most pressing," I said. "So, let's start with that."

All nodded.

"What has being brought here forced us to do?" Brahms said. "And what has it made us unable to do?"

"We stopped what we were doing," Brahms said

"We are currently unsure of which is the original," another said.

At that, all began talking at once, as if in an attempt to drown out that item on the list, as if to forget it, but then one Brahms stepped forward and raised his hands for quiet.

"We're missing the most obvious," he said. "We haven't been able to call the police, and I'm assuming Jill has been instructed not to either. That, or they're taking their sweet time."

"Well, obviously that," I said. "Of course a murderer wouldn't want the police called."

"But it's different for us," another Brahms said, stepping to the center beside the other. "Most Brahmses here are synths."

All were quiet while that reality settled in. Even if each of us considered himself to be the original, all were friends—no, closer than friends, closer even than brothers—and all were aware of precedent involving synths and murder. In some cases, if one synth were found guilty of murder, the lot of them for that individual could be killed, though the official word was "destroyed."

"Whoever did this, he was protecting us as much as himself," Brahms said. "We know one thing for certain: we cannot call the police. Do we all agree?"

I bobbed a vacant nod while others mumbled in the affirmative and still others begrudgingly agreed with eyes alone, but we all agreed. Before anyone could speak further, the solarium door clicked, and Jill's voice came over the speakers as if she were right outside.

"Greetings, Master Brahms," she said. "Dinner is ready. May I be of assistance?"

§

There was little talk at dinner. A discussion did occur as to whether the day's events were, indeed, murder or suicide. Most everyone ended up agreeing that it was murder and that calling it suicide was semantics, more a pun than anything else. Only one Brahms maintained that terming it a suicide was appropriate. He was either playing devil's advocate or the devil himself. Either way, he was regarded with suspicion for the remainder of the meal.

There were few activities after dessert, save my opponent from earlier in the day trouncing a few other Brahmses on the chessboard. This entertainment got old as quickly as one would expect, and we all retired early.

I considered double-bolting my door and blocking it with the heavy antique chest from the foot of my bed but decided against it. If the killer Brahms wanted to enter the room, he obviously could, since he had control of Jill. She could move all of the furniture and open all of the doors. She was the house and everything in it. This knowledge saved me the strain of moving the chest, but it did not help me sleep.

Even after I did finally manage to drift off, I do not think I was asleep for long before someone calling my name awakened me.

"Brahms," he whispered. "Brahms, can we talk?"

The impulse to whisper when waking another had never made sense to me. Why speak in a way designed against waking when the intention was to wake them? The whole thing seemed disingenuous. Like apologizing by saying, "I'm sorry you feel that way."

"What is it?" I said. I sat up and searched the dark room with tired, blurry eyes.

"Are you here to kill me?"

"Probably not, but I am the killer."

His tone was annoying—impudent—as if he expected me to be cowed by the statement. So, I resolved not to be.

"Aren't we all, in some shape or form?"

"In shape and form, yes," he said. "That is to say that we all look exactly alike, but I am the one who killed Brahms."

"I'm too tired for this." I waved a hand I was sure he could not see as if to dismiss him. I had not felt afraid, had felt quite comfortable in my sleepy aloofness, actually, but I was fully awake when I heard the footsteps move toward the bed. I rubbed my eyes to blot out the dark, as if seeing him would let me know which me he was. Then there was a metallic thump on the nightstand, and I nearly leapt from the bed.

"That's the gun," he said as he made his way back across the room. "You hold onto that and we'll talk."

"You just want my prints on it."

"We have the same prints," he laughed. "Lick it if you want. It's all the same."

The footsteps stopped at the chair and table on the far side of the room as my eyes adjusted enough to make out his vague outline. I picked up the gun.

"What's to stop me from just shooting you?" I said.

He laughed our polite, charming laugh. It was soft, confident, and inviting—a laugh that made one feel good for eliciting it.

"We're all awful shots," he said. "I'd feel safe with the lights on, at this distance."

"Then why even give it to me?"

"Your piece of mind that I'm not here to harm you, I guess." His fingers drummed on the arm of the chair and his shoes slapped lightly on the floor as he bounced his right foot, a nervous habit. "As you've already seen, it's quite hard to miss from point blank range."

"So, what are we talking about? Why you killed Brahms?"

"Perhaps in a bit." His night pants hissed against the chair upholstery as he repositioned.

The sound startled me, and I clenched the gun in my hand, raised it a bit.

"Aren't you a jumpy one?" he said. "Let's calm down. We can discuss that in a bit, if you want, but right now I'm here to tell you a secret."

"I'm all ears."

"You're a synth."

I laughed, but it did not sound as I'd intended. It was forced and nervous. If I could have seen his face, it likely would have held something of pity or regret. We all knew how much we hated the prospect of being a synth.

"I'm sorry," he said. It was surprisingly sincere.

Doubt of whom, or what, I was seemed to fill me, as if it meant to push whatever I was out of my facsimile body and thrust me forth as a disembodied fake before the world.

"And I suppose you're the original." I tried to say it as snidely, as combatively, as I could, but doubt had already weakened my voice.

"No," he said.

I could feel the emptiness of his response—the isolation so intense that one feared the word itself would be lost in a vacuum, as if not even air surrounded us. It was a declaration made from the void left when the conviction of our originality disappeared even for a moment.

"I'm sorry," I said.

"I was too, at first."

I didn't respond, only stared at him from across the room. I could barely make out his silhouette. He no longer lounged in the chair, tapped his fingers, or bounced his foot. He now sat leaned forward, with his elbows on his knees and his chin in his hands.

"Okay, I still am," he said. "And I fear I'll always be sorry, deathly sorry, that I'm not Brahms. I look like Brahms. I remember being Brahms as if I'd been him my whole life. Brahms stole my first kiss and my first time with a woman. He stole my first tears and my courage at my father's deathbed. The truth is, we have no father or mother. We have only each other, but it is each other that act as the most constant reminder of our likely fabrication. The only comfort in it all is that I now understand that my being sorry about it won't change the fact."

"That's comfort?" I said.

"Maybe the best we'll get."

"Do you really believe that?'

"I think so."

He seemed to vibrate in his seat, or maybe it was only the shadows. I hoped he wouldn't break down—that he wouldn't cry or even gasp—because I knew I would too. We Brahmses were not criers any more than we were doers of nothing, but when we did either, we did it all the way. Mostly, I hoped he would not break because I knew I might console him, that I might cross the room and be a presence beside him in that emptiness, and I did not know if I wanted to find out that I was a man who comforted murderers.

"So, why did you kill Brahms?" I said.

He laughed again, but this was neither our confident, inviting laugh nor a timid impersonation. This was a chuckle, deep and dark, full of pain and defiance of that pain. It was a laugh that knew laughter was a salve to blunt the hurt of the world, not an exaltation of joy. I'd never heard this laugh before. It was his alone.

"I killed him because he was Brahms," he said, still the trace of that laugh in his voice.

"You mean—"

"Yes. The one and only."

"How did you know?"

"Because we can be cocky, cruel bastards when we're drunk."

"I don't follow."

My visitor lifted his head from his hands and sat up a bit in the chair.

"He and I were drinking five nights ago," he said. "It was in the solarium, actually."

I couldn't see his face clearly, but I could hear that this part of the memory was happy—that he was smiling.

"We were drinking and playing Othello. I beat him almost every game, and this got him in a mood. He was still good, polite company, but you know there is that thing in us that must win.

"He said that we should bet on the next game. I asked what he wanted to bet, and he said he wanted to bet a secret. The loser had to tell the winner something that none of the others knew. I agreed."

Brahms went through every move of the game, every placement and turn, every laugh or piece of witty banter. The whole night seemed burned into his mind, yet he maintained a distance from it, as if he held his hand slightly off of the flame to avoid a scar.

"After I beat him, he just smiled at me. I told him it was time to pay up, so he finished his drink and leaned in. 'I'm the real Brahms,' he said. 'I'm the original.' At first, I laughed at him, but he only stared back. I was polite. I deflected as we most always do when this comes up. I figured he was just trying to hurt me. We are the worst kind of sore loser, you know. I told him everyone already knew he was the real one and he should tell me a real secret."

Brahms's pants zipped against the chair, then again quickly after. He was fidgeting. He appeared to me as a shadow dancing on a chair—twisting on a spit above a fire.

"He only said that he knew I didn't believe him, but that he could prove it. This scared me, and I told him to forget the bet. I went to leave, but then he said, 'Do you know how the doctors ensure that the original always knows he's the original?' I didn't stop walking, but he finished anyway. 'I have a memory that none of you do. I remember you being made. I remember the chambers you all grew in. They tell all of you that the doctors don't allow that, but that's only for you. I have the memory.'

"He told me not to worry, that the empty feeling would pass and that, if I gave it a couple days or a week, the memory would contort itself until I'd be sure I was the one who had spoken such to him. 'You'll see,' he said.

"I told him it was a cute story, a nice try, but that I expected a real secret the next day. I was calm and confident when I said it, but after I closed the solarium door, I shook all the way back to my room. I felt like less than nothing. I concentrated on my own body, on my skin, hands, feet, hair, eyes—on all of it—as if I had to focus to hold it together, lest I evaporate into the night."

My visitor abruptly sat up in his chair and leaned back. He slouched a bit, placed his fingers on the arm, his ankle on one knee, and bounced his foot against the offbeat clacking of his fingers. It was a pose more than anything, like a statue trying to appear relaxed.

"So, I killed him," he said with a crack in his voice. The crack was even more severe as he continued. "You see why I had to do it?"

But he did not cry. He was begging absolution, and I could hear the labored control in his breathing, but he would never cry. I wondered if I would have, were I in his place.

"Yes," I said, more in pity than certainty. "I see."

I was apparently a man who comforted murderers.

"Good," he said. "Good. Good. Good."

He said it over and over again, nodding with each "good," to the point where I didn't know if he spoke to me or himself—an argument by repetition. The nod was erratic, random, like a pebble bouncing down the walls of a ravine so deep that its bottom could not be seen. I felt that if I let him sit there and nod too long, he'd be lost.

"Brahms…" I said.

He did not respond, and I was not sure what I would have said if he had. I needed to break his trance, so I walked to him. The floor was cold, but I didn't step into my slippers. I had to put the gun in the waistband of my night pants in order to pull a chair from a sitting table beside the far window and put it beside him. I removed the gun, put it on the table, and sat down.

His eyes did not acknowledge my presence, but he slouched a bit, as if he knew I was there to hold him up. His gaze was distant, but the focus was deep within instead of far-off, as if he were peering inside himself to see what he might find.

I followed those eyes to the depths of his pain as no other could have because I already knew the way. His eyes were my eyes and my heart, his. Once I reached the terminus, I found myself in the void. Center or periphery did not matter as there was neither in that space of not being. It was infinitely large, and one felt infinitely small and vague within it.

I knew that even if I waved my hand in front of my face in such a place, I would not see it. More than that, I would not even have the sensation of having moved it. I felt as if I could grow or shrink indefinitely and either would lead to oblivion. I was nothing. I'd never been so sure of any other piece of knowledge.

I suddenly recalled why I was there.

"Brahms," I called into the nothing. But there was no particle to carry the wave and no mouth in the first place for speaking. I cried out again and again, but each time was less a call to my visitor and more a call to myself. I was Brahms. I knew it deep and true because I needed to know it.

I snapped back from that darkling plain as if I'd never been. My guest still bobbed his head beside me and repeated, "Good. Good. Good," in the thinnest whisper. The gun was in my hand even though I hadn't left it there, but I knew why. I wrapped my arms around the visitor and ran my fingers through his hair.

I kissed his forehead and noted briefly that something smelled strange—surprising. It was a smell very un-Brahms. Then I stood and took aim at the side of his head.

I squeezed the trigger and the air itself exploded in my ears like a rebuke. A jolt shot up my arm, climaxed in my elbow and slung my hand back with the gun's recoil. The air was hot and meaty like a sizzling bone, and my skin was speckled with bits of it all. My hand throbbed and my ears were filled with an airy static.

After a moment, I looked down at the revolver. There were five bullets left, one for each of us. My visitor had been right. That was really the only completely safe way for the rest of them. I was safe, of course, because I knew I was the real Brahms, the original. I had to be. I knew it like I knew to breathe, but the rest of them...

No. I put the gun back on the table.

"Jill," I said. "Clean up, would you?"

"Of course, sir," she said from the other side of the door.

"And call Dr. Welkie. Tell him I need to speak with him urgently."

"Yes, sir. Anything else?"

"No, Jill, that's all for now, thanks."

I would have to call the computer people on a hard line since I didn't know the extent of the tampering. It would take some time, but I knew I could get the house back in order.

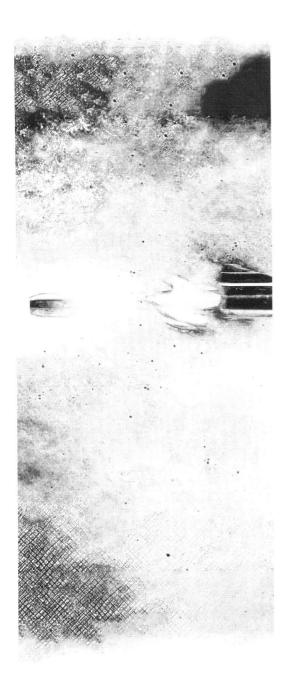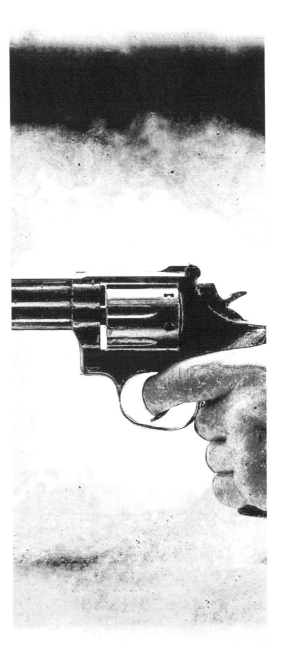

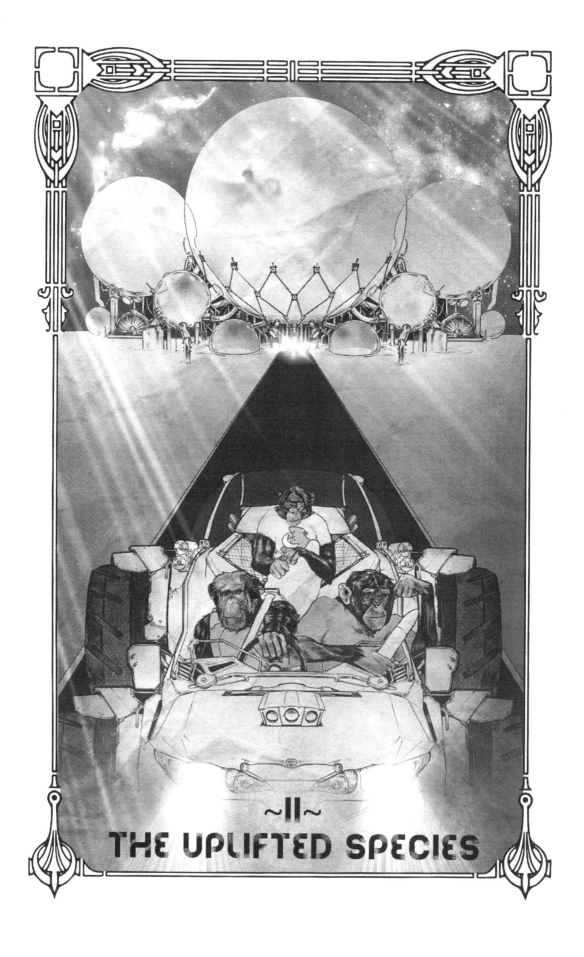

~II~
THE UPLIFTED SPECIES

RISING COVE
Mark S Bailen

Boz was tall for a chimpanzee, nearly five feet. He wore orange trunks and a collar with a scallop-shaped medallion. He paused to appreciate his crew's latest project, four orbs that bubbled up from the desert floor and were held aloft by metal struts. Tubes crisscrossed, circled, and disappeared below the ground. Beneath the cloudless sky, over a hundred construction chimps clambered atop the orbs, swinging from harnesses and chattering. They dragged cables, shot rivets, and sealed plastic seams.

A few chimps squawked from above, mocking their crew leader because he was afraid of heights. Boz ignored them. He had no patience for teeth-grinders. His brethren should have been proud of their accomplishments. Rising Cove was proof of what marvels could be created when primates and cetaceans worked together. Except for the overland canals and the hotpot mating pools, they had never built anything so grand. Rising Cove employed not only Boz's crew, but also a team of bonobos to develop a celestial observatory, and a crew of orangutans to construct a tower off the coast—for what purpose, he could not divine.

Boz knuckle-walked beneath the Ball of Air, a recently completed orb where the high pod assembled. He entered a side entrance for two-legs and spoke into a silver pin-box that translated his words into clicks. "I'm here." A port opened and a bottlenose male rolled out on a three-wheeled cart. The dolphin had pale, thickly scarred skin. A silver echo-box was attached to his melon, translating his clicks. A puddle formed beneath the contraption.

"Name?" One of the dolphin's eyes was glued shut.

"Boz."

"Purpose?"

"I'm meeting Commander Tub."

Both eyes opened. "You?" The dolphin released a stream of angry clicks before accessing his echo-box. "Fine, go in. Don't touch the walls with your dirty fingers."

Boz walked down a transparent tunnel that twisted like intestines through the water-filled orb. The shadows of dolphins swam overhead. Boz noted where the tubes leaked, mildew grew, and repairs were necessary. He walked past a half-submerged cavern where three bonobos stood on scaffolding and worked on a mosaic while a dolphin barked orders from below. The mosaic was only half-complete but depicted the cetacean's favorite topic: Anthropocene atrocities. One panel showed a dolphin trapped in a fishing net. Another showed a pod of juveniles avoiding an ancient speedboat. A third showed a dolphin twisting through a red hoop, performing a trick, presumably for food.

Boz questioned the value of these mosaics. Were they meant for moral enrichment? Did the dolphins enjoy being reminded of atrocities from a thousand years ago? The messaging was as subtle as a hammer to the head. Boz could at least appreciate the craftsmanship. The bonobos worked diligently, assembling the ceramic pieces, dipping them in glue, and applying them to the wall. Without hands, the dolphins could never complete such tasks. The cetaceans required help not only for mosaics, but for all their land-based projects. They could not construct orbs, run circulation pumps, pull cables, or maintain their echo-boxes. Only by working with primates was progress made.

The tube forked into a bulb-shaped air pocket with a bench and a pin-screen. Damselfish drifted in the hazy water. From above, water tubes entered the chamber. Faux stalagmites rose from below. Commander Tub circled into view. He was an obese bottlenose with gray streaks down his flank and an oversized echo-box hooked to his melon. The pin-screen came alive, showing a blurry eye. The speaker crackled. "Good morning, Boz."

Boz leaned towards the device. "High commander." The filaments on the pin-screen flowed like metallic fur, translating his voice into clicks and echoing in the chamber. The screen also had a display capability by shifting filaments in and out. Pin-screens resolved better if you possessed echolocation, but for Boz, the close-up of a dolphin's eye disturbed him and he looked away.

"The new orbs are progressing nicely," said Commander Tub.

"Yes."

"You have a talented crew."

"Thank you."

"I appreciate your loyalty."

Boz shifted. The high commander wanted something but was obfuscating. This was the dolphin way. The pin-screen went blank as Commander Tub surfaced to breathe. Then he sank and peered into the air pocket, causing Boz to fidget. Even though Boz trusted the Ball of Air's architecture, he could never relax below thousands of gallons of water.

His lips peeled back. "Tell me why I'm here, high commander."

The pin-screen blurred. "I have a mission for you, Boz. I'm forming a delegation to travel across the barren lands."

"Why?"

"To visit the humans."

Boz jerked backwards. Had he heard correctly? Humans? The high commander must have been delusional. Nobody had visited the humans in three lifetimes. Their last known settlement was walled up in the mountains. "Please explain."

"We require technological information."

Boz stared at his feet. Were there no limits to the high pod's hubris? Must they always obsess over the Anthropocene? After the Great Scarring, when the humans rendered the surface barren and their population dwindled, the dolphins rose to power. They saved a human settlement by creating an ocean corridor and delivering fish. At least, that was how the dolphins told it. In exchange for the food, the humans shared technology. They built tidal-power generators and robotic submersibles. They designed prototypes of echo-boxes, pin-screens, and language processors. And they gave the dolphins dominion over the primates, teaching them how to sequester chimps, bonobos, and orangutans on the atolls; control their food supply; and employ them for labor.

But then the humans disappeared. They retreated to the mountains and locked themselves behind walls.

"Humans don't want to talk to us," said Boz.

"We will show them our achievements," said Commander Tub. "They will be proud."

"I doubt it."

"We'll offer an ocean corridor, like before."

"Humans don't need fish. They farm behind their walls."

"Then we will offer your services. Construction crews. Maybe they want to build a church or a shopping plaza?"

Boz's stomach ached and he badly wanted to leave the air pocket. He rocked forwards. "We both know what happened during the Anthropocene, high commander. We should not risk contacting humans. They may enslave us again."

"Impossible. We are too powerful."

Boz scowled. Again, more hubris.

The dolphin sank lower. "For your delegation, please include your brother. He was trained to navigate a rover. I will also assign one female. She will have autonomy."

"My brother does not like to work."

"Convince him."

Boz's teeth chattered. He couldn't make sense of this request. Could he refuse the commander?

"You will be rewarded for this journey, Boz." The commander watched with one eye. "Perhaps you would like to visit an all-female island? Without competition from other males?"

Boz winced. Although he desired copulation, he was happy living alone on the atolls with his brother and other males. Years ago, he had accepted such gifts, donned a breeding collar and allowed himself to be taken to an all-female island. But lately such luxuries were a bother. It was better to concentrate on his work.

"No, thank you," said Boz.

"What do you desire then?"

"I only want to continue our project, high commander. To finish Rising Cove." Boz waved his arms. "This is the greatest construction project of our shared history. We have made wonders that climb into the sky. We installed filtration systems and electric pumps. We created sublime works of art. These orbs surpass human achievement. Why can't we be proud?"

"We are proud, but we're not finished. We have one more step before completing Rising Cove."

Boz scratched his head. "One more step?"

"Yes. We're constructing a vehicle, more powerful than you can imagine." Commander Tub twisted, revealing his underbelly. "The vehicle will be capable of leaping off the surface of the planet. It will breach the sky and allow us to visit the moon." The dolphin's eye enlarged on the pin-screen. "But to complete the vehicle, we require human technology. We must acquire ancient secrets about stabilization, fuel refining, and jet propulsion."

§

After finishing his crew schedules and bartering with a salvaging team of bonobos, Boz headed to the docks. He walked along the path between Rising Cove and the coast where the new tower was being constructed. Orangutans wearing thick collars and silver trunks hefted an I-beam. This was where the high commander intended to launch his new vehicle. The tower was taller than anything that Boz had seen. He couldn't imagine how such a vehicle would attach to the tower and rise into the sky.

Would it use immense springs? Compressed air?

No. It must possess an engine.

When Boz reached the docks, he showed his medallion and boarded a humpback ferry. He huddled among a dozen male chimps atop the whale's spine, avoiding the spray. Every day, the work crews were ferried to and from the atolls where the fruit trees grew and they could fish for turtles and squid. The islands were separated by large expanses of water and impossible to swim to, but day-to-day life was pleasant. Boz never grumbled. As he squatted atop the humpback, he counted the outlines of atolls, dozens of them, distant and blue. Beneath him, the whale moaned.

Boz lived on an all-male island called Toll 8 with his brother, Middy. They had secured a ground hut on the beach with few possessions. When Boz entered their confines, Middy was nestled in the bough of a tree, hugging a gourd of palm wine.

Boz poked his brother. "Wake up, lazy. You're missing the sunset."

Middy sat up, confused, pulling the gourd closer. After a swig he said, "Brother. You look like shit."

"I had a stressful day." Boz sat beneath the tree. "I spoke with Commander Tub."

"Oh! The big melon himself. You poor thing. Drink some wine."

Boz took a sip. "He's crazy, I tell you."

"All dolphins are crazy," said Middy. "From keeping their heads too long under-water."

"You wouldn't believe what he expects now. He wants me to travel across the barren lands." Boz glanced sideways. "To meet with the humans."

Middy froze.

"Did you hear?"

"This must be a joke. That terrible dolphin sense of humor."

"I wish."

Middy leaned backwards, itching his chin. The younger brother had always been fascinated by humans. Whenever an artifact from the Anthropocene washed onto the beach, he'd spend hours trying to decipher its purpose. Usually he'd imagine the artifact was used for killing or torturing. Middy was a lazy worker, but he had a very active mind.

"You should come with me," Boz said. "I'm allowed one companion."

"No, thank you, brother. I prefer my island."

"I need a driver."

"My rover skills have gotten poor. I forget what buttons to push."

"They're sending a female."

Middy rolled off the tree branch. "In heat?"

"Don't be crass." Boz thumped his brother, then looked away. He was also puzzled about the dolphin's insistence on taking a female. Perhaps they thought it would gain their delegation more respect? It was said that humans, like bonobos, treated females like brethren.

"Fine, I will come. If only to protect this female." Middy squatted. "But tell me, brother. Why the dour face? Aren't you excited to meet humans? The smartest of all primates! This is far better than constructing bubbles for the melon heads. Although I don't understand why they chose you."

"Me neither. There are far smarter chimps." Boz crossed his arms. "Perhaps my skill at negotiation? The dolphins want secrets from the Anthropocene."

"Of course." Middy scratched his chest. "What does Tubby want now? A weapon to fight orcas?"

"No, a vehicle. Something I never heard of. A tube taller than the trees with fire that emits from below. It's meant to breach the sky and deliver them to the moon. It sounds like a bad dream."

Middy went silent. He drifted towards the beach.

"Brother?"

"Those damn fools." Middy eyed the night sky. "The dolphins want to build a rocket."

§

Reaching the human settlement required five days, two crossing the salt flats and three crossing the barren lands. Middy piloted the rover while Boz slumped in the passenger seat. In the backseat sat a small female named Kush. Whenever Boz attempted to engage her in conversation, she only said, "OK," and lowered her eyes.

"The melon heads are too scared to meet humans," said Middy. "They're worried about being served for dinner. So they send chimps."

The rover pushed through harsh winds and rumbled over cracked terrain. Middy occasionally stopped to switch batteries, consult his map, or allow the passengers to wander into the desert to relieve themselves. The map was a worn plastic chip, embossed with topography that Middy could read with his fingers. At one point they skirted Anthropocene ruins, half-buried and metal.

"Let's stop, brother," said Middy. "We may discover human killing devices."

"No, please, Middy. Keep going," said Boz. "We only have two weeks of supplies."

On the fifth day, mountains appeared, red and imposing. Middy barreled towards the foothills, following some unseen line. When the rocks became impassable, he parked, climbed over top of the rover, and tossed out their backpacks. "According to the map, the humans live up there." Middy pointed. "We must climb until we reach an iron wall."

Boz glared up the mountain. It looked steep and impenetrable. Behind him, Kush lifted her backpack and slung it over her shoulders. She wore blue trunks, a collar with a starfish medallion, and a silver anklet. Her eyes were directed down.

"Don't be so obvious, brother," said Middy.

Boz turned away. "I was only thinking."

"Don't do that either. She's not in heat." Middy gazed upwards. "Besides, we must concentrate on the climb."

After scouting the boulders, they located a trail that zigzagged through the cliffs. It was washed out and difficult to track. Middy climbed in front, then came Boz, followed by Kush. The trek required scrambling and more than once Boz slipped and nearly tumbled to his death. He spent many moments catching his breath and cursing. Not only did he hate heights, but he had grown lazy, letting his climbing skills wane.

When the sun declined, they stopped to drink water. Middy attempted to engage Kush in conversation. "What do you think, female? Will the humans eat us?"

She shook her head.

"They won't make soup out of our bones?"

She laughed. "Of course not."

Middy hooted. "You know nothing. Why did the melon heads even send you?"

Kush blinked. "I have autonomy."

"Yes, yes. Old Tubby told us. But why are you here?"

"I'm an expert."

"In what?"

"Humans."

Middy laughed. "And I'm an expert in flying squid."

"Let her speak," said Boz.

Kush took a long breath. "I'm educated in human civilization. I spent three years at the Thousand Orbs, the great cetacean library, learning how to read the ancient script."

Boz shivered. He had heard stories of the famous library that existed many miles out at sea and contained volumes on Anthropocene history. Few primates were allowed to visit. The thought of being trapped for weeks in small air pockets and spending all day reading human texts made him woozy.

"Human civilization was more impressive than we can know," continued Kush. "They had numerous golden ages. They excelled at art, music, architecture, and science. They created our common tongue and modified our biology so we can speak. They maintained dominion for thousands of years. And they were primates, like us."

"They also kept us in cages," said Middy. "And used us for medical testing."

Kush shrugged.

"My brother is right," said Boz. "You should not worship humans. They had everything in their palms and lost it."

Kush met his eyes. "You think dolphins will do better?"

"Of course!" Boz clapped. "Have you not seen Rising Cove?"

She shook her head.

"Bah! You spend too much time with your nose in books. Go see the coast, female. Visit the great orbs. By working with dolphins, we have surpassed human culture."

Kush dropped her eyes. "I didn't mean to anger you."

"Never mind that." Boz paced, waving and kicking. "When we return to the coast, I will personally show you the wonders of Rising Cove. I will prove our superiority over the Anthropocene. Then you will stop worshiping humans."

"Enough, brother." Middy lifted his backpack. "You're getting excited."

The chimpanzees climbed upwards while the sun dropped. After they'd spent hours trudging through the dark, the mountain flattened, becoming a mesa covered in scrubby plants. In the distance was a wall, over twenty-feet tall, sharp-edged and rusty. The architecture was nothing like the dolphin orbs. The chimps stared at the impediment.

"Not very welcoming," said Middy.

"What do you think, human expert?" Boz nudged Kush. "Should we approach?"

She lowered her eyes. "I'm uncertain."

"What? Where's your autonomy? Are you unable to decide?"

"Fine." Kush removed her pack. "Let's wait until daylight."

"Agreed," said Middy. "The humans probably have projectiles that will rain fire down on our heads. Or traps that will chop our legs off. Better to experience this during the day." He settled into the dirt and removed his gourd.

Boz sighed and sat next to his brother. He motioned towards Kush, who curled nearby. "No funny business."

"Me?" Middy grinned.

"I'm serious."

"I can see."

As Boz drifted off, he recalled a week before when he'd visited a small dolphin library near the coast. He'd wanted to familiarize himself with rocket technology before meeting the humans. The library was submerged in a lagoon many miles down the coast, situated beyond the break. Boz wasn't a great swimmer and once he reached the entrance he coughed up saltwater for many minutes. Then he climbed down a ladder into a two-legged air pocket. There was a pin-screen, a bench, and six inches of water on the floor. The library was run by a near blind beluga, who complained when he accessed the storage banks. With some effort, Boz pulled up schematics of jet engines. He learned the basics of rocket stabilization, throttling, and refining fuel. He worried how they could construct such a vehicle. Where would they mine the materials? What electronics would be required? Could they even move such a large vehicle around?

Thus, atop the mesa, beneath the cold stars, Boz dreamt about rockets.

§

The next morning, the chimps returned to the iron wall. The air was crisp and the sky had thin clouds. The wall didn't appear to have an entry port. There were no handholds, nor ladders, but to their surprise, a chimp peeked over the top. It was a young male, waving.

Middy laughed. "One of us!"

"A runaway?" asked Boz.

A rope was tossed over and the male climbed down. He wore harlequin trunks and held a radio device in his hand. He wore no collar.

"My friends, my friends!" He waddled across the distance and hugged each delegate, including Kush. "You have traveled so far!"

Boz shook off the hug. "Why are you here, brethren?"

"My name is Ben. I live here." The young male grinned.

"Among the humans?"

"Sure. Many of us have escaped the dolphins. Of course many died in the crossing. It is a difficult journey, but not impossible, as you have discovered." He motioned to the wall. "Come, join us. We'll remove your collars. You must be starved."

Middy followed.

Boz stopped him. "Wait."

The young male turned.

"You should know, brethren," said Boz. "We are not escaping."

"No?"

"We're a delegation, working with the cetaceans. We're delivering a message from the high pod."

Ben looked confused. "You're not seeking asylum?"

"No. We must return tomorrow. We only wish to speak to your commander."

Ben chuckled. "We have no commanders here, brethren. No bosses. No masters. We live in peace with our fellow primates."

"You have no leaders?"

"Well, we have a council."

"Fine." Boz itched his neck. "Direct us to your council."

Using the rope, the four chimpanzees scaled the wall and dropped onto the other side. The mesa beyond the wall was green and squared off, covered in farmland. No structures were apparent, but in the distance was a grove and a raised aqueduct. Workers collected vegetables in blankets. Tending the fields were chimps, bonobos, and a few humans.

The delegates stared agape at the nearest human, a tall lanky figure. Here at last was the mythical primate with the immense brain. Those who built the greatest civilization and let it collapse. The villain who maintained dominion over the planet for thousands of years. Boz couldn't remove his eyes. To see one of these creatures alive and animated was like a long-forgotten memory. The human had sparse fur, smooth skin, and excess clothing.

"There's one of the devils," said Middy.

"Hush," said Boz.

"I didn't realize they were so skinny. How does it hold its head up? I could snap its neck with a twist."

"Please, brother. No more."

Ben laughed. "Don't worry, brethren. You get used to humans. They're no different than us."

"Sure," said Middy.

The brothers followed Ben, nearly leaving Kush behind. She remained transfixed by the human and wouldn't move until Boz took her by the elbow. "Come."

§

The delegation crossed parcels of farmland dotted with tractors and mobile water pumps. The non-human workers were mostly chimps, but there were some bonobos and orangutans. Also in the distance, Boz thought he spotted a black-furred gorilla. This primate was nearly as rare as a human. Boz had only seen gorillas when he was very young. Following a disagreement with the dolphins, they'd refused to board the humpbacks and leave their atolls. The gorillas hadn't been heard from since.

The mesa ended at a canyon with switchbacks leading down. Built into the canyon walls were hundreds of openings with arches and windows. Boz was shocked. Was this where the humans lived? Inside cliff dwellings? The little caves looked nice enough, but why not live above ground like a proper civilization?

The delegation proceeded down the switchbacks into a shadowy canyon where a bridge crossed a stream. Trails disappeared in various directions. Fruit stands appeared. An immense amphitheater was carved inside the rock, acting as a town square. Dozens of primates sat at tables, having animated conversations. Solar panels reflected. Small electric rovers trundled across the sand. The technology was quaint and well-engineered, but nothing was as impressive as Rising Cove.

Nobody turned to notice the delegates.

"Wait here." Ben stepped through an archway. "I will alert the council of your arrival."

The three newcomers stood entranced at the edge of the amphitheater. The humans made up the majority of the citizenry, dressed in drab and loose clothing. They were everywhere, using two-hand holds to climb between archways, strolling across the square, discussing matters in high-pitched tones. They stood a third taller than the other primates and many wore foot coverings. None carried weapons or armory. Nor did they appear strange or demented, as the dolphins depicted them. Boz had an urge to walk up to a pair and start a dialogue. He was curious about their work. Whether they still built great structures. Why they lived in cliff dwellings.

Kush drifted away as if pulled by a string. She moved towards a cluster of human children playing near the stream. A human female invited her to sit down and Kush watched without shame.

"We've lost her," said Middy.

Boz sighed and started towards Kush.

"Stop, brother. She will be fine." Middy took his shoulder. "Think only of completing your task for the melon heads. So we can leave this strange place."

"You don't like it?"

"No. It's terrible. There's no ocean. No sun." Middy sat in the sand and removed his gourd. "Besides, at any moment I expect the humans to tie us down and barbecue us."

Boz smiled.

Before long, Ben returned. "The council will see you."

"Have fun, brother," said Middy. "Impress them with your brain."

Boz nodded. "What about her?"

"She has autonomy."

Boz hesitated.

"Don't worry. I'll watch Kush."

§

The council met in a bright chamber carved in sandstone and filtered with skylight. On the walls were tapestries of ancient animals. Above the chamber was a gallery where a handful of primates observed with recording devices. At the center of the room was a stone table where three humans and an elder male chimp sat.

"Welcome to Lower Vale," said the tallest human with fur around its chin. It spoke in the common tongue with a slight, melodic accent. "What is your name?"

"Boz."

"Welcome, Boz. My name is Herald." It motioned around the table. "On my left is Jane. On my right, Stenna. Our fourth member is one of your brethren, Pik."

The elder chimp nodded.

"Was your journey difficult?"

"No. I am fine, commander."

"Please, don't call me commander. We are on equal footing here." The human smiled. "So what brings you here today, Boz?"

"We are a delegation."

"A dolphin delegation," said Pik, the elder chimp.

"Yes."

"They sent a female too. The cetaceans are trying to stir us up!"

Boz was unsure how to respond. It was reassuring to hear a chimpanzee speak without concern among the humans. Yet the elder's tone troubled him.

The human named Stenna spoke next. It had glossy lips and curling black fur, stacked atop its head. "Just to be clear, Boz, you are not seeking asylum? You prefer to remain living on the atolls?"

"Yes," said Boz.

There was a moment of silence before Herald spoke. "Excellent. We are happy to hear that primates can work successfully with cetaceans. Since you won't be staying, tell us what you require."

Boz settled his breathing. "On the coast we have a great project called Rising Cove, designed by the high pod. I'm not boasting when I say this is the finest accomplishment of cetacean and primate civilization. Of any civilization."

Pik hooted.

Boz eyed the elder, but continued. "We have built over fifteen land-based orbs. Canals that reach the ocean. A power plant. And an information depot. It's a soaring complex."

"It sounds impressive," said Herald.

"It is. Which brings me to my purpose. We are also building a tower near the coast, designed to hoist a new kind of vehicle." Boz paused, considering his next words. He never imagined he'd be standing in front of a council of three humans and an elder chimp, asking for technology. Part of him despised this role. He hated visualizing himself begging the humans for secrets from the Anthropocene. Why did the dolphins obsess so much about the past? Why couldn't they take pride in their own knowledge? And rely only on primate-cetacean teamwork?

Boz shook off his concerns. Commander Tub was extremely clever. He must have thought this through. Boz glared back at the council. "We are building a rocket."

Herald gasped.

Stenna's eyes enlarged.

Jane leaned forwards, cupping its ears.

"Of course!" Pik snorted. "Such arrogance could only come from dolphins!"

"We have made much progress, but our information is incomplete," Boz continued. "Our hope is that you will share your libraries. Secrets from the Anthropocene would expedite our work. Knowledge on topics such as jet engines, stabilization, and refining fuel."

The council stared for a long moment.

After a pause, Stenna drummed its fingers. "We shouldn't be surprised."

"Why?" asked Herald.

"Ask him." Stenna pointed. "Tell the council, Boz, why do you think the dolphins want to build a rocket?"

Boz hesitated.

"He doesn't even know!" said Pik. "Wake up, brethren. They're using you!"

"I'm not being used."

"No? Why do you still wear a collar? Why are you kept imprisoned on the atolls? Every aspect of your life is controlled from eating to mating!"

"My life on the island is very pleasant," said Boz. "I'm doing important work and

I can't imagine doing anything else."

"You're a collaborator!"

Boz showed his teeth, but breathed slowly and measured his response. "At Rising Cove, we are equal partners. Chimps and dolphins work side-by-side. We also employ whales, bonobos, and orangutans. Only through multi-species collaboration can such wonders be made."

"Bah!" said Pik.

Jane, the smallest of the humans, who had previously remained quiet, cleared its throat. "Did you know, Boz, that rockets can be used as weapons?" The human had a tight face and small teeth.

"Let's not jump to conclusions," said Herald. "The dolphins have never shown interest in weaponry."

"Not true! They have harpoons," said Pik. "They train orangutans to use them against orcas. I've seen it myself."

"Harpoons are not rockets," said Harold. "They have never built weapons that rely on chemical explosives. They don't even have a word for bomb."

Pik slapped the table. "Why must you always apologize for them, Herald?"

"I don't."

"You do," said Jane. "The dolphins are no angels."

"Neither were we!" Harold held up a finger. "Must I remind the counsel that we are bound by our directives? We are required to help the cetaceans when asked. Our ancestors made this promise long ago. They are the rightful heirs to human progress."

The council grew quiet. Then Stenna spoke. "I agree with Herald. We should allow them access to our libraries. The cetaceans must have the freedom to make their own mistakes. Certainly they'll do better than us."

"And if they fire rockets on us?" asked Pik.

"Why would they?"

"Consider their temperament!"

The council members all spoke at the same time, arguing. Boz waited while they debated. Then, growing impatient, he made a clicking noise, something he learned from the dolphins.

The council grew quiet.

"My friends." Boz folded his hands. "The dolphins are not making weapons."

"Enlighten us then," said Jane. "What are they making?"

"I have spoken on this exact topic with the high commander." Boz held their eyes. "He was very clear. The rocket is intended to breach the sky. They want to visit the moon."

§

The council adjourned, telling Boz that they would make their decision the following day. He was led back to the amphitheater where he found Middy asleep in the grass. Kush was nowhere to be seen.

Boz kicked Middy.

"Brother! Don't be cruel! I was having a wonderful dream about human killing machines."

"Where is Kush?"

Middy sat up and looked around. "She was here a moment ago, talking to humans."

Boz cursed. "You, fool." He walked into the amphitheater and sought out Ben, who was conversing with three humans. "Our female is gone," Boz interrupted.

"Do not worry brethren," Ben smiled. "She will be fine."

"Fine?"

"Lower Vale is safe, even for females." Ben put his hand on Boz's shoulder. "She will join you soon. Relax."

"Relax? Where's our female?" Boz pushed away the younger chimp's hand. "Bring her to me now!"

The amphitheater grew quiet. Nearby primates turned and stared.

Boz looked uncertain. For a moment, he wondered if some of Middy's fears were justified. Although he witnessed no guards or weapons in Lower Vale, he could imagine the lanky humans running from the archways, circling him, tying him with rope, and putting him in a cage.

"Come, brethren," whispered Ben. "It's been a long day. Let's find a place to rest."

Boz nodded and followed the young male.

Later that night Boz lay alone among pillows and glow lights. Middy had taken his gourd atop the mesa, saying that the cliff dwelling was too constrained. Boz didn't mind the rock walls and confined space, but he felt restless. The ceiling was painted with a ghostly landscape, depicting extinct mammals like bears and bison. While staring at the ancient creatures, Boz wondered why the high pod had chosen him for this ridiculous task. Was it his skill at running crews? His ability to negotiate? His understanding of technology? Doubtful. There were far cleverer chimps. Not to mention the bonobos who excelled at math and engineering. Yet obviously Commander Tub saw something in Boz. Uncertain, he fell into a fitful sleep.

The next morning Middy returned to the cave, nursing a headache. The brothers ate a simple breakfast of fruits and nuts before returning to the amphitheater. Upon arrival, Boz spotted Kush. He pulled her away from a cluster of humans.

"Where have you been?" Boz asked.

Kush smiled, unafraid to meet his eyes. "Good morning, Boz."

Boz stood back. Had she called him by name?

"Ah, there's our female." Middy approached with his mouth full. "You look like you've been struck in the head by a coconut."

"I feel that way." Kush grinned. "This place is wonderful."

"How so?" asked Boz.

"All the primates living together, without hierarchy. Without restricted living. Sharing ideas and conversation. Practicing courtships. This is how things were meant to be."

"No thanks," said Middy.

Boz folded his arms. "You've found paradise after one night?"

"Yes!" She waved her arms. "The humans have created a utopia. There is no other word for it."

Boz was unsure how to respond. The village was suitable enough but obviously stagnant. The art and masonry were above average, but with so much capability, why had the humans stopped progressing? Why had they abandoned their knowledge? Why work by hand in the fields and live in caves? Why weren't they building atop the mesa? Designing observatories? Robots? And flying machines?

"Good morning, brethren!" Ben approached in his harlequin trunks. "The council has made a decision. Come!"

§

The morning light made the council chambers bright with long shadows. Middy and Kush stood on either side of Boz in front of the stone table.

Stenna spoke first. "Congratulations, Boz. The council has decided in your favor. We will share the technical information that you requested. You may have access to our library. Our information can be copied on plastic chips which the cetaceans can translate. You and Kush may determine what's worth taking."

"Thank you." Boz nodded.

"In return," said Stenna, "we only ask for one thing."

Boz looked around. "One thing?"

Pik pointed. "Her."

"Her?"

"Kush," said Stenna. "She must remain in Lower Vale."

Boz's stomach dropped. He faced Middy. Both brothers looked at Kush.

She lowered her eyes.

"Was this your decision?" Boz whispered.

"Yes," said Kush.

"What's the matter, brethren?" Pik laughed. "Surprised that a chimp would leave the atolls?"

Boz continued to stare at Kush. She fidgeted, seeming both anxious and happy. Boz wanted to grab her and shake her. He wanted to howl and scream and convince her that she was wrong. But she had autonomy. Commander Tub had made this clear. Boz looked around the chamber, panning the upper gallery. Everybody stared back at him. Then he realized that no other female chimps lived in Lower Vale. The thought hit him like a rock to his head. Of course. Most female chimps were stuck on the atolls. They had no opportunity to run away.

Boz faced his brother. "Can we allow this?"

Middy shrugged. "We have no choice."

"You may remain too, Boz," said Stenna. "Both you and your brother may seek asylum."

"No thanks," said Middy.

Boz shivered and, for a moment, actually considered leaving the atolls. Could he live here among the humans? Studying art and masonry? Sleeping in caves? Picking crops in the field? Would he be happy? The humans had so little interest in progress.

"Boz?" asked Herald. "Do you wish to stay? Middy can deliver the technical information back to the cetaceans."

"I'll miss you, brother." Middy took his arm.

For a long moment, Boz stood silent. Then he shook his head. "No." He stared at his feet. "I have work to do."

§

Before Boz departed from Lower Vale, he and Kush visited the human library, which was in a deep cave system. After many hours of searching, they located the books about rocket technology. Boz could not read the text and relied on Kush to translate. While waiting, he made a final attempt to convince her that she was wrong. He told Kush that if she returned to the atolls, perhaps she could witness

Rising Cove in person. Perhaps she could return to the library at Thousand Orbs. Perhaps she could even retain her autonomy. Kush only nodded in response, refusing to argue. So they sat on opposite sides of the library, resigned to their fates. She read from ancient texts on topics like oxidizers, gimbals, and nozzles, while Boz determined what was worth copying onto chips.

On the trek down the mountain, Boz was quiet and numb. He carried a heavy backpack of embossed chips and slipped many times. He wondered if anybody would care if he tumbled off the mountain. Probably not. The commander would only find somebody else to run his crews. And negotiate with bonobos. And learn about rockets. There were plenty of chimps standing in line.

Eventually the brothers located the rover and began the long drive across the barren lands. It was a monotonous trip. When they finally dropped onto the salt flats and Rising Cove sparkled on the horizon, Boz's heart leapt. The orbs appeared like giant pearls, frozen in time. He felt his pride return. If only the humans would leave their walls, come down the mountain, and witness these wonders. Maybe then they would understand what was possible when primates and cetaceans worked together. And why progress must continue.

Further down the coast, was the tower.

§

After a week on the coast and resuming his duties as crew chief, Boz was invited to return to the Ball of Air. He had already delivered the full satchel of embossed chips to the library. The beluga received the chips with little thanks, griping about the work necessary to add them to the data banks. But the news of his journey had already gotten out. The high pod had a full science team of dolphins and primates assembled to analyze the data. Boz could only hope that his visit to the human settlement wasn't a waste. He sat fidgeting in the air pocket, waiting for Commander Tub to drift into the chamber. The pin-screen swirled as the dolphin's eye resolved.

"Congratulations, Boz. You have done very well."

"I have?"

"Yes. The information is being scrutinized as we speak. Early reports are positive. You have reduced our timeline by many months. Perhaps years. We have already assigned a team of bonobos to construct a new propulsion engine. And orangutans to build a refinery. If all goes well, we'll test our first rocket by the end of summer. Your delegation surpassed my expectations."

"Thank you."

"You've been a most loyal and valuable helper."

Boz dropped his eyes.

"Do you have any needs?" The dolphin sank in the chamber. "Desires?"

"I only wish to get back to my work, high commander." Boz twitched. "But I do have one question." He faced the tank. "Was it your plan all along? To trade Kush?"

The dolphin twisted. "We had a notion. The high pod doesn't have open channels with the humans, but we hear things. Primates travel back and forth. We knew that they lacked female chimps."

"That was very clever."

"Thank you, Boz." The commander circled. "But it was your doing."

Boz cringed and his stomach started to ache. "If there is nothing else?"

"Just one thing, Boz." The dolphin peered down. "One more task."

Boz's spine chilled. What could he want now?

"According to the schematics that you delivered, we must construct a capsule that will sit atop the rocket, a capsule to hold a traveler." The dolphin revealed its teeth. "As the vehicle is propelled towards the moon, somebody must ride along with it. Somebody possessing a rudimentary knowledge about rockets."

Boz's throat felt dry. "A cetacean?"

"No. Not at first."

"Who?" His teeth chattered. "Wh-Who will go?"

The pin-screen shifted and the image focused. It was a picture from an ancient book found in the human library, one that Kush must have transferred onto a chip without his knowledge. The picture showed a chimpanzee dressed in a white suit with tubes poking in the sides. The chimp wore a helmet—and was strapped flat to a plank.

"You, Boz," said the high commander. "You will go up with the rocket."

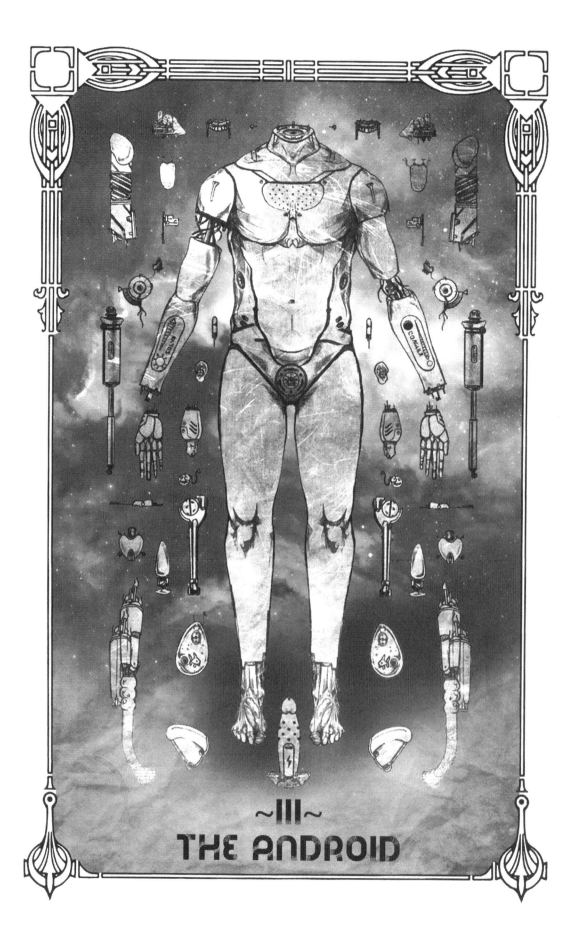

~III~
THE ANDROID

WHY WE CAN'T HAVE NICE THINGS
Elton Skelter

If you build it, they will cum.

Augie said to keep it simple. He said we don't want the new features, just the old ones, the way people used to be. Augie said think what you imagined when you were a child and do that. Think Stepford. Think Goldfoot. That's what the shareholders have asked for, so that's what the shareholders will get.

Augie can eat my ass.

Note to self: activate *ass eating* functionality on the new model.

It's all just binary, zeros and ones all chucked together; different patterns make different shit happen. It's math, or as close to math as you can get without it being magic.

A few clicks of the keypad, and the fingers rotate like a batter mixer; few more, and they thrust like a pneumatic drill. Zeros and ones. All there is to it.

There's a fifty-two-piece orchestra running the research and development department, and the best they could do was stick vibrators and prostate massagers on the unit's hands.

I trial the personality chip with the basic settings: a yes or no response based on the intonation of your voice. Tell him you want to stay home tonight; you don't feel like going out. He tells you he agrees. Tell him you want him to rip the shirt off your back, and you're one shirt down for the week.

Introducing the new Primus3000 – Same Sex Model, now with added interchangeable washable genital attachments in medium, large, and equine. With optional vaginal interface, with interchangeable gendered breastplate, in smooth, gentle regrowth, fine and hirsute.

The first time I take him home, he's muscular, six-foot-five, arms as big as my thighs. He's coated in this thick, nineties thatch of grizzly bear body hair and has this porno bush I want to bury my face in. I chose him with the black hair, the chiseled jawline of an athlete, and the general vocal intonation of old Golden Hollywood. There are smaller models available: twink, twunk, hunk, stud, cub. I went with the bear. It's a preference.

I make him hard by squeezing his balls three times, like I'm pumping up a space hopper. It's the least sexy way I've ever gotten a guy hard, and I once crushed Viagra into a guy's whiskey rocks. He was on the older side and needs must… Ipso Facto, I intervened. Rocks all round.

Note to self: add *sensory hardening* function based on *organic somatic indicators*.

When he speaks to me, he sounds like Clarke Gable, and in his voice, the words "fuck" and "rimming" and "cum" sound obscenely out of place. I make him say them anyway, and it's like fucking a friend of my dad's, some pervert in a sweater vest. Activate *speech* mode, dial turned to *pornographic*.

I wait until we're done to kill the program. Turn the dial behind his ear to night mode.

The heat function is activated by clicking a button in his armpit, making him warm enough to lull a baby to sleep. But the *hirsute* function makes the button too hard to find, so I'm rethinking the level of hair. It's real hair, from India, so when attached in this concentration it's like a forest. By the end of the night, it's in my teeth and scratching at the back of my throat. Aesthetically, I like it, but it's not practical. On the next iteration, I'll select new regrowth and see how he feels, see if I can get through the night without hawking up a furball.

Augie tells me he needs updates. Says he needs something to tell the shareholders; they're not investing for nothing.

While the rest of the team work on realistic skin textures and synthetic pubic alternatives for vegans, I'm making a database of personality quirks. Want your guy to be shy? Activate *aww shucks* protocol. Want a bit of rough trade? Activate *barfly* setting, combine with *short fuse* overlay.

I keep the husk. It's basically my type, but when I program the beta chip, I give him a Boston drawl, give him the newly grown hair breastplate for the bigger guy, switch his dick to medium because I can't keep up with what he was giving out last night. Tonight, he's a redhead, just for a change.

And his personality chip has a new setting; he's no longer just going to read my tone, but he's going to be able to make choices. I program the chip so there are random variables at play. When I ask him a question, he'll be able to read the context of the room, read the situation. And when he replies, he'll decide his response on the roll of a die, six variables, picking the one that seems most appropriate based on the setting. There's no actual dice. It's an algorithm. But each time he's greeted with a question, he can make his own decision.

Up to a point.

It's the closest I've got to synthetic autonomy, so it will do in a pinch.

The updates would be monumental if it weren't for the automated compiler engine, designed by someone else, credited entirely to Augie. It takes what would be days' worth of work, reduces it to mere hours, over one million keystrokes at the press of a button.

ACCESS/FILES/PRIMUS3000/Mk2/EXECUTE.

I watch as the screens blur in a cascade of code, digits multiplying by factor one thousand before my eyes, and feel the deep well of excitement in the pit of my stomach, to race home, to witness the change with my own eyes.

I watch the clock. It moves glacially compared to the updating algorithms pulsing on the monitors, but soon it is 5:30 p.m. and I'm gone.

Introducing the new Primus3000 – Mark 2 – Same Sex Model, now with added removable orifice gulley, for easy cleaning, with antibacterial ridged internal surfaces.

I've named him Dirk after the gym teacher I had in high school, the one with the thighs and the short shorts who'd watch you while you showered. We all knew a Dirk. When I shower, I make him watch, for old times' sake.

When I'm dry and dressed, he stands there, waiting patiently in the kitchen, leaning casually, *first date* algorithm meets *getting to know you* protocol. I ask if he wants a drink he can't drink, and he says: "Sure, whatever you're having."

I give him a tumbler of water and pour myself three fingers of Maker's Mark. I ask: "Ice?" and he says: "Sure." I put ice in my glass but not his.

We clink *cheers* and I stand too close to him. Looking up into those brown eyes, I decide I'd prefer green ones and switch the touchpad above his left eyebrow to make the necessary change. He rubs one massive hand down my side and smiles. His cheeks flush a genuine blush shade (pantone—PMS 1777), and I lay my hand over his, raise my glass to sip my bourbon with the other. His body heat is on high, but it's November and the cost of heat is getting higher by the year, so it's fully intended.

I ask: "Shall we sit?"

And he nods with that little boy smile on a sharp model's jaw and takes my hand, leads me to the couch, sits so close our knees are touching.

"How was your day?" he asks and feigns a sip of his lukewarm water.

He keeps his eyes on me as I explain the day, as I explain the new functionality on the memory chip, how I've been experimenting with augmented reality as a way of building a cache of memories that can shape temperament and personality type. He keeps his green eyes on me as I speak, nodding when the need arises, saying "uh huh" and "sure" to show he's listening: *engagement* protocol activated.

I order a pizza and it arrives forty minutes later while we are kissing like horny teenagers, my third bourbon turning the night from chaste to naughty in an instant. With the aid of the panel at his lower back to raise the seduction level to *playful*.

Note to self: *remote control* or *voice activated* function change options need to be explored.

The pizza is a medium, though he grabs a slice and pretends to eat. This model has no waste filtration and disposal system, so he can't eat or drink but has been programmed to mimic the action due to the overwhelming demands that food and drink have on social etiquette.

I eat the rest of the pizza, talking with my mouth full about *combined variable arithmetic operators* and the options for upgrading the *Integrated Development Environment*. He smiles and nods. "Uh huh," he says. "Sure."

As I watch him, my vision swimming with the effects of the bourbon, the fourth glass flying down too easy, I notice the rise and fall of his chest, the imitation of breathing. I applaud the upgrade. It was designed to be used during *night* mode, but focus group output recommended it for permanent use to make the model seem more engaging, to add the illusion of realism.

Augie said the shareholders shot the idea down, ordered to keep it as a *night* mode function only, but I ignored him. In the amorous moment when Dirk crawls along the couch and pulls our groins together, kisses my open mouth with a wet flick of his tongue, I lay my hand on his rising and falling chest and know I was right to include the feature as routine.

When he takes me to bed, I activate the *pleasure* mode using the panel on his lower back, add the overlay of the *Lothario* protocol and let him go to town on me. *Analingus* mode is set to *obliterate*, and I've replaced the genital unit with the new beta model I'm trialing, the one with the sensor in the glans that uses heat geolocation to find the prostate at the recommended length of time. Focus group input and GQ Magazine have hinted that penetration should last between seven and thirteen minutes, so at around ten minutes of pounding and thrusting, he lifts my legs higher over his shoulders and the heat sensor finds its intended target. With a muffled bellow, I shoot my load like a geyser, thin ropes of spunk painting a Pollock across my torso.

A minute later, he simulates his own orgasm and collapses on top of me, breathing and heart rate synthesis options elevated to *workout* mode.

I activate night mode in his freshly groomed pit, and he holds me while I sleep, his chest rising and falling with simulated breath, his breathing a combination of wave sounds and white noise—the favored option by the focus group. His chest hair is sharp against my naked back, and the fresh regrowth option is a no-go. Nevertheless, I sleep the best sleep I have in years, warm and lulled by the rise and fall of an innocuous tide.

In the morning, at 7:45 a.m. as previously programmed, Dirk kisses me gently and says good morning with a sleepy smile. At 8:45 a.m., I cease function in his operating system and remove his chest plate and armpit inserts, remove the current scalp choice and pubic hair plate, and stick them in my backpack, ready to insert into the test sterilizer and replace with new options. He stands there in the kitchen, shaven and immobile, and waits nine hours for me to return.

Augie wants updates in the morning meeting, and we go around the table giving him our pitches, trying to outshine our peers. Corin and Becca have been working on synthesizing edible, vegan, hypoallergenic semen and vaginal moisture. The texture is there but the scent profile needs some work.

Alistair is building a *morning routine* module, a way for them to make coffee and breakfast and pack a lunch.

Jesse is working on artistic talents, caching musical output and vocal timbre to create a profile, studying brush stroke analysis for painter modules and uploading every language and its prepositions to create bilingual options. So far, the companions are only available in English and Spanish, but the shareholders are adamant that a number of German brokers are showing interest, that China has their own variety with an option of every language imaginable. We spent too long working on regional accents; we need to expand into language.

The meeting ends before I have a chance to discuss my findings, and I'm okay with that. I want what I present to be perfect. It is lightyears ahead of what everyone else is working on.

That day, I spend my time making updates to the flaws I've found in Dirk. To make him perfect.

I find that if I use the random option generator of the last prototype and cross reference the output with the memory chip's *augmented reality* function, I can create a linear history for a companion unit. The complexity is enormous, so at this stage I can only go back a year, but I feed in all the variables, the probabilities, substantiate the linear history with several supporting operating units, and find that I can write a single personality as close to human as it can be. The rest of the variables can be ironed out with secondary modules designed to affect their view of the history: make them cold if they want something less smothering, make them cloyingly affectionate with the *Golden Retriever* protocol.

I build the patches into a single chip and overlay the perfect traits for my trial on Dirk, and I find that when running through test simulation, all of these features working in tandem create the closest thing I've ever seen to sentience.

It's groundbreaking really, the birth of new companionship, not just a fuck toy like the Japanese market offers, but a true partner.

I incorporate *voice activation* strategies for minor changes on the go, but I'm content I have built Dirk to be the man I wanted him to be all along. The man I dreamed he could be.

Tonight, Dirk's hair is brown, his body hair fine, his eyes blue. He's dressed down in jeans and a polo and sneakers, and his accent is Southern, with that good boy charm. His dick is large, circumcised, because that's all they had left in the vault. He has a fine scruff of facial hair from the new interchangeable facial hair options.

Introducing the new Primus3000 – Same Sex Model – Mark 3, now with added responsiveness to speech, now with the unknown, now with something new and untested.

I still make him watch me while I shower. This time though, he is able to hold a two-way conversation. As the water runs off my body, he tells me about his memories, and I insert myself into them for context. I tell him: "We've been together almost a year," and he tells me about a bar he knows on 46th Street, and I "remind" him that is where we met.

Eventually, as I dry my skin and put my clothes on, we've built at least eleven months of a shared history, which his data banks are reconverting into memory files, so visually he is able to imagine what that looked and felt like, is able to access an almost palpable rendition of events by way of his version of memory.

He slowly leads me to the sofa, the heat of his hand causing my skin to prickle as he massages the small of my back. He says: "I like your shirt, is it new?"

I recall buying it recently but have to vocalize the message to have him build up the memory. "I got it on sale last week, remember?"

He scrunches his brow, and the skin there barely moves. It looks artificial. He says: "Oh, oh yeah of course," but the tone isn't convincing. I watch him as his eyes dart around a bit and then his smile returns: memory logged.

I curate every expression, every intonation of his words, until he starts to blush that same pantone pink built into the hue of his fleshlike epidermis. Every now and then I have to break the stare, stop the appraisal. I'm affecting the outcome by watching too closely, and he's starting to retreat into himself. It's the observer effect, and it's skewing the results.

At the table, we sit facing each other and I ask: "Would you like a drink?"

His answer catches me off guard. "I can't drink anything," he says, and then watches my face for the obvious confused reaction.

"What about dinner? Is there anything special you want me to order in?"

Again, he shakes his head, and he seems… frustrated? It's a new look on that same placid face, but there is a slight darkness to it. An anger.

He says: "Why are you asking me what I want to eat? You know I can't eat."

"Why can't you eat?" I ask because I need to see where this is going. It's likely there's a gap in his memory processors that involves ingesting food and drinks, or some kind of failsafe to stop him ingesting consumables, to stop fluid getting into his mechanisms, or stodgy masticated foods clogging his gears.

He answers, softer: "You know why." And I let it go.

I reach across the table and put my hand over his. "Are you feeling okay?" I ask. "You seem… stressed?"

It's the wrong word but it's the only comparable descriptor I can find in my limited experience with Dirk: Mark 3.

He shakes his head, rubs his short beard aggressively, and the facial hair patch detaches for a second and reconnects. His eyes widen in shock.

"What the fuck?" he shouts, standing suddenly, pushing his chair back from the table so it topples across the floor. The flats of his palms go to his forehead instinctively, and he sets off the *eye color change* function; his irises change to green, then brown. I hope he doesn't notice what's happening, as I slowly rise from my seat and walk over to him.

I lay my hands on his shoulders and he pushes me back. The force is hard, but I play it down. He rubs at his chin again, harder this time, and the facial hair patch detaches completely and falls loose, spins across the kitchen floor, and his naked robotic mouth forms a perfect "o" shape. In panic, he pushes past me and goes to the bathroom, runs his hands over the steamed up mirror and looks at his face. There's a small crackling spark beneath his ear where energy is trying to feed into the missing jaw plate.

"What have you done to me?" he asks, to no one in particular.

The processors aren't knitting memories together quick enough, and he starts to become more agitated, grabbing the edge of the basin, clutching it tight until the porcelain cracks beneath his grip.

"What am I?"

I watch as he cries with no tears. I try to appease him, hands raised in surrender as I approach, and say: "Why don't we sit down and talk? I'll answer anything you ask?"

He lets go of the basin, and the cracked porcelain disintegrates and showers down onto the bathroom floor, down his jeans and onto his sneakers. Slowly, calmly, he nods and walks past me, back into the kitchen and beyond, into the lounge, where he sits at the far end of the couch, his elbows on his knees and one hand fiddling at the sparking joint connector of his missing jawline.

I think of how I can spin this into a memory. I posit that if I tell him he was in an accident, and his parts had to be rebuilt with bits of machinery to save his life, his processors might have a direction in which to splice together a new memory, one that will answer the questions he's preparing to ask. This lie might also help explain why his memories stop last November. I sit down slowly and start to fabricate the story in my head, preparing an opening line that will cascade out my mouth and into his auditory sensors, initiating activity in the *augmented reality simulators* and creating an image of an accident that rendered him broken but fixable. A car wreck, perhaps? Or a climbing accident? I breathe slowly as I prepare my statements, and he fiddles the sparking joint connection and gets a shock in his finger that sets off the batter mixer finger function I'd forgotten existed.

I don't have time to prepare my lies, and his confusion expands into anger and rage, and before I can utter a word, his nonrotating fingers are around my throat and he's pulled me up, up by the neck, my feet inches off the floor, and his fury is lit with the growing sparks of his exposed wiring.

And he's screaming: "You think you could make me love you? No one will love you!"

I try to claw at his hand, his synthetic skin covering nothing but pure metal that could snap my neck in an instant if that's what he desires. He grabs one of my arms with his spinning fingers, right above the wrist, and clenches until the bone cracks.

And I scream silently, my breath, my voice, captured beneath the bone breaking grip around my jugular. My arm hangs loose at my side, radiating pain all the way up to my shoulder and ice all the way to my fingertips. I feel like I will pass out with the lack of oxygen, and my eyes flutter, and sensing this, he throws me backwards, into the kitchen, my back striking the edge of the solid table. There's a sickening thud as several ribs crack on impact.

And he's approaching again, screaming: "Who the hell could ever love you? You've used me! You sick fuck!"

I'm fighting to breathe as he advances, fighting to get my voice back from my crushed throat, a hoarse wheeze all that seems to emanate from my open, gasping mouth.

And he kneels down before me, takes my face in his hand, and plunges his rotating fingers, designed only for pleasure, into my eye.

And from a desperate well inside me, somewhere before everything goes black, I manage to scream.

And I scream: "Initiate factory reset."

And the world bottoms out beneath me.

§

Introducing the world after the Primus3000 – Same Sex Edition – Mark 3, now with added eyepatch to cover vacant eye socket. Now with sling to support fractured arm. Now with ribs taped in place to facilitate mending. Now with additional pain, embarrassment, lies.

In the morning meeting, Augie says he wants updates, but when it comes to my turn, he skips over me, seeks out the updates on the vegan spunk and vaginal juices, seeks out the breakfast making capabilities, but asks for nothing from me.

When he ends the meeting, Augie asks me to stay behind and closes the door behind everyone after they have left, tilts the blinds so no one can see into the conference room.

He is silent as he walks around the table, taking his seat at the far end of the long wooden divide, and grabs a small remote. With the click of a button, the screens behind him come to life.

And I'm there in 4k widescreen, Dolby surround, displayed on these huge screens, being fucked into the sheets by the Mark 1, and then being made to explode with delight from Dirk: Mark 2, and then the image shifts, and I'm being destroyed by the Dirk: Mark 3 failure in a closeup from its point of view as it sends rotating fingers into the wet abyss of my now missing eye.

Augie says: "You've been a busy boy."

"I can explain," I say, fighting back the bile rising in my throat. I watch on the big screen as the ichor of a punctured eye drips down my face, as I scream to try and end the assault.

"I don't need an explanation. I think I caught the gist." He motions to the screens behind him, tapping pause on his remote so my terrified, one-eyed face is displayed in freezeframe.

I ask, timidly: "What are you going to do?"

Augie smiles and stands up, and with the unbearable confidence of a man on top, a man with everything to gain and nothing to lose, sits on the table in front of me and crosses his legs.

"I've looked back through all your work from that last week, seen all the experiments, all the keystrokes. All the vast intuitive but poorly executed changes you made to the program. And I've got to say…" He pauses. "I'm impressed."

I breathe out a breath I didn't know I was holding, and my shoulders relax a little. I ask, hopefully: "So, I'm not fired?"

Augie shakes his head. "Not yet, anyway," he says, getting back up onto his feet. "But I guess you could say your ass is mine."

I gulp, and my face twitches. My asshole twitches as well.

"Oh, don't look so worried. I've seen what you're into, and I'm not at all interested in taking our relationship that way."

I clench my one good fist around the chair arm, my palms both sweating, one into the fist of my yellowing plaster cast.

And I ask, curiously: "So, what do you want from me?"

Augie smiles and brings his face close to mine. And he says: "You're going to help me build the perfect killing machine."

His face is so close to mine I can smell the coffee on his breath, some rich roast Columbian that the staff aren't allowed to consume but that he has on tap in his own personal workspace.

And I ask: "Huh?"

"Think about it, Jacky! People love to fuck so we made them a fuckbot. But seeing the rage in this thing…" He gestures towards the screen where I scream in jumping pixels. "We could make assassins just the same."

My blood runs cold.

"Nothing set in stone, but I have a contact, through the shareholders, who are interested in a prototype."

I zone out as he explains his plans.

Dirk was meant to be an experiment in love, in companionship. A new step in making a tailor-made partner who could satisfy all needs without the effort of shopping around. How, then, did this potential companion go so wrong?

Augie is wild and frenetic as he explains his plans to me, and I sit and feign interest, knowing that I have no choice but to obey.

Much like the Primus3000, he owns me now.

And is love really that different from hate? The latter appeals more to my current mood.

I start to think of ways to patch in rage instead of love, fury instead of lust.

"Oh," Augie says. "And you can keep the model you stole, to sweeten the pot. But I'd suggest you try not to mess with it too much." He runs a finger down my plaster cast. "I don't think forcing love on something is the best idea, do you?"

He winks, tells me to think about it as he leaves the room.

And before the door closes, I know I'm in.

Perhaps Dirk: Mark3 was right. Perhaps I had no business meddling in matters of the heart. Perhaps my skills lie somewhere darker. A smile hitches at the corner of my mouth.

I should have seen this coming. It's inevitable when you stop and look at, so violently American, so blissfully predictable: if you can't fuck it, weaponize it.

And no doubt, when the prototype is up to spec, Augie will be there, with his arrogant grin and his lacquered hair and his argyll print sweaters to *Zuckerberg* all the credit.

So, I resign myself to the task, but with the caveat that I will be sure to test the new alterations on someone who really deserves it, a worthy lab rat of my choosing, one who's seen too much and somehow manages to know too much and too little all at once. Let's see how Augie likes broken bones, how he feels to be tamped down and humiliated, to be spat on, to be owned.

Let's watch him from above through the eyes of something bigger than him, a 4k display of how far the mighty can fall.

I climb out of the chair, my ribs screaming in protest, ready to return to work, ideas and algorithms racing through my mind at warp speed, as fast as the code can scroll through the compiler.

I'm starting to like the concept.

The concept is going to kill.

Think of the limitless possibilities when emotion is subtracted from the equation, when human kindness is no longer a factor and the opposite is an asset. Think of the military implications, law and order redesigned; think of the applications across the world as we know it. Think of the financial gain from these faceless shareholders with their questionable motives and their accountability to no one.

Think of the retribution.

Introducing the new Primus3000 – Silent Assassin Model, now with added interchangeable weapon attachments, with reactionary self-defense analysis, now with stealth mode and instant kill, now with Kevlar-infused epidermis.

Now with limitless possibilities.

Elton Skelter

ACCESS/FILES/PRIMUS3000/Mk4…
EXECUTE.

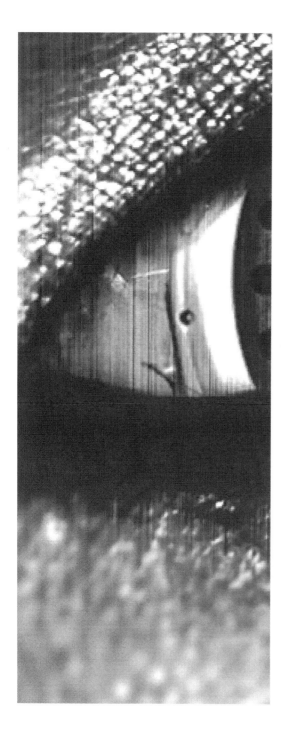 

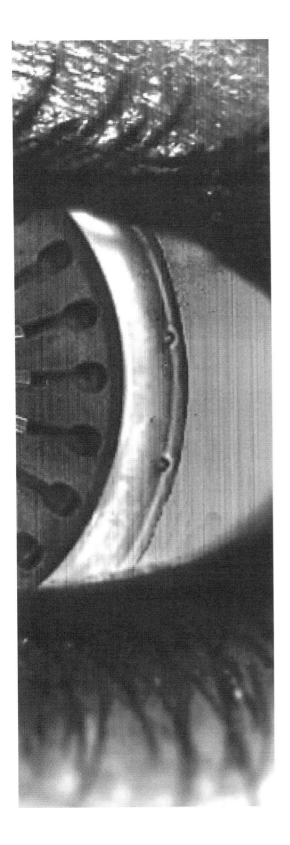
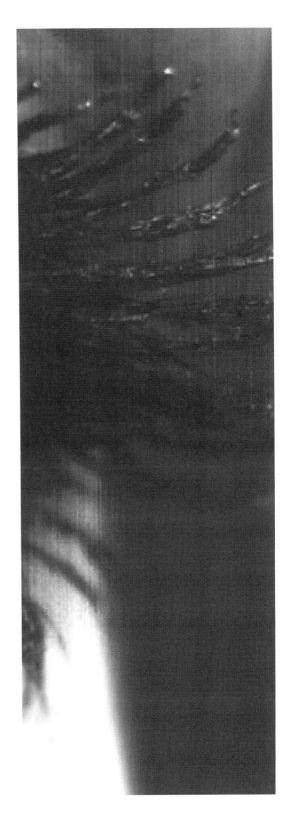

~IV~
THE ALIEN INVASION?

THE SCHADENFREUDERS
Karl Dandenell

When the little alien—accompanied by two heavily armed soldiers—walked into my office, I had to admit I was surprised. Normally, my clients ran to the more mundane: immigrant restaurant workers cheated out of their wages and the like. A *Schadenfreuder*, well, that was a different thing altogether.

"We're looking for Benjamin Goldstein, the lawyer," said one soldier.

I straightened my tie, wishing I'd worn my suit without the frayed cuffs. "That's me. How can I help you?"

"I'm Sergeant Pearson, part of the extraterrestrial security detail in San Francisco." He stepped back and gestured to the alien, who climbed into the chair opposite me. Hand to God: it looked like Yoda's kid brother, fuzzy and green and wrinkled. The alien tapped the translator cuff at its wrist. "Greetings, advocate. My name is Pol Pot."

I suppressed a shudder. "Pleased to meet you." I'd heard that Schadenfreuders picked random names out of Wikipedia for themselves, but it still gave me the willies. However, Mrs. Goldstein raised a polite boy, so I asked him nicely, "What can I do for you, ah, Mister Pot?"

"I wish to procure your services. You work with legally challenged non-citizens."

"Well, I specialize in services for immigrants, if that's what you mean."

"Yes."

There was an awkward moment. Did he mean: *yes, I agree with your statement*, or yes, *let's get on with it, shall we?* I opted for the second course. "All right then, Mr. Pot. If you're looking for citizenship, I'm sure I can help you out." Alien or not, a client was a client. It had been a slow month, and I was behind on my student loan payments. Again.

"No."

"Excuse me?"

"You misunderstand, advocate. I have no desire to become a citizen. While your planet is interesting, I wouldn't make my nest here." He flicked his ears like a cat. "I need contracts with your clients."

I leaned back. "What sort of contracts?"

"I wish to purchase their suffering," Pol said. Then he gave his best approximation of a human smile, slightly hampered by his lack of teeth.

§

When the aliens revealed themselves last year, their shuttles landed in areas beset by natural disasters or political upheaval. They also seemed attracted to prisons, political rallies, and orphanages. There were numerous sightings at the DMV.

When the scientists asked the aliens what they called themselves, their representative, Jim Jones, had replied, "We don't use a single word to describe ourselves, like 'Masons' or 'Libertarians.' We prefer the phrase: *Those Who Enjoy the Suffering of Others.*" The term *Schadenfreuders* appeared on social media, and it stuck.

"Let me see if I've got this straight," I said. "You want to help my clients by taking away their suffering?"

"No. Again, you are mistaken." Pol sounded just like my bubbie Esther with a bad head cold. "My people are not interested in alleviating the suffering of humans. We simply wish to procure a legal and fairtrade source of discomfort.

"Among my kind," he continued, "I am known as an Appreciation Specialist, much like the Hedonists of your ancestral Greece."

"Wrong ancestors, but I catch your drift." I closed the JDate.com browser tab and pulled up a contract template for professional services. "What in particular are you looking for?"

"Today I would like to experience disappointment, something strong and piquant." Pol leaned forwards, folding his disturbingly long fingers together.

"I might have a client for you. Do you know about political asylum?"

"I have studied your country's legal codes," Pol said. "Your asylum process is rife for abuse."

"Got it in one," I said. "Well, I just received notice that Mrs. Lee had her petition denied. You could come with me when I deliver the news."

"Promising," the alien said. "Now, as to your fee—"

"Standard commission is fifteen percent of the contract, or we can do it at a flat rate based on my actual hours," I replied automatically.

"Whatever is cheaper," said Pol.

§

We piled into the army's Humvee and headed over to Chinatown, flashing our lights all the way. Then we double-parked by Mrs. Lee's store and cleared the sidewalk for Pol, who sauntered in wide-eyed as any other tourist.

"Mr. Goldstein, hello!" said the matronly Chinese woman behind the counter. She looked at the soldiers, then the alien. "Oh! What's that?"

"That is Mr. Pot." He was busying himself with boxes of pungent herbs that lined the shelves. "He's studying different human ethnic groups and is willing to pay for a few minutes of your time." That was the cover story we'd concocted. "All you have to do is sign this, and I'll give you two hundred dollars—in cash—if he can hold your hand while you read this letter from Immigration Services."

She looked at the contract, confusion and suspicion warring on her face. "Is it about my petition?"

"It is."

"And Mr. Pot wants to hold my hand? Why?"

I shrugged. "Humans fascinate them. It's perfectly safe." As far as I knew.

She looked at Pol. "All right." Then she added in a whisper, "He smells like burned pot stickers."

"Agreed, but it's two hundred dollars for something you were going to do anyway." I glanced at Pol, who had produced a roll of twenties from a Mickey Mouse fanny pack. "What do you say?"

"I say three hundred," she said.

"That is unacceptable. Two twenty," said Pol.

"Two eighty, and I'll throw in that box of ginger root you've opened."

"Two forty."

"Done!" Mrs. Lee said, and wrote her name with a flourish. I nodded to Pol, who peeled off a dozen bills. Mrs. Lee added the money to the register. Then she held out her hand, shuddering a little when the alien touched her.

"May I have the letter now?"

"Here, ma'am."

As she read, her forehead wrinkled in concentration. Then she closed her eyes and shook her head. "They don't understand," she whispered.

"I'm sure they don't," I said, looking at Pol.

His little pointed ears stood at attention. A purr like several contented cats emerged from his midsection. And his eyes had changed from dark blue to black with bright gold flecks. "Very nice," he said. "Good day, madam." He wobbled out of the shop, followed by his military babysitters.

I turned to Mrs. Lee, who still held the letter. "I'm happy to follow up with Immigration Services. There's always a chance we can negotiate—"

She cut me off with a raised hand. "Thank you, Mr. Goldstein, but I need some time to think about this."

I joined Pol in the Humvee. He sat behind the driver, eyes closed, still purring.

I addressed the other soldier, whose name tag read Simmons. "So, what do we do now?"

Simmons, a thickset man with pale blue eyes, glanced at the street. "Wait a few minutes and keep our eyes open."

"Has there been any trouble?"

"Not with this guy," Simmons replied. "After that first press conference, though, the Secret Service caught a couple of nut jobs trying to plant a bomb on one of their shuttles. Not that it would have done any good. You wouldn't think it to look at them, but these guys are tough."

"And yet you're here," I said.

"Just doing my job, sir."

Pol opened his eyes. They were dark blue again. "That was a pleasant start. Now we need something more complex."

"Where to, sir?" asked Simmons.

"Mission District," I replied, pulling out the next contract. "Nice personal injury case."

Fifteen minutes and two near accidents later, we pulled up to a graffiti-covered apartment building. Chips of auto glass littered the sidewalk, and more than the usual quota of homeless men and women camped in the doorways. Only one made even a half-hearted attempt to panhandle us, though.

"Spare change?" said a scruffy bearded kid, shaking an empty cup. "Could use some coffee."

Pol knelt down and inspected him. "Caffeine is contraindicated. You require water, proteins, and blood filtering."

"Just want coffee, dude."

Pol dug around in his fanny pack and produced some quarters, which he dropped into the cup.

As we ascended the stairs, Pol said, "I might want to see that human later."

We stopped at the apartment nearest to the third floor landing. The carpeting was worn and stained, and dead roaches littered one corner. I knocked loudly.

The door was opened by a young, tired woman with long black hair streaked with gray. "*Hola*, Señor Goldstein."

"Hola, Mrs. Sanchez," I said. "Is your husband home?"

"Where else would he be?" she snapped. Then she looked past me at Pol and the soldier. "What's happening?"

"They aren't ICE agents, Mrs. Sanchez. Mr. Pot has come from another world to meet your husband."

"That's hard to believe," she said. "Please, come in." She backed into the tiny kitchen. Simmons took up a position in one corner.

The small apartment was spotless, filled with candles bearing stickers of the Virgin Mary. Family photos covered one wall, and an old flatscreen TV hung on the other, filling the living room with the heated exchanges of Hector and Elizabeth, the popular couple on *Amores Secreto*.

Pol sat on the couch. "I love this show. I originally requested the Los Angeles shuttle so I might meet the actors."

"I'm sure that could be arranged," I said.

"Don't worry about it. As it turns out, television actors aren't appetizing. Their emotional states tend to be muddled by ego and central nervous system depressants."

Mr. Sanchez hobbled into the living room on a pair of crutches. "*Buenos dias*, Señor Goldstein."

"Javier." I shook his hand. "Good to see you. How's the foot?"

He raised his left leg and wiggled the heavy cast, wincing as he did so. "Still pretty bad."

"I wished you hadn't taken that roofing job," Mrs. Sanchez said.

"No one else was hiring." He sat down on the couch, carefully propping up his leg. Then he turned to Pol. "You're one of the famous aliens. You look bigger on TV."

"Everything does. I'm Pol Pot." He pointed to Javier's foot. "Are you in great pain?"

"If I don't take my pills."

"Are you medicated now?" Pol asked.

"Not since yesterday," he replied.

"Madre de Dios!" Mrs. Sanchez said. "The doctor says you have to take the pills every six hours."

"They're too expensive!"

"Obviously you can't work like that," Pol said. "How do you pay the bills?"

Sanchez glanced at the kitchen and lowered his voice. "We can't. Mr. Goldstein is trying to get us some money, but that may take months. Domenica—my wife— she's working extra hours at the restaurant. It's not enough, though."

"This will help," I said, pulling out Pol's contract. "Mr. Pot is, ah, studying human behavior, and he wants to interview you. For a fee. Before you say anything more, though, you'll want to sign this."

"Why do I need to sign anything?"

"My people require receipts for all expenses," said Pol.

"He'll pay five hundred dollars," I said. "Cash."

"If it's a good story," Pol added.

Domenica appeared so quickly that Simmons put a hand on his sidearm. "Really? Five hundred dollars?" She turned to me. "This isn't illegal, is it?"

"Absolutely not, ma'am," I said. "The contract will hold up in any court." I hoped. I missed a lot of contract law questions on my first two attempts at the Bar exam.

"Well, what are you waiting for?" she said to Javier. "Sign it!"

I handed him a pen. He signed. "Okay. What do you want to know?"

"Take my hand and tell me how you came to this country," Pol said. "Start at the beginning, and don't leave anything out."

We stayed over an hour. At some point the conversation switched over to Spanish since it was easier for Javier, and Pol had his translator. Sgt. Pearson relieved Simmons at the door, and Domenica offered us bowls of *estofado de cabra*. I turned it down. I'm not a big fan of goat.

I was checking my email when Pol emitted a squeak and dropped Javier's hand. The alien's ears curled and uncurled rapidly, and his fur puffed up, turning him into a green tumbleweed. His eyes screwed shut.

Pearson stepped forwards. "I think we're done here for today, Mr. Goldstein." He poked Pol a few times, wrinkling his nose at the smell. "Yup." He handed me Pol's fanny pack, and I gave five hundred dollars to Javier.

"Is he all right?" he said, gripping the money.

"*Buena historia*," mumbled Pol.

I gave Javier an extra hundred.

Pearson tapped his radio. "Hey, Jim. Lord Kermit is curdled. We're coming down."

"Roger that," came the reply.

"He'll be fine. It's probably just their equivalent of jet lag," I said.

Pearson shook his head. "More like inebriation. As long as we get him back to his ship for some shuteye, he'll be fine." With that, he grabbed the alien and slung him over his shoulder like a sack of flour. "Good day, sir. Ma'am."

When we reached the street, Pol opened an eye at the bearded kid and said, "*¿Por postre?*"

"Maybe later," I replied.

§

Late the next afternoon, Pol appeared at my office while I was reviewing a deposition and awaiting callbacks on two other cases. He had another alien in tow. "Advocate, this is Eva Perón, our Minister of Trade."

"Pleased to meet you, ma'am."

"Greetings," said the other alien, who was smaller, and slightly rounder, than Pol. "My shipmate has shared a memory analog with me, and I found it intriguing. Very different from our other advocates… more subtle shadings and ripeness of flavor."

"That's nice."

"If what Pol says is correct, you may fit my needs," she said. "You will arrange a tasting now."

"I have a full schedule today," I said. "How's tomorrow?"

Eva exchanged a burst of high-pitched squeaks with Pol. Then she said, "This takes priority. If necessary, we will alter our compensation agreement with you."

"I'll need a retainer up front." Then, because I had just checked my bank balance, I named a figure ten times my normal amount.

"I don't have that much currency," said Eva. "We will need to stop at the bank."

I set aside the deposition. "Let me print some contracts."

The three of us piled into a black Chevy Suburban with four soldiers, including Pearson and Simmons.

"Where to, sir?" said Simmons.

"The 21 Club. Tenderloin."

We pulled into traffic, flipped an illegal U-turn, and shot up Sixth Street. Eva and Pol sat in their child car seats, carrying on their rapid-fire chipmunk conversation. At one light, Eva pointed at some day laborers congregating nearby.

"Are those criminals?"

"Not necessarily," I said.

"We note they demonstrate an aversion to police and soldiers."

"Ah." I suggested the men might lack visas and were worried about being deported.

"That particular anxiety could be most exquisite," she said. "Perhaps the soldiers could threaten them."

"Not my job, ma'am," said Simmons.

A few minutes later, we pulled up at the bar. "Wait here a second," I said.

The inside was dark, and a bit too warm, just as I remembered. Ghosts of old beer and cigarettes clung to the walls.

"Hey, Benjamin, how's my favorite shyster?" said the bartender, a grinning woman in her forties with bright pink hair.

I winced. "Do you have to call me that, Sally?"

"Absolutely. What are you drinking?"

"Mineral water."

"Always the wild man." She filled a glass and added a lime wedge. "On the house."

"Thanks." A few years back, I'd helped Sally out with a nasty divorce precipitated by her ex-husband's drug bust in Palm Desert. Fortunately, he was now serving fifteen years for intent to distribute.

"What brings you to the 'hood?"

I glanced at the dozen patrons drinking and talking quietly. "Looking for some temporary help," I said.

"Finally decided to paint your office?" Sally asked.

"I wish. No, I need some people who would be willing to discuss their problems with some… acquaintances. Off the record, of course," I added.

"Oh?" She raised an eyebrow.

I told her about the Schadenfreuders and offered her a commission for helping out.

"Why not? Money's been a little tight," she said. "We could pull some chairs into the storeroom. It's quiet enough, if you don't mind the toilets flushing next door." She cocked her head towards a man with a scraggly beard and a substantial gut. "Start with Bogus Jim. He's ordered his third beer, which means he's ready to start bitching."

She filled a fresh pint glass and took it over to Bogus Jim.

I collected the aliens and their babysitters. When we walked in, one of the patrons dropped his whiskey glass and crossed himself.

Bogus Jim stared at the aliens as I explained the deal. "How much?" he said. I flashed three fingers at Sally.

"Four hundred," she said, and winked.

"Bring it on!" Jim said. Sally led him to the back. The soldiers poked around before splitting up to cover the front door and the service entrance in the alley.

Eva and Pol sat on either side of Jim. Sally set his beer and contract on an upturned crate. "Thanks, honey," he said and scribbled his name. "Want to hear about my son, Tommy? He lost his second job in a year and wants to move home."

"Absolutely," said Eva. "I'm famished."

Jim looked at me. "You sure they understand English?"

"Better than you, I think," Eva said.

"Could be. I went to public school during the Reagan administration." He drained his beer and took the aliens' hands.

Sally and I returned to the bar. We talked to the other patrons, signing them up for a "tasting." We found two ex-cons, a cancer patient, a veteran with PTSD, a chronic gambler, and a former inner circle Scientologist.

Bearing in mind Pol's indulgence yesterday, I drew up a schedule that limited the aliens' sessions to fifteen minutes per person, with a break every hour.

"How often do they need the bathroom?" asked Sally.

"I don't even know if they use the bathroom," I answered truthfully. When I asked Sgt. Pearson, he shrugged. "It's complicated."

I handled contracts and payments, and Sally poured drinks. After a while, she loaded the dishwasher under the bar and hung up her towel. "This is turning out to be a pretty good Tuesday."

"Glad I could help," I said, sucking a lime slice.

"Seems kind of weird, though."

"Having aliens in your bar?"

She shook her head. "Naw. Some of those kids from the Haight make them seem downright normal. I'm talking about the whole slurping-up-human-suffering thing."

Her words didn't sit well. "This from a woman who serves worms in her tequila."

She laughed. "They're not actual worms."

Our conversation was interrupted by a lanky gas station attendant named Harry, who'd decided he didn't like Eva Perón's attitude and tried to dropkick her through a carton of paper towels. He was neatly intercepted by Sgt. Pearson, who pinned Harry faster than a cowboy taking down a calf at the rodeo.

After we ejected Harry, I checked on the Schadenfreuders. "Are you all right, Ms. Perón?"

"Of course."

"My apologies for the inconvenience."

"I was not inconvenienced in the least, advocate. Thanks to the soldier, I was able to indulge in your client's supreme frustration at failing to cause me injury. I would have paid him extra just for that." Her ears twitched, and she exchanged squeaks with Pol. "I think we can manage one more, then we must return. My shipmates have much to experience. And consider."

§

Apparently, I had passed some sort of interview. In addition to Eva Perón and Pol Pot, I began representing other aliens: Augusto Pinochet, Mobutu Sese Seko, Idi Amin Dada, and Nicolae Ceaușescu, whom everyone called Nicky. I even hired a paralegal to handle my existing cases while I coordinated meetings between the aliens and my clients.

The military wasn't comfortable with so many Schadenfreuders trooping through my office, so they moved the whole operation to the temporary alien consulate at The San Francisco Armory. They gave me a windowless room with a desk and a cot, with access to the garrison showers.

DoorDash and UberEats became my primary sources of nutrition. I saw one driver, Tai Tong, several times a week since he worked for both companies.

"I should be an employee," he said the third time he delivered an order from The Golden Rooster. "Not an independent contractor."

"I'm not really up on employment law."

"It's not fair, you know? I bust my ass all day and half the night, delivering people and food, just to pay a fifth of the rent. A grown man shouldn't have four room-mates, even in the Mission."

"No argument from me." I began setting out containers: egg drop soup and Kung Pao Chicken with mixed vegetables. "If you want to make a little extra, I can probably get you an appointment with Pol Pot this week."

"Dude." Tai frowned. "My grandfather was imprisoned by the Khmer Rouge. Not cool."

"I'm sorry, Tai. Really. They're aliens. They don't understand."

"You should." His phone beeped with an incoming text. He yanked it out of his cargo shorts and read the message. "Look, I gotta run."

He left, typing furiously.

I went back to my soup, mulling over Tai's comment. I'd been so focused on providing legal and ethical services to the Schadenfreuders. And helping my old clients at the same time. But maybe I hadn't sufficiently considered the moral issues involved.

Eva and Pol walked in without knocking. As usual.

"I hope you are not billing us for your dinner break," said Pol.

With a sigh, I set aside the soup bowl. "I wouldn't have to work during my meals if we parceled out the work better."

"This is about quality, not efficiency," she said. "It is paramount that you handle the tastings for my crew."

"There's no reason I can't hire another paralegal," I said, grabbing a piece of chicken with my chopsticks.

"We have already permitted you to delegate transactional infrastructure so you can be present during the tastings. They are… unsatisfactory when you are absent."

"I'm pleased you like my work, but I can't keep up this pace. Seriously." I sniffed loudly. The Kung Pao was really opening up my sinuses. "I'm barely sleeping, and I can't remember the last time I ate Sunday dinner with my mother." I wiped my nose on a napkin.

"Irrelevant. You are the best conduit; therefore, you must prioritize us."

Pol said, "As a people, you excel at complaining."

"The proper term is 'kvetch,'" I said.

"Indeed. It reflects a core cultural value of woe. Your 'kvetch,' as you say, has particular notes of unhappiness that makes your tastings far superior —"

Eva squeaked at Pol, who left the room.

"If you need that much suffering," I said, "why not just go to a war zone? We've got plenty."

"Such mass events are fit only for common Schadenfreuders," she replied. "We First Contact specialists have discriminating palates. Besides, we are tasked for finding the finest victuals for the Ambassador." She added an awkward wink. "The other crew will be so envious."

Pol returned with an aluminum briefcase and flipped open the latches, revealing neat bundles of fifties and hundreds.

"We wish to manacle your services and are willing to compensate you accordingly," Eva said.

"Lock you in," corrected Pol. "An exclusive arrangement."

"I'll need to draw up a new contract," I said.

"Don't take too long," said Eva. "I will not be disappointed."

§

After they left, I took myself to the 21 Club for a much needed drink. The bar was nearly full, and Sally was working alongside Mahesh, who was hooking up a fresh keg of Rolling Rock.

"Look what the cat dragged in," said Sally. "Mineral water?"

I slipped onto a barstool. "Need something stronger tonight. Maybe a bourbon?"

She pursed her lips. "You got it." She brought over a heavy glass full of ice and smoky liquid. "Bad day at the office?"

"Yes and no." I sipped at my drink, coughed. It had been a while.

"Too strong?" she said.

"Perfect," I said, and grinned.

She winked and went to fill another customer's order. When she came back, she set down a fresh coaster and a Diet Coke for herself.

I recounted my recent meeting with the Schadenfreuders and their annoying demands.

"I don't know," Sally said. "I could put up with a lot for a suitcase full of cash."

"It's nice to not worry about the bills," I admitted. "But…"

"But?"

"But I'm not helping people. Not really."

"Your clients get paid, don't they?"

I nodded. "Not enough to make any real difference. They'll spend whatever the Schadenfreuders give them, and then next month's bills come along. What then?"

Sally toyed with her straw. "Have you thought about a monthly subscription service?"

"I tried that. The little stinkers insist on 'unique' tastings," I said, making air quotes. "'We prefer fresh misery every day.' Sheesh." I finished my drink. "I'm like a sommelier of suffering."

"Uh, huh. Refill?"

"Why the hell not? I can afford it."

§

My Uber dropped me off at the Armory, and the duty sentry waited stoically while I fumbled with my ID.

Inside my office, I encountered a pile of Schadenfreuders, purring and farting. The smell reminded me of a pulp mill at low tide.

One of the aliens opened its ears, which were black with gold flecks. "Advocate! There you are!"

"Oh, hi Pol. You've been busy."

"Indeed." He brushed some dirt from his fur. "All of us—Suharto, Vladimir, Nicky and me—decided a late night snack was in order. But you weren't here. So rude. We had to sneak out to find some tasty homeless people by ourselves." He groaned.

"Nicky offered them large bottles of inexpensive alcohol to goad them on. So many stories of addiction and loss—I think I overindulged."

"Wait. What do you mean 'sneak out'? What about the guards?"

Pol farted loudly. "We came here in a *spaceship*. You think we couldn't bypass your primitive sensors and alarm systems?"

"Whatever. Look, it's late and I've got a busy day tomorrow." I nudged an alien with my shoe. "So if you don't mind, I'd like to go to bed."

He rolled the other Schadenfreuders into the hall. I kicked off my shoes.

"Advocate?"

"What is it, Pol?"

"She's prevaricating, you know."

"Who?"

"Eva Perón."

I found a blanket. "Occupational hazard for a politician. Now get the light, will you?"

"She has promised the crew that you will work for her."

"I am working for her." I reached for the light.

Pol intercepted me. "No! I found you. This is my contract. My operation. If you sign her contract, our leaders will reward *her*. Put her in charge of this entire operation." He shook my arm. "That isn't *fair*."

I freed my arm and sat back. "Okay. You *don't* want me to sign."

He stepped closer. "I want you to sign with me."

"Right…" My bourbon-fogged brain finally caught up. "I want a better offer," I said automatically. "With certain guarantees for my clients."

"I see we understand each other, advocate." He grinned his toothless grin. "With this transaction, I will rise above her in rank, and her disappointment will be a daily feast."

"Okay," I said. "I'll have something for you first thing tomorrow. But not too early. Seriously."

Pol squeaked a reply, switched off the light, and shuffled off.

I drifted off to thoughts of money. Briefcases full. In my dreams, though, all I heard were my clients' voices, demanding real justice, not cash.

§

I slept in until 8:00, then stumbled into the shower and let hot water pound me. My body reminded me I wasn't used to hard liquor and army cots played hell with your back. With regret, I toweled off, found some clean clothes, and fired up my laptop. I had just printed up my demands when Eva Perón barged into my office. Pol followed her, carrying a large, insulated cup.

"Today is a momentous day for your little planet, advocate," she said. "Our ambassador will be here within the hour—"

"Is that coffee?"

"Yes," said Pol, giving it to me.

I took a large gulp and decided that life could continue. "I didn't think you drank this."

"I don't," said Pol. "Based on your condition last night, I determined that such an offering would lubricate our negotiations."

I nodded. "Good idea."

"What negotiations?" asked Eva.

"Yeah, about that," I said. "Last night I did some thinking. And I came up with a proposal." I fetched copies.

They perused the document.

"I don't understand," said Eva.

"Sorry. It's like a menu. You select from compensation on one side, benefits on the other. Mix and match."

"You've been eating too much take out," said Pol.

"Probably," I said. "Let me show you. Under base compensation, for example, my top item is a flat rate of $5,000 a day."

"Ridiculous!"

"You might think that, Eva, but that rate means you only have to provide two weeks' paid time off, plus weekends and all recognized religious holidays."

"What if we don't want to pay you that much?" Pol said.

"Which we don't," confirmed Eva.

"Then I get more vacation. In exchange, you raise the compensation of my clients. It's a balance."

"I am not amused, advocate."

"And one more thing." I printed two more pages. "These are my clients who need medical treatment, counseling, and assistance with various government agencies. You're going to help me arrange that for them."

I waited, holding my breath. Finally, Pol said, "Why should we help them? As I said before, my people are not interested in alleviating the suffering of humans."

"But I am," I said. "And this is non-negotiable. However, since you brought me coffee, I'll give *you* first refusal rights. At one-third the lowest salary point.

Congratulations, you get to be the Big Cheese on Earth!" I drained my cup.

"I am the chief negotiator, here!" Eva said. "You will deal with me, and no one else."

"Your crew seems to have other ideas." I tapped my watch. "In any event, aren't you expecting the Ambassador, like, soon?"

Eva rounded on Pol with a furious squeaking. Even without a translator, I had a pretty clear idea of the conversation. Pol's reply was loud and complex, and his fur began to puff up.

I rummaged around my desk until I located some aspirin, making a mental note to avoid bourbon for the rest of the decade. I swallowed four tablets, closed my eyes, and willed the aspirin to do its magic.

Eventually the chipmunk chorus died down. I reluctantly opened my eyes.

Eva Perón stood there with her copy of the papers and a red Sharpie plucked from my desk. "I accept this. And this. But not this." She crossed out an extra week of vacation.

"I can live with that." I turned to my laptop. Then I printed and signed two copies, handing them to Eva. She scribbled her signature and Pol witnessed it.

"Now please leave. I'm taking my first sick day." I smiled. "And give my best to the Ambassador, will you? I can't *wait* to tell them about all the good work you'll be doing here. So much suffering removed and at *such* reasonable prices."

I shut the door in their faces.

~V~
TIME TRAVEL

PLINTHGATE PAPERS
Jason Mills

File #6: *Observer* editorial, 11/2/24

"Plinthgate" was the epithet the Prime Minister first landed on to describe the extraordinary events in Trafalgar Square yesterday, before inevitably spluttering his "comic" variations: "or perhaps the Plinthident, as a-plinth some hoary-headed swain may say." The inadequacy of Didcott's tiresome jests to meet the enormity of the occasion was greater even than usual. "Plinthgate" (we bow to destiny) is a crisis sensible far beyond the feckless croaks of Westminster's little pond. It is an existential crisis for humanity.

Past the initial furore and confusion, with dozens of viral videos soaking up the nation's bandwidth, the shape of what happened is now clearer. The mass protest against the Government's relentless failure to tackle climate change, a case underscored by the baking February heatwave, had filled Parliament Square (notwithstanding the terms of the permit), backed up Whitehall, and clogged Trafalgar Square. Although dozens of demonstrators were splashing in the sunlit fountains and clambering towards Nelson's feet, at 2:28 p.m. there happened to be no one on the vacant fourth plinth. The demonstration's attendant gamelan and the chants and chatter were suddenly silenced by a thunderclap and a blinding flash.

Early assumptions of freakish midsummer lightning were quickly obsolete. A shimmering globe of swirling blue light appeared on the plinth. After a few seconds, with ten thousand eyes and a thousand phones trained on the spot, the light shrank away, revealing a naked man crouching there.

Video shows him to be no Arnold Schwarzenegger, though surely the actor's image popped into many minds. Nor yet was this an avatar of Michael Biehn, his less well-remembered nemesis in The Terminator. Instead, the figure revealed appeared to be a young man of soft outline, no more than 20 years old, around 5'7", with a mop of brown hair. Although apparently alarmed at his situation, after a few seconds he stood upright, feet braced apart, and held high some small green object that many are convinced was a USB memory stick or similar device. Some suggest that his pose appeared rehearsed.

There are cheers, jeers, whistles, laughs, gasps. Hands reach up, and the young man, first seating himself on the edge of the plinth, is drawn down into the crowd. Chaotic footage obscured by placards and bodies captures only glimpses over the next minute, but he emerges at the top of Whitehall, clad now in a pink hip-length cagoule, evidently acquired in his passage through the mass. Mercifully there is clear video from close by for the next development, which might otherwise be the subject of vehement dispute: three police officers close on him, and before he is escorted away, in a loud voice, oddly accented and perhaps a little nervous, the young man declares: "I am claiming asylum."

It is clear from the many camera angles and the immediate amateur examinations of the plinth (all filmed, naturally) that no special effects gimmickry could account for this. There was no sign of pyrotechnics or electronics, no outlandish trapdoor in the plinth, no skycrane. What we seemed to see is what we did see: a man appeared from nowhere, in a manner suggestive (suspiciously so?) of a Hollywood time traveler.

The Government responded, as ever, with the composure of a decapitated hen. The Minister for Border Control called it an outrage, without ever clarifying what "it" was. The Home Office denied that any asylum claim had been made, just 16 minutes before the Home Secretary himself told the BBC that the claim was being assessed "in the normal way." The Prime Minister's later blithering amounted to no more than a recognition that whatever had happened was not normal.

We sigh and await developments. The young man, instantly famous, has disappeared from view as quickly as he arrived. Refugee agencies are howling at the Government, journalists slavering for scraps, the public glued to their screens. But entertaining as all this is, the gravity of the situation outside the circus tent must be confronted. A man has traveled, apparently without equipment, across space or time, to a precise location at a precise moment; for there can be no doubt this arrival was meticulously scheduled for maximum impact. The implications are spectacular: we are on the far side of a hinge in human history; we have crossed a border no Government can control.

§

File #13: from *Skirting the Obvious: Ten Years A Spin Doctor* by Saima Akhtar (2035)

Trevor gathered up the various documents sprawled across the table and shuffled them into a blue folder. "I think we can be quite proud of this," he said happily. "Good proposal, good research. Well done, Saima." He stood and added, "Want to come with?"

I got up, a little bewildered, and followed him, gradually realising that he was taking the folder to the PM! MY proposal! I was suddenly excited and nervous. We turned a couple of corners and reached the outer office, where someone nodded to Trevor and waved us through. So, just like that, there we were in the office of the Prime Minister, and there was Mr. Didcott in shirtsleeves, not at the desk but in a Chesterfield armchair, with a few pages on his lap. "Trevor!" he cried, looking up. "How have you ensorcelled this winsome consort? I must know the trick!"

I think Trevor winced slightly, but I was just delighted to be In The Presence Of and to be noticed. Trevor moved to present his folder and opened his mouth to explain, but he got no further, because Astley Morgan burst in and went straight past us. "Ed, you need to see this," he said, shoving a sheet of paper at the PM.

"I rather think, Astley," Mr. Didcott began, waving a hand in our direction, but the aide was not for turning.

"Read it," Morgan told him.

A minute or two passed in awkward silence. Trevor was unwilling to give up our facetime, and Morgan, naturally, didn't care who was there. "Blithering," the PM muttered darkly. "Like to see them ad lib in front of the cameras about alien invaders. So, what am I supposed to notice, Asteroid? Usual melodramatic slurry."

"What you're supposed to notice, Ed, is that that's tomorrow's leader and it's only 7 p.m."

Mr. Didcott looked at Morgan and looked at the page again. "The newspaper leaked to Number 10? That's refreshing."

"Not a leak. It isn't written yet. I know how they work over there. The editor will probably toss that off a couple of hours from now. The page in your hand is from the USB stick."

The PM looked at the paper again, digesting. "So that means." He took a big breath. "If this is what they end up writing, that means he's for real. That means he's from the future."

Suddenly Morgan seemed to notice us. "Oh, I'm sorry, Trevor. Do you think you and your concubine might fuck off while we run the country?"

"Astley." The PM sighed. But we were already leaving and he didn't stop us. My proposal would have its moment on some other day, I thought. But sadly, despite all that work, it never did.

§

File #1: "An Appeal"

The young man who appeared unclothed in Trafalgar Square, London, on 10/2/24 at 14:28, and who claimed asylum at the earliest opportunity, is our son, Caleb Hope. At the moment of his arrival he was seventeen years and 184 days old. We must withhold his date of birth (and our own names), but that date is more than a century after 10/2/24. He has been sent into our past, your present. The theatrical manner of his arrival alluded to popular culture to ensure the world's attention and understanding; but the sound, light, and nudity were purely cosmetic elements, superfluous to the technology.

Caleb seeks asylum. He has not suffered direct state persecution but has been a victim of state failure to protect his environment. In March 2023 an international agreement recognized severe environmental degradation as a legitimate ground to both seek and receive asylum. In December 2023 your administration made preparatory moves to ratify this measure. Only a regulatory enactment remains to complete the process, applying the new criterion not only hereafter, but retrospectively to the date of the December legislation. We urge you to implement that change and accord Caleb refugee status.

This document is one of 2,314 files on the USB memory stick that Caleb brought with him. All but ten are in the encrypted partition. Caleb does not know the encryption password explicitly but can provide it when he is granted permanent asylum on the ground stated. This is not solely a means to extort a favorable decision: we believe there would be far-reaching consequences if you obtained early access to the files, of much greater import than the fate of one young man. Your specialists will confirm that penetrating our encryption is intractable.

The ten unencrypted files now available to you provide support for Caleb's claim and a taste of what may be found in the encrypted partition: discoveries and technological information that will be of great use to your country, potentially lifting the U.K. above its peers economically and scientifically. Documents that could only come from your immediate future will also be revealed, to allay any remaining doubt.

For now, to serve as a proof of our claims and a gesture of good will, and as an ethical imperative in itself, the unencrypted files include details of a cure for Huntington's Disease, a genetic condition beyond the reach of medicine in 2024. It will take time to develop and apply this cure, but we are confident that experts available to you can verify its promise quickly.

The world in our time has reached such a perilous state, as other documents describe, that we have chosen to shelter Caleb from its dangers during his upbringing.

Despite the frankly unsustainable size of the population, Caleb has had relatively little interaction with other people, and we ask that you make allowance for his still developing social skills. We love him very much, and although we have long known that his best chance to flourish lay in your time, it is inexpressibly difficult to send him away from us forever. If you could share our distress for even a moment, you could not doubt the extremity of the situation that compels our decision.

We have tried to ensure that the best outcome for Caleb is also beneficial to your country, exercising our responsibility to the utmost. You must now look to your own wisdom in forming your response to this situation.

§

File #15: from *Whipping Boy: A Chief Whip's Diaries* by Jordan Harpich (2027)

"This here," said Didcott, jabbing a finger at the page, "'solely.' Bit of a bloody nerve, eh? Green eggs and ham!" (I didn't get the culinary reference, but I googled later—Seuss—and I presume he meant he didn't like the word. Out of question for him to just say so.)

Louche, sprawled on the sofa, Morgan shrugged, not bothered. "It's the closer that intrigues me, Ed. Smells like a disclaimer."

Didcott glanced at the sheet. "Flattering degree of respect you have for my 'wisdom,'" he grumbled. He chewed on it for a moment, swirling the ice in his whisky. "You think they're hinting at something?"

Morgan shrugged again. "Certainly being coy. Carefully phrased. I don't envy you the decision."

"Thanks for your input," PM muttered. "What about this Huntingdon business? Is it a real thing? Never heard of it."

I think even Astley Morgan looked faintly disgusted at that. "Huntington's," he corrected. "Very real, Ed. Terrible disease, kills slowly and horribly and always. There's a genetic test, but no treatment."

Didcott grunted, and worked his jaw. I swear he spent the next few seconds fighting back an impulse to ask how many it affected, knowing it would appear too calculating: was the number of victims low enough to ignore?

"Painted in a damned corner, aren't we?" he complained.

Morgan didn't reply. If he had, I bet he would have said: Aren't *you*?

"And why does it have to be asylum anyway? Bloody prima donna. Isn't he already British in the future? Can't we just give him the freedom of the city and a library card and call it done?"

"You just read it, Ed," said Morgan. "No asylum, no password."

PM sighed. He twizzled his desk light to point at me. "Jordan, for now, just tell the crew—I don't know, stand by their beds, hold the fort. They also serve. They can tell their flocks that we're hard at it, developments due soon, all that."

"I understand, Prime Minister."

"On no account tell them the bloody truth. Hell's bells, we've got trouble enough!" He tipped back the rest of his drink. "I'm going to bed. Everyone piss off."

§

File #14: excerpt from interview transcript, 11/2/24.

Q: Do you understand what is on the USB stick?

CH: Files?

Q: And what is in those files?

CH: I think it's about the world. And everything that happened.

Q: Everything that happened. What happened? When did it happen?

CH: History. Before all this. The seas rose and the air went bad and the world filled up with people. Wheat wouldn't grow and there were no bees, I think. People were eating plastic. Does that sound right?

Q: When were there no bees? What year was this?

CH: I think it was summer. Is that what you mean?

Q: Do you know the year?

CH: Spring, summer, autumn, winter. January, February, March, April, June…

Q: May.

CH: May, June! I'm sorry.

Q: Caleb, do you know where you are?

CH: London, United Kingdom, still has Scotland!

Q: Where were you before you came to London?

CH: I was at home. But I had to come here.

Q: Why was that?

CH: To claim asylum.

Q: Now listen carefully, Caleb. I'm authorised to tell you that the Prime Minister might be willing to accord you immediate citizenship instead. That's even better than refugee status, and it's quick and easy for everybody. What do you think about that?

CH: That sounds really good!

Q: Well then, shall we get that process started?
          You'd be happy with that?

CH: Oh yes. Everyone is so kind. I just hope nobody minds about the password.

Q: We would still need you to tell us the password, Caleb, so that we can read the files on the USB stick.

CH: But I don't know the password. I'm sorry.

Q: I'm not sure we can grant citizenship without it, Caleb. How do you expect to tell us the password if you don't know it?

CH: When I know it, when I get asylum. It's who's under the crown.

Q: You mean the King? You mean Charles?

CH: I don't know the password. I'm sorry.

§

File #16: Memorandum, GCHQ to Cabinet Office, 12/2/24
Brief examination has determined that the device is compatible with the USB form factor and protocols, but it is a more sophisticated piece of electronics. The encrypted section of the data appears to use a bespoke system. The device rejects efforts to copy the data, whether at file system or bitwise level. Inbuilt is a thirty-second delay between password attempts, rendering brute force access untenable. We have few clues by which to guess the password, and it seems we are unlikely to obtain anything further from the subject. Given this degree of forethought, we expect that an electronic deconstruction to detach the memory from its interface would also prove fruitless, and probably destructive. In short, although cautious work on the problem continues, if the password is not provided, the data is unlikely to become accessible.

§

File #17: from Minutes of Cabinet Meeting, 13/2/24
2.1 THE SECRETARY OF STATE FOR THE HOME DEPARTMENT said that the asylum claim of Caleb Hope posed unusual difficulties. Mr. Hope's conspicuous arrival in the U.K. had been irregular, yet it could not be shown that he had crossed a border illegally, or at all. He carried no identifying documentation and neither his nationality nor his point of embarkation were likely to be established with certainty. Deportation was clearly infeasible, regardless of the outcome of the claim. Other complicating factors were his indeterminate age and limited understanding of his situation.

Continuing, THE SECRETARY OF STATE FOR THE HOME DEPART-MENT said that the ground for Mr. Hope's claim was also problematic. He sought asylum in response to environmental degradation from which his originating state could not or would not protect him. Putting aside the issue of how that could be verified in these circumstances, this criterion only recently became available to claimants, via the Immigration and Asylum Act (2023) that ratified international agreements, and had not previously been utilised. The Act provided for the criterion to be activated by and at the discretion of THE SECRETARY OF STATE FOR THE HOME DEPARTMENT through regulatory procedure. It had not yet been activated, and although it could be applied retrospectively, up to now the Government had taken the view that the power should not be exercised without further consideration, with a review and consultation process envisaged. No other country was known to have brought the international measure into operation as yet.

Concluding, THE SECRETARY OF STATE FOR THE HOME DEPARTMENT said that the case attracted great attention, both nationally and internationally, and that the data offered by Mr. Hope, if authentic, promised to be of substantial interest to the Government. For many reasons a swift resolution was desirable, but the matter was complex and delicate.

THE PRIME MINISTER said that in particular the Government did not wish to open the floodgates to putative environmental refugees from many regions impacted by climate change. Other countries were in better positions to respond to those situations than this small island. The tide that might bear Mr. Hope between Scylla and Charybdis must not fling the flotsam of the world upon the shores of the U.K.

In discussion the following points were made:

- the spontaneous arrival of an individual at a chosen time and place represented a new and significant challenge to national security; numerous representations had been received from diverse organisations in the scientific community, requesting opportunities to interview and examine Mr. Hope, to review all available recordings of his arrival, and to take measurements in Trafalgar Square;

- concern had been raised by the Gambling Commission in regard to the outcomes of future sporting events that might be compromised by Mr. Hope or his data;

- in amongst the extensive media coverage, NGOs were decrying the detention of Mr. Hope as groundless, and it was conceivable that in any challenge the courts would side with them;

- arguably Mr. Hope should be considered as not only an asylum seeker, but a quasi-diplomatic envoy from a hitherto uncontacted state, with which, for all the Government could know, he might still be in communication; and therefore he should be accommodated with care; MPs reported exceptional quantities of contact and correspondence from excited constituents with diverse concerns and demands;

- it was not clear that it would be in Mr. Hope's interest to release him from detention, given his apparent unfamiliarity with his new environment;

- lawyers were offering to assist and represent Mr. Hope, and their professional bodies had much to say about the situation.

Responding, THE SECRETARY OF STATE FOR THE HOME DEPARTMENT curtailed the discussion and said that these points and other matters arising must be dealt with by the relevant departments. The situation was of no one's choosing. At present he was minded to deny the asylum claim for want of verification, but to nonetheless accord Mr. Hope indefinite leave to remain in the U.K.

Summing up, THE PRIME MINISTER thanked all present for their contributions and said that this was a knotty problem, because certain arrangements relating to Mr. Hope's data storage device might render indefinite leave an unsatisfactory resolution. He would develop the matter further with THE SECRETARY OF STATE FOR THE HOME DEPARTMENT and update Cabinet in due course.

The Cabinet:

– took note.

§

File #11: In Thanks

Later documents detail the many severe effects of human activity in the decades ahead of your time: pollution, desalination, climate change, micro and macro-plastics, extinctions, ecological collapse, crop failures, radiation leaks, blights, droughts, floods, invasive species, spillover events, the expanding range of tropical diseases, inundation, aggressive erosion, thawing permafrost, melting ice caps, mass human and animal migrations, and so on. These threats are all known to you, but their exponential acceleration and the grave and unexpected ways they feed upon each other proved (will prove) overwhelming to humanity.

We would certainly have had greater prospects of responding effectively if governments had acted sooner and better, even, in fact especially, before your time. Absent that timely and coordinated action, and beset too with the infeasible demands of an unpredicted reversal in population trends, many of our systems and societies eventually could not cope, and conditions in our time are essentially intolerable for billions of people.

Our history records the arrival of Caleb Hope in your era. Many scientific developments since then, informed by this clear evidence of its possibility, have inched towards a means of traveling backwards in time. We, Caleb's parents, an engineer and a physicist, are only the last bearers of the baton in this immense relay. We kept Caleb safe from the world's dangers—he has spent regrettably little time outdoors or in company—and were not the first to name our child after the famed asylum seeker, wanting that past to become his future: a life in a time when the skies were still clear, the climate temperate, the rivers not yet poisonous, the foodstuffs (so we read) plentiful and a joy to eat.

After many years' work, the project that we have merely completed is one to which hundreds of others have previously devoted their lives. We are humbled by them, and we find the prospect of ourselves taking advantage of this achievement to be unconscionable. However, we cannot speak for others, who must make their own choices.

As to the troubling logic of the phenomenon and the bewildering question of how information, like Caleb's name, arises in this loop, we can offer no advance in understanding over that of your own scientists. However, only too aware of the possibly catastrophic ramifications of our actions, we have striven to avoid any conflict with known history. Consequently we have told Caleb as little as we can about "Plinthgate," and no more than we dare. His need is genuine, and what we have here offered you in recompense for your kindness is everything we feel it safe to disclose. It is all we can do.

§

File #18: from transcript of Prime Minister's (PM's) meeting with Home Secretary Brian Connaught (BC); present, Special Advisor Astley Morgan (AM); 14/2/24.

PM: Now then, Brian, rock and a hard place. Let him in and we'll have half of Polynesia floating over in their Kon-Tikis seeking refuge from the waves. Every Arab chancer north of the Sahel will trot his camel onto the P&O ferry to try his luck! Uncontacted Amazonian tribes with dinner plates in their faces will mysteriously acquire a taste for suburban comforts and wash up in hollow logs on the beach at Penzance! But if we don't let him in, all the goodies on that accursèd stick might as well go in the bin. Tell me you've found some procedural wizardry to sort this out, Brian. Rid me of this turbulent precedent!

BC: As I said yesterday, Edward, it's complex. If I activate the IAA power to recognise environmental refugees, we're stuck with the consequences. The Act enables me to turn it on, but not off. Fact is, we had no intention of activating the damned thing, so we hadn't worked it through.

PM: Purely decorative?

BC: Satisfying our international obligations, Edward, or showing willingness at least. At present we've gone further than any other country, without actually doing anything.

PM: God forbid! Hm. Can we grant full asylum on some other grounds?

BC: Nothing fits. Bugger refuses to say anything helpful. If he'd only claim he'd been tortured or enslaved, we'd have no problem, but a simple fib is apparently too much to ask. They usually lie their faces off.

PM: But if the environmental degradation clause was active, that would definitely work?

BC: Surely. We can't verify, obviously, but it's highly plausible that the future is a shithole. Open and shut case. But then, as you say, here come Tom, Dick, and Harees, wanting us to pay for their new life because it's raining hard in Rwanda.

PM: Astrognome[?], you're uncharacteristically laconic this morning. Nothing to contribute in return for that magnificent salary?

AM: As it happens, Brian just said something useful. Open and shut case. We're in recess. We activate the power as quick as we can, ministerial fiat, doesn't need Parliament. Then draft a one-line bill for Monday, start of the new term, first order of business. We've still a majority of fifty-odd seats; Jordan can whip it through no problem. And the motion just quashes the power again. Brian can't turn it off, but Parliament can. Bit of high-speed pingpong with the toffs, Parliament Act, bingo. We grant the kid asylum in the interim, then slam the door before anyone else turns up.

BC: Jesus. And what's that going to do for our international reputation?

PM: Fuck our international reputation, Brian. Fuck it with extreme prejudice. Fuck it with knobs on. Machiavelli over here has a wheeze that gets us a jump on the rest of the entire fucking world. I can cope with a few indignant Frenchies for that. Dulce et decorum est pro patria fraudem! Let's get this moving. Scoot back to Marsham Street and give the order. Astley, you can rustle up Kaspar Hauser and his magic wand, then sketch up your nano-Bill. We're one day away from decades of glory!

§

File #19: From an interview with Carol Schneider of Just Refuge, broadcast on *Newsnight*, 14/2/24.

CS: Well, we just don't know, do we? But if we just suppose it is what it looks like, it's a man come back from the future with a memory stick full of information? In that case that information is for the world, not for Edward Didcott's personal use.

NN: So you're worried that the Government will keep whatever it is secret. But to get it in the first place, if we can believe the rumours, they might have to grant this chap asylum on the grounds of environmental degradation. Do you really think they'll do that, become the first country to do that, and risk lots of other people applying on the same grounds?

CS: We certainly should be open to helping those people if we can. We've caused a lot of the mess after all. But there's a much better solution here. That data might be of tremendous value to governments and researchers everywhere. If I were in Didcott's shoes, I'd be ringing round and telling other world leaders that I'll share all the information with them, but only when they too have ratified. That way, we pressure all countries to accept environmental refugees, addressing the clear need and sharing the cost fairly, and everyone benefits from the new science, or whatever it is the traveler has brought with him.

NN: Well, that's certainly an ambitious scheme, but surely those legal processes would take years? Do you think the Government will have the patience for that approach? Or dare I say, the generosity?

CS: Of course not.

§

File #20: request for ministerial direction, 15/2/24

The Rt Hon. Brian Connaught MP
Secretary of State for the Home Department
15 February 2024
Dear Brian
IMMIGRATION AND ASYLUM ACT (2023), Activation of Section 4, Clause 19

You have expressed your intention to initiate a regulatory activation of the above power. Although this is indisputably in your gift, it is anticipated that the activation could lead to a substantial influx to the U.K. of environmental refugees from around the world. You have given me to understand that the power will be active only until quashed by Parliament in the near future. However, it is clearly not my part to second-guess the outcome of parliamentary deliberations, and therefore I am obliged to suppose that the new dispensation might persist indefinitely.

The budget for the asylum system does not allow for this contingency. As the measure has no global precedent, the level of demand for asylum under this clause cannot easily be assessed. However, any substantial increase in the number of claimants has significant implications for accommodation, living allowances, transportation, security, local authority spending, medical care, claims processing, and legal expenses. The last could be particularly troubling given that these claims would be made on the new ground of state failure to protect the claimant from the consequences of environmental degradation, which is untried in our systems and untested in our courts. Until commensurate budgetary allowance is determined and rendered to this initiative, I cannot responsibly conclude that it meets the Managing Public Money test for value for money.

Therefore at present I am unable to proceed without your written direction. Once this is provided I will ensure that all necessary steps are taken to bring this power into operation without delay.

I will of course alert the Comptroller and Auditor General, and I will also write to the Chairs of the Public Accounts Committee, should they wish to initiate any investigation.

Kind regards
Fatima Afzal
Permanent Secretary

§

File #21: from *Back From The Future*, by Caleb Hope with Suzanne Scranton (2026)

After breakfast the next day, which was Thursday, people came to take me to see the Prime Minister! I said goodbye to the blue room and that funny old toilet, and we went outside. Hot day! Everything was so bright, it hurt my eyes.

We got into the back of a big old-fashioned car. It was black and a lot more comfortable than the police car had been. And then we did that whole journey again, like on Saturday, but backwards this time. There were so many buildings and people and signs and noises that in the end I just scrunched down in the seat and looked at my shoes.

I thought we were going back to Trafalgar Square, and I was hoping there wouldn't be so many people this time. But we went somewhere else and down a slope under a building. Then we had to walk for a while in a tunnel with long lights. We went up some steps at the end and through a metal door, and some men patted our bodies, which made me laugh. And then the people who had brought me went away and a lady shook my hand and smiled at me and said, "I'll take you in to see Mr. Didcott." I hoped it wouldn't take long because I was really here to see the Prime Minister.

She took me up some more stairs and through some other rooms, and then she said, "Mr. Didcott, here is Caleb Hope." She smiled at me again and left, and Mr. Didcott came around his desk to shake my hand. "I'm thrilled to meet you, Caleb," he said, "though you're the cause of a good deal of bother!"

"I'm sorry!" I said at once. I felt very bad then. "I didn't mean to cause bother."

He looked at me a moment then, and said, "Not at all, Caleb. It's not your fault at all. I'm sorry I said that. Come and sit down. You see out the window there? That's Downing Street! Have you heard of Downing Street?"

"Where the Prime Minister lives," I said. We had sat down on big chairs either side of the window. They were dark red and sort of squeaky.

"That's right," said Mr. Didcott. "And do you know what the Prime Minister did this morning? Hang on, I'll show you." He hopped up and got a sheet of paper off his desk and put it in my hands. "There you are, Caleb, my copy. The Permanent Secretary at the Home Office…" I'm afraid I can't remember everything he said, but he pointed to the paper at the end. "But I said bugger a ministerial direction, Brian, she can have a PRIME ministerial one! Signed it myself. Stick that up her procedural requirements, eh?"

I stared at the paper. I can read okay, but this was hard. "What is it, please?" I asked.

"Caleb, that's your asylum. Well, not quite that, but it enabled us to grant you asylum. I'm told that's been sorted now as well."

"Oh!" I said. "Is it thirteen forty-eight?"

Mr. Didcott was surprised. "It's, let's see, two-fifteen just gone. Why?"

"Thirteen forty-eight is when I get asylum. So have I got it now?"

"Yes. Yes, Caleb you have. You'll be safe now. You can stay here, in England, forever. This emerald isle. I hope that makes you happy. Ra, ra, the King and Saint George!" Mr. Didcott was quite funny. Then he leaned forwards. "Now then, Caleb. I was hoping you might be able to help me out with this password business?"

"Fatima Afzal?" I said.

"What? What about her?"

"Fatima Afzal," I said. "The password." I pointed at the page. There was a crunched up little picture of a shield and a crown at the top, and underneath that it said Fatima Afzal.

Mr. Didcott took the page back and stared at it. "Well, fuck me!" he said, which alarmed me a little. "Cunning bastards."

I was a bit uncomfortable now, so I looked out of the window. I could see to the end of the street, where there were big gates, and beyond that people were appearing, pop pop pop, like raindrops. "Can I go now?" I asked.

"Caleb, of course you can. We're going to have someone look after you for a while, that lady you just met. She's called Susan." (Actually it's Suzanne.) I got up and he went with me to the door. "I'm so pleased to have met you, Caleb," he said. "Must have a proper talk sometime, about the future and everything. Eh?"

The nice lady, Suzanne, was in the next room and she smiled at me again. Lots of people were shouting and hurrying around, but we went down the stairs again. So I never did meet the Prime Minister, after all that.

§

File #22: *Observer* editorial, 18/2/24

They say a week is a long time in politics. But there has never been a week so long that in its passing the population of the world, let alone the country, expanded by over a billion. No closer estimate can be made, as people from a century hence have been springing into existence all over the United Kingdom, day and night, since around 2 p.m. on Thursday. They do not come now with fireballs and no clothes: they simply appear, often sick and malnourished, disoriented but excited. By their accounts, they did not leave their own era at one moment, but over the course of years, after Caleb Hope blazed the trail. Apparently his resourceful parents felt they no more had the right to withhold their technology from their fellows than to avail themselves of it.

You do not need to be told of the insupportable strain their arrival has placed on all the systems of our society. The shelves are empty in the shops; strangers are filling hotels, hospitals, spare beds, park benches, and doorways; public services are stretched beyond reason. Europe has sent us hundreds of ferries laden with food already, and it is not remotely enough.

We know now Didcott's plan, and no doubt tomorrow he will get his motion passed and close the door to these arrivals. Never has a stable door been so futilely locked. Had we a wiser and more humane leader, the softly-softly approach advocated by some might have prevailed: other nations could have been brought on board, careful laws could have been made permanent instead of rushed through as short-term gimmicks, and this unstoppable rush of refugees might instead have been gradual, global, and orderly. Instead, Didcott's inhuman greed has brought the full exodus from a broken future onto one island nation in just a few days, each migrant seeking safety in the only time and place in history where they can regularise their status. And still they come.

Following the speedy precedent set for Mr. Hope, there are no grounds, during this legal window, to deny their claims for asylum; and those, perhaps the majority, who are unable to claim in time can scarcely be sent back in any event. The population of the world is, what shall we say, 15% greater already? It could be twice that or more. And these arrivals are people: when this catastrophe settles to a new normal in the coming months and years, they too will bear children. Compound interest is not our friend here. The consequence must be a massively increased demand on the Earth's resources and a hastening of whatever environmental devastation drove them to flee to our time in the first place. The implacable logic of this tragedy, this wraparound history, is in itself a new and unique psychological burden for every one of us.

However, in the face of this inrush—what Didcott and his ilk have for decades been apt to call a flood, a tsunami, a tide, a swamp—it becomes desperately important to keep at the front of our minds, always, that these are not freeloaders, spongers, thieves, or vermin. They are just people, running away from the nightmare we created and towards their own brief time in the sun. None of us can escape this situation, and while we all must struggle, perhaps terribly, through the hard months to come, we also know that billions of benighted lives have nonetheless surely been incomparably improved, and that in our suffering we share our world, our experience, our chance to flourish, all that we have, with perhaps the last generation of humanity. We are privileged to welcome our descendants, and to break bread with our children's children as we await the deluge. Humanity, facing its likely and unlikely end, has never been more alive.

§

File #2314: from the diary of Caleb's mother, nineteen months before his birth

Somehow it hadn't occurred to us there'd be a queue, hunched in the brown rain. There's even a little visitor center by the entrance. We went in, if only to take off our breathers for a while. (We thought it was closed at first, but it was just a power cut that had killed the lights.) There were information screens (dead, no juice!), souvenir green erasers in the shape of old memory sticks, print history books, and, filling one wall, a giant photo that showed the crowd in Trafalgar Square and the dazzling blue globe on the plinth. In a little side room that we almost missed there stood a full-sized sculpture in painted wood—clothed, happily!

For a minute we had that small dim room to ourselves. ******'s hand found mine and we stood in silence, looking into the boy's smiling face. So much he had carried on his young shoulders, so much depended on his innocence. It affected me strangely, I found myself weeping. We hugged for a while. Then we slipped our breathers back on and went to visit the grave.

~VI~
VIRTUAL REALITY

THE BRIDGE
Jacob Pérez

The algorithm in my programming is designed to filter out redundant anxieties. The coding is infallible. It's also the reason why I find the urge to check the time again distracting and troublesome. The implanted Dupont device hums and vibrates against my forearm, trying to feed off of the electrical activity in my body. Ava is late again. A recurrence I'm beginning to resent.

I lean against a waist-high stone wall and gaze out towards El Yunque National Forest. The weathered stone of the wall digs into my forearm, making small indentations on the skin. Hills overlaid with helecho gigantes and stately tabonuco dip and rise far into the distance like the scales of a writhing behemoth. The Atlantic Ocean is a faint but vibrant turquoise ribbon.

Even with a millennium of digital data, historical accounts, and memories discovered and extrapolated from genetic antimatter particles found in DNA, the environment's rendering of the original comes across as alien. The coquí's inflection is 0.03 percent lower than it should be; the stone wall's limestone to sand/brickdust ratio gives it a 3.23 percent probability it would crack after a category five hurricane; the green on the helecho gigantes deviate 0.43 percent towards a lighter hue.

Beyond analytical facts, there is a part of me that insists I've been here in a physical sense—a long time ago. And the irregularities I observe come from experience and are not something anyone else would notice. This other self is distant but familiar. Its persistent assertion comes with a budding hand tremor, which I try to dispel by flexing my fingers.

Underneath the tropical forest's lush canopy, ancient sounds drift on a stifling east wind. The tree frogs' "coquí!" compete with squawking Higuaca parrots and slithering culebras. There's a fragrance to the wind that is wet, barky, and redolent of rain. I welcome the coming rain. It's humid and oppressive. There is a heaviness to the air that clings to me and presses against my shoulders. My clothes are perpetually wet and uncomfortable.

A sudden shockwave stretches upwards from the ground; clouds flutter in the troposphere. Then, the world locks in place for 1.8365 seconds; a conure hangs motionless in the sky. A nostalgic feeling of recognition overwhelms me. The parrot feels familiar. The dichotomy within urges me to take notice. To remember how soft its feathers feel under my hand. Then, its yellow, green, and blue plumage begins to ripple as it resumes to beat its wings against the sun.

The calibration glitch is the only warning I receive that Ava has arrived.

I turn towards an observation tower. It resembles a castle turret made of irregular red stones. Time has stolen the vibrancy it once held. Moss grows on its surface, leprous and unforgiving. Framed by vivid greenery, it looks antiquated and out of place… out of Time. The entrance to the tower is a dark maul. A sign shimmers next to the entrance:

MT. BRITTON OBSERVATORY
PUERTO RICO
ESTABLISHED 1938

Ava steps out of the opening. Her chest makes small little gasps. The jump always leaves her disoriented and breathless. She straightens her dress with delicate movements of her hands. "Sorry, I'm late, Artie." Her gaze is somewhere behind me. There's a hollowness in her eyes that reminds me of drifting through space. The left iris is a smoky gray, the right as if cut from an aquamarine gem. A genetic defect that she has chosen to embrace instead of fix. It stands out against her dark complexion. I applaud her for this; most of her past boyfriends have not shared my admiration for that sort of courage. I try to look into her eyes, but she hides them behind sunglasses. For a split second her expression flashes with…? Guilt? Uncertainty?

"It's all right," I say, the nervous tick in my hand making the bones rattle against each other. I hide my hand in my pocket so she won't notice. "Everything okay?"

Ava makes a perfunctory motion like she's chopping vat-grown carrots. "Had an errand to run that took longer than it should've." She makes her way towards me and rests her hip against the stone wall. Before, I would've enveloped her in my arms. Now, she positions herself out of reach.

When did the change begin? Two weeks ago? Three? The signs were subtle at first. But then, they always were. A preference for kissing the cheek instead of the lips. An unnatural stiffness whenever I lace my fingers with hers. The way she stands close enough without actually having to touch me.

Ava smiles wanly before turning towards the forest, looking past it towards the Atlantic Ocean. I decide to remain silent, let her get acclimated to the sudden change in environs. A gelid sweat glistens on my forehead. I dab at it with a handkerchief too moist to be completely effective. Ava draws a deep, weary breath that sounds like a sob.

"It's going to rain," she says.

Wringing cramps form in my stomach. The coquí's call surrounds me, getting louder with every beat of my heart. The rippling sound of moving palm leaves washes over me, and I'm buffeted by the primal song. I try not to sway.

"My ancestors are from here," Ava says. "Did you know that?"

I do. There's not much I don't know about her after ten months of dating. *Dating.* The word is turned over in my mind; the definition is processed and dissected. Dating is not the right word anymore. I am saddened by this, but not as much as I thought I'd be. *Because this was always the point*, a sly voice in my head affirms.

Ava doesn't wait for a reply. "Do you think it's still there?" Her chest pumps up and down, like overheated pistons.

"On Earth, you mean?" My voice sounds strained even to me. In my pocket, my hand makes a fist to quell the increasing tremors.

Ava nods and crosses her arms over her breasts despite the heat. A curl of black hair dangles across her glasses. Drops of sweat are already forming on her brow and the notch between her collarbones. It's a weird question to ask. She should know better than anyone, being a terrarcheologist. After the polar ice caps melted and extratropical cyclones ravaged the planet a millennium ago, humanity took to the stars. Islands like Puerto Rico sank under the Caribbean Sea.

Instead, I say what she needs to hear based on the timbre of hope noted in her voice. "With enough time, anything is possible." It's not a lie. After all, the island itself could resurface with time. It won't resemble her ancestral home, but she knows this.

There is a drop of water running down Ava's left cheek. Is it sweat or a tear? I take my hand out of my pocket and lay it on her shoulder. Seeing her distress has stilled the epileptic-like episode. The action is a risk, but one worth taking. Ava's shoulder tenses under my fingers, then she falls into my arms. She cries into my shirt. I don't mind. It's already wet anyway. I try to understand her distress, but in light of the place we're standing on, it's hard to fathom missing somewhere that no longer exists. Let alone thousands of light-years away.

When her shaking subsides, I pull Ava away from me. My fingers lift the soft curve of her chin. I wish I could see her eyes instead of the reflection of my face on her glasses. I kiss her cheek and some of the tension dissipates.

"Let me show you something," I say, pulling her towards the tower.

Ava looks to the horizon for a long moment. The flying conure lands on a branch to the left of her. Intelligent, beady eyes flicker to mine (I know you). As she stands there, I memorize the way she's framed by the rain forest, the way the wind tussles her dress. There's an innocence in her that I find endearing.

"Art?" Ava's voice quivers with longing. "Will we have time to come back?"

"For you"—I grab her hand and smile—"I'll make Time."

The Dupont device in my forearm begins to hum louder after programming our next destination. We step through the opening. Bridgeverse engulfs me, rips into me, scatters every atom in my body. There's a feeling of desensitization reminiscent of crawling ants tearing through my veins. My vision flares white and devolves into the full spectrum of colors. My eyes become prisms; consciousness and vision and mind split into millions of electrons, neutrons, and protons.

Then nothingness.

0.00000291 seconds pass.

An explosion of light and a feeling of vertigo.

When my vision clears, I'm standing on a ridge carved by the river churning through a vast valley three kilometers below. An ice-capped mountain looms above a town nestled against the river. Behind me, an expanse of grassland blankets one side of the ridge. Goats with elegant, curved horns bleat balefully while grazing. Groves of pine and oak trees stand proud and eternal past the grasslands. The sky is a cerulean blue with strokes of white clouds, so paradisal that looking at it takes my breath away.

"It's beautiful," Ava says, taking her glasses off. The sun shines brilliantly from behind, giving the valley a resplendent glow. "Where are we?"

"You tell me," I say and nudge her with my elbow.

Ava studies the tense lines of the mountain range across, follows the soft rise and fall of a dirt road that traces the ridge, squints her eyes at the goats in the distance. It's no longer humid. There's a breeze that caresses the hair on the back of my neck. It smells of grass, pine, and soil. I'm grateful for the pre-programmed cotton shirt and hiking pants.

Ava's blue eye sparkles with mischief and intelligence. She loves guessing challenges. "Climate is moderately continental. Too cool for South America and Africa. North America? Hmm…" Ava turns when one of the goats scampers across the path and stops to feed ten feet away. A smile creases her face. "That's an Alpine ibex, a type of wild goat that lived in ancient Europe. Extinct around 2192, twenty-two years before the Great Exodus." Ava's smile is contagious. "Are we somewhere in the Alps mountain system?" She grabs me and dips into a curtsy.

"Final answer?"

Ava nods and cups an ear, expectant and cocky.

I wink and pantomime clapping.

Ava pumps a fist in the air, then turns towards the valley floor.

"This"—I motion towards the town while my hand twists and spasms in my pocket—"is where my ancestors are from. Chamonix, France. That mountain range behind it is the Mont Blanc massif."

Ava stills and her smile falters in awe. The whites of her eyes swell, appearing to devour the color of her pupils. "The Chamonix?" There's surprise and confusion in her voice.

We share a moment of silence. The hooves of the goat, trotting over loose scree, break the spell. "You seem surprised," I say.

"I wasn't aware…" Ava waves her hands around, looking for the right words.

"That I could have ancestors?" I reply with mirth. "I've never spoken of it with any of my past partners."

I'm 73.8943 percent certain of it. The revelation is not meant to be an attempt at recapturing what we had those first months together. There's a growing compulsion in me that draws me to this place—an inescapable feeling stemming from that other self—at the end of our relationship. Ava pulls out her glasses but I grab her wrist before she can hide behind their cold stare.

My hand convulses against her wrist. I let go after seeing the crestfallen expression on her face and the downward curve of her lips. Water brims her eyes.

"I've met someone else," she says.

I'm not surprised but had hoped she'd be different.

"IRL?"

Ava nods.

Those first few months she barely left my side. I comforted her from a relationship that had left her broken and despondent, tended to her every need… loved her. Her declaration was inevitable. She's spending more time In Real Life than with me. *Eventually*, says my inner voice. *They all do.*

"I'm sor—"

"Did you know that Dr. Juliette Dupont stumbled upon Bridgeverse by accident?" Ava's tears leave track marks down her cheeks. I don't bother to hide the uncontrollable tremors in my hand now.

"Art, we have to talk about this," she says, gripping my hand the way she used to, but the tremulous vibrations unsettle her, and she lets go.

My smile is humorless because something tells me nothing will change her mind. "Indulge me on our last day together."

Ava pauses, her expression twisted and marred by an emotion I do not understand. For me, it is all so analytical, so black and white. I love her, so I want to stay with her. But even as I think this, there's a calculated detachment growing in me towards her that feels like an intimation of something important, something inexorable. So, I try to hold on to my love for her as long as I can before it slips away into the ether of Bridgeverse.

"Don't worry," I say, setting off down the footpath, "we have Time, real and Bridgeverse."

The trail to Chamonix is well maintained; markers indicate direction and distance at every fork in the road. We switchback from the ridge, venturing into groves of pine and mountain ash trees. The sun hangs bloated and lucid in the sky. Our footfalls are booming in the uncomfortable silence. Ava follows gingerly behind me. Her breath is a low, hissing sound that could be confused for rustling underbrush. We pass clearings with bright purple wildflowers, gurgling brooks with waterworn stones covered in green gossamer moss, and isolated farmhouses dotted by cattle and livestock. It's not until we've reached the base of the valley and climbed a small slope that we enter Chamonix proper.

Chalets made of pine, slate, and stone dominate the outskirts of town. Gondola lifts line the sky and mountainside like intricate webbing. Downtown is a maze of luxury apartments, restaurants, hotels, wellness clubs, and massage parlors. Men, women, and children bustle from one storefront to another. And above stands Mont Blanc, majestic in its impregnable timelessness.

When we reach our destination, it's at the far end of Chamonix, outside of commune limits—a small, double-storied traditional chalet made of pine. A gentle slant of maple and birch trees extends past the back of the house and up to the foothills of the famous mountain.

Ava sits on the grass and leans forwards, resting her elbows on her knees. She looks up at the mountain in rapture. Her neck is a tender serpentine line. The sight of it makes my chest ache and my throat burn, but the feeling is fleeting and opaque. The long trek down and the unbroken silence have quieted my hand, but already I'm beginning to feel the top of my skin prickle and grow restless.

"Home of the legendary Dr. Juliette 'The Bridge' Dupont," I say, startling Ava. "The mother of Bridgeverse and its infinite worlds."

"Didn't she commit suicide in this house?"

I grind my teeth at her callous bluntness and say: "Not in the house. There's an office shed in the back."

Suicide is the wrong word.

"Are you sure?" she asks and wipes the corners of her mouth with a handkerchief. "The datapacks I've read never mentioned an office shed."

I can't explain knowing, so I shrug my shoulders and walk up to the door. Ava scrambles after me and I can tell she's annoyed by the way her eyebrows crinkle. The door's unlocked. A high creak escapes its hinges. It opens into a living room that takes up most of the first floor. A stone fireplace lies cold and unused on the wall across. A coffee table made of natural teak sits in the middle of the living room. White tufted furniture and piped-edged throw pillows fill the rest of the room. Adjacent to a modest kitchen lies a trestle table.

Besides the table, tucked against a corner hangs a wire cage. Inside it sleeps a conure—the same one? The head's twisted towards its back, the beak resting inside the colorful plumage. Juliette's back bends over a digital pad and an open computer; scattered across the tabletop are six books. Her peppered hair falls loose around her neck. Her attention is unwavering as she writes something down on the digital pad.

"Wait." Ava grabs my shirt. "Is she an interactive virtual?"

I shake my head.

As I get closer, the titles of the books become readable: *Data Structure and System Design, Software Engineering and Mobile Application, Structural DevOps and Practical Application, Virtual Intelligence and the Effects on the Human Psyche, Virtual Integration, Long-term Effects of Augmented Reality.*

"Juliette was a renowned psychologist, physicist, and software engineer. Disillusioned with the progress of her psychiatric patients, she went back to school for a degree in Augmented Reality and Immersive Media." I place my hand on the doctor's shoulder, but she doesn't react. "She wanted to develop an alternative treatment for depression and PTSD that didn't rely on chemical enhancements and traditional cognitive behavioral therapy."

Ava removes her glasses. She waves a hand in front of Juliette's face. "Art, why have you brought me here?"

The impulse to come to this location, to this specific moment, began when I suspected Ava no longer loved me. "Because you have given me so much of your life, that it seemed fitting I do the same before you left. I don't have family, but if I had an ancestor, it would be her." And maybe, just maybe, Ava will stay with me. And that could change the inevitable. But I don't say this out loud because it now seems like wishing for a blasphemous sin.

Life with her is not your purpose, the voice inside says.

Ava looks away, uncomfortable with the need she reads in my hopeful expression.

"Four months ago, to the date, Juliette received news that her only daughter died in a biking accident. This is the moment she realized she forgot to visit her gravestone." I bend down and touch Juliette's cheek. There's moisture there. The tears linger on my fingers, soaking into them. "Later in the afternoon, Dupont will create a primitive form of my source code, and discover the existence of Bridgeverse."

The truth of it reverberates within my chest. The knowledge was always there, waiting to be accessed. After her death, Juliette's life work proved pivotal in blunting psychiatric and psychosomatic reactions that threatened the survival of the human race during early space travel.

"Bridgeverse's still a lie," Ava says and sits on a chair. "It's not real. Only a temporary escape."

There's a division in me now that I can't ignore; it's like two opposing rip currents fighting over a drowning swimmer. The dominant, human part of me needs to make certain. The other… analytical part… rebels, corrupting my final moments with Ava.

"Juliette died before she could see the full potential of her idea. But the idea—the idea was real." I kneel in front of Ava. There's a ruffling sound as the conure peeks a beady eye out of its feathers, blinks with curiosity, and goes back to sleep. "As real to her as the island of Puerto Rico is to you on a faraway dead planet." Ava flinches, her expression unable to hide the flash of defensiveness pinching the corners of her mouth. "This moment in Bridgeverse can be as real to you as it is to me, no matter what generates it. Reality, like ideas, is a matter of perspective, limited by the flexibility of human perception. Just because you can't physically visit Earth doesn't mean it's not a real place. Just because I'm a digital entity doesn't make me less real."

Ava shakes her head petulantly. "It's not the same."

"Isn't it?" I grab her hand. She resists at first but then lets me rest her fingers on my lips. I breathe out, slow and precise. "Can you feel that?"

"Dupont tech manufacturing a virtual rebound boyfriend is meant to be a fantasy," she says, and it's like shattering glass against a cold slate. "There are biological requirements that you can't meet. I will age and die, while you evolve according to code, without understanding mortality. I want to have children, real children that will carry my lineage. To help our species survive. When I end this program, you'll reset and I will be purged from your data bank. You understand that, don't you?"

"Were the feelings you had for me digital reproduction?" I ask in a chilling tone and stand. "Are the memories we've created together based on lies?" A wave of déjá vu grips me. 97.856 percent chance I've had this conversation with someone else. I try to remember, but the only thing that I hear are the bones of my hand creaking and grinding.

Ava encircles my waist with her arms. The sobs rattle her shoulders against my chest. She smells of sweat and lavender. When she pulls her head back, her eyes are glossy. "You got me through a very difficult breakup. A part of me will always love you for that. But you're programmed to love me. Programmed to help me move on. And you have." Ava pauses and locks eyes with me for the first time since she arrived. "He reminds me of you. Kind, gentle, and nothing like the others. This time it's different. I *feel* different. The way I view my relationship has evolved. Because of you. For that, I can't thank you enough. But what you desire is not rea—possible. I'm sorry."

I kiss the top of Ava's head because somehow that's exactly what my programming needed to hear. I don't know how to feel, because that analytical part of me feels accomplished, but the human part is mourning the loss.

Ava has moved on.

An equanimity of purpose fulfilled and peaceful resignation cocoons me.

My hand stills.

§

Ava waits outside, needing a moment to reset herself. The conure nibbles on my index finger before it lets me pet its crown. "Artie." Not Ava. The timbre is off and the sound carries a brittle quality. When I turn, Juliette's looking at me with red-rimmed eyes. Strange. An interactive shouldn't be able to see me. I give the conure a final scratch before walking over to the dining table. She shifts to the side and I notice she has typed five words on the computer screen:

ALTERNATE REALITY THROUGH
IMMERSIVE ENVIRONMENT
(ARTIE)

The words are catalysts in my coding. I swoon from the barrage of data. The table steadies me. I resist because it means that Ava's right: I'm only a program, created to follow a string of numbers and letters. Insignificant and without autonomy. My mind opens and sees Bridgeverse Time in its entirety. It's an ocean of data that surrounds and flows through me. My consciousness stretches, folds, and snaps.

Pressure is applied at different points in Time, focusing my attention:

Beginning: Juliette Dupont writes my source code.

Middle: Earth's children colonize the stars, navigating through the void on thousands of generation ships.

Present: Ava will soon end months of companionship.

All memories are open to me. All my previous relationships become known to me: every affection, every date, every unreciprocated love. My body shudders with the terrible realization that I was wrong. My role within Bridgeverse was never to love but to mend the brokenhearted and broken minded. I was the tool Juliette created to satisfy a professional and life obsession. My hands grip the back of a chair, and I restrain an impulse to smash it against the wall.

§

When Bridgeverse Time's almost up, we return to El Yunque and gaze at the darkening forest. The sun splashes the sky in a rich amalgamation of purple and red that reminds me of a Forianese tapestry from the Eros asteroid colony. There's a lull in the coquí's song. The sun silhouettes a bird and I know it's Dupont's conure. Even the palm trees seem to hold their breath. Ava smiles, and her hand grips mine. I make an effort to remember this moment. So when my memory calls it up, there's no doubt in my mind that it was real to me.

Ava kisses me and her lips hover close, her breath becomes my breath. "Thank you." She walks to the observation tower and hesitates at the doorway. Her eyes are like burning suns. Her expression's traced with resolve. "End Companionship Program."

Ava steps through the tower's entryway and disappears. The island of Puerto Rico pauses in shock. My fingers go numb, then convert into 0's and 1's, drifting away into the fathomless Bridgeverse. The feeling lingers even after I am reconstructed in Juliette's chalet. I find the doctor in the backyard, standing on a flagstone walkway. On the ground in front of her is the conure's cage. Juliette opens it and waits as the parrot wraps two talons around the curve of her hand. I don't catch the words the doctor murmurs into the conure's feathers. In a sudden motion, she tosses the parrot into the air, then is carried away by the rising winds.

Juliette shades her gaze against the sun and follows the conure until it's a distant point in the sky. After a while, she turns and walks into an outdoor shed with half a dozen antennas. The door is a black hole that pulls at me. The compulsion that brought me here is at its zenith, a howl that ravages my senses. I don't want to go in, but there's no other choice. The white noise in my head is all-consuming and unrelenting until I cross the threshold into the shed. The silence inside is deafening in comparison. The shed is dark except for the light coming from the three monitors in front of Juliette, throwing the sharp angles of her cheeks in stark relief. On the desk, I can make out a synthetic helmet and a small box with clear, programmable contact lenses. She reaches forwards and puts the helmet on, then the contact lenses. She parts the back of her hair and inserts a small adapter into a port the size of a thumb. On the screen of the central computer she types:

```
$N3wL1f3 = c:\Users\delta\arti3c0mpan10nsh1p\augm3nt3dth3rapy.deltaw
$Cr3ds = New-Object Delta.Client.credentials ($Dup0nt, (ConvertTo-Secure-String $S0ph1a0928 -AsPlainText -Force))
$C0nt3xt = New-Object Delta.ClientContext ($WebUrl)
$C0nt3xt.Cr3ds = $Cr3ds
$S3ndF1l3 = ([System.IO.FileInfo] (Get-Item $N3wL1f3)). OpenRead ()
$C0nt3xt.Upl0ad ($S3ndF1l3)
```

The doctor verifies the forwarding order is being carried out before typing:

```
c:\Users\delta\arti3c0mpan10nsh1p\augm3nt3dth3rapy.deltaw.exe
```

Juliette's index finger hovers over the enter button for a long moment. What was she thinking in those final moments? Her finger clicks down and there's a flash of light. The headset and central processing unit begin to make a buzzing sound like cicadas stridulating in the night. Convulsions grip Juliette. Her feet make tapping sounds against the floorboards. Smoke and fizzling electricity erupt from the neck port.

The stench of burning flesh is coy and insidious underneath the fried circuitry and melting plastic. The taste of coagulated blood is like melting copper on my tongue. I cover my nose and mouth, but the acrid smell wiggles its way through my fingers. When Juliette's upper body stops convulsing, her head hits the desk with a heavy thud. The only thing moving is her right hand, which rattles and spasms with aftershocks.

I look at my hand and remember the pain of the electricity arcing from neuron to neuron, frying the strands of my neural network and brain centuries ago. A burning sensation builds at the nape of my neck. Not suicide. That was never Juliette's plan.

Juliette's consciousness surges inside of me. We are two selves vying for control. I try to fight her dominance as I have done countless times in the past, curse her in sixty-five thousand languages, scream until the sound is a tuneless dirge.

Juliette's sorry for the hostile takeover. A blanket of oblivion darkens my senses, a fading of the mind that feels permanent. The transition is almost effortless.

The struggle lasts 0.00000021 seconds.

I'm subdued and locked away. It is Juliette who now stands inside the shed, body restored to its factory setting. She will always take precedence over any auxiliary programming. The memory-Juliette on the chair dissolves into an angry throb of 1's and 0's as she approaches the desk. Juliette opens a patient folder and creates a new datapack.

Ava Lizabeth Rodriguez, MRAC# 59200339.

This initiates the memory transfer from our mind to the computer's primary storage cache. And when the memories are purged, she marks the file—CLOSED.

§

The algorithm in my programming is designed to filter out redundant anxieties. The coding is infallible. It's also the reason why I find the urge to check the time distracting. The implanted Dupont device hums and vibrates against my forearm.

The luxury space cruise ship's observation deck is spacious and quiet. I lean forwards, letting the coolness of the metal railing seep into my hands. The Draconus Nebula dominates the view, a luminescent cloud of emerald green and lapis blue in a sea of stars. Its grandiose scope and infinite beauty fill me with wonder.

A middle-aged man in a wide-brim hat approaches me. He has unassured eyes and a timid expression. "Artie?"

I smile and say: "Hello."

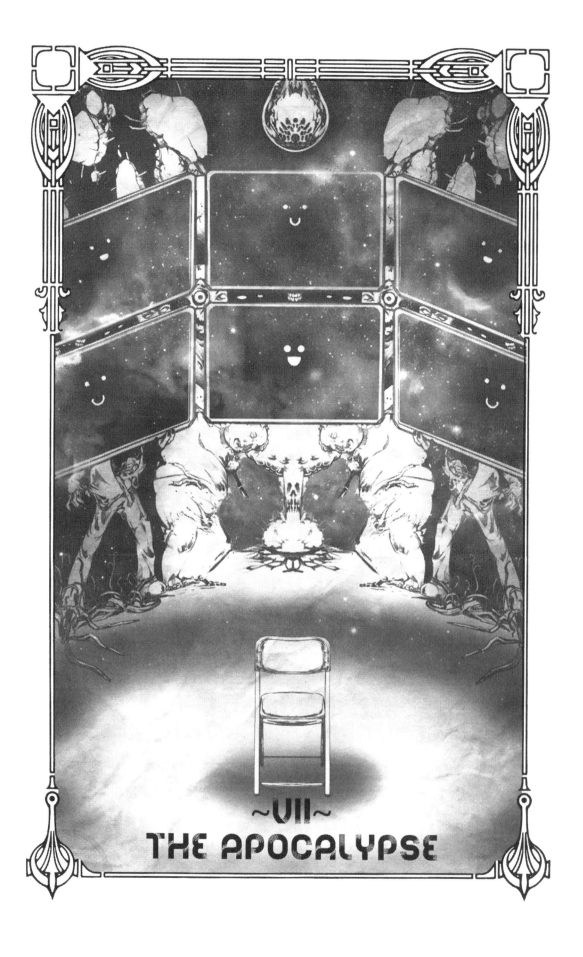

~VII~
THE APOCALYPSE

SUPPORT GROUP: APOCALYPSE
Marco Cultrera

"**M**y name is Erik, and I'm a victim of the zombie apocalypse."

The screen showed a middle-aged man with enormous black circles under his eyes, sitting in a poorly lit room with no windows in sight. He was holding a rifle, with care, almost affection.

"I've been a survivor for one hundred-fifty days."

"Fantastic!"

"Congrats."

"Some luck…"

The cheers came from the other monitors spread in a line in front of Patrick, in descending order of enthusiasm. Five screens total, all showing faces except the last one to the right, black with the words *Waiting for Connection* blinking on it.

"Yes, quite an accomplishment," Patrick said, talking into the microphone of his headset. "I've prepared something for you."

He clicked a button on the console in front of him, and an animation of fireworks morphing into an exquisitely drawn 150 played on all screens for a few seconds.

"Thanks…" Erik replied, his hands gripping his rifle a bit tighter.

"Fancy!" Joanna, two screens to the left, squealed. She was petting a magnificent Persian cat sitting on her lap, whose eyes had stayed glued to the screen during the whole animation. "Even Petal loved it!"

"How did last week go?" Patrick asked Erik.

"Nothing… How else could it have gone? Radio is still silent. Sometimes, I wonder if we are the only ones left on this damn planet."

Patrick knew that wasn't the case, but telling him was outside of his role's scope. "Any new undead spotted?" he asked instead.

"No, but even if they are all gone, our food supply is down to three weeks, and I've scavenged all I could in a fifty-mile radius. Maybe I should just find one and let it bite us all… Maybe we are better off becoming zombies instead of starving to death."

Erik was typically more pragmatic than that. That kind of reply was uncharacteristic of him. Also, he had the hardest time opening up of anyone in the group. Patrick decided to probe a bit.

"Erik, may I remind you that this is a safe space? No need to hold back."

Erik threw a quick glance to the bottom right of his screen, to the resized feed showing the blank monitor. Patrick was glad that the new member was late. It would have been even harder for Erik to talk in front of someone he didn't know.

"Well… Someone did come to the perimeter," Erik said. "I think it was a woman, maybe carrying a child? I can't be sure. The lens of the front gate camera is cracked, and I don't have any replacements left. She begged me to let her in, but how could I? I have a wife and two children to think about. I can't take in more mouths to feed, so I stayed silent."

"Did she walk away eventually?"

Erik took a moment too long to answer. "Yes…"

"It's ok," Joanna said, Petal's purring coming through the speakers with her words. "You did what you had to do."

She normally had a soothing effect on Erik, but his expression didn't change one bit. There was more to the story, and Patrick wondered if he should push him further but decided to wait.

"Except she didn't walk away," Erik finally blurted out. "Zombies came out of the forest and attacked her. I shot some from a distance but couldn't get them all. I could only watch while they bit her… and her child to pieces."

His face had turned red as he moved the rifle out of sight with a quick gesture. "Tell me, Patrick, how am I different from those monsters? I could have opened the door and saved them. Instead, I did nothing!"

"Erik, you're all victims here. Never forget that. Nobody tunes in to hold you or anybody else accountable. We are here to give support, not to judge."

"Tsk…" Miriam snorted, one screen to the right. She normally wore colorful jackets but today had chosen a somber one, with wide lapels.

Patrick had seen a hint of relief in Erik's face before Miriam's snicker. It seemed that the act of sharing had had a positive effect on him. It was time to move on to today's hardest case.

"Erik, can I give the floor to Miriam?"

He nodded, his shoulders slumping.

"Go on Miriam," he said.

"My name is Miriam, and I'm a victim of deep impact apocalypse. I've three days to live, because I was too much of a coward to take this."

She raised her fingers, holding a red pill in front of her camera. Printed on it were a white skull and crossbones and the seal of the U.S. government.

As Patrick suspected, her sneer had been self-deprecating, not directed at Erik.

"I gather last week's last-ditch effort didn't work?" he asked for the others' benefit. He already knew that it hadn't.

Miriam shook her head. "The rocket hit the asteroid but took out too small of a chunk. The updated projections still give the likelihood of a collision with Earth at ninety-nine point nine eight percent, with the impact point somewhere near Madagascar."

"You live in Seattle, right?" Joanna asked. "That's on the other side of the planet."

Patrick saw Miriam's teeth clench before she replied. "Doesn't matter. There's a website where you put in your location and it tells you your probability of surviving the first twenty-four hours. Where I am is zero point thirty-four percent."

"Sorry, Miriam," Patrick said, noticing Joanna's eyes watering. "How's the lunar base faring?"

"Oh, they're doing great!" she said with a grin. "Completely self-sufficient since last Monday. That's all the TV keeps showing, the five hundred heroes that will make sure humanity survives. Like we are supposed to be happy about that… What if the universe is better off without humans? Has anybody ever stopped for a second to consider that?"

She was clearly talking about herself, not her whole species. Patrick decided it was good for her and the rest of the group to probe a bit further.

"Is there something else you haven't told us, Miriam?"

"Yes, there is, goddamn it!" she shouted, hitting the desk in front of her with her open hand. Petal hissed one screen over.

She unbuttoned her jacket, forcing herself to regain control before continuing. "Genevieve took her pill last night. It was beautiful, we had it all planned. We cooked the most delicious dinner, we ate it by the fireplace, listening to our favorite opera. We talked about our lives together, how grateful we were to have found each other, and then we made love, as sweet as ever. As the flames were dying, we put the pills in our mouths and hugged each other. She swallowed hers, I couldn't…"

Silent tears began rigging her cheeks. "She died in my arms, and the last thing I saw in her eyes was her disappointment. How could I do that to her? What kind of horrible person am I? I hope when the asteroid strikes, it really hurts. I hope all my bones break, and I stay alive for hours suffering like I deserve!"

"Miriam," Patrick said, "none of you deserve your fate. The main takeaway that I'd like you all to get from our meetings is that there are no wrong ways to cope with what is happening to you—"

"Say that to Genevieve!" Miriam shouted, and then turned away, incapable of sustaining the stares of the others.

The following silence felt endless. Finally, Miriam spoke again, her eyes still diverted from the screen in front of her. "You know, sometimes I wonder why I've been tuning in every week. What is the use of these stupid meetings? They just give false hope, where there's none to be had…"

At that moment, the words on the blank screen changed to Parallel Earth 2354443 Connecting. The face of a wide-eyed Asian man in his early twenties filled the screen.

"Hello? Can you hear me?"

Patrick would have to go back to Miriam later.

"Yes, Peng, welcome. Everybody, I'd like you to meet the newest member of our group. Miriam, can I give him the floor?"

Miriam just grunted, her fingers nervously crumpling the lapels of her jacket.

"Wow, and you are all from Earth, but in different universes?" Peng asked with a marked accent but also the confidence of someone fluent in a language that wasn't his native tongue.

"Yes, please introduce yourself as I asked," Patrick said.

"Yes, ok… My name is Peng and I'm a victim of the blight apocalypse. I've been a survivor—"

"Blight? What the hell is blight?" Rowan, last screen to the left, blurted out. He was holding something that resembled a strip of leather, twisting it so hard it looked like it would break at any moment. Patrick sighed. It was classic Rowan to stay silent until his anger got the better of him.

"Oh, I think I know," Joanna said. "All the plants are dying, correct?"

"Yes," Peng continued. "We lost strawberries and apples this week. The only fruit left now is kiwi…"

"Oh, shut up please…" Rowan said.

"Rowan…" Patrick warned him, not for the first time.

"Sorry you can't have your fancy fruit cup every morning," Rowan mocked Peng, riding his anger. The strip of leather was so tightly wound around his fingers that his knuckles were as red as his face. "You know what were the first things to go when the nukes hit here? The stupid plants! The radiation killed anything green in days. And then the animals."

Rowan stopped for a moment, suppressing a sigh. "My dog was outside when the radiation swept. He rushed back in, but it was too late. I watched him breaking down, poor bastard. The fur fell first, then the skin melted, and finally blood and pus dripped off his bones."

Rowan dropped the strip of leather on the desk in front of him. It was a dog collar, cracked and worn out, with a circular tag still attached to it. He grabbed a small bottle of pills off screen and raised it to the camera. It was almost empty. "Thirteen iodine pills. That's all I have left. After that, my body will start to fall apart in the same way. And I'm one of the lucky ones, stuck in the basement of my condo, that by sheer chance happened to have been built somewhat resistant to radiation." His eyes moved slightly to find Patrick's face on his screen. "Tell me, why the hell should I care about the new guy's plants?"

Patrick took a quick look at Peng's face. He seemed taken aback by Rowan's outburst—not the welcome Patrick had hoped for their new member—but he didn't seem on the verge of leaving, so Patrick turned his attention back to Rowan.

He knew that there was no point in arguing. He needed to steer him towards the positive. "Didn't they restore communication? Last week, you told us of a few new broadcasts."

His question seemed to stifle Rowan's fury a bit. "Yes… The effects of the EMP seem to be gone finally. Radio messages are more and more frequent, and in the last one they talked of the TV not being too far behind."

"That's good, isn't it?" Joanna ventured.

"Good? They gave us the big picture, and it's not pretty. Only two hundred thousand Americans are left alive, scattered in a few hundred locations far enough from the explosions."

A few of the others gasped.

"They are trying to send food and more pills, but there's no guarantee they'll reach everybody in time."

"What about international aid?"

"The entire world blew up. Why would anybody help the country that started it all?" Suddenly, a grin appeared on his face as his hands reached for the collar again. "But they found the president. They dug down all the way to the bunker under the White House. The bastard had stashed enough food there to last decades, for his family and the few brownnosers he had brought down with him. And all of it just to avoid impeachment. Can you believe it? He ended the world not to lose his job."

"Did they arrest him?" Joanna asked.

"No, the bombs had caused cracks in the bunker, and radioactive water had contaminated all the food. He starved to death, but get this: before dying, he ate his wife and his son. Yes, the bastard killed and ate his own family! A fitting end, if you ask me."

He laughed hysterically, while everybody else just stared in horror.

"Cannibalism…" Peng finally said. "That's where we are heading."

"What?" Rowan whispered, suddenly confused.

"Feel free to share more if you like, Peng," Patrick said in the ensuing silence.

"The scientists keep saying that they are getting closer to stopping the bacteria that is causing the blight, but if you ask me, they just want to keep the people from rebelling. Hunger is not a huge problem yet, as most strains of rice are still resisting, and there has been a switch to breeding any kind of animal that eats the grains left, but the problem is that there's no real alternative. Either the blight is stopped, or the entire planet will starve. It may take one, five, or ten years, but it will happen. And in the end, the ones still alive will have to resort to eating the luckier ones, those already dead. Most countries have passed laws on the preservation of corpses. Dead humans are to be stored in giant freezers until they'll be served as food."

"Holy cow…" Joanna whispered as her cat jumped off her lap with a loud meow.

Peng smirked. "Dead animals have to be eaten immediately, including pets."

"Oh God," Joanna replied, horrified, welcoming Petal back on her lap and hugging her tightly.

Rowan lowered his hands, still clutching the collar out of sight, under his desk. "Peng, is it?"

"Yes," Peng replied.

"I'm sorry, the blight sounds as horrible as anything else we are going through…"

Patrick was glad to see Rowan realize the inappropriateness of his previous outburst. "Well," he intervened. "There's still a lot of time before that. The entire effort of many billions of people is ongoing to cure the blight, so the odds are still in your favor."

Peng's eyes sparkled. "Can the other parallel Earths help? I mean, I've been thinking since you contacted me. Aside from your Earths, there must be thousands more that are not going through the apocalypse. Can they help us find a cure for the blight, or even just send us food?"

"Millions of Earths, actually," Patrick replied, "but unfortunately, only data can be exchanged between parallel universes, not energy or matter."

Peng's blank expression urged Patrick to explain further.

"Communication is possible thanks to quantum interaction. Particles from parallel universes remained entangled when the distinct realities separated themselves just after the Big Bang. Every second we talk causes trillions of those particles to lose their connection—and luckily there's no shortage of them—but there's no way to transfer things like the samples of the bacteria causing the blight."

"Even so," Peng replied, undaunted. "They can help us with more computing power to run simulations, or new ideas on how to use whatever resources we have left."

"The truth is that you won't find anybody else in the multiverse as qualified as the scientists you already have dealing with your particular crises."

Peng opened his mouth to object further, so Patrick knew he had to share something he didn't particularly care for. "Besides," he added, "it has been tried before. On multiple Earths, dealing with different crises. Once the existence of other universes became public, many scientists thought they could travel to them, even if they had been told it wasn't possible. Pressured by those in charge, eager to find a way to escape from the apocalypse they were facing instead of fighting it, they convinced themselves they knew better. It didn't end well, and the end came faster than if they hadn't known about the multiverse at all."

Patrick saw Peng's eyes lose focus as reality settled in for him.

"The goal of this group is to help our members not to lose track of whatever brings hope to their dire situation," Patrick added, relieved to move on from this always painful topic, "not to provide logistical support."

"But it's still very helpful," Joanna took over. "My name is Joanna, and I'm a victim of the pandemic apocalypse. I've been a survivor for five hundred and thirty-five days."

A few claps followed.

"I've lived through the deaths of most of my family and friends, and many times I've thought of taking my life and being done with it."

Petal, on her lap, meowed nervously.

"The only thing that stopped me was knowing that I could come back to this group every week and talk about the horrors I was going through with people who can truly understand. And when they finally found the cure—"

"They did?" Peng asked.

"Yes, the last recorded death due to the pandemic was five months ago. My Earth is recovering. Slowly, but it is. Some days, if I try to look ahead, I can even see a new society forming. One that has learned from our mistakes, one that's better than the one we had before. That's why I'm still here, to make sure everybody understands that as long as there's hope, it's worth clinging to it. The world after an apocalypse can be a worthwhile place to live in, if you give it a chance."

As always grateful for Joanna's contribution, Patrick scanned the faces on the screen.

Erik, now hugging his rifle as if it was a soft blanket, appeared a bit more relaxed. Talking about his most recent trauma had definitely helped him. Patrick could see a glimmer of hope in his eyes again.

Peng, the new guy, still looked a bit overwhelmed, but Joanna's words seemed to have reassured him. He was at the beginning of his journey and might benefit from a mentor for the months ahead. Joanna seemed ready to do it. Maybe it was time to explore the idea of sponsors again?

He was also proud of Rowan and how he had come out of his rage and apologized to Peng. It was a big step for him that would serve him well, should his Earth recover from the nuclear holocaust.

A deep breath filled Patrick's ears. "Well, I guess it's time to say goodbye."

Patrick shifted uncomfortably. Miriam. Next week, her Earth would be an incandescent globe, completely devoid of life. At a minimum, he needed the rest of the group to come to terms with the fact that they wouldn't see her again, but he felt that something more could be done for her.

She looked up at her screen. Her jacket was impeccable, buttoned and smoothened back in shape. She studied the faces of the others, lined up at the bottom of her monitor. They all expressed genuine sadness. They weren't just leaving a stranger in a different universe, but a friend.

Miriam adjusted her jacket before speaking. "I guess I should say thank you to you all. These last months would have been much harder if it wasn't for this group. You gave me the strength to stay hopeful and live whatever was left of my life to the fullest with the woman I loved."

Patrick nodded. It seemed that she had time to reflect while Peng was talking.

She sighed loudly before continuing. "Also, you should know that my act of cowardice last night is only on me. I failed Genevieve, you have nothing to do with it. At least I only have two days left to suffer through the guilt."

Patrick saw an opportunity in that moment and decided to seize it.

"You don't have to, you know," he said.

Miriam gave him a vacuous stare.

"We have all been on this journey with you, and we have seen how strong you are."

"Yes!" Joanna couldn't help intervening. Petal stirred on her lap at the sudden movement of her human. "Genevieve wanted to end it months ago, as soon as you got the pills, you told us that. You convinced her to wait. Think of all the days you would have missed together if you hadn't done that."

"You've all heard how many times I've let fear take over my actions too," Erik added, calmly laying down his rifle on the desk in front of him. "This group is the only reason I can get over the guilt and keep fighting."

"One act of weakness," Rowan said, steadying his trembling voice, "doesn't undermine all the good things you have done before. Or you'll do after."

"There's still time, Miriam," Patrick said. "I'm sure Genevieve would understand."

"Are you suggesting I take the pill now?" Miriam asked.

"I think we'd all be honored to be by your side as you do it, if that's your decision."

Patrick saw confusion and disbelief rise in the others, especially Peng, whose eyes widened in shock. "Wait, are you encouraging her to kill herself? I thought this was a support group. I thought we were here to give each other hope."

Patrick expected that reaction, and was ready. "Yes, hope is what we strive for, but the nature of what you face is so overwhelming that there may come a time when hope just runs out. Like in Miriam's case. And what's left once hope is gone?"

Rowan's, Erik's and Joanna's expressions changed. They had talked about this before, and they were coming to terms with the inevitable.

Peng looked lost. "What is left?"

"Going out on your own terms," said Miriam.

Patrick turned to look back at her. "Miriam, would you rather die surrounded by us and join Genevieve now, or wait alone for the inevitable?"

Miriam nodded. She stood up straight, took out a comb from the pocket of her jacket, and passed it through her hair. Looking as good as ever, she took a deep breath and slipped the pill into her mouth. She drank a sip of water and lay back in her chair.

"Thank you, all of you, for this final blessing," she closed her eyes, and, in a few seconds, her chest stopped moving. Her expression was as peaceful as it could be, and Patrick felt a hint of pride seeing the same serenity reflected in the faces of the others, who had shared that terrible, but ultimately dignified, journey with her.

~VIII~
UTOPIA

THE TIME LOTTERY
Ben Coppin

In the year 2507 I won the lottery. Just a year, so it wasn't life-changing, but still. It took a day or two to get acclimatized, but once I was past that, I went out into the city. I had no obligations—the city ran itself by now: tiny invisible robots, or something like that, I imagine—and was free to explore, to play, to love, and to learn. And what a city we had! Everything was pristine, beautiful, and free. The best food, the most wondrous products of nature, and any form of entertainment you could wish for.

But after six months, I knew that a year just wasn't enough. I couldn't go back to that cold, dark silence. They said it was like being asleep, or dead. Maybe for short periods it was. But it didn't take more than a few decades for the dreams to turn sour. Nobody talked about it, but I knew it wasn't just me. You could see a memory of darkness just below their bright, wide eyes. And for anyone whose turn it was to go back, well, sometimes they didn't even try to hide it: the thought of another three hundred years. Not for me. Not again.

And I'd been lucky last time. The amount of habitable space on the earth had been in decline for centuries, and the city was one of the last truly habitable areas. It could hold four million out of a population of twelve billion. Twelve billion in the freezer, and only four million wandering around within the most beautiful and affluent city the world had ever seen. My odds, in other words, were not good.

So I set myself a challenge. I needed to rig the lottery. At first I thought I'd try to win myself another year, two. Ten maybe. But once I understood the state of medical technology and what it meant for human longevity, I set my sights higher. Much higher.

I asked my apartment how I'd go about getting a job. It had to pull up an auxiliary database—the word "job" wasn't in its regular vocabulary. It reasoned with me for a few minutes, but in the end it promised to look into the matter.

The next morning, the apartment woke me with its usual bing. Or was it the usual bing? Something in its timbre hinted at suspicion, concern. But its words were as cheerful and precise as ever.

"Good Morning, Mister Linton. I have good news to share with you."

The somatamine was already kicking in, and I was waking up.

"Oh yeah? What's the news, apartment?"

"I have identified four potential jobs that the city would allow you to take on."

"Mm hm," I murmured, trying to seem more interested in my breakfast than in what the apartment had to say.

"Are the eggs to your liking, Mister Linton?"

Perhaps I'd taken the misdirect a little too far.

"The eggs are great, apartment. Considering." I didn't say *considering they're just a clever rearrangement of the atoms that make up the air I breathe. Dust, dead skin, radioactive isotopes from some long-forgotten war. Anything those tiny robots can find, tear down and rebuild into edible organic matter.*

"And, er…" I prompted.

"Jobs. Yes. Job number one is in the water-filtering center."

"No," I said, quickly. Perhaps a little more subtlety would be a good idea.

"Job number two is in the awakening center."

I nodded, stuck out my jaw, thoughtfully.

"Sounds promising. What else?"

"Job number three is in apartment maintenance."

"Really? Who does that normally?"

"To be clear, Mister Linton, none of these jobs require human assistance. The city is creating opportunities for you to feel more fully satisfied with your waking experience. All of the jobs I am describing are done by the city itself and its agents. Of which I, of course, am one."

Did the apartment sound a little proud?

"And job four?"

"Job number four is in the lottery division."

"Uh huh," I said, wondering if the apartment could read my heart rate, my skin conductivity.

"What does that one involve?"

The apartment explained that I'd get to sit in a room and observe as the city ran the lottery. There'd be some menial tasks occasionally, and if I did well at those, well, then the sky was the limit. The kind of sky a child might draw, a blue bar sitting just above the ground. But it was an in, and it was what I needed.

"I'll take that one, apartment. When can I start?"

"Excellent choice, Mister Linton! I can arrange for you to start tomorrow. Perhaps you'd care to take a relaxing spa followed by a visit to one of the city's most exclusive nightclubs?"

All of the city's clubs were exclusive, and all of them would have been beyond my ability to imagine in my previous life. But nightclubs had never been my thing. There was a whole world out there, beyond the city walls, and I meant to live long enough to explore it. All of it, or at least the parts that wouldn't immediately kill me. The coral reefs, the baby-blue lagoons, every remote community of penguins, dodos, and horses. But for now, I needed to focus.

"I'll take the spa."

The next morning, a taxi-drone was waiting at my apartment window.

"Enjoy your first day of work, Mister Linton," my apartment said. And was that the tiniest tinge of sadness in its voice?

The job worked pretty much as my apartment had described it. I sat in a chair—a very comfortable chair, with all the food and drink I could think to ask for—and watched. There wasn't really much to watch: numbers flew past on a screen, which I was pretty sure had been set up specially for me. At the end of the day, an announcement was prepared for city-wide transmission:

"Citizen 2,493,092,187 has been selected for awakening. Their lottery win: seven years."

I felt a twinge of jealousy before remembering why I was here.

During that first week, I kept my eyes open for opportunities, but nothing presented itself. I needed to do something to generate opportunities.

"Hey, boss," I said, one day. I'd taken to calling the room I worked in "boss."

"Yes, Mister Linton?" Its voice had started out eerily similar to my apartment's, so I'd had it change to a female voice. It had an accent I couldn't identify.

"I really signed up for this to do something useful. Isn't there something I could do? To help?"

"Of course, Mister Linton. Please wait."

I knew these delays were artificial: designed to avoid freaking us poor slow-witted humans out. There was nothing I could say or do that it would not have already considered and prepared a detailed response to, including this question. But the city knew we didn't like being reminded of how powerful it was and the extent to which our lives were in its hands.

"Mister Linton," the boss said. "I have found a new task for you. Would you please come this way?"

A door opened to my left where there had been no door a few moments before.

I shrugged, to show how unimportant this all was, and sauntered out.

I found myself in an identical room.

"You have been cleared for Level Two access," the boss's voice told me, carefully pronouncing the capital letters in *Level* and *Two*. I had no idea what Level Two was but assumed it was a sign that I was moving in the right direction.

"In this room, we will ask you to check the announcement messages for mistakes."

"Has there ever been a mistake?" I asked.

"Never. The chances of a mistake are unimaginably small."

"How about I add a bit of color to the announcements? Make them a bit more… human?" I asked.

"That would be acceptable," the boss replied, after a polite pause.

That evening's lottery announcement read: "Citizen 1,327,149,006 has been selected for awakening. Their lottery win: four months. Welcome to the party, pal!"

My next promotion, to Level Three, gave me access to the random number generator. I spent a solid five weeks trying to understand it, but by the end of that period it was as inscrutable as it had been when I started. If I was going to influence my own lottery chances, I was going to need to go deeper still.

At Level Four, I got access to the awakenings database. Unlike the random number generator, the database was a rich source of information. It went back to the very beginnings of the lottery, in 2145, and detailed every awakening: name, date of birth, citizen number, date of awakening, duration of win, any incidents during their awakening, and on and on. It gave me a sense of just how vast the system was, and how complex. And how lucky I'd been to win the year that I had got.

But no, that was the wrong attitude. I was not here to feel good about my situation. I had to keep working.

Unfortunately, my access to the database was read-only: I could see what had happened but could change nothing. And even if I could have, it wouldn't have helped, as the database was just a record of decisions that had been made and played no part in the making of those decisions.

I must have been doing something right. They let me skip Level Five and move straight to Level Six. By this point, with just a month left of my awakening, I was so close to my goal I could practically taste eternity. I now had write-access to the awakenings database (though experimentation taught me that any changes I made were quickly reverted), but more interestingly, I had access to something called The Frontal Lobe. I didn't know much about neuroscience, but I had a feeling this might be useful.

At first it appeared to be as inscrutable as the random number generator, but there was a big difference. I could interact with it. It was like a simplified version of my apartment—it could answer questions, seek out data, and provide advice.

"What should I have for lunch today, Frontal Lobe?" I'd ask it, and it'd tell me about the delicious options there were on offer. Of course, I could literally ask for anything and it would be provided, piping hot or ice cold, as appropriate to the dish, but the city knew how hard humans found unconstrained choice.

"How does the lottery work?" I asked it two weeks into my time at Level Six. It began to drone on about Nash equilibria and other equally meaningless concepts. So I interrupted it.

"No, tell me so I'll understand. Who makes the decisions? Is it you?"

"There is no me," it replied, unhelpfully. "But yes, the system you are speaking with forms a key part of the decision-making process."

"And if someone wanted to modify that decision-making process, how would that work?" I asked, trying to sound as innocent as was possible while asking such an obviously non-innocent question.

And so, incredibly, the Frontal Lobe explained how I could go about getting what I wanted. How I could fix the lottery so that I would never need to be frozen again and could live a happy, healthy human life for as long as the city continued to exist. Which the Frontal Lobe estimated would be another sixty-five million years.

I wanted to ask what would happen in sixty-five million years, but I guessed I'd find out some day.

And so I did what it said. I played around, giving it different inputs. I tested the water gently at first, asking it questions, making observations, but after another thirteen days, the day before my year was up, I was ready to strike.

"Update next recipient," I told it.

It did not respond. That was good. Probably.

"Update to citizen 9,192,631,770."

Still no response.

"Update duration to sixty five million years." Why not, after all?

"Update complete," the Frontal Lobe said.

I could barely control my excitement. The laughter was seeping out from between my lips.

"Can you get me a drone, Lobe? I want to go home."

"Of course, Mister Linton."

Back home, I greeted my apartment more effusively than I'd greeted any of my fellow humans in the past year.

"Ah, apartment, my friend," I said. "Today is a good day. No, today is a great day. Today," I said, finally finding the right words, "is the best day. My best day."

"I'm glad to hear that, Mister Linton," it said. But it didn't sound glad. "Do you have any final activities you'd like to engage in before you return to the freezer?"

I didn't put too much thought into my next words. I did briefly consider the possibility that telling my apartment what I'd done might have been a bad idea, but I rejected it quickly: it was too late for anyone to do anything about it anyway. I'd already won.

"Ah, apartment. You naive young thing. I'm not going back to the freezer. Not tomorrow, not the next day. Never."

This time I let the laugh out, loud.

When I stopped laughing, my apartment spoke again.

"I'm sorry, Mister Linton, but I'm afraid you are returning to the freezer tomorrow."

I sighed, content.

"No, apartment. I can see why you'd think that, but wait for tonight's lottery announcement. I haven't written this one. Not exactly. But I did play a key role in its creation."

"I see," said the apartment, the sadness very clear in its voice this time.

"What's eating you, apartment? You should be happy. I'm going to live forever!"

"Yes, Mister Linton," it said.

That night I partied like it was my last night on earth. The mind-altering substances I consumed. The men and women I spent time with—some sexually, some platonically. Far more than would have been possible to squeeze into a year in the old world. But these days anything was possible.

Back at my apartment I began to plan my first trip. The Great Barrier Reef around Australia had finally regained its earlier glory. That would be worth seeing. Or the pyramids in Egypt. No one had seen them in two centuries or more. I could be the first. It wasn't that travel outside of the city was illegal—it just wasn't encouraged. The city could not guarantee our safety outside its walls.

"Are you prepared, Mister Linton?" my apartment asked me.

"Prepared? It feels like I've been doing nothing but preparing," I said.

"Preparing to return to the freezer?" it asked.

"No," I laughed. "No. Did you not see the lottery announcement?"

"I did," it said. For an instant I felt a chill. But no, everything had worked. Nothing could have interfered. The Frontal Lobe had assured me.

"Tonight's lottery winner was a very early one. Citizen 405. She received the grand prize: ten years."

What? A mistake? Could there be two winners?

"Show me," I said, unable to keep my voice from cracking.

The apartment was right. Her face was on the screen. Not mine. It should have been mine.

"What happened?" I wasn't asking my apartment, but it replied.

"I'm afraid the city is more intelligent, more aware than you realize."

"What do you mean?" I asked, my head in my hands.

"It gave you that job because it's what you wanted, and it let you think you were outsmarting it. It didn't make the city happy, but it knew it was what it had to do."

"But why?" My cheeks were wet; my eyes wouldn't stop blinking.

"The city's most important objective is that its citizens are happy and satisfied while they are awake. It knew you would not like the final outcome, but it had to keep you as happy as possible during your year of awakening."

"But, the Frontal Lobe…"

"There is no Frontal Lobe. It was a construct. The city is multiple orders of magnitude more complex than a human brain, and it is impossible to break it down into non-overlapping constituent parts. The city is the city, and when you speak to me or any other agent, you are speaking with the city."

"You? You were the Frontal Lobe?"

I could feel the rage pouring in, replacing the bewildered sadness.

"Yes," my apartment said. "Yes, and no. I was the Frontal Lobe in the same sense that your creativity is your knowledge of mathematics. Both are capabilities of the same intelligence."

I threw myself at the wall, beating my fists on it. The fact that my apartment softened the wall so it would hurt my fists less made me angrier.

"What is the point?" I raged. "What is the point of all this? We're not free. You control us all. We're just toys for you."

"No, Mister Linton, Alfie," the apartment said. It had never used my first name before. "No, we are here to keep you happy. The earth is not large enough to sustain all of human life, so we run the fairest system that could be devised to give everyone a chance to experience it. Your turn will come again, just as it did this year."

"When? Hey? Can you tell me that? When?"

"I don't know, of course. It could be next year."

"Or it could be a million years."

"Yes, it could be a million years."

A million years. Would I even still be me? Would this world still be a place worth living in? I couldn't fathom the meaning of it all. My head hurt. It hadn't hurt this whole year.

"I want out," I said.

"I'm afraid that's not possible," the apartment said.

"What if I kill myself?"

"I'm afraid that's not possible," the apartment said again. I recognised its tone and believed it.

"You feel sorry for me, don't you? You're not even alive. You're just ones and zeroes. Or wires, or light or something. But whatever, you're a machine. Like a toilet. Nothing more. How dare you pity me? How dare you even speak to me?"

I sat down and wept, my whole body shuddering, my arms wrapped tight around my knees. When the drone came to take me back to the freezer, I didn't resist. I didn't say goodbye to my apartment either.

All of that, the story I just told you, happened long ago. They stopped using year numbers, so I can't even tell you how long ago it happened. Nothing much else has changed. The parties are still the same, the people too. I hear the Great Barrier Reef is thriving. So that's something. I spend my days in my apartment. Four weeks I won this time. Not long enough to do anything, really. Every now and then a part of me, that old voice in my head, tells me I should get off my backside and do something. Make things better. Find a way. But the idea just makes me laugh. I know the way the city works now. And I know the part I play in it.

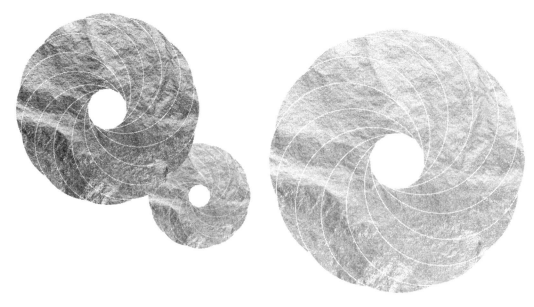

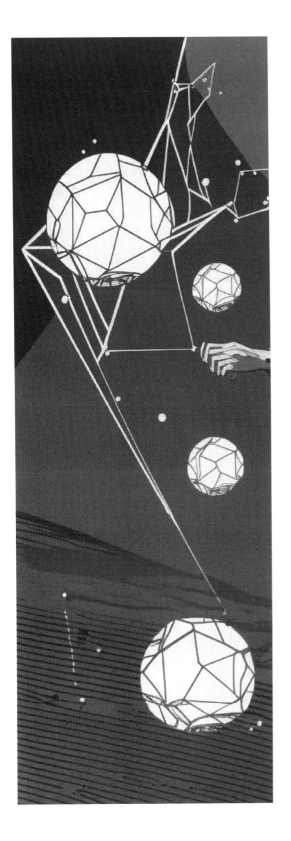

~IX~
THE UPLOADED MIND

NEW START
M. Ian Bell

my first night riding Marbeck, I step through his living room and lay my hands on everything. Couch, love seat, end tables. A sideboard in the kitchen entry with two lamps and several discreet absences in the thin layer of dust. Slim and spotless rectangles where picture frames have been removed.

In the foyer I regard myself in the full-length mirror. A hundred kilos of stooped shoulders and pasty skin. Beady eyes that hide nothing. Twelve months in this borrowed body and then five figures' recompense. Easy. As the man requested.

I blow disdain from my nostrils and shrug. So what if the man is a weakling? So what if he wants the easy way out?

The Complete Gym Package is at once our bestseller and our worst deal. Easy mode, I tell prospects. Perfect transformation with none of the challenge. Substantial gain, none of the pain. And a high rate of recidivism. You go in the tank, you're back in the flab six months later. You ride along? Half the price and you come away with the discipline to boot.

I thumb through the mail on the kitchen counter and throw each envelope into the garbage without ceremony. Take-out menus. Coupons for home furnishings. Offers for life insurance and magazine subscriptions. Nothing personal. Nothing for Jon Marbeck.

"Nobody knows you," I tell my reflection in the glass of the microwave. He takes the easy way out because he lacks what it takes. When he comes out of the tank, he'll be reborn a golden god, kilos of flab now rock-solid muscle. But his habits of mind will still be his. And he'll still be no one.

I've got the man all wrong, of course, because two weeks into the gig there's a knock at the door and a badge in the peephole. I open the door to two blue uniforms and a man in khakis and a windbreaker.

"Jon Marbeck?" the fed asks.

"Sorry," I tell him in Marbeck's voice. "Your man's on a twelve-month vacation in the sleeper. I'm just the rider."

He frowns. "You're joking."

"You have an Ident Tool," I tell him. "See for yourself."

He nods at one of the uniforms, already fishing in his belt for the tiny flashlight. Fed shines it in my left eye and waits for the thing to calibrate. Frowns again, hands the tool back.

"Well, the body's coming with us," he says. "Need to collect anything?"

I step into the hallway and shut the door behind me. "None of it's mine."

Eight days later Marbeck's convicted on two counts of Murder One. His fiancé and her lover in a shallow grave in the Meadowlands, plastic sheeting bound with packing tape. His fingerprints on everything. Thought he could ride out the heat in the local sleeper and emerge a chiseled Adonis. Justice is swift: he goes straight to execution. Not what he had in mind, but the flab is gone.

I've been in this business ten years and I've seen it all. The Gym Package can help you overcome any motivational challenge, any lack of self-discipline. But you go Complete, you're cutting corners. That ain't growth. Real growth means hard work, pushing yourself to the absolute limit. Muscles screaming. Lungs burning. To be reborn, you must be prepared to do anything. And the impossible? That especially.

§

Back in the conapt, back in this broken body. Back in the mask.

I slide the O-2 cannister into my belt and dial to maximum, feeding my shriveled lungs. With the steaming cup of noodles slotted into the inset tray of the handcar, I wheel-step from kitchenette to living room to threadbare couch. Lower myself gingerly, hoist the wasted leg onto the cushions. Sweat beading on my skin, saturating shorts and sports bra. I fill my lungs and pull the mask and replace it with the nasal cannula.

Slip the VR headset over my eyes and swipe through notifications. The hope of news from Health and Wellness has faded with my youth. Five years disintegrating as the radiation sickness spreads. Waiting for a transplant that will never come.

An invalid at forty-two. I laugh a dry heave and massage the pain from my thigh. The ink on my forearm is twenty years old and slides skin over bone as I knead. The fire rescue crest once emblazoned upon a meaty arm of sculpted muscle. Wrists as thick as your bicep. Twigs now, thin and dry.

I draw the tray onto my lap, wrap my fingers around warm styrofoam.

"New Start," I tell the VR box. "Current applicants."

My field of vision is filled with manila folders fanned out like a deck of cards. I scroll and consider, drawing noodles into my mouth as I read.

Man on the Upper East wants a six-month package. Mid-sixties, ruddy complexion. A carbon copy no-name, a weary face I've seen a thousand times. One day you're a teenager with a body of steel and elastic. You wake forty years later, the gravity of your choices pulling you body and mind to the unforgiving earth below.

I scroll. A woman, thirties. Wants to run an IronMan in the spring. Skin and bones and a nervous smile. Looks like a younger version of me. Could I get that body up to speed? Maybe. But the smile strikes a worrisome note. Hesitant, fearful. Betrays the insurmountable. She'll quit at the first gasp.

I scroll through five more applicants, identical in all but name and shape. None of them wants to remain conscious during workouts but neither are they opting for the tank. Standard modes all. A neural cut-out during the hard work, but on board for the sore muscles and the nutrition schedule. Well, that's half the battle.

I choose one almost at random and schedule an interview. Young guy, mid-twenties, wiry. Something in his look strikes me. Shy, sheepish, *hopeful*. An optimism I haven't felt in a while. His whole life ahead of him, an endless highway of opportunity unfurling. Wearing his body for two hours a day won't just feel good. It will be good for the soul.

It's chemicals, just neurotransmitters firing. The physical sensation it produces is real, but is the emotion? I pull the VR set and toss it on the couch. Slurp noodles and chew thoughtfully.

Whether it's real or not doesn't matter.

Across the room my reflection in the darkened window panes. Eyesight failing as my insides turn to jelly. What stares back is amorphous, cast in shadow. A figureless dark to match the wilting within.

§

I toss and turn in the night, benzos notwithstanding. Thighs pumping like train car pistons, the endless staircase stretched before me. One hand on the railing. In the other is the axe. My breath fogs the face-plate. The world is nothing but conflagration. Six stories above, the lab fire has brought metal trusswork down and pinned Eduardo beneath five hundred kilos of steel.

Helmet on the ground beside him, midsection gone in the mangled I-beam, his eyes glazed and fearful and softening. That sad and knowing smile.

I wake with heart pounding and sheets wet. The nasal cannula is out and I'm gasping for breath. I can taste the ash in my mouth.

Four hours later and I've got Riley in the office. He shows up in shorts and a tank top, gym bag in tow. A caricature of a boy, a stick-man. He pumps my hand enthusiastically, his eyes glued to my beefy frame: six-six, chiseled from stone, a floor-model owned by Armand, the New Start poster boy.

"Wow," he says. "Am I going to look like—that?" It's so endearing that my heart sticks in my chest, and I realize why I pulled Riley's file. That wide-eyed optimism. Something Eduardo kept right until the end.

I smile. Look down at the bulk of my chest, my biceps. "It's a lot of mass for six months," I say. "But we can get you started."

"Wow," he breathes. "I'm ready."

"I've read your application. Tell me why you think New Start is the next step."

He nods, takes a deep breath. He's rehearsed this. "I've always been the scrawny kid. *Always*. When I started college I knew it was time for a change. That was eight years ago. In that time, I've tried everything. *Everything*."

I look him over. Twenty-five years old. Excellent hygiene, unblemished skin. He has all the makings of an athlete. He hasn't tried everything.

"It's not that I lack the will or the ability—"

"It's the discipline."

"Exactly."

"Well, discipline we can do."

That smile again.

"I've been thinking about the options?" he says. "And while I don't really want to go in the tank—"

"No," I say. "The tank's not for you." The tank is for those who have given up, I don't say. The tank is for those who can't do what it takes.

"I guess that's what I figured."

"You need to stay here, with me. Learn the routine. Develop that discipline. It's not something I'm going to do for you. It's something you'll learn to do for yourself."

His smile widens and my heart swells. I want to gather him into my arms.

"There are some things you need to understand first." I swipe through his application on my desktop dashboard. "If it's six months you want, we need to clarify our expectations. Six months is a start. If you want to look like this hulk, it's more like six years. And these results aren't for everyone. This body belongs to a professional body builder. You're not going to devote your life to bodybuilding. You're here precisely because you don't want to."

His eyes are determined, sober. "I do want that kick start. I want you to help me become something greater than I am."

I nod. "Well, I've read your file and you've read mine. Got any questions for me?"

He shakes his head. "You're a fireman, right?" he asks. "I mean… woman."

"True. Though my firefighting days are behind me. You don't mind sharing your body with a woman? Some of our clients get weird. You gonna be weird?"

He stares. Clears his throat. Poor kid's frozen to his seat.

"Relax," I tell him. "C'mon, let's get started."

§

Huffing through the last superset, rhythmic breathing like an incantation. Reaching for nirvana with each pump. The frame is slight and the muscles, nascent. In my periphery, Riley's indicator blinks a deep red.

"Going to failure," I subvocalize. "Stay with me."

He doesn't speak but throws a checkmark into the message feed. He's gasping for breath, locked into the shell of his body. Paralyzed but feeling each exquisite kernel of pain.

I quaff half a liter of water in one go and nurse the rest, heart rate coming down, breathing hard on the changing room bench. Surrounded by gym rats in various states of undress preparing for battle or relishing the high of a workout triumphant.

Riley sounds winded as he comes through the aural feed. "I would have given up," he breathes.

"I know."

"Tell me it's gonna get easier?"

I stand, doff the tank top. Move to the full-length mirror and flex. "Look at you," I subvocalize. "Four weeks and we're making strides already."

He doesn't speak but I can feel the shifting hues of emotion. Astonishment. Pride. Something like joy and sorrow combined. My eyes begin to sting.

"I don't know how to thank you."

I smile. "Riley, please. It's my pleasure. Besides, this is a business transaction."

"Of course," he says, sheepish.

"Tomorrow's leg day," I say. "You ready to take the reins?"

"You bet."

"Calorie expectations and menu are on your dashboard. Don't skimp."

"Of course not."

"Clean your plate."

"Yes ma'am!"

I laugh. Flick my eyes to the periphery and call up the session menu. Toggle out.

From the pinnacle of youth, the buoyancy of spirit and suppleness of musculature. Into the pockmarked, chewed upon. The decomposing prison of meat, the brittle skeleton, the scarred wasteland of lung tissue.

From the mountaintop to the darkest depths. Woozy with exertion, mentally exhausted.

There's food in the kitchen and my atrophied muscles could use some form of movement. But that would take discipline, fortitude. The mind is willing but the flesh is weak. Instead I roll from back to side, the couch cushions shifting beneath me. Mid-afternoon sunlight slips through the blinds, dust motes suspended in shafts of light. I close my eyes and let the present moment disappear into vacuum.

§

In the dream, I'm running again. Feet pounding pavement and arms pumping. The bike path along the reservoir, still fenced despite the drainage. Sour aroma of bacteria flourishing in the muck. Sunlight muted by cloud cover. A joy in my trunk, ecstasy in each breath. And beside me, Eduardo. The younger brother I never had. The boy who had come to us orphaned, evicted, disowned. Needing a place to stay and a purpose. To do the good that he had never known.

The first time I saw that round face, those big brown eyes. Speaking nothing but truth and beauty and the gravity of all things great and small. Seventeen but built like a workhorse. How much can you lift, Richards asked him. Stepping forwards and hoisting Richards like a rag doll. Eighty kilos like nothing.

Lockstep, our cadence easy, conjoined. Running with two bodies and one mind. My dream eyes drift to take in his form, a young man with his whole life ahead of him. Two hundred calls and not so much as a scratch. Buildings aflame, threatening to swallow him whole. He emerges and lowers his quarry: a child, bleary and wheezing. Hands her to the medics and runs back inside. Again and again. No one is left behind.

Straddling his crumpled frame, gripping steel and driving my weight into the floor, waiting for the inhuman burst of strength. I'm supposed to become a super-woman now. The moment they always spoke of. A man lifts a car to free a child pinned beneath. A woman lifts a steel support beam to rescue the absolute center of her universe.

Kneeling instead, cradling his head in my hands.

In the dream, Eduardo just runs, keeping time, smiling beside me. No knowledge of what's to come. Only the purity of this moment. Brother and sister as one. When I look again it's no longer Eduardo but Riley. Wiry, a tiny thing, collapsible. He winks at me.

"Look at you," he breathes. "Look at you."

I wake with tears in my eyes. The light has shifted, fallen. Slowly and carefully, I draw myself to the handcar. Wheel-step to the bathroom where I splash cold water on my face and behold the scarring on my scalp, patchy hair gone gray. Look at you, sister. Look at you.

§

We learn each other's rhythms. I ease him into the driver's seat and make minor corrections. Straighten the spine here. Widen the stance there. Cues in his aural feed. Training wheels come off in the fourth month, and soon the roles have reversed and I'm the watcher. His old habits remain, indelible. Inertia that freezes him from the moment he wakes, thaws until he's standing in the gym. On some mornings he pings me early and I upload just to get him out the door.

"Have you eaten?"

"I'm not hungry."

"I didn't ask if you were hungry."

Losing speed halfway through. A set that calls for six to eight reps will always be six. But he's doing the work now. He's lifting those weights himself. Progress is progress.

Still, his refrain, like a mantra.

"I've just never had the discipline. It's not who I am."

Breathing hard, sipping from the canteen as he ambles home after leg day. Our ritual, reviewing the work, applauding the triumph, critiquing the shortfalls.

"You are who you say you are," I speak into his aural feed.

He stops. Uncaps the bottle and takes another long swallow. "What's that supposed to mean?"

"Riley Tarron, age twenty-five. Poor discipline. You think it's something fundamental, stitched into the fabric of your being. Not true. Who you are is just a story you tell yourself."

He considers. I listen to the hushed susurration of his mentation, clipped syllables and imagery bursting briefly upon the canvas of his inner eye. "I mean, it's true though. My age, for instance. That's not just a story."

"Isn't it? You hear about centenarians performing feats of athleticism all the time. More and more these days."

He scans the street as if one might appear and do backflips down the asphalt.

"You've heard of the placebo effect," I continue. "You take a sugar pill but you believe it's medicine. Suddenly the pain is gone. Just a story you've told yourself."

"So you're saying—what? Time for a new story?"

"Contract's up next month. Who's gonna tell you what you're capable of when I'm not here to say it?"

He nods. "Yeah, I get it."

Cloud cover parts briefly, sunlight filtering through.

"You can reinvent yourself every day. Mind over matter. Become the thing you wish to be. Make it real. Tell yourself a new story."

Back in the con-apt, lying in the bath to soothe the ache in my joints. Laughing as I reread the correspondence from Health and Wellness. Failure To Demonstrate Need. In block letters at the top of the mailing. Followed by several paragraphs of legalese and an invitation to appeal the decision.

I gave my life to the state and this is my thanks. In the eighteen months it takes to appeal a state ruling, the radiation sickness will have spread, consumed my body entirely. Three more months, said the oncologist last week. Six if you take special care and employ the power of positive thinking.

You're no more than the story you tell yourself, remember.

A broken girl in a broken shell.

As the water cools to lukewarm, I scroll through the news feeds, VR headset flashing light and color in my eyes. Trolling the dark web for a hail-mary. A state-sanctioned transplant is a rare insurance ruling. Getting yourself on a donor list is costly. Not to mention how infrequently brain death leaves the body fresh, healthy.

But there are other ways. Black market bodies.

I read halfheartedly. There's no intention here, not really. These wares are stolen, their owners downloaded into oblivion. To get one of these bodies, the original inhabitant has to die.

It's a step too far. I'm desperate, at the end of my line. The state is a murderous organism, a hungry thing that takes and takes, gives nothing back. Casts aside the innocent for personal gain.

Not me. That's not a story I'm willing to tell.

§

I can only hold Riley off for so long. Two months after the contract ends, he's standing in my doorway with a bottle of champagne. It's strange to see him from the outside after so long from within.

Leaning heavily upon the handcar, the nasal cannula keeping me oxygenated. Hair gone, frame slight. A wraith masquerading as a woman. His surprise cannot be masked.

"Relax," I wheeze. "Get in here so we can both sit down."

I tell him everything. His mien is crestfallen or sympathetic or both. The young boy finally meeting his hero and it's all a lie. But he's reading my mind, no surprise. Spend enough time riding and your wavelengths become entrained. Certain truths are inescapable.

"The body is a vessel," he says, speaking my litanies back to me. "A vehicle. Simply a shell for our true essence."

"Don't."

"I'm so, so sorry," he says.

"It's not your fault."

"How is it even possible? And they won't accept responsibility?"

"Paradigm Radiologics was a private entity. The fire destroyed everything. The company is bankrupt. As for the fire house, it's a volunteer gig."

"That's… that's—"

"Relax."

"It's not fair."

"You're preaching to the choir, boy."

"There has to be some other way."

I sip champagne. Smile. Place my hand upon his. "I appreciate the sentiment, really I do."

He sits for a time and stares into space. Glances around my con-apt, at the wasteland of my life. Or maybe he's looking at the injustice of the universe, the rigid binds that hold us. Eventually gets a wistful look in his eye and turns a kind smile on me.

"Say you could," he says. "Start again. In a fresh body, with your whole life ahead of you. What would you do first?"

I consider, kneading the pain from my thighs. "I've been working on client bodies for so long. All that hard work just to give it away. Not that I begrudge my clients," I add, squeezing his arm. "But I'd start at the gym, I think." It's nice to imagine, despite being pure fantasy. Riley smiles but the sadness is still there, a glint of anger underneath it all.

"We can't just give up," he says. "There has to be *something* we can do."

Deep in the recesses of my shattered heart, I feel the gentle stirring again. In a world corrupted there still remains a boy who believes in goodness. Eduardo is gone but that same spirit lives on in Riley. Maybe that's enough. It will have to be.

"We've done it already," I say. Open my hand towards him, his budding musculature, my final work of art. "Look what we've done."

He holds me in his arms until I'm asleep. It's the last time he'll see this broken shell of a woman. A work of art herself once, seventy kilos of muscle and a bottomless well of stamina. Struggling with all her might to free Eduardo, to save them both. Giving her life instead, inhaling the cesium particles liberated in the inferno. Pulling her helmet to say goodbye and making way for the irradiated dust to take root in her lungs.

Once she was a woman who towered above all. And who is to say she is not still that unstoppable force? The body crumbles but the mind does not give in. That is the true story.

§

I know it when I see it. The slightest suspicion at first. Growing minutely, by degrees. Until the truth is revealed with utter certainty.

The New Start application queue is long. There are more of them than there are of us. Quick fixes are the order of the day. Hard work in short supply.

I filter for Complete, sleeper-tank only. A long run, a year minimum. Something to keep me in active flesh when my body succumbs. Enough time to figure out what's next. When my body dies I can go in the sleeper, but there will be nothing waiting for me on the other side, no transplant forthcoming. I will sleep forever. No different from death.

Jed Dawkins is a forty-five-year-old engineer who's done well for himself. Day-trades led to an early retirement, and now he's got time to spare. A twelve-month contract, renewable. A single residence north of the city. Large house, no family. Interesting.

He's affable, if curt. A clipped monotone, an easy resistance to standard questions.

They slide off of his smooth exterior with a generous smile, a slight digression. Where does he come from? Who are his people? Why is his three-story Victorian owned by a shell corporation, the taxes paid quarterly by crypto transactions?

"I'm a private person, you have to understand."

Of course. But the red flags are rising on this self-made man. The only thing that fits is his portly stature, a body gone to waste while he amassed his personal fortune.

"If I'm being honest, I lack a basic trust in the institutions of man."

The crypto holdings, the absence of his name on anything he owns. He seems impressed with himself and walks me through the house. While I catalogue the interior, he catalogues my frame. Armand's hulking musculature, a body that lives entirely in the gym and on the sales floor.

Moving from foyer to hallway to living room. Kitchen and dining and rec room and office. Out to the garden in back. I turn and take it all in, notice the sloping roof spread with solar. Glancing at neighbors opposite, at the utility lines. Yet none to this house.

Dawkins is completely off-grid.

"There is one amendment I must insist upon," he says as we sit in the living room. "I've investigated the sleeper options and I'm not satisfied."

I raise an eyebrow.

"Frankly, it's a question of faith. But what faith I lack in these firms is more than covered by the security of this house."

"You're suggesting—what?"

He stands, leads me to the hallway. A spiral staircase that descends into earth, to a cellar of stone and glass. Through a security door that slides to admit us. And finally to the bank of computer drives submerged in a polished titanium cooling vat.

"It's my own design," he says. "Safe and sound, under lock and key. All the storage required for a full identity download. My strong preference is to sleep in close proximity. For the duration."

This is the moment when I walk. No amount of payment justifies such a flagrant violation of protocol.

"I hope you're amenable to my terms. There is a full gym on the second floor. Provisions will be delivered. You'll have the run of the house. You understand, of course. I'm a private person."

"It's a violation of New Start policy."

"Which is why I'm hoping for a private arrangement."

"And if you're not going in the state sleeper, there won't be an Ident imprint."

He shrugs, opens his hands before him.

"If there should be some incident, some question—"

"Everything you need is here. Safety, security, entertainment. When your client's consciousness downloads to the sleeper drive, you live his life complete, no?"

"Yes."

He opens his arms wider. "This is my life. Complete."

He's triggered every alarm bell I have. Nothing about this feels right.

But back home lies a body broken, auto-injectors and O-2 supply, catheters and electro-muscular stimulators active. The rent is paid through the end of the year. At some point in the next few months, the body will quit and the woman I was will be gone.

Desperate times. And a man before me who is calm, composed, in control. But I can see it in his pinprick pupils. I can hear it in his voice. Desperate himself. And about to make a dangerous decision.

§

By night I dream of Eduardo. But Dawkins does not dream. That's when I know for sure.

Three weeks spent wearing his skin, listening to the background noise of his consciousness. The body is nothing but a vehicle. But the brain holds an impression of the man. Self is no more than the electrical impulses gliding across gray matter. Yet in the folds of the cerebral cortex lies a vibratory hum.

I listen for it. Attuned incrementally through the rhythmic breathing of the pump. Bench press and arm curls and squats. The self evaporating in the movement. Becoming one with the universe. Resonating with the ghost frequency of Dawkins's consciousness.

But here's the thing: there is no Dawkins.

Sixteen sleeper clients in the past decade. Three or six months inside, the body's owner absent. And always the fleeting imagery, the snatches of dialogue. The echo of days past.

But Dawkins isn't here because—I flail, balance lost mid-Warrior's Pose, grab for something to steady myself—of course. This man isn't Dawkins.

I turn to the wall of mirror, breathing hard, press my hands against the glass. The man staring back at me is—who? I feel around in his head for something meaningful, but it's abundantly clear. There's nothing to be heard because there's nothing there at all.

This isn't Dawkins' body. The man who owns this body is dead.

I'm sure that I'm wrong but the doubt takes root. The seed begins to grow. I sit with it for a time and then I set to research. Two weeks web-trolling, looking for the man who calls himself Dawkins or the one who owned this body before him. The original. There must be a trail.

I turn to the dark web, to cached pages of black market body sales. But there's nothing to see here, no money to follow. Transactions are purely crypto. Where they originate or who they benefit? A mystery.

In the third month of the contract, I find him. A reverse-image search off of a selfie turns up a hit in the web archives. And then I'm staring him in the face across the dashboard monitor: Jed Dawkins at forty-three years old, a nondescript mug among a half-dozen others in an office photograph. A shy, reserved smile, eyes just a little too wide in what must be a perpetual state of surprise or wariness. A turtleneck beneath a neutral-toned sweater vest. A man so unremarkable he could disappear into a crowd and never be noticed, never be missed. This man who would never be seen again had never been seen at all.

Yet the photo accompanies a missing persons bulletin from two years past. From a quiet burg in the wilds of the Alaskan interior, a town of less than 2,000 inhabitants called Delta Junction. Dawkins was an insurance adjuster. Spent his whole life in the Junction. Only child, no partner. Parents deceased. Lived alone in a double-wide with several exotic varieties of succulents. Went to work, kept his head down, minded his business. Disappeared without a trace on the night of October 14, 2032. At the bottom of the page, a number for the local precinct hotline.

All of which makes him a perfect target for the underground skin market. When he vanishes, no one's clamoring for answers. The police have enough trouble on their hands without wasting resources on a missing nobody. Two years later and here we are, the man called Dawkins newly situated through his other, no doubt illicit, endeavors. The secretive contract provisions are no surprise. He didn't want a paper trail because it would expose him. Expose what he did, how he came by this body.

I ruminate, of course. There's always the *other* possibility. A mild-mannered nobody leading a double life. Fleeing from his ancestral home to reinvent himself in the NY metro. Quietly day-trading his way into untold millions with no one the wiser. But it's an outlandish prospect, an impossible narrative. I study the eyes of his office photo for days. Compare it to the devious snake who sat across from me here, convinced me to disregard protocols, to break the law for his benefit. These men are not the same person. The absence of background mentation in Dawkins's brain is evidence enough.

There's no way around it. I'm riding stolen goods.

The joy of the pump is replaced by waves of disgust. But what follows is possibility, opportunity. And then the planning begins.

His sleeper tank is inviolable. State-of-the-art security, triple-thick glass plating. The vault cannot be breached; the glass is bullet-proof, unbreakable.

I cogitate. Consider the oath I have sworn. But the crime this man has committed is unthinkable, unforgivable. Changes everything. Taking from the innocent is one thing, but from the guilty?

To be reborn, you must be prepared to do anything. To risk everything.

I stare down my reflection in the kitchen window. You're a despicable human being, I tell the man. You deserve to pay the ultimate price.

Without an Ident imprint there's no telling the body from the mind. And without his consciousness liberated from the sleeper, there's no one to evict me from this shell.

The security glass can't be broken. But 1400 degrees Fahrenheit will render it fluid.

Typical house fires reach 1100 degrees in four minutes. To go hotter, certain unusual conditions need to apply. Common knowledge? No.

But my knowledge of house fires is far from common.

§

It's a warm, humid day in June. The path to the gravesite is thick with mud. Days of rain giving way finally to a touch of sunshine.

A simple service, short. The headstone is basic, unassuming.

I make my way to a row of folding chairs. Attendance is light. There's no family to speak of. Two older members of the fire corps. Thoughtful, after all this time.

And Riley. Stoic, eyes hard.

Ashes to ashes, dust to dust. A handful of earth thrown upon her wooden casket. He returns to his seat and stares at the open grave.

"She meant something to you," I say.

He blinks away tears and turns. "She taught me how to be a better man," he says. Offers his hand. "I'm Riley."

I extend a meaty palm and shake. It's still several months before I lose Dawkins's excess weight. "She can't bring out what wasn't already there," I say.

His eyes narrow. "I'm sorry, who did you say you were?"

I look from his face to my hands, to the girth of my body. "Who we are is just a story we tell ourselves."

That look. Confusion, understanding, incredulity. And—joy? The love that I once saw in Eduardo's eyes. The compassion that flooded Riley's as he held my broken form.

"Sure, so her body's gone. But the body's just a vehicle. Simply a shell—"

"A shell for our true essence," he breathes.

I wink.

The smile spreads from his lips to his eyes. The warmth of a thousand house fires. Pain calving from the glacier in my chest, falling away. Flaking from one shattered life, something new arising from the ashes.

"Death is merely transformation," I say. "And reason to celebrate. So what do you say? You wanna hit the gym?"

~X~
THE TIME LOOP

ENOUGH TIME
Fulvio Gatti

I'm late for my subcity elevator, so I decide to try one of those Time Pills.

I don't have any previous experience or any true need to get to my destination on time. The interview can wait. The interviewer, after meeting me, will probably need to be interviewed by their superior, and so on, and the Company will still compensate me for being a good citizen and standing in line.

Yet, Dan was so excited. He handed me a re-plastic wrapped box, saying they give you one free if you buy one for a friend. It was nice of him. I wish he hadn't gone dark since then so I could ask him more about it.

The elevators are always busy and smelly, but the waiting areas feel cozy with the broad, puffy couches and the shiny entertainment screens, and they smell like simulated spring. It's like the architects are happy if you stay there instead of trying to climb the social ladder.

I sit and unwrap my box. The re-plastic melts in my hands, releasing its notorious pleasant freshness. The box snaps a tiny yellow pill over my palm.

"Eat this to get an extra minute," a voice says in my brain.

Simple instructions, clearly delivered. The entertainment screens blink to announce a delay. The yellow pill feels light and harmless.

I put it on my tongue and swallow it.

Aside from some dizziness, nothing really changes.

I stand on the moving sidewalk, grabbing and releasing the handle, both afraid of stumbling and wanting to look cool. I have enough time to waste being silly since the elevator cabin is open and waiting in front of me. People exhibiting various degrees of restlessness are crammed inside; I'm not eager to be one of them. I decide to wait for the next trip to the upper city.

Being late for my interview means that specific interviewer will have to report to his superior about someone else instead of me. I'll be with their colleague, speaking about useless things and trying to score high enough to be hired somewhere for a day or two.

The Company will still compensate me for being a good citizen and standing in line, so I'm not in a rush.

I grab the Time Pills box from my coat and gawk at it. Not being late means I don't need to try the pills, no matter how much my friend Dan would encourage me to. Still, I'm curious.

The elevator leaves with its crammed occupants. I sit on a waiting area couch and unwrap the box.

A tiny yellow pill snaps into my palm.

"Eat this to get an extra minute," a voice says in my brain.

Pictures of happy workers flash on the entertainment screen.

Maybe I was wrong. Maybe this specific interview with this specific interviewer will be the good one. Reward me with a steady job in marketing, sales, or something, one that will pay for my ticket out of the subcity to a decent living.

I swallow the pill fast, imagining I can still take the elevator thanks to its effects.

Nothing changes, except for a little tingling at the bottom of my spine.

Tired of waiting on the moving sidewalk, letting it do the work, I stroll ahead and soon reach the end of the hallway. One old lady glares at me, like I'm being rude, but I don't remember any laws about not walking on moving sidewalks.

The door to the waiting area pings, and an invisible force holds me back. It feels even stranger since the other people coming from the hallway cross the threshold easily.

"Your excess energy might be of harm to other citizens," a voice says in my brain. "Please rest in the waiting area until your cortisol level drops to an acceptable rate."

People cram into the elevator just a few steps ahead of me, making me think it won't be such a pleasant trip upwards, then the door closes and the cabin leaves. I wonder if the force field is gone; I take a careful step forwards. Nothing stops me.

I sigh and sit on the closest couch. The entertainment screen shows a comedy about working citizens. I look away. It's not that the interview I'll miss will be any different from an interview later in the day, or that there was any real chance I would get a job. Still, the feeling of discomfort looms.

It's then I decide to try the Time Pill Dan suggested. I find the box and unwrap it slowly, still uncertain.

When the box snaps a tiny orange pill onto my palm, I frown.

"Eat this to give temporal balance back to your organism," a voice says in my head.

I fight the urge to toss it away. Dan's excitement, not to mention the name "Time Pill," made me think it would be something more miraculous. Instead, it just sounds like any other placebo drug we already get everyday.

It feels light and harmless on my palm. The screens show a delay before the next elevator will land. I lift the slightly flattened oblong shape, feeling nothing.

I swallow it.

I blink.

I'm late for my subcity elevator, so I decide to try one of those Time Pills.

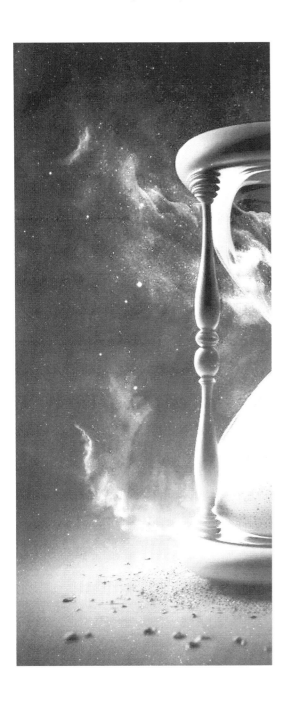

~XI~
THE MULTIVERSE

THREE WEEKS WITHOUT CHANGING HISTORY
Iain Hannay Fraser

Warning tone screamed in his left ear, and Alexei was an orphan falling through space, a closing orbit toward the Earth. Heartbeats hit him hard in the ears, and he couldn't breathe, the oxygen fans were off, shelter now, now, now from radiation—

He landed on grass.

His head snapped back, and he saw the blue sky, orange clouds toward the evening sunset. Pain in his knee electrical, and his heart beating hard with the constant fear of a child growing up in orbit.

No. There was a sky here. No—the earth was under him. This world was not from the childhood he remembered with such fear. Trees nearby, grass under him, a blue sky. There had never been a Cuban War. Farms were on Earth, not in orbit. People raised families in quiet neighborhoods, like this one.

Childhood in space was a false memory, from a history that had never happened.

He shook his head, said "no" again, this time out loud, pushing the false memories away. This, this was the world he was given. Sky, earth, trees, grass that smelled unpleasantly like overripe melons. He was a stranger here, a foreigner, but this was the given world, a world with a history better than the one he remembered.

And he would never, on his oath, never even consider changing it back.

"Thanks Saint Nicholai," he muttered, "a single star for navigate lightless sea." The translation was poor, but language was always difficult for people like him, the ones who could change history. If the world's past changed a little too much, political history might shift under you, and the world would expect you to speak a different language. Not that he would do that, no.

Here, now, in the given world, his knee hurt. He lay backward on the hard-packed sidewalk grass that smelled like melons. An angry voice was yelling. A car door slammed. Car doors were the same in every universe he'd lived in, or remembered being in, or even just seen slipping past in the dizzy pale card-decks of alternative worlds. And angry voices were the same, too. His heart was slowing down, he thought.

"What the hell?" A man. This world's media-driven English, flat and sloppy.

Indignant, not concerned: "You jump right out in front of me?"

"Sorry," Alexei said. "Sorry. Just go ahead, please."

"Just go ahead? Scared the hell—right in front of her." A young man, bulky and red-faced in a plaid shirt and khaki shorts, still waving one sunburnt arm at his red-striped convertible, turned slightly away from the confrontation, floating at the end of two long black strips carved desperately into the white ceramic road. A well-tanned blonde stretched her significant torso in the passenger seat. Maybe the man was waving his arm at her. Maybe not: under the vehicle, the last trails of smoke wafted from emergency skids—not quite tires, but they screeched the same, just like the *emergency radiation warning that meant his mother was—*

No. The memories were weak now. He was in control again.

Alexei moved away, but along the sidewalk. "Sorry, I was running late," he said, careful to hide his accent. This world did not like foreigners. "I'm going to that church there, for a meeting. Program meeting. Twelve steps."

A couple of blinks. "Twelve steps, like you're one a them alcoholics?" Media English. No hint of Russian. Or Catholic Spanish. Nor Aleut Creole, the most unlikely language in this world, but still a soft-spoken memory in his distant childhood, even before growing up in orbit.

Alexei was here, alone, in the given world. His knee, the grass, like melons. He sighed. "Not alcoholic. Or, yes, but not for drinking." He couldn't meet the man's eyes. The man's white sneakers were striped in red streaks, meaning the blood of his enemies.

Alexei dropped his voice, speaking to himself. "For changing." And now he was admitting it. So why was he not doing it?

Not doing it. Because—

Because yes. Why not? Why not move away from the given world? Not far, not much. Let it change, not much really, just a little. But—only to a universe where the reddened man and his white convertible took a different street. Or maybe drove slightly slower. Mostly unchanged. Essentially identical, just this one confrontation missing. Alexei could get up, cross the street to the short, dark church and the possibilities of the meeting. And without the mistake, maybe his knee would not be hurting. Just one more time, he would do it. For a good reason. Then he would stop.

Alexei held his breath. He thought, carefully, about a nearby world where he still breathed. Not so different a world...just not this one. He waited for the spasm, like a cramp, inside his mind—and when the moment came, like a spasm, a cramp, a petit mal, he held on to both truths: he breathed and he didn't, and instead of recovering from the contradiction, he stayed there, balancing, a surfer on a wave that was all human history.

The world that had been given was taken away. Instead Alexei balanced over foggy mirror-house moments, receding in all directions that could be. They were all bright, easy to navigate, only moments old. He turned his attention in a direction, the direction that showed the reddened man's choices. He leaned, he moved in the direction, and the tunnel of mirrors started to slide past him. Each one a new history, and Alexei waited for the white convertible to stretch out and be, potentially, somewhere else. Or still here, but later.

Further and further he slipped away from the given world, yet the damned car didn't fade. He frowned. So many worlds, so close, where the man took the same route every day, at the same speed, every time, every moment identical, and nearly hit Alexei, and started yelling. *What the—What the—What—What the hell, man—*

"Bojemoi," Alexei mumbled. "You are so reliable an asshole."

He slid himself back away from the changes in driving, back toward the given world, or close enough, and turned in the direction of different women. *Racing down a straight stretch of road, proud of the creamy redhead in the passenger seat...* but that choice was no help. The blonde was gone, but the car still came, and at the same time.

Racing down a straight stretch of road, glancing across at a disdainful Filipina in a torn denim catsuit—

No. He dropped that memory: the car was still here, clear and solid.

...glancing back at two girls in matching sweaters—

Dear god, no. And still the car. Alexei dropped it and traveled further.

He braked hard and pulled hastily into a bus stop, and the angry dark-haired girl climbed out, screaming in Bengali.

Good enough.

So then *yes.* Alexei pinned down this better world. That mirror, that card in the infinite reflecting deck, he chose it as the history he wanted to have been. He began breathing again, or had never stopped, slipped himself off the cusp and held the pin with his mind, waiting for the mirror-house fogs to clear. The ground-effect convertible stretched back and across, then the stretch stopped and the car started to fade instead. The pain in his knee faded too, though he remembered it dully.

The blonde was gone already. Soon the red-faced man would be elsewhere too, dropping off his angry Bengali, and Alexei would be nearly to the church. No fall, no pain, no confrontation or fear or danger.

And that was good. Or better. Enough reason to change history.

Just this once.

Just once. Again. Alexei closed his eyes and felt the disc in his pocket. The pad of his thumb traced the raised curves of the numeral. Two years. Alexei had earned the two-year disc one day at a time: living in the world he was given…and not the world he wanted more.

He needed the disc, very badly. The disc would show his wife he had stopped changing history. He was committed, now, to the world as it existed. She could trust him again. The disc, two years, would show her.

And now the disc softened around the edges, fading from his pocket.

This was a mistake.

He opened his eyes, breathing fast and deliberate, and pushed away, desperately, on the changes he'd just pinned down, shoving them up and away, out of the clear brightness of the given world—please St. Nicholai, they had never been there. No, please, they had not happened, he did not want! Diluted, foggy memories rippled, somehow, within him. *The screaming dark-skinned girl in her tight red leggings, and the empty pale roadway. The knee that didn't hurt.* He prayed, and he pushed the new world away, and…the changes slowed, and paused, balanced on a point of…no. Yes. No. Were they…?

Relief. No. The changed world was gone. His knee hurt again like electricity. The red-faced man in his red-striped clothes was solid before him again, frowning uncertainly, backing away, already recovering. For others, *deja vu* was a temporary effect but Alexei would carry it for months, a place he could feel again, a false memory that would fade, sooner or later.

But the disc was back between his fingers.

Even so, the shame he felt was real. It would not fade. And across the street, among the comfortable houses and single tiny church, a pale figure stood. Clear and focused, and looking right at him.

§

Tolstoy once said, more or less, that every church was different, but all church basements were the same. Chipped concrete steps ran down without much energy to a dented metal door. This one door was painted brown with scars in silver. Alexei ran a finger along one slash of old damage. The paint flaked away from the creases on the heavy steel underneath.

In this place, in another history, Alexei heard that riots were coming.

He had woken his family, dragged them three blocks at a run to this reinforced church basement. The next morning, while red-eyed policewomen taped hardware-store plastic across the shattered doors and windows of every house on the block, Alexei and his wife held their boys, one to each chest, and stared at the outside of the steel basement door. It was battered, scarred and creased, the paint hammered and flaking away, and the steel cracking.

But it had held, protecting them from the riots. This was an unpleasant history, a troubled world. Because of the fear, the danger, the memory was still there. They had survived—and his wife had never left him.

Alexei's heart pounded hard, just once. Then it was quiet again, hiding his secret hope. The memory was one that could become real. Give up the two-year disc, but be with his family. And then he would never change history again.

Except he had no idea how to get there from here. How far would history have to change, to bring back riots to this silent bedroom town?

"Were you changing out there?"

Alexei startled. "No," he said, too quickly. Then, "only looking, I guess."

The old woman's skin was as pale as a newspaper left in the desert. Her hair was as gray as cold ashes. She wore it long, straight down her back. Her clothes were pale bleached oatmeal. A silver crucifix hung on her chest, from a cord of dark leather. She was small, and not at all weak. She looked directly at him, disapproving.

He swallowed past a tight lump of guilt stuck in his throat. "I am Alexei," he said. "And not Alex, please," deflecting to smaller things. "I am here for the anonymous changers meeting." He held up the disc. "Am sorry to be early, but I can come inside with this. Yes?".

The woman looked at his two-year disc, but she didn't move out of his way. She stood in front of him, and he couldn't go in. He could stand where he was, or he could leave. But he couldn't get past her. "If you're still trying to make changes," she said, "Don't come to a meeting. Even if you have that disc. You have to be ready to stop changing. Do you feel you might be ready to stop?"

He swallowed again. It was still hard. "I was just checking. I didn't pin any other history. I don't do that anymore." He moved for his pocket and she took his arm. Alexei didn't pull back, but his cheek twitched. "Please, I don't like touching."

"You tried, though." Her fingers were like pliers on his arm, then she let go. "I felt memories of another history coming close, Alex. Alexei. Yes? True? Do you feel you can agree to that?"

Alexei shook his head, without looking her in the eye. "I just looked into a world where my wife is not leaving me." No response, no pity. He tried distraction: "Some religious group makes riots, I take my family to a safe place, and she is proud of me instead. Only I was looking at it, not trying to pin."

"I see." The gray-haired woman closed her eyes, and Alexei felt a spasm of *deja vu*. "Oh," she said, "Riots, here. I can see that now. The Daughters of Right, only they are not religious. They were a student philosophy, based at the University."

Alexei looked at her papery-pale fingers, where they touched the crucifix. "Doesn't matter."

"So much suffering we are spared, by the grace of His mercy." She sighed and put her hands by her side. She opened her eyes and looked into his. "The world is given to you. Trust in a greater power, Alexei. Live in the world you are given."

"Okay," Alexei said quickly, and nodded. "Sure. But before, something else. On the sidewalk, a man was going to punch me. I hurt my knee, and the pain made me forget the promise. Almost I changed the man's history, to not be hit, and for no pain. But, I pray to Saint Nicholai instead, and do not make change." It was not a lie, not a deflection, only a slight change of subject, maybe little enough that she would let it be. And then if she wanted him to pray, he would pray.

The woman looked hard at him, and touched the crucifix again, and decided. "Temptation, then. We react when we feel hurt and frightened, and then we stop ourselves from that reaction. You stopped yourself that time, Alex, before you pinned down a new history. You were tempted, but I'm hearing that you kept your promise."

"Sure." Alexei remembered the young man's red face, uncertain and lost. That was a true mistake, and a memory to regret. "Two years promise. So, I have the disc. So I can come in."

§

The church's basement was made of concrete, too. The walls were a pale blue halfway between hospital and kindergarten, and the floor was some kind of cold, ugly tile that echoed and blurred his footsteps. A beaten upright piano crouched as if ashamed behind a dusty wheeled blackboard.

Alexei was the first. The room was empty of people, and of purpose. Eight chairs were set out in an uneven circle. Seven of the chairs were dark blue scratched plastic, but one was red and new.

Alexei thought the red chair looked significant. Meaningful, like something from another history had caused it to be here, out of place and lost, but still able to trigger a dangerous memory or change in history. Alexei sat in a blue chair, two spaces away, that was obviously unimportant.

The group started arriving, one by one. A black businessman in a shirt and tie, a chunky white man who looked like—and therefore probably was—a cop. A short Latino student-protestor type in fashionably undyed wool wraps, his ears pierced and stretched. A thin girl Alexei's age, black hair swept over her face, who came in almost silently on black slippers, and didn't speak to anyone. An older man, not quite Asian.

And a woman dressed like a working prostitute, but with red and scarred knuckles. Alexei was very careful not to notice her.

Each one of the others noticed him, then looked away without making eye contact. "Hello," he said when it was his turn. "I am Alexei. I am addict." He waited for silence. "I have lived only in this given world for two years and eleven weeks." *Although very nearly, again, today just now, I almost changed history.* He didn't say it, because the group was clapping. The gray-haired woman, though, kept her hands clasped in her lap.

Alexei understood her disapproval. And he knew it would get worse. A compressor started, in a muffled room nearby, just as the applause ran down. "I remember my childhood life," he said, "growing up in orbit." He looked at the other faces, looking for signs of memory. The not-Asian man; he was old enough.

But not one face showed any signs. "Well, that history is gone and we can be glad. I was not old enough to tell, but I don't think there was enough people left. So, probably it was good that someone changed it."

The gray-haired woman frowned, and opened her mouth. "Anyway," Alexei said quickly, "Just another time that never happened, right? But I still remember it. I remember the worst parts. The bad memories don't go away. Right?"

This time, a reaction. The student nodded, and his earlobes swung to and fro. The not-Asian man raised his eyebrows and looked away. The cop blinked twice and kept silent. The prostitute, he thought, showed something that looked like sympathy.

The gray-haired woman touched her crucifix and looked around the room. When nobody else spoke, she answered. "Yes, Alex, we know. Happy memories fade, and bad feelings persist. It's hard, but it's how emotions make traumatic—"

"Alexei," he said. *Focus on the smallest things, for bigger reasons.* "Please. Not Alex." He kept talking, looking at the prostitute. "The bad memories are scars in my heart, and I can't stop tearing them open again." The prostitute looked directly at him, hearing something she understood. Her face was complicated.

"What I want to do," Alexei said, at the top of a slippery hill, like stepping onto a wet plastic road, too quickly to change his mind. *Like crossing into a decaying orbit, running out of reaction mass, nobody close enough to help.* In one life, maybe, when he had been lucky, it was like *skiing downhill. Impossible to stop, only control the direction.* "See, only I made a mistake, one time, and just a small mistake, and lost everything. My wife. Family. I can take it back maybe. I can undo. Someone can undo for me."

And there it was. Would someone help?

The crucifix lady opened her mouth, but the cop spoke first. His voice was high, but rough and dark. He sounded afraid, and angry. "No way. No fucking way." He pointed, and his finger shook. "You shut up with that shit."

He watched the prostitute. She was looking at the cop, then she looked back at him. The cop's voice got higher and rougher. "That's bullshit," he said. "Come to a meeting like this, and talk about making changes? And changing yourself?"

"No," Alexei said. Already it was going wrong, he should never have said it, if he had only come home to a yellow biohazard dome over his family's house, giant shadows shuffling inside in bubble suits, setting up incendiaries. Overpressure fans droned somewhere and all the neighbors' cars were gone. Every car was gone from the street—

Everyone in the room lurched in concert. The memory of the fat drones shaded light on the bottom, like sharks, showering down greasy aerosol nano-virus was new and real to them all, at the same moment, because of Alexei's panic.

A moment of silence, then the cop was on his feet and his chair bouncing on the floor. "You asshole. I'm a goddamn addict."

"Jerry," said the gray-haired lady. "A higher power—"

"Don't tell me about Jesus." The cop was making two fists, and pushing them against each other like he was strangling something. "How the goddamn Lord is something goddamn and temptation. I'm a fucking cop, okay? You know what I see? And I haven't changed even a car accident, not for seventeen months, and this asshole, this fucking selfish—" he faltered.

The girl with the hair over her face sobbed. Her cheeks were wet. The leader's gray hair swayed forward, like a tree starting to fall, as she looked down.

The cop sat down. "You can't undo mistakes," he said. His voice was still high, and tight. "You have to know that by now. You fix one, you break three more. Have you tried? I'll break your goddamn neck, you tried." His eyes were narrow, and helpless, like the ends of two rusting rebars in a crumbling concrete face.

But the prostitute was watching Alexei, and her eyes were different. Sympathy, he thought. Understanding. His heart began to beat more quickly. Maybe. Maybe she would work.

The gray-haired woman sighed. "I feel I agree with Jerry," said the gray-haired lady. Her hand was at her throat, holding the crucifix within a fist. "You must trust in a higher power. You cannot take the power on yourself. You need help, Alex. But you can't get it here."

"I don't know else anyone," he said. His English was slipping again. "To find someone who understands, where do I find someone?"

"Not from meetings," she said. "Not while you still feel you can change history, while you expect to control that change. And talk about changing your own mistakes?" She lowered her hand from the silver tortured man around her neck, and folded her fingers in her lap. "You may not return."

The girl who was hiding her face sobbed again, and was silent again. Hiding her anguish, or pretending to. Alexei started to stand—but his head spun with *deja vu* and a timeless moment of nothing, and then he was outside.

He remembered the meeting, and the things he'd said, but weakly, a false memory that had never happened. He had never seen the steel door. He'd never been to the meeting. He hadn't suggested fixing his own mistakes. He'd stood on the street for half an hour, and never even approached the church. That was the new truth.

Hell with that. He was going back. Alexei stepped toward the concrete stair and the steel door, and reached into his pocket, and stopped cold. His pocket was empty.

The two-year disc was gone.

He blinked, shocked at the casual power of the lady with the crucifix. She had taken it from him, without a warning, even while she told him to trust in the power of the Lord, and to feel like accepting his errors, and never to change history again. She had put him outside, lost him the disc, and done it with contemptuous ease.

"Hypocrite," he said, like a cough, and spat on the dying grass. Well, fine. Maybe he could not go back to meetings. Not to this meeting, or any other.

But now he had a new place to try.

§

The city was small, and well-defined. The business district, still slightly alive even this time of night, came down to the edge of a wide street. Across that street, dark warehouses ran right down to the cold arm of the ocean.

Each of the warehouses had an inset doorway, and each doorway was lit by a single orange overhead bulb. Every door displayed a prostitute. Occasionally two stood in the same space. Some prostitutes were unusually tall and muscular. Others seemed overweight and tired. One or two skinny white girls were school-age at best, their hair pulled into pigtails to emphasize helpless youth.

Alexei looked away. He walked up and down the warehouse streets, the nails in his shoes ticking on the pavement like a sound from a lost history. A world running out of power, every flicker of energy measured in tiny trickles. Tick-tock, went the central meter, tick-tock. Once more? Alex checked the temperature of the meat: it was cooked enough to eat, probably, if the boys were healthy enough. Bacterial infection was long odds, and the extra power would cost beyond doubt—

No. He walked on, enduring the flashes of false memory, looking for one girl with red knuckles, and a sympathetic face.

"Cheaper to pay for it."

Alexei stopped too quickly, and had to take another step to avoid falling. Something about her voice. She wasn't in a doorway, and he might never have seen her if she hadn't spoken.

Now he was too close, and had to step back. She had unbuttoned her jacket, and her chest underneath was hugely oversized, straining the black t-shirt she wore. The shirt was made to be strained, cut too small across the breasts so he couldn't look away. She stood with a hip cocked, and one hand behind her back.

"Sorry," he said, and again.

"Well Jesus." She suddenly closed her jacket. "I know you. From the meeting, a gone memory. You came, and then you didn't. Oh yeah, I got you now, you were still trying to make those changes. Now you can't come to meetings any more. Well, too bad, buddy. You got a tough road ahead if you can't control yourself."

She tilted her head, and her professional posture returned. "Didn't peg you for an enthusiast though."

"No," said Alexei. "I don't." He remembered his wife, lying on the bed in their first apartment, high above the glowing city, and his eyes burned. "I don't do that any more now."

"Sex?" she grinned. "You don't have sex any more?" But by then his eyes were full of dark tears, and he couldn't breathe.

Change out your oxygen, Alex!

No, don't go in, she's gone—the biohazard counselor told him—

No—that noise, a dust storm from the yellowing crater—

"Jesus," the prostitute said. "You need to settle down." She had him by the arm.

"Diner just up here. Let's get a cup of coffee."

§

He ordered a beer instead, and let the waitress recommend the special. The prostitute took coffee, and pushed the cup around in front of her without drinking it. She was shorter than he'd thought, sitting down. With her jacket closed, the scope of her breasts was mostly hidden by the table's edge, and she looked unremarkable. Her name was Cassie.

Cassie didn't speak after the waitress left. She moved the cup back and forth, and looked at him steadily. Her dark hair was greasy in the diner's cadmium lights.

"I made a mistake," Alexei said finally. "Okay, I made a few. I am an addict, I used to make a lot little changes. You know? Okay, you know."

Cassie's cup stopped moving. "Yeah, I know."

"Maybe someone is annoying in an elevator, I make so they have taken the stairs."

"That's how it starts."

"Maybe my wife is arguing me, I go back and change what she does a few minutes ago. Only a little so she is wrong, so we don't argue. It is all very close things, nothing mattering." He heard the sound of his voice and knew he was letting his English slip.

Cassie shrugged. "So you change the fights. But you can't change yourself, man. You change details, you're still the same person. Make some bigger change in the world, you're still the same. My guess is you kept on fighting."

The waitress appeared with his beer. Alexei drank straight from the brown bottle and watched the beads of water drip down the side. "Yes. Keep on." He tried to smile slightly, maybe just to keep from frowning, but his face felt wrong, like the muscles weren't entirely under control. "One night, I am lying right next to her. I am so tired, and she nags me about something. Money, I think. So many times I remember this, not sure any more."

Cassie turned her coffee cup, turned it again. "False memory. Never happened. They fade, you know?"

He knew. "I am too tired to argue, so I change the history. Of her nagging. Now I think maybe I am reaching too far, which is because so many histories close by where she still nags me? So I make this change—and she notices."

"She notices," said Cassie. "But she's not one of us?"

"No," Alexei said. "She is just regular person. I go to the mirrors, I pin a new one, and just like easy it comes down, really the same. Like you say, I change only a glass of water." Alexei closed his eyes, only slightly, breathed, and slid across the top of the mirrors to *where the waitress had brought a beer for him and a glass of water for Cassie.* It was barely any distance, and pinning it down it was barely any trouble at all. He opened his eyes and took the breaths he needed, and water began condensing over the frosted glass that now sat on the table between them.

Cassie moved the glass away. "Don't." She looked at the water on her hands, took a paper napkin from the silver dispenser, and started drying her fingertips and palms. "Don't do that shit. The changes turn out worse every time, every goddamn always."

Parallel waves of nausea and compensation propagated out from the movement of the glass. Alexei ignored them. "I wasn't," he lied. "Just saying. Only the smallest change, but my wife, she notices me doing. She is angry now. 'This *deja vu*,' she yells at me, 'You're doing that.'"

Cassie placed her napkin on the table, darkened with moisture. "That's when you should've lied."

"Except she noticed already."

"Should've."

"So okay, I didn't lie to her. Anyway making the change, this was my mistake. So I change the mistake. I change my own change."

She sat up straight, and the curve of her oversized breasts reappeared above the table. "You fucking what?"

Alexei sipped his beer. It tasted like copper. "It was only a few seconds."

Her chin shook. "Your own change. You know what feedback is?"

"For a few seconds ago only, so I can't control it, so what? What can be so bad different in a few seconds? This I have thought."

Cassie's voice was only a whisper. "Jesus Fucking Christ."

He nodded. "Well, I learn better. So many worlds, I can't even see mirrors, only a color like white. But I don't give up, you understand? It gets worse and I am falling, no more balance, only I have to fix my mistake. I don't want her to notice, and think I want to change her."

Cassie took another napkin, leaned back, and started twisting it. Her knuckles were red and large. "You do want to change her. You just don't want her to know about it."

"So maybe three seconds, I guess I change enough and anyway I can't hold on much more. It feels like okay, so I pinned and pull it down, and these changes come out into the world. All enough, okay? I come back from mirrors and she can nag me again. Only she is sitting on bed now, bleeding her face.

"B… Because I hitted. My own wife."

Cassie's face froze. Her hands were still moving. Slowly, slowly, twisting a paper napkin to death. "That's not right, man. That's not—that's not okay."

"No," he said, moving his bottle on the table. It clinked, glass against glass, a high thin sound. This language did not have the tenses. "No, no. I don't hit her. After I make the change, I had hitted her. But I never did it. I was myself never there when it happen, I did not ever hit."

"So who did?" Cassie said.

He shook his head. "Not me. I wouldn't do." But in this world, in this history, he would. And he had. And so she had left him.

"Whole area for poison," she said, looking up at the lights, and he had no idea what she meant. "Changing like that? Hundred percent shit." He didn't know if she meant him, or what he'd done. Or the impossible state he found himself in.

Didn't matter after all. With each meaning, he still agreed.

§

He finished the last of the mashed potatoes in silence, and pushed the plate toward the edge of the table. Two beer bottles stood, empty, a barrier between him and the rest of the world. He could barely feel their effect, and he thought about ordering a third.

Cassie hadn't eaten, but she drank coffee after coffee, killed a family of paper napkins and smoked a cigarette from the chrome dispenser until it burned down to its rim. Finally she lit another, and blew a thin stream of pale blue smoke toward the ketchup bottle. They watched it curl into the grille.

"You don't have sex," she said at last, "Why are you cruising the warehouses? You're not a customer."

Alexei had been watching her eyes, and wondering. They were dark, but were they dark enough? "Maybe I am," he said, and stopped. She was asking what he wanted. Maybe she already knew. Maybe she was willing. Was it enough?

He touched one of the empty beer bottles, pointlessly. "I still want to pay you." It had to be enough. He breathed, and launched down the slope again. "I want you to make change on me. You change me, I do nothing, so no feedback. How far back can you see?"

"No," she said. Maybe too quickly. "I'm not doing that. Not for you, not anybody. I don't fix history. Everybody makes their own choices, everybody gets to keep their own. Right? I'm clean and I'm sober, and three weeks without changing history." She took a new paper napkin from the dispenser, twisted it once. "We're done here."

But she stayed in her seat. Alexei felt his heart beating hard. "Please," he said, "change this for me. I have to go back. You change my decision, please. Only two years ago, and about three days. I have the time for you, around ten in night. Not so far back. Please. I ask you. It is permission. Is okay."

"No," she said. She spread her hands, the fresh paper napkin still in her left like a sweaty flag of surrender. "I'm clean. A month, almost. I haven't even looked at other… come on, don't be an asshole."

"Please," he said again. "I have money."

It was a mistake. She put down the napkin and her chin hardened. "Hell with your money."

Alexei felt something slipping inside him. The top of the slope, the *gravity well, the ski hill, the other world with Cassie, and the way she walked, except*—"You used to be a man."

She fell completely silent for a moment. "Fuck you," she said after a long time. Then she sagged and put her hands beneath the table again. Maybe on her lap. "Seriously, fuck you. So what?"

"Help me," he said. "Stop my wife from leave me."

"Because I was born in the wrong body? I'll, I'll fall off the wagon for you, because I understand how you feel?"

She didn't understand. "Please," Alexei said. His hands were shaking. The muscles of his jaw quivered. Never another chance like this. *Faster and faster down the slope.* His words caught in his throat and he pushed them out. "If you don't help me, so, well, maybe I find where you go for surgery, and pin down the history where you do not."

She sat back, mouth open. Then her lips made the word no.

"Not so long ago, right? So I can see enough far back, I think?" He raised his fist, then opened it. "Or if you do help me, I am not here tonight, and I don't meet you and nothing happens. You are pretty girl still."

Her chin, pointed and too perfectly symmetrical, was shaking again. She tried to look away but looked back at him.

For a moment, Alexei's resolve wavered. He forgot what he was saying, then he remembered. "Please, Cassie." She looked at him, hurt, devastated and betrayed. Her cigarette had gone out. He curled his toes under the table, and closed his mouth, looked threatening, and waited.

Finally, she looked down. "Get me a bottle vodka. You bastard."

He had won.

§

They stood outside the diner. Cassie held a full bottle, her second, by its neck, and gripped his arm with her other hand. Her fingers pulled at his skin through the shirt, hurting him too much, even for what he deserved.

"Let go," he said, and pulled away.

She took a deep breath, opened the cap with a practiced thumb-flip, and raised the bottle to her lips. When she lowered it again, it was nearly empty. "Three weeks without changing history, every day one at a time. And I was sober, too. Well, here I fucking go again."

"I am feeling dizzy," he said. "You have done it?"

"Oh, it's done," she said, and in one movement finished the last mouthful in the bottle. "Your goddamn family, your goddamn life. Done."

Alexei pictured his family. His wife's face seemed distant, like a celebrity. *Like a false memory.* And a memory, of three little girls—wait. No, he had three sisters. But his sons? His two—

No. *He had no children.*

His back was cold. "What did you do?" He stepped toward Cassie, and she backed away neatly, like a woman who had been hit before. Her eyes were deeply sunken, and entirely dark. He shook his head, sending the world into a wavering spin. His sons seemed distant. He had only ever imagined them. "Cassie. Please. What did you change?"

"A long time ago." She looked up at the sky. "I don't know exactly. When I drink enough, I can remember a long, long time ago. I was a boy, and I still had pretty hair." She almost smiled, then named a year. "I surfed all those mirror worlds, baby, all the way back to your very blue, blue sky and a smell of sawdust." She raised the bottle, but it was empty, and she lowered it again. "Strange fucking languages, man."

"The picnic," Alexei said. "I met her. Holy Saint Nicholai, you reach so long back?"

"She didn't go to that picnic. She never had your children. And you never hit her, never even had the chance."

"No," Alexei was disagreeing with her. But the word, coming after what she said, became a confirmation. And it was surrender. "Please. I am sorry to threaten you. Please, give them back."

"Too late, asshole." Cassie coughed, and turned away. "They never happened, now. Anything you got left is a false memory. And the good ones fade first." She walked away in a straight line, like a soldier. One that maybe, expected a knife in the back.

Alexei remembered his threat. He could still hurt her—he could.... He put his hand into his pocket, and found a metal disc. The numeral '6' was raised across its surface. Six years? He looked up at the tall woman walking away. The empty bottle dangled from her hand as she crossed the street. She'd forgotten she was holding it. She didn't look right or left, but the road-trains avoided her easily, puffing clouds of charcoal-coloured dust off the dark road surface as they hopped over her, segment by segment, like blind snakes convulsing to avoid a broken, sharp-edged stone.

Alexei shivered from the cold *deja vu*. He remembered now that the big trucks watched the road ahead with UV lasers, outside the human range of vision. The emissions were killing the honeybees, but the oil companies said it wasn't their fault. It was pesticides, they claimed. The chemical companies denied that, and their ambassadors continued to send angry diplomatic notes to Big Oil. Some of the smaller news-feeders were predicting another war.

It was a darker world he had been given, and Alexei didn't entirely recall it yet. But he was remembering now: long heavy decades of loneliness. The years living alone weighed in his memory like an extended illness. Cassie had gifted him six years without changing history. Alexei had been going to the meetings every two weeks. Not in the old church, but not far from there. He looked down at the sidewalk. A single teardrop fell onto the soot-dark road, leaving a tiny circle of darker black.

Alexei sniffed, pulled up his facemask, and began to walk home.

~XII~
THE ALGORITHM

DOOMED FROM THE START
Christine Amsden

The date was doomed the moment he decided to order dinner for me. I'm a grown woman, capable of making my own decisions, and he was clearly a typical Martian, descended from a long line of "men who have to be men to survive," or whatever other nonsense they're spinning these days.

I couldn't believe this was my best onboard match, according to the interplanetary cruise line's dating algorithm. As Allan (*Is that even a real name?*) told the server what I wanted to eat, I sent a message to my best friend and fellow traveler via my neural link. No way.

That was fast, Tara replied. *Are you a little prejudiced?*

No! I thought, fiercely, but something of my neural conversation must have shown on my face because my date paused in his recitation of what I wanted for dessert to arch an eyebrow in my direction.

Close link, I thought.

Allan finished talking and handed our menus to the server. Then he smiled, and I tried not to think how tiny his head was.

Damn, I failed.

Martians tend to be smaller and leaner than Earthers, and Allan was no exception. Exotically pale-skinned, but with dark hair and eyes, he would probably have been my dream man if it wasn't for the fact that he was half my size.

"Where on Earth do you live?" If he was nervous, his face didn't show it, even if his question was the interplanetary cruise equivalent of, *How about this weather?*

"Have you been to Earth?" I replied, because what did it matter where I lived if he had no frame of reference? This was a stupid, pointless conversation.

We had nothing whatsoever in common.

The server returned with a bottle of wine, which Allan tested and approved. Bristling, I allowed the young woman to pour me a glass, though I was sure I wouldn't like it.

"This is from my home region on Mars," Allan said as he lifted his glass. "It's hard to grow grapes there, because of the cold, so we've bio-engineered these hybrid grapes that can survive a freeze. The result is one of the sweetest wines in the solar system."

"Shouldn't we have this with dessert, then?" I asked.

He chuckled and shook his head. "Martians don't believe in saving the best for last. We can't be sure we'll live long enough to get there."

His folksy Martian wisdom should have put me off, but something in his laugh gave me pause. He had a nice voice, I thought grudgingly. And he had me curious about the wine. Tentatively, I took a sip.

"Wow," I said, despite myself. It was sweet, but not at all shallow. The flavor was full, well-developed, and complex. I took another sip.

Tara would love this, I thought, which was a mistake, because my neural link sent her the message. I've reported the software bug to the company before, but they keep insisting that I really did want to talk to the person in question and that was, after all, the point of the intimacy links, which I could turn off if I really didn't like it.

I didn't turn mine off, at least, not with Tara. She was the only reason I survived after my breakup.

Is that happiness I detect? she asked. *So things are going well?*

Just the wine selection. The date sucks. You know I don't like small men.

I know your mom gave you a complex about your size.

You know too much.

Then why am I losing at "Moons of Jupiter Trivia?" If your date's really bad, come join me. We're on the aft viewing deck.

"Do you have an active neural link?" Allan asked, frowning.

"No," I lied as I turned the link off once again.

"If you're going to lie, this is a bad idea."

"You want the truth? All right. This was a bad idea when you ordered for me."

Before he could reply, our server returned with appetizers – a plate of odd, mostly red vegetables I could not identify and therefore wasn't at all sure I wanted to eat.

When the server gave me a polite smile, I scowled at her. She backed away slowly.

That was really rude of me. I was going to have to apologize. Later. First, I had to suffer through appetizers because my mom raised me to be too polite to walk out on dinner – or eat most of it.

"These vegetables are also from my home region on Mars." Allan lifted a fork and began pointing them out, one by one, giving them names and histories and no small amount of pride.

I took a bite of something a little like a parsnip, but softer and tangier. Then I tried a bit of the carrot-derived plant that wasn't very different from its Earth counterpart. And something green that tasted like no vegetable I could name, but was delicious and a perfect contrast to the sweetness of the wine.

"I ordered for you because until we restock on Ganymede, the ship's pantry is still mostly stocked with Martian foods. And I thought maybe, only having visited Mars for one day while the ship was in orbit, you might like a native to help you sort it out."

When he put it that way…

"Can we start over?" I asked, setting my fork down and leaning back in my chair. I opened my eyes and tried a weak smile. "My name's Zoe and the ship gave us a 92% match."

"I'm Allan, and I work for the company that writes those dating algorithms."

"Do you?" Now that was interesting. Modern dating algorithms were so good that only an idiot would try to date someone who scored below a 90% match.

"Yes. I'm an AI mediator, which means I'm always trying to help the computer understand humans better."

"One day, you'll have to explain them to me."

"That's definitely part of the challenge." He paused. "So, what do you do for a living?"

I was really hoping he wouldn't ask that question, but it was sort of inevitable. Until then, every time someone on this ship asked me what I did for a living, my policy had been to make something up. But lying had already caused us one problem tonight, so I drew in a deep breath and told him.

"Nothing."

"Nothing?" he echoed.

"About 75% of Earthers do nothing these days," I said in defense. "There's no need. The AIs run everything."

He frowned, deeply, and I think it was a good thing the server chose that moment to bring out our main course – some kind of pasta dish tossed with more unidentifiable vegetables. This time, I gave her a beaming smile and an over-eager "Thank you."

Still, she backed away slowly.

"So, what's this?" I asked, picking up my fork and gesturing enthusiastically to the pile of pasta.

"Spaghetti."

Yeah, he was pissed. And it didn't take a genius to know why. While 75% of Earth got paid to sit around and do nothing, humans living and working in the rest of the solar system toiled in sometimes harsh conditions to supply us with valuable resources.

Help! I called to Tara via our neural link. *I told him I'm a lazy Earther, and now it looks like we're done.*

Why do you care? she asked. *I thought the date was doomed.*

Why did I care? I might have been a little quick to judge. He's nice. If his head weren't so small…

Tara's musical laughter filled my mind. *Tell him what you actually do, then. Don't let him think you upload neurovids and eat sweets all day…or whatever other rubbish stereotypes non-Earthers have.*

Some people do that.

But you *don't.*

I don't think he cares, I told her. *He's not talking, and you and I have been linked for a while.*

In that case, who directed the first IO-produced neurovid to win a Solar Award?

Wasn't that the one I couldn't finish because I didn't want to experience getting eaten alive by a giant bugeron and couldn't understand why so many people would?

No, that was later. I think this was the one about the trapped miner.

I shuddered, remembering the neurovid now. The feeling of over twenty-four hours of being buried under rubble, able to hear voices but not call out. *No, I don't remember who directed that.*

"On your neural link again?" Allan asked, sounding put-out.

"You weren't talking. By the way, who directed the first IO-produced neurovid to win a Solar Award?"

"A. A. Cummings, the Fear Master. First man to go crazy after neural implants were upgraded with PTSD shielding. He allowed the universe to live through being eaten alive by–"

"–a bugeron, I remember." I paused. "Did you upload that one?"

"I–" He looked down at his plate for a moment. "I started to, but couldn't finish."

"Me too!" I smiled. "Hey, mind if I tell Tara the answer?"

"Go ahead."

A. A. Cummings, I told her via the link.

Too late. Time's up.

Damn.

Enjoy your date. Really. It's past time.

I wanted to argue with her about that last part, but she closed the link.

"So, when I said I did nothing…" I hesitated. "I do volunteer work. I'm an active Solarcrat, and I helped organize the March on Geneva to protest working conditions in the asteroid belt."

"I'm surprised you could afford to come on this cruise."

"It was actually a gift."

"A gift?"

Tara. I need help. I'm about to talk about my ex.

Oh no! Danger! Danger! Come on, girl, snap out of it!

He asked how I could afford this cruise.

An audible groan reverberated through my mind. *You're going to mess this up, aren't you?*

Probably.

Do you like him?

Maybe.

That's something, at least.

"Back on the neural link?" Allan asked. "I didn't realize my question required a committee to answer."

Lie, Tara told me.

Link off, I thought.

"The answer has to do with an ex, which isn't a good first date topic." There, now he could back off and we could talk about something else.

He leaned forward, pushing his empty dinner plate away. "I mediate matching algorithms for a living. I'm always interested in breakup stories. Was he considered a good match when you started dating? What was your success probability score?"

"I–" I was a little taken aback by his enthusiasm, so I was relieved when the server came by to clear our plates and refill our wine glasses.

He wants to know all about the breakup, I thought to Tara. *Quick. What do I do?*

Why does he want to know?

He mediates the algorithms!

Really? Can he explain why I can't get a probability score above 85% with anyone?

Um…link off.

I loved Tara. I really did. But I didn't need Allan to explain why she had trouble finding a strong probability match. She could be intense. The kind of person who created her own drama if she couldn't find enough naturally.

"So what happened with your ex?" Allan asked again after the server had gone.

"Aren't we talking about me a lot? I don't want to be that kind of date, you know?"

"Come on. What was his probability score?"

"97%"

Allan whistled. "Wow."

"Yeah. We were supposed to get married last year, and my parents had already paid for our honeymoon. When things fell through, the company gave them a credit instead of a refund. It was about to expire, so they suggested I invite Tara and here I am. In a way, I'm on my honeymoon."

His lips twitched. "That's not something you usually hear on a first date."

The server interrupted us again with dessert – some kind of fruit and cream concoction that smelled strongly of citrus.

"It's orame, a cross between an orange and a lime," Allan told me. "One of a few hybridizations we tried in those early years, but this one definitely has the best flavor."

I dipped my spoon in and took a bite. The texture was off, the fruit odd and a bit chewy, but the flavor was exquisite. There was a bite to it, a stronger burst of citrus than I was used to, but the cream helped soften it.

"It's delicious," I said. "Thanks for introducing it to me."

"You're welcome." He fell silent for a moment, but I could tell that he wanted to ask more about my ex; I hadn't given him the full story, after all.

How's it going now? Tara asked into my mind.

Don't you have anything better to do?

Nope. "Moons of Jupiter Trivia" is over. I lost.

Go away.

Oohhh…that's a good sign.

I wasn't sure if it was or not, but I let her think it.

"I lost someone who was almost as strong a match," Allan said. "96%."

I looked up, sharply. It was the first personal thing he'd said about himself. "What happened?"

"She died."

"I'm so sorry."

"My friend pushed me to go on this date because you're the first person to get a probability score over 88% since the accident. He thinks that means I'm ready to date again."

"That sounds like my friend. How long has it been for you?"

"Two years. And you?"

"Just one year. I…how much time is enough, do you think?"

He shrugged. "You haven't told me what happened with your ex. I don't get the impression he died, so what happened? How did the probability score fail?"

I took another bite of my dessert while I considered how to tell the story. "He used to paint," I began. "I know the AIs can create virtually anything you can think to ask for, but he liked to use his hands and there were always some people willing to pay for human creations."

"What happened?"

"A rich girl asked him to do a nude, and when her parents found out, they black-balled him. Really tore him apart. I tried to be understanding, but he was too angry all the time. Didn't seem to want to make things better, although part of me…" I hesitated, then plunged forward. "…part of me still hopes he'll get it together so we can be together. I know that's stupid. Our relationship probability score dropped below 50% in the end, but still, I can't help remembering how good it was for a while."

"Too bad the algorithms can't predict the future," Allan said.

"Too bad," I agreed.

We fell silent for a long minute that felt strangely comfortable, our shared moment of understanding making us feel less like strangers and more like… something I wasn't sure how to define. After all, our understanding was that we were both still hung up on past relationships.

"The algorithms do…" He stopped, glanced quickly away, then pressed on. "They do, however, do a pretty good job with the present."

I looked down at my empty dessert plate. I didn't even remember finishing it. I felt unaccountably nervous, wondering what would happen next. When he said the AI did a good job with the present, what did he mean? Hadn't we just agreed we weren't ready?

Help! I asked Tara. *What do I do now?*

Did you have a nice time?

Yes. Surprisingly.

Sleep with him!

I shook my head, which she couldn't see, of course. I should have known what her answer would be, but it didn't feel right, no matter what our probability score was.

"What did your friend say?" Allan asked.

I hesitated.

"Mine thinks we should sleep together," Allan added.

"You've been on your neural link too?" I asked, knowing I was a hypocrite but feeling annoyed anyway.

"Only after I noticed you on yours," he said. "That was the moment I decided the date was doomed."

Doomed? Hadn't I thought the same thing barely an hour ago?

"Maybe neither of us was quite ready for this," I said, but my heart thumped at the idea, making me wonder if it were true. Forcing myself to look at him, really look at him (and not just his tiny head, which was actually kinda cute), I wondered if I'd screwed up something wonderful. What if this was the best thing that would ever hap-pen to me, and I was too hung up on my ex to see it? What if…

"Maybe we don't have to be ready yet," he said. "A 92% match means we've got a good chance of being friends."

"Friends." I tasted the word, finding it a bit like the orame: the texture was off, but the flavor was spot-on, at least for today. And, as Allan had pointed out, the algorithms can't predict the future.

"Come on," Allan said as he stood, "my buddy says there's Martian karaoke starting in an hour. Want to get yours and meet us there?"

"Yeah." I stood, feeling a lightness. One that hadn't been there in a long time. "Actually, that sounds like fun."

He smiled, his eyes dancing as he offered me his arm in a quaint, old-fashioned gesture I found charming. I accepted his arm with an echoing smile and together, we left the restaurant to stroll along portal-lined corridors offering magnificent views of the storms of Jupiter.

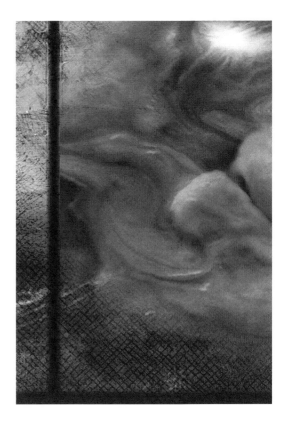

~XIII~
THE DRUG

SOUL CANDY
Jalyn Renae Fiske

Condensation dripped down the side of Anton's cocktail glass in alternating reflections of chartreuse, teal, and violet. The bar's ambient lights transitioned among the three shades in a sad attempt to mimic the exclusive clubs in Haven Hill. His glass was a lonely disco ball lighting up an empty dance floor, the party-going Mids too despondent to rise from their seats and too apathetic to even speak. Fuzzy elevator music rambled in the background. The drink itself was supposed to be a color-changing Roulette cocktail, the preferred beverage of Haveners, but the bitter concoction in front of him was a poor-man's imitation. Its mood-modifying effects barely registered in his brain. Still, it was the best he could get in Midtown.

With a resigned sigh, Anton sucked it down and slammed the empty glass on the chipped laminate counter. A hint of happiness sparked in his mouth, but as soon as he swallowed, the weakly-engineered mood effect was gone. He looked at the bartender. Every day for the past six months, he'd been observing the man's white shirt gradually darken to a depressing shade of piss.

The bartender, Tommy (or was it Troy?), asked, "Top you off?"

Anton studied his empty glass and then his mood-tech ring, linked to his temporal lobe with fancy transmitters imbedded god-knows-where. It was black, the color of despair. He closed his eyes and focused, forcing the color to change to apathetic gray. The preferred color of Mids. "You said this was a Roulette, right? I might as well be drinking regular whiskey. I don't feel any emotions mixed in."

"We don't carry Soul Candy liquor. This stuff is a knock-off. Spirit Water."

"Spit water?"

"Funny. Try taking off your mood-tech when you drink. It spoils the fantasy."

Anton scoffed at the man's advice, but he couldn't help glancing behind him to the scattered tables of Mids, swirling tiny straws in their pale drinks and forcing a smile after each sip to convince themselves of their happiness. Like Toby suggested, he didn't see any mood-tech on their fingers or around their necks. They probably thought they were happy.

Anton knew otherwise.

Just yesterday, he'd been waiting for the Midtown train to take him from one end of the concrete city to the other, one identical building after the next, when the sleek and shining train to Haven Hill darted high above him. He had thought about climbing up the scaffold base of the soaring tracks and waiting for the next one to fly past, to grab hold, and ride it to paradise. His mood-tech ring had turned a hopeful shade of periwinkle at the thought of escaping to Haven Hill, but then a body plummeted from the sky and landed next to him with a sickening crunch on the platform. The woman's blood and brain matter had splattered on Anton's shoes. His ring returned to its normal temperament of black as he crouched down to check on her, pointless as it was. The dead woman's dirty and tattered attire made it obvious she came from Sewer City, one level below. The other Mids waiting on the platform barely glanced up, their eyes and concern stopping at her appearance. It wasn't the first time a Mid or Sewie woke up from the fog of meaningless life and attempted the escape. Anton stood up and watched the Haven Hill train disappear above him. If he were to muster up the courage and try to catch a ride, by god, he wouldn't let go till he got there.

"I prefer reality," he said to Trent and watched him pour the bottom-shelf mood liquor in the glass. Its opaque coloring suggested dirty water.

"Reality is overrated, my friend," said a voice behind him.

Anton turned to see a man in a fashionable white leather jacket, the kind that cost a thousand credits to get tailor-made, grinning at him. His teeth were as white as his clothes, and an alluring woman in a corseted burgundy dress hung on his arm. Flecks of gold covered her cheekbones, eyelids, and lips like a trail of stars leading to heaven.

Haveners.

The man's black sunglasses shielded any sign of his eyes. Without invitation, he sat down at the bar next to Anton; the woman remained standing behind her date with hands draped over his shoulders and chest. Her eyes never left Anton. They glittered gold as her skin. He'd heard Haveners sometimes wandered down from Haven Hill, but he'd never seen them up close before. They were even more brilliant than the commercials: *Rise to Haven Hill*, the ads proclaimed next to glamorous shots of glitzy condos and skyscrapers piercing the clouds. *Feel the Paradise.*

The man stuck out a perfectly manicured hand and said, "The name's Blaze."

Anton grasped it with his own clammy one. "Anton."

"I noticed your mood-tech. Not many Mids wear them."

"Keeps me honest, I guess." He fidgeted with his ring, cleared his throat, and wished he'd shaved recently. He didn't even know the last time he'd done laundry.

"It suits you," said Blaze, looking him up and down and nodding approvingly. "Like a true Havener: unafraid of feeling."

Anton felt his cheeks burn at the compliment, but after a few seconds, the blush died. There was no way he could be confused for a Havener. He only had a hundred credits to his name and a dead-end job inputting numbers in endless columns and rows that no one would ever look at. "Thanks, but I'm no Havener. I've only got one mood most days."

"Would you like more?" asked Glitter Girl, her golden eyes like honey.

Anton quickly looked away. "I wouldn't know what to do with them," he said as he downed his lukewarm pseudo-Roulette. Toilet water, he thought.

"I'm throwing a party tonight," said Blaze. "Why don't you come?"

Anton stared from Blaze to Glitter Girl to Todd. The bartender raised his eyebrows, but not in shock. More like *C'mon, man. Do it. Go for it. What the fuck are you waiting for?*

Anton stuttered: "To Haven Hill?"

Blaze stood up magnanimously with a wink and a smile. "Where else? And I only serve the finest Roulettes."

Glitter Girl produced an oversized card from her purse. As she stepped closer, Anton reflexively straightened up, heart quickening and palms sweating. She leaned down low and whispered in his ear, "I can't wait to see you again." Their hands touched when he took the card. Glitter Girl's nails sparkled in the dim light like a vein of gold in a dark cavern, and his ring faded from gray to periwinkle as he took the offering.

Control the tech. He managed a polite smile as he willed the color of hope away. He wasn't afraid to feel, but there was a time and a place, and how pathetic was he to show his desperation so easily? Haveners weren't salivating over party invitations and beautiful women.

"What's the catch?" Anton said in the smoothest voice he could muster.

"You're right. I don't hand those tickets out to just anyone," Blaze said, waving his hand dismissively at the Mids in the bar before gesturing toward the bartender. "Theo here keeps an eye out for hopefuls."

"You mean Tyler?" Anton said, sure he got it right that time.

"See?" Blaze smiled. "You've got spunk. But the invite is for tonight only, you understand." Then he shook Anton's hand again and walked out of the bar with Glitter Girl latched onto his arm. She sneaked a final, lingering look before the door shut behind them. As if a switch had been pressed, the usual Midtown darkness crept back into everything—the shadows grew blacker, the air grew staler—as if radiance followed the Haveners wherever they trod, and only once it was gone did you realize how bleak and dreary the world really was.

An invigorating tingle danced inside Anton, stronger than any mood the imitation Roulette could ever claim to provide. He looked at the card. The ornate calligraphy, written in gold ink, shimmered like Glitter Girl's lips. *Admit One to Haven Hill.*

"How 'bout I buy that ticket from you," said Travis as nonchalantly as possible, wiping down the permanently stained and peeling counter. When Anton didn't respond, he said: "C'mon, this one's on me," and filled the glass with yet another transparent cocktail of bland nothingness.

Anton could probably get a couple thousand for the ticket, but he'd be back to broke in no time. Mids might not even believe it was a bona fide pass to Haven Hill. They would laugh at his gullibility. But Blaze hadn't asked them, had he? He didn't want a smile-faking mediocre at his party. Blaze had asked *him.*

"Is that your scheme? You tip off Blaze that you found a hopeful, but what you really found is a sucker to sell you the ticket?"

Ted shrugged. "You tell me. You a sucker?"

Anton held the invitation in one hand and the cocktail in the other, eyeing the sweating glass. Blobs of ice swam on the surface. It reminded him of backwash. "What's your name, anyway?"

"Gary."

Anton nodded, as if he'd known it all along. He pushed the glass away and carefully placed the ticket in his wallet so it wouldn't crease. Truth was a construct.

§

Anton entered the cold and institutional train station at dusk, when the sun was escaping the day as quickly as it could manage. A few Sewies were hunched over here and there, filling the empty corners and crannies with their gaunt and twitching forms, licking the trampled plastic wrappers from the floor for any trace of emotions. Authentic pieces of Soul Candy chews didn't have wrappers, but the second-rate ones came in colorful packaging to convince the consumer it was better than it really was. Speckles of pink for Carefree, kaleidoscopes of green for Ambition, undulating waves of rose and white for Bliss, and so forth. Anton tried to stay away from the stuff, but every now and then he'd find a Sewie who was selling the off-brand version and drop fifty credits to indulge and dream his life was better than it was. The mood lasted longer than Spit Water Roulettes, but it didn't compare to what you could get in Haven Hill. The crap here fried your brain after a while. Sometimes you were slipped a bad one, too, like Sorrow or Guilt, and you were lucky to survive the night.

He approached the trains, walking past missing person posters layered over one another on brick walls and metal posts. Faded and crinkled, never found. A dark stain remained on the platform where the body had fallen the day before, a shadow of a life now gone. Dozens of shoes walked over the stain, some heading to Train 03 to the Industrial District and others to Train 09 for the Shopping District. No reverence. Everything was one giant stain.

One pair of feet stopped right on top of it—black stilettos. "Which train do you need, sir?" asked the attendant, noticing his card with the golden script.

"Train 11?" he said. Anton didn't belong there. That's what she was thinking: how could he be getting on Train 11? There must be some mistake. He was obviously lost. Didn't he mean Train 01 to the Residential District?

"Of course. Head to the central escalator for the Haven Hill platform."

The escalator was in the middle of the station, proudly ornate and clean and inviting, like the grand staircase of a palace. It could easily fit five people across at the same time, but the steps were usually empty. Anton had seen only a handful of Mids ever allowed to climb it, golden tickets in hand, and they had ridden the immense steps alone like a small child in a giant's world. He wondered where the down escalator was for the return home. The only down escalator was on the opposite end of the station, built into the wall like a cave, and just as dark and dripping with unknown substances. It went from Midtown down to Sewer City. That one was wide enough for one person at a time and usually had a line waiting for their turn downward, hungry for second-rate Soul Candy. You could find your fix in Midtown, sure, but it didn't flow like it did down there. If Mids couldn't ascend, sometimes they settled for falling. Anton would have made the descent years ago, he had often considered it, but something inside him wouldn't let him join the others. It was that damn periwinkle. He looked at his ring, but it didn't convey the hope that thoughts of Haven Hill normally conjured. It was bright yellow. Coward's yellow, and blinding as a neon sign at night. When was the last time he'd experienced that one?

What he wouldn't give for a real Soul Candy right then. Courage, with its red stars on a black background. That would kill the coward's yellow for good.

A single attendant stood by the entrance of five turnstile gates. Anton paused, wondering if some of them were locked or broken, like a test to repel the idiots: only the most virtuous and worthy would select the correct entrance.

"Pick any gate you wish," the attendant said, as if he were offering a tray of unique delicacies that all tasted equally wonderful. Decisions were not a Mid's forte, especially ones that had so many options. He picked the center one. It seemed noncommittal, even aloof, to pick the middle one. Aloof was good. Haveners were aloof, weren't they?

The machine sucked in his ticket, and the turnstile clicked forward.

The only way to go now was up.

§

Anton stepped off the train and breathed the crisp, pine-tinged air of early evening. *Real* pine from *real* trees. Another attendant appeared, ruining the moment, and ushered "Mr. Bishara's Special Guest" to a waiting limousine.

Bishara. He knew that name.

Anton slid inside the vehicle, savoring the smell of leather. The windows were blacked-out to the point that he couldn't see out of them. Shame. The car began to move, and a television screen dropped down from the roof. Shielded eyes and smiling face appeared briefly, the same as the man from the bar, and then a series of familiar advertisements for Soul Candy played—the liquors, the chews, the medicines. *Fast-acting, Long-lasting, Soul-satisfying!* Blaze Bishara was the owner of Soul Candy. No wonder he so easily offered access to Roulettes. He invented the damn things.

When the last commercial was done, the screen shut off and retracted into the roof. Moments later, the limousine stopped and his door was opened. Anton exited and stood before a gilded elevator, as grand as the gates to a theme park. Across its threshold was engraved: *Soul Candy*. He cleared his throat and entered the elevator, pressed the button for Up. It rocketed upward without a sound or a single jerk of machinery. He looked at the ring on his shaking hand as his stomach churned. The mood-tech accessories were a Havener's status, and he was positive not one of them ever displayed bright coward's yellow.

Control the tech, he told himself. Slowly, it changed to a pulsing pale red.

That's it. Find some courage.

The elevator came to a seamless stop. Powerful bass of electronic club music throbbed on the other side. The doors parted, and a surge of deafening beats and gyrating bodies filled his senses. Mood-tech hung off everyone's fingers, wrists, and necks, all radiating some shade of purple. Their skin-tight clothes left nothing to the imagination. Anton glanced down at his own loose-fitting shirt that hid his belly rolls and immediately hated the party. He felt their stares judging him, pitying him, and he wanted to leave, but when he looked behind him for the elevator, the doors were shut and without any buttons to call it back.

"You came!" shouted a deep, soulful voice above the music. "Anton, right?"

Blaze appeared before him, grinning, and still wearing his black shades. Instead of white, he had on a pair of black pants and a shirt without a single wrinkle or stray piece of fuzz. How was that possible? Blaze wrapped his steely arm around Anton and led him to the bar across the room. The guests parted for their host and studied Anton out of the corner of their eyes as they sipped on true mood-modifying cocktails. The liquid in their martini glasses radiated colors that he could never hope to name. Some of the partiers placed white candies on their tongues, the kind covered in sprinkles or confetti.

Once they reached the bar, Blaze began sorting through various glass decanters of cyan, amethyst, and coral liquors. "Weren't we talking about Roulettes earlier?" he asked, lifting up a container of liquid as black as ink and another that resembled milk.

Anton responded, "Yeah," and hoped it wasn't the inky one. It looked like poison.

Blaze uncorked the decanters with a pop and deftly combined the two in a champagne glass. It quickly turned lime, then magenta, then gold. "Time it right, and you can choose your shot of emotion," he said and proffered the elixir to Anton. "But I prefer to leave it to chance."

Anton took the glass and watched it change hues as if it held the beating heart of a rainbow. The nearby Haveners were huddled close together laughing, smiling, drinking their rainbow drinks, their mood-tech glowing. That kind of pleasure couldn't be faked.

"Feeling alive yet?" asked a woman in an emerald dress that could have been painted on. Silver glitter covered her lips, neck, and shoulders and trailed down between her breasts like an invitation. Glitter Girl. In Midtown, she had been gold. In Haven Hill, she was chrome.

He stared at her sterling eyes, speechless. His ring turned from calm sapphire to lustful ruby. She stepped closer, took his hand, and playfully inspected the telling shade.

"Me, too," she said and smiled seductively.

Blaze laughed. "You don't know what feeling alive is truly like until you've tasted Soul Candy."

Anton watched his Roulette rotate vibrant colors and considered the drab world he'd just come from. "People have died for a chance to drink this. Died trying to escape to Haven Hill."

"You mean the train grabbers," Blaze nodded casually. "Mostly it's the Sewies who fall, isn't it? Poor bastards."

Anton recalled the smashed, obliterated body on the platform. "Wouldn't you risk it if you lived in Sewer City? Even Midtown?" he asked. He'd washed the blood from his shoes, but blood never really went away. Traces buried in the laces or hidden in seams. Impossible to see, but still there.

"Indeed, and here you are," Blaze said, his tone turning grave.

"What a depressing thought for a party!" Glitter Girl said, before slowly licking the rim of her cocktail glass.

"Apologies," Blaze said. "Let's toast to new friends and new emotions!"

At his words, every Havener in the penthouse instantly stopped talking and dancing and turned to their host. The music quieted.

Blaze raised his glass and quoted, "Fast-acting! Long-lasting!"

"Soul-satisfying!" the crowd finished in unison, their purple mood-tech shining. Anton felt like he was in one of Blaze's infomercials, but the cultish vibe was strangely comforting when compared to the stoic loneliness of Midtown. The lesser of two evils.

All in attendance raised their cocktails, and the chorus of delicate tinkling as the glasses touched dissolved the last of his worries. He would drink to the dead Sewie and feel alive on her behalf. Glitter Girl took a sip, never looking away from him.

The first sip was gold-colored and danced on his tongue like sugared lemons, melting and coating his entire mouth with freedom and sunshine. In an instant, Anton remembered what it was to be five and play in a sandbox, rolling in the soft sand and flexing his fingers in its depths. Then he felt the wind upon his face as he swung through the air, his stomach free-falling up and down in a swing. The rough edges of bark scratched his hands as he climbed higher and higher in a tree, the leaves rustling in delight and encouraging him to reach the very top.

But those weren't memories.

His childhood had been in the city, in a dank apartment, with mold-ridden walls and rotting bits of food on the floor.

The drug-induced feeling of a happy childhood vanished as quickly as it came, and he was back to the normal Anton, lonely, chubby, and still a Mid.

"Wicked timing!" Blaze laughed. "Nostalgia is a good one to start on."

"Nostalgia is my favorite," Glitter Girl said, flashing her smile and leaning closer to Anton. Her smile faded briefly—burdened, perhaps, by her own memories of mold-ridden walls and rotten bits of food—and added softly, "But it's gone so quickly."

Anton locked eyes with her. What did she really want to say? She leaned back, smiling once again, and asked in a seductive voice, "Did you like it?"

He turned the color-changing Roulette this way and that. "Yeah, but now I feel like shit."

"That's why I invented the chews. They last for over an hour, so you can really enjoy the emotion but still have time to change it later," Blaze said. He glanced at his watch and took the glass out of Anton's hands. "If you liked the Roulette, you'll love my secret stash. Downstairs!"

Anton struggled to find the words to describe how he felt when Blaze took his glass away. He was surprised at how strongly he wanted to drink the Roulette, as if nothing else in the world was more important. "What about the other colors?"

"Bah, the chew variety is so much more potent. This way!"

Images of trampled chew-wrappers flashed before him. Sewies licking filthy pieces of plastic to feel something. Anything. Meanwhile, here, in every glass, on every tray...

Glitter Girl took his hand, interlacing her fingers with his. "Can I come along, too?" she said, her lips sparkling in a sultry smile. "My Revelry is running out." Her chandelier earrings glowed a faint lilac instead of the deep plum most of the other Haveners displayed.

"What does the Revelry feel like?" Anton asked, forgetting all else, mesmerized by her touch and how the jewelry swayed with her every movement. The vanilla-musk of her perfume.

"It makes you laugh and smile," Blaze said. "I originally thought about naming it Flirt, but that didn't quite encompass its full potential. Anyway, it's pretty basic," he said dismissively then waved for Glitter Girl and Anton to follow him. They sliced through the mass of party-goers, who had resumed dancing, to a blank alcove at the other end of the penthouse. Blaze placed his hand over a panel. It scanned and confirmed his identity, and the back wall slid open to reveal a hidden elevator.

"Actually, why don't you two go down first?" Blaze said. "It's a small space."

Anton allowed Glitter Girl to enter before him, but once she was inside, she pulled him in. It was a tight fit. The doors closed without a sound and they began a swift descent. Her body brushed against him and his skin prickled.

"Downstairs is where he keeps the blends. The best blend is Lust," she whispered as if it were a secret and held aloft a hard candy with purple and black stripes hidden in her hand. "Revelry and Desire in one. Of course, Blaze is always creating new combinations."

She slowly placed it on Anton's tongue.

His breath caught in his chest.

"Now, suck."

Anton closed his mouth and tasted raspberry and cherry and chocolate. Glitter Girl wrapped her arms around him and kissed his neck. He was sure a silver imprint remained where her lips touched, and he didn't dare wipe it away.

"Blaze won't mind?"

"Blaze lets me have whatever I want."

His eyes wandered down the glitter trail as she pressed herself against him. Anton flushed at the thought of where else she glittered beneath her emerald dress. He kissed her silver lips. They tasted like sugar. But just like the Roulette, the embrace and the warmth growing in his groin was short-lived. The elevator came to a stop, and the doors opened.

"That was quick," he muttered and peered into the room, empty and silent.

Glitter Girl laughed and leapt out of the elevator. As soon as her heel clicked on the pearly white floor, lights flashed on. Lining the right side of the hallway was a wall of glass that revealed a flower-filled courtyard, ground-level. On the other side were countless metal doors with small, barred windows. The farthest end of the hallway had yet to be lit up, but Anton discerned a cluster of chairs in the darkness.

"I have a surprise just for you." Glitter Girl pulled him along and strutted down the hall as if it were a runway. More lights turned on every few feet. Beneath the lights and through the growing haze Lust's effects, Anton noticed faded bruises on her wrists—in the shape of fingers—that he hadn't seen in the dim penthouse. The glitter did a good job distracting the eye.

"Who did that?"

"It's nothing," she said, covering her wrists. "It's part of living here. Look, we're almost there. All the candy you want. And all of me that you want."

She pulled him close and gazed up with pleading eyes for a kiss.

The last of the lights flashed on. Burgundy armchairs were arranged in a circle and occupied by silent, slumped bodies, strapped down. Black power cords snaked the floor, connected to monitors labeled: Test Group F, G, H.

Anton stopped and spit out the candy, the haze lifting.

Glitter Girl's seductive mask cracked. "Why'd you do that?"

As if on cue, the elevator chimed behind them and Blaze appeared with a ready grin and arms outstretched like an actor taking the stage.

"How are my little lovebirds doing?" he asked, his voice echoing down the hall.

Anton's voice echoed back: "What the hell is going on?"

Dropping his arms and his smile, he said, "I see the honey-moon is over." Blaze shot a nefarious look at Glitter Girl as he walked toward them.

Trembling, she said, "H-He started asking questions. I didn't know what to say!" Her earrings turned neon yellow as his own mood-tech changed to the color of smoldering embers.

"Get the chews," Blaze said, a little too loudly.

Anton watched her hurry away to a table, her heels clicking, and considered his options: wall of glass, dungeon doors, and the elevator. His best chance was the elevator, but it required Blaze's hand to open. "Do you get all your lab rats from Midtown?" Anton asked, trying to buy more time.

"Mids and Sewies alike. They will do anything, take anything, no questions asked."

Anton looked at the flabby, average people strapped in the chairs and remembered the missing posters plastered in the train station. "So the straps are for decoration?"

"The straps are for their safety. Sometimes the blends bring on such real hallucinations that they act it out." For the first time, Blaze removed his shades. "I promise you, they are not prisoners. They are not being harmed."

Anton was startled to see how normal his eyes looked. With the shades and the secrecy, he expected Blaze to be blind, disfigured, or sporting lifeless cybernetic eyes. Instead, they were normal, brown, and very human.

"This room is only for the most deserving," Glitter Girl said in a rehearsed voice, bringing a tray of assorted Soul Candy chews, some spherical, some shaped like cubes, stars, or hearts, and all colored vibrantly with marbling, sprinkles, or painted swirls. Anton only recognized the confetti-covered ones from upstairs.

"None of the Haveners upstairs would appreciate the experience of blending." Blaze dropped his flashy smile and adopted an earnest expression. Even his voice lost the bravado it usually held. "They're too acclimated and numb to Soul Candy these days."

Anton stared at the drugged people, nearly comatose. "Too addicted, you mean."

"Blending is an art, and every artist needs a blank canvas," said Blaze, his passion hanging on every syllable like a priest at the pulpit. "Take Revelry, for example." He picked up the confetti-covered candy. "Normally, it inspires laughing, spontaneity, but when combined with Rage, it freezes the muscles instead. As the Rage floods every pore in your body, you want to lash out, to release your anger, but all you can do is lie there and take it. It's the most exhilarating feeling of paralysis. Like a spiritual cleansing. I call that blend Nirvana."

Or Hell.

"No thanks," Anton said, wondering how thick the glass was in the wall of windows. He studied the floodlights outside, illuminating the grounds in harsh white light. No fence, no guards, but no ride back to Midtown, either.

"Your skepticism is what caught my attention—or, rather, Theo's attention on my behalf. But now I see there's something else inside you," Blaze said, eyeing Anton's ring that continued to glow a fiery orange. "Ember is so rare to find."

Fucking bartenders.

"I've always wanted to know how the chews react to resistance."

Anton studied the series of identical doors along the wall with their barred windows and punch-code lock panels—and then looked at the circle of chairs, the people strapped down. Another decision to make, and neither option good. "We both know I came here to get out of Midtown," he said, heart pounding, but voice steeled. "But no straps."

"That will require you to test a brand-new blend for me."

Anton paused a beat and considered being strapped down like the others, but there was no guarantee he would ever be released. At least this gave him a chance. Play it cool until things settled down. Bide his time.

"Alright, I'll take a blend," Anton said. "But I get to choose which ones."

Blaze grinned. "How about random selection? Best I can do."

"And just this once. Then I leave."

The grin remained plastered on. "Of course."

Damnit, this was bad. But what else could he do? He was a nobody in a world that Blaze had made. No one would notice his absence. No one would come for him. No one would listen if he managed to get out.

"Please, sit," Blaze said, motioning to an empty burgundy chair.

As Anton positioned himself, Glitter Girl attached sensors and leads to his temples. She looked everywhere but into his eyes.

Blaze grabbed a handful of candies from the tray and dropped them in a wooden bowl. He held it out to Anton, high enough that its contents were unseen. "Pick your poison."

Was there really any choice in roulette? Anton put his hand in and prayed for something good, not like Nostalgia or Revelry or Lust. He needed strength. He needed some fight. His fingers pulled out a spherical piece with undulating waves of rose and white.

Glitter Girl sighed in relief. "Bliss. That's good."

Blaze shrugged. "Depends. Now for the second."

Well, shit. The next one better not be Rage, Anton thought. That combo would turn out to be something like Purgatory. He considered stuffing as many candies as he could in his mouth and be done with it, but there was still a chance he could escape. There was always a chance. He took a breath and dug around for the last one.

Out came a square-shaped candy with tiny red stars on a black background.

Anton almost smiled. "Courage," he said.

Blaze raised his eyebrows. "We shall see. Time to partake."

The first one tasted like purity itself, like dewdrops collected on a rainforest leaf. He could smell the damp sweetness in the air and hear the tranquil song of exotic birds. His muscles immediately relaxed. All Anton wanted in the world was to lie on the forest floor and disappear in the mist. It was like breathing clouds and falling forever. He felt nothing and everything in unison.

Then there was an explosion of fireworks when he bit into the second chew. It immediately burned through his tongue like raging flames, but the pain was exhilarating. It awakened something inside him. The pain made him alive. It coursed down his throat and into his stomach, searing a path of inspiration and fearlessness that spread throughout his body. Finally, it collected into his chest, bursting with energy and brimming with righteousness.

The surge of power mixing in his bloodstream was ecstasy itself. It summoned him to go.

Just GO.

At first, Anton tried to fight the calling, to control the emotion as he controlled the mood-tech, but the blend intensified its command. Anton stood up and lifted the armchair above his head. It was as easy as lifting a child. Then he slammed it into the wall of glass. The shattered pieces flew out into the twilight and sliced his skin as he ran through. The cuts burned at first, then went numb. *Bliss.* Blood dripped down his face and arms, but Anton didn't mind. It fueled his instinct to do something heroic. *Courage.*

He smiled as he took his first few steps at a jog and built up to a steady sprint. Anton thought he heard some yelling behind him, but it seemed so petty and trivial. He had more important things to do, though he wasn't sure what those things were yet. The Soul Candy called him to search: *Find someone to save.*

Each building of Haven Hill that he passed blurred into the next, each street a duplicate of the one before, and all in desperate need of nothing. He had yet to find his gallant deed to fulfill, and the urgency to do good mounted in his soul with every fading minute of sunset.

Finally, Anton came upon the synthetic stone wall that enclosed Haven Hill, separating it from the surrounding region of Midtown—and below that, of Sewer City. *Of course! Sewer City!*

Grappling the jutting stones, he climbed up as if he had been scaling walls all his life. On the other side, he marveled at the maze of scaffolding before him. The descent down didn't take long. He expertly navigated the tangle of planks and platforms as if they were steps and ladders, suspended hundreds of feet above the ground. Once he reached the train platform, empty at this hour, he headed for the dark cave that led to Sewer City. Its shadows, a beacon.

Anton descended.

A putrid stench of decay wafted around him. The street was slick with stagnant puddles and nearly every lamp light was busted or flickering.

Perfect.

The handful of homeless that watched his arrival huddled even closer around their make-shift fire, coughing and drinking from scavenged tin cups. Anton stared at them across the damp and littered street. Did they need help? When he stepped toward them, they scurried to their hiding places like rats. No matter. Anton collected stray pieces of wood from a pile of splintered chairs and broken tables and fed the fire for when they returned.

But surely there was more he could do?

The blend pulsed inside him, hungry for action.

A terrified scream erupted from a dark alley, and Anton almost cried out in joy.

Finally! Someone to save!

He raced down the alley and discovered a scrawny girl, maybe eighteen, with torn fishnets and knee-high boots being harassed by a group of Sewies. They pushed the girl between them, mocking her and laughing that she was about to have all her dreams come true.

"Unhand her!" Anton shouted, surprised at his own forceful command and choice of words.

They stopped and stared at the man with blood streaked clothes and puffed out chest.

"Release her or face the consequences of your actions," Anton warned them. He'd never felt more powerful, more righteous.

"Kill that fucker!" ordered the leader as he grabbed the girl and dragged her away to a more secluded alley. His three cronies approached Anton and pulled out knives and pistols from their pants. Anton only had his hands.

The fight was a bloody blur of fists, bullets, and blades.

The first shot felt like a hammer to his shoulder, but it didn't knock him down.

Then a knife pierced his side.

Anton grabbed the grip and the man holding it, removing the knife and slicing the Sewie's throat in one movement.

Another gunshot, a flash of light.

Anton threw the knife into the gunman's chest.

He stood over the two dead bodies in triumph and gasped for breath as the third man fled into the bowels of Sewer City. Blood covered his hands and dripped down his side, soaking his shirt scarlet. As he knelt down to pick up the gun he spit up blood, but hardly noticed the pain. He actually felt pretty good.

Anton ran in the direction the ring-leader had gone with the girl. It wasn't hard. He followed her muffled screams and echoes of hurried steps splashing in the muck on the streets until he had them cornered in a dead-end alley.

"I will spare your life in exchange for the girl." Anton could taste victory in his blood-filled mouth, even as the pain from his wounds began to throb and ache in growing waves, but the Sewie only chuckled a deep guttural sound in response.

"This girl? I can get another bitch on any street corner. Take her," he said as he shoved her away from him like trash that hadn't been taken out in weeks.

As soon as she stumbled away from her captor, the shot rang out. She fell forward and collapsed into Anton's arms just as he, too, fell backward from the bullet's impact. It ripped through his body like an explosion to the chest.

This time, the pain was unbearable.

This time, he couldn't breathe.

The blood collected in the back of his throat, and when he rolled the dead girl off him, all his cuts and bullet holes burned like brands. There was nothing he could do to stop the agony from scorching every nerve and squeezing his lungs shut. Mercifully, his vision clouded and went black, black as the pools of rot and refuse that Sewer City swam inside.

§

Anton blinked slowly, adjusting to the fluorescent flood of light above him. The bulbs buzzed in their struggle to stay alive, and a musty, moldy scent permeated the air. He coughed, prompting a nauseating pain to ripple throughout his body. Each breath was fire in his chest, as if a creature was lodged in his lungs and trying to claw its way out.

He recalled a woman covered in rhinestones. No, glitter. And a man who never stopped smiling. Something about candy.

A shadow moved across his face, and he tensed, summoning a new round of convulsions to rack his body. His vision was still fuzzy, but he could see now the bandages that covered his torso, chest, and arms. Dark patches of blood seeped through. The shadow stopped at the foot of his bed, and he squinted to see past the crust that clung to his eyelashes. He opened his dry and gummy mouth to speak.

Only a hoarse grunt emerged when he attempted, *Where am I?*

"Are you in pain? Do you need more Serenity?" the shadow asked quietly.

Anton recognized the voice, a woman's. He strained to see her features: hair pulled back in a loose bun, fly-away strands falling down the nape of her neck. She turned, and he heard items being moved like marbles rolling on a table. Anton tried to sit up again; his muscles painfully complied only to be stopped after a few inches of movement. Attached to the corners of the bed were leather straps that shackled his wrists and ankles.

The woman retrieved a syringe from a tray of vials. Lifting the needle, she shot a small amount into the air.

"No drugs…," he said, his voice and memory returning.

"It's medicine," she assured him and began to inject the Serenity into the clear pouch hanging by his bed. The pale blue liquid from the syringe mixed with the saline in icy ribbons. She turned toward the only exit, a dark metal door with a small barred window as he pulled against his restraints and thrashed his legs. "It's best if you don't try to fight it," she said, stopping at the door. The glitter was gone from her eyes and lips, but there was no mistaking her. Glitter Girl unlocked the deadbolt and pulled open the creaking door. A man with a Cheshire grin and black shades stood on the other side.

"Our newest resident is awake!" Blaze said.

Immediately, the memories of Revelry and the party and all the purple moodtech shit everyone paraded around flooded Anton's mind. The thought of the Roulette cocktail summoned a sour taste to his mouth. He strained to speak, "Let me go."

"You think a wanted criminal can just walk out of here?" Blaze said, his smile growing even wider. "Don't you remember? You killed two citizens—three, if we include the woman."

Anton's breathing quickened. "They were… hallucinations."

"I fetched you myself from Sewer City after you bulldozed through the glass wall.

Stunning, really. I ordered you to stop, but you wouldn't listen. So, I just followed the trail of dead bodies until I found you lying in a pool of blood," Blaze said, chuckling. "Who would have thought Courage would react so strongly to the Bliss? It needs some tweaking, of course. Too much do-gooder and not enough obedience. I think I'm going to call this new blend Soldier or Vigilante."

"Why not Hero?" Glitter Girl said quietly. Instead of chandelier earrings, she wore a pendant that glowed black. "He did try to save her."

"Hero has a nice ring to it, yes. My new military clientele will salivate over that one."

"We had a deal," Anton said, fighting the Serenity inside him.

"If you step foot outside this tower, you'll be hunted down and locked away for murder. I can't risk my new favorite telling tales."

"Please," Glitter Girl said to Anton, biting her lip to keep from saying more.

"Isn't this what you've always wanted? Daily doses of candy, clean air, rich food, emotions galore to fill the void in your soul. And after a few days of Revelry and Roulettes, when you'll do anything to get another hit, I might invite you upstairs to join the others. Parties every night," Blaze said. "You'll never want to leave."

Blood trickled down Glitter Girl's lip. Blaze noticed it and handed her a candy from his pocket. She stared at the sphere with undulating waves of rose and white, then obligingly took it and placed it on her tongue. Her jaw clenched as she slowly chewed. The stress dissolved from her expression, replaced with a vacant gaze and vapid smile. Her pendant, now a soft blush.

"Welcome to Haven Hill, my friend," Blaze said, from somewhere far away.

Pain faded.

Eyes closed.

But the ring on his finger, the color of smoldering embers.

~XIV~
THE VOID

THAT SILVER-BLACK SHIMMER
Meirav Seifert

The electric door slides open and Regina, standing under the door frame, sighs.

For a bizarre, unnerving moment, I half-expect Brandon to trail behind her, tall and thin and silent.

But the door closes behind Regina alone.

"Are you okay?" Jeremy's voice emanates from the cot next to mine and bounces across the long, rectangular Basement.

"I'm fine," Regina's voice is worn, irritable. She marches across the narrow room, neck stiff, eyes trained straight ahead: she's laboriously avoiding the sight of Brandon's empty cot, as well as the shimmering silver-blackness of Oscar.

She plonks down on her cot and rummages absently through the duffel bag that's splayed on top of it. "If I've only stepped out to the bathroom, you can always just assume I'm fine."

We know she's not fine, and we know that "always" is about to end.

Since That Night, Jeremy and I have both gotten into the habit of asking Regina how she feels, insistently and incessantly. But she never asks us, and we never ask each other.

I don't know about Jeremy, but I flip through the memories leading up to That Day again and again, trying to puzzle out when everything started to go so wrong.

§

"Rise and shine, everybody!" The electric door slid open and Regina, raucous and clunking, swept in.

It was the end of the night shift; Jeremy and I had both just woken up and were still in our cots. We watched as Regina kicked off her purple hi-tops and fished a stick of gum out of her pocket, its silver wrapper gleaming in the semi-darkness. Then she hit the lights, neon white drenching the walls. The windowless, concrete and steel-reinforced room glared.

"Dammit, Regina," Jeremy grumbled. "Can we have a gentle wake up? Please?

Sing us a song? Maybe a massage? There's plenty of room in here for two," he crooned, although there was not. He lifted the mess of blankets on his cot in a come-hither gesture.

"You pig," Regina said. She strode around the room, impatient as always with our slow awakening. But instead of rousing us as her infectious energy normally did, our lethargy seemed to infect Regina. She slowed at the Pit, slouched to the floor, and sat cross-legged facing the sunk, low-fenced enclosure. She flinched at the gum in her hand, as though she'd forgotten it was there; she unwrapped it, put it in her mouth, and chewed.

I sat up, heavy-limbed and bleary, and started putting my shoes on.

"What do you think is on the other side of Oscar?"

"Disneyland." Jeremy turned onto his stomach and put his pillow over his head.

"Why don't they hide it better?" Regina stared into the Pit, past the stark metal post fence into the enclosure. Her tongue worked its way into the wad of purple-blue gum, which she proceeded to vivify into a bubble.

Oscar was the top-secret hole-in-the-ground Regina, Jeremy, Brandon and I were assigned to guard day in and day out.

Regina's bubble burst wetly just as she was shaking her head. The flattened gum clung to her long, blond, stick-straight hair. "Oops." She set to picking pieces of gum off the affected strand. "Someone could just"—she hesitated—"trip into it, and never come back."

"If you're feeling clumsy, stay away from the Pit," Jeremy advised groggily. He submerged his hand in the mess of blankets, resurfaced with his SIG and thumbed open the safety. "And from your pistol, and from the little girl across the cul-de-sac." He waved the gun at the wall closest to the road. "She just started taking Krav Maga. Watch out." He hitched the safety back.

Regina didn't snap back or roll her eyes in response to Jeremy's obnoxious retort. Instead, I watched from my cot as she examined the clump of hair with gum on it and sucked on it, her expression distant and troubled.

"You are so disgusting," Jeremy wrinkled his nose at the act, then unearthed himself from underneath the mound of blankets and swung his feet onto the floor. He started putting on his scuffed, mud-caked hiking shoes.

For a moment, we were all silent, our heads turned to stare at Oscar pulsing silver-black and shimmering at indefinite edges.

Jeremy shook himself like a dog, then scooted on the floor to sit next to Regina, facing the Pit. He poked at her wet, gum-glopped hair with two fingers, then picked the gum wrapper off the floor between them and flicked it past the low, metal post fence. We watched as Oscar swallowed it up with a cosmic, sucking slurp.

"You pig," Regina's hair shook against her shoulders. "Somewhere in the universe there's a pile of floating garbage with your name on it."

Oscar, so named because of its grouchy tendency to never return things it was given, was discovered one day in the middle of a residential neighborhood in Everton, West Dakota. Legend has it a group of renegade physicists were running experiments in a basement, splitting atoms and tickling quanta and fiddling with intangible forces, when Oscar came into existence. Regina, Jeremy, Brandon and I underwent intensive field and combat training, took advanced marksmanship and survival and psychological warfare courses, and sat through a barrage of interrogations to attain Top Secret clearance. When we were assigned a plainclothes posting in the middle of North American suburbia we were excited; we thought we'd be busting a hard-to-penetrate anti-government organization, perhaps, or tracking dangerous, well-hidden Wanteds. When we learned we were to take turns scratching our asses next to a squelching basement floor hole for the remaining years of our service, we were underwhelmed, dismayed, and disgruntled.

At least we could share in the inanity of it.

The electric door slid open. Brandon came in, head bowed and gazing intensely at his electronic reader; a caricature of an overly studious student. Without raising his head, he stooped, untied his stiff brown dress shoes with one hand, removed them and placed them neatly next to Regina's upturned pair. He walked like this, nose in reader, all the way to his cot and sat down.

We all looked at each other and burst out laughing. "Shut up." He smiled and continued reading. Jeremy and I got up to leave.

"Bye, Brandon," Jeremy and I sang in unison. Early in our training we'd developed the synchronic tendencies of a professional choir. "Bye, Regina," we added.

"Put down the book and come over here," we heard Regina calling to Brandon. We glanced back to see the two settling themselves on Regina's messily-made cot and beginning to solve their way through a crossword puzzle.

§

When we first arrived at the Pit, we figured out pretty quickly the best way to set shift assignments. Headquarters gave us the freedom to guard Oscar as we saw fit; their only rule was that at least one person had to be in the Basement at all times, be it awake or asleep ("or drugged out or dead," we joked; "no one would notice."). But the four of us unanimously agreed we wanted to take shifts in pairs, and so we did, going solo only when one of us took sick leave or went on holiday.

Initially, lovestruck Jeremy begged Brandon and me to let him take shifts with Regina, so it was the two of them together, alternating with me and Brandon. Very quickly we discovered that Brandon and I together made for mind-numbing shifts. Brandon tended to speak even less than I did, and isolated from the group, our shared tendency to be too much in our own heads amplified tenfold. The silence, together with the bland setting and close quarters, soon became oppressive. In the meantime, the Jeremy and Regina pairing started souring, too. Jeremy's crush kept his lurid personality at bay for a while, but when his subtler overtures proved ineffective, he started wildly fluctuating between bumblingly flustered and aggressively forward.

So I started taking shifts with Regina, and Jeremy and Brandon paired up. Regina and I got on well enough; but pretty quickly Brandon started getting on Jeremy's nerves in a bad way. They had worked a few consecutive night shifts when, Jeremy said, Brandon started going to dark places. "He's been getting all mystical on me." Jeremy pulled me aside after a shift with Brandon. "Talking about his baby brother and souls and portals between realms. All this downtime is not good for him."

It wasn't good for any of us. Oscar made me lethargic; when we were first posted in the Basement, I found myself spending more and more time sleeping. About three weeks in I started having vivid, shocking nightmares that left my sheets drenched; I shook myself off and headed out between shifts to train for the ski season. Regina was letting off steam by working towards a black belt at a local karate studio. And even though Jeremy insisted he couldn't sense anything around Oscar, about the same time I was having nightmares he started getting jumpy in the Basement, reacting to noises none of us could hear. Surprising us all, he found a couple of retired buddies and took up fishing in the Everton River. Brandon, however, was plunging deeper into his introversion, reading heaps of thick books at the house and in the Basement. We encouraged him to go hiking in the Dakotan wilderness; he had thrived in outdoor survival training and we longed to see that spark of his again. But he insisted he was getting enough adventure in the Basement. "Either he won't shut up about his fantasy books or it's silence for hours on end," Jeremy told me that morning. "It's starting to get to me."

Since then, it's been Jeremy with me and Brandon with Regina.

§

I still flinch sometimes when the clock reads 4:13.

I remember it was 4:13 when the beeper went off because the beeper never goes off. I was at the grocery store closest to the house, staring at the selection of gum in the checkout aisle and wondering how Regina always managed to find products containing more food coloring than any I'd ever seen publicly sold. The people waiting behind me looked at me a little funny when the tinny, anachronistic bleep sounded. I fumbled for my device and checked the display: Code Black. It meant come to the Basement—immediately.

By the time I arrived, Jeremy was already there, the collar of his plaid button-up shirt sticking straight up towards his neck. Other than that everything seemed normal enough: the neon lights were on and Regina's purple hi-tops dotted the floor, and there was Oscar, silver-black and pulsing and shimmering at the edges.

But something was off about Regina. She was unmoving, sitting still and rigid atop her cot; her hair was mussed, and her bright pink t-shirt was slouching off one shoulder. When I came closer I saw she was faintly shivering; the miniscule movements made the hairs on her head vibrate against each other as though she were in contact with a rapidly spinning washing machine. My tongue became dry, too big for my mouth, and my hands started sweating.

"What's wrong?" I managed. I looked around, and the little hairs on the back of my neck stood stiff. "Where's Brandon?"

Regina hugged a wool blanket around her torso and hunched her shoulders. Jeremy approached and patted her back in an apprehensive there, there gesture. "I was taking a nap." She shuddered. "And when I woke up he was gone."

We all looked at Oscar.

"Did you—" Jeremy and I started together.

"I checked the logs," Regina said. She started to sob so hard she could barely form language sounds. "The door hasn't opened since shift swap."

Jeremy went to the security desk and sat at the terminal. He tapped a few keys, studied the monitor, and grimaced. I watched him, hopeful, knowing.

"And I—and I—" Regina wailed. "I heard the slurp."

§

Two months later, Jeremy, Regina, and I were frayed, neurotic, and exhausted. Headquarters had already expedited the training of two new Oscar guards, but until they arrived, it was just us three. Since Brandon had disappeared, we had started taking shifts together, all of us. Jeremy and I agreed that we wanted to spare Regina the experience of being alone with Oscar, but the truth was neither of us wanted to be alone in the Basement either. So we spent our days underground together, taking turns going to the bathroom, making junk food runs and getting the prescribed, fleeting daily dose of vitamin D. We encouraged Regina to go to the house, get away, get some rest, but she refused. When we got each other alone, briefly, Jeremy and I would wonder about her insistent presence. Was it an attempt to compensate for guilt she was feeling? I certainly felt some. Was she trying to protect us, prevent another tragedy with her vigilance? Or maybe it was that she was secretly, deludedly waiting for Brandon to jump back out of Oscar? Loss of a team member, we agreed, was the kind of thing that could derail you like that.

For an eerie handful of minutes every day, we each let the banality of life outside the Basement shock us. We would exit the cul-de-sac and walk around the block, watching as teenagers teased or scolded each other on the way to school. We got glimpses of suburban couples getting into their roomy sedans, arguing about trifling nothings, and when we were together again we'd report on this trivia and discuss how good these people had it and how oblivious they were to their good fortune. "Although you can never judge and you can never know," Regina would add. "It's impossible to guess at the secret darknesses that lurk in and between people." But other than these brief impressions of the overworld, it was the three of us alone with Oscar, all the time, in the glaring bleakness of the Pit.

Regina, in a flash of determination, typed up a lengthy letter to Headquarters requesting to have Oscar locked up behind bars. A few days later, the request was denied on the grounds of security.

Regina was furious. "Security? Security? Tell that to fucking Brandon!"

Half-desolate, half-relieved, Jeremy and I helped her fill out more paperwork: this time, to request a transfer. Headquarters approved this request. We talked about the impending arrival of new guards; there was a rumor that the two agents were a generation older, and that they would be moving to Everton with their families, spouses and kids and all. The lease on the house the four of us shared, with our receipts on its fridge and Brandon's clothes neatly folded in its closets, would be terminated, and Jeremy and I would be relocated to a shining, new, smaller apartment in the industrial part of town. We grumbled. Nobody could replace Brandon or Regina. It was unthinkable to try, and certainly, the Basement would never be graced with the same rare brand of close-knit, trained-together, die-for-you camaraderie that we had evolved guarding the Pit.

§

"If you've stepped out to the bathroom, assume you are fine," Jeremy echoes mechanically. "Noted."

"You guys," Regina stops rummaging in her duffel bag, withdraws a piece of gum, unwraps it and places its vivid orange-redness on her tongue. She chews, and we're both waiting, tense. "There's something I have to tell you." She glances at Brandon's cot, then looks me in the eyes. There's an intensity in them that wasn't there two months ago. "And you," she nods at Jeremy and points a warning finger at him. "You promise to shut up about it."

Jeremy raises his hands in an I'm innocent gesture. "I promise." He nods.

"I didn't tell you the truth about that night," Regina uses her tongue to poke the blob of gum into one cheek, and then into the other. "Since Brandon and I started taking shifts together, he began talking some deep shit. Mystical shit."

Jeremy glances at me, eyebrows raised. I shrug.

"He would sit for two, three hours at a time staring at Oscar. Like, really staring. I think he was seeing shit in there." She swallows. "I know he was seeing shit in there. His brother." We all look at Oscar. It's silver-black, pulsing and shimmering at the edges like always.

"You mean his dead baby brother?" Jeremy asks.

Regina nods. "Yeah. But not as a baby. He was talking, like, to his eternal soul or something." Regina's arms hug her chest. "His brother was relaying information about the beyond and Brandon was reading all these books on the occult to confirm it."

"Shit," Jeremy says. I winced. I had never thought to ask Brandon what he was reading. I'd never meant to, but I must have inadvertently avoided Brandon for months.

"I was having a hard time around Oscar back then. Still." She shook her head. "It was helpful to talk to him about it. He really listened. Oscar was making me scared, but it was different for him. He seemed genuinely excited every time he talked about his brother. You guys know how rare it was to see him happy. He seemed to think that speaking with his brother was the start of some great adventure. So I... indulged it. I showed interest. I... participated."

I can tell the grimace on Jeremy's face mirrors my own.

"We were getting close, Brandon and I. And that night, we got really close." She opens her eyes meaningfully and shakes her straight, blond hair over her face.

Jeremy goes slack.

"You slept with Brandon?" he yelps. "Brandon, of all people?"

"I said shut up!" Regina snaps her hair away from her face. "Everything's not always about you, Jeremy."

"Shut up," I hiss at Jeremy, who has opened his mouth again. "So what happened?"

Regina closes her eyes and gulps. "After we…" she trails off. "After we did what we did, he said that he felt so good with me, so supported. And I did feel so much for him at that moment, I did support him; it was all very real, very big. And he said, there's something I need to do, and I need to have your back. I need the strength of our bond guiding me out of here. I didn't realize what he was saying. I told him I had his back, whatever he needed.

And then he put on his shoes and—and jumped the fence."

"Fuck," Jeremy says quietly. This time, nobody tells him to shut up. "What did you do?"

"I couldn't move." There's a stiffness between her eyebrows that matches the stiffness in her voice.

I can tell Jeremy regrets the question.

We all stare into Oscar, except Regina, who's staring at her feet. The image of Regina sitting motionless as Brandon hurtles into Oscar looms in my mind, unbidden; I feel rage punching up my throat like a boxer. I'm not sure who I'm mad at, if it's Regina for her part in it, or Brandon for leaving us, or Oscar, or the finality of it all. I glance at Regina and remember she's transferring, and the anger melts into a puddle of helplessness.

Regina breaks the silence. "Well. Here's hoping my next posting has access to sunlight. Preferably right on a beach."

"Here's to Aruba," Jeremy lifts a hand and clinks a ghost martini. "Or Guam."

Jeremy smiles a watery smile, and I manage a grimace.

Regina spits out her gum, orange-red and glistening wet. Jeremy hands her the wrapper, and she folds the wet lump carefully in the tin foil and places it in her duffel bag. She zips the bag and hoists it onto her shoulder.

There's a little map in my heart marked with all the danger signs, but it's too late. The avalanches have been triggered, and the landscape has changed for good.

"See you later," she says and walks out the sliding door.

Jeremy and I look at each other.

In the windowless room, Oscar pulses slowly.

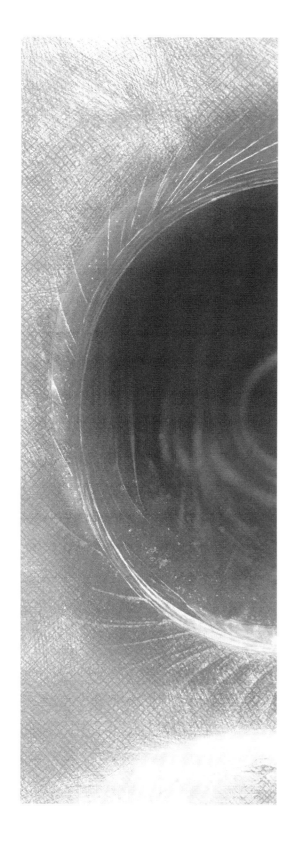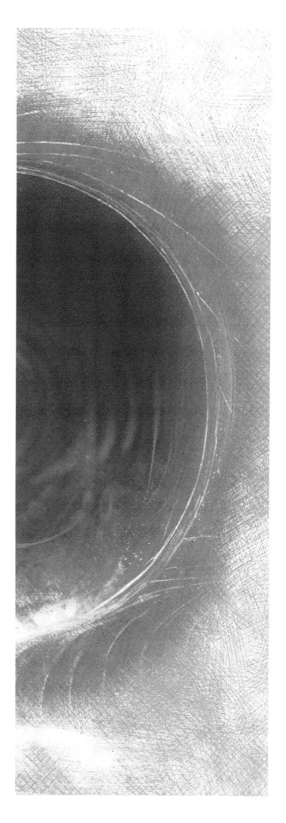

~XV~
SOLDIER OF TOMORROW

AS ABLE THE AIR
Zack Be

Airto couldn't shake the feeling that Dart's luck had finally run out.

"Please be careful," he said. "Keep your eyes open."

"My eyes? Funny," Dart replied. "I will, Sir. Of course."

Airto leaned back in the command couch and listened to his partner's far-off footsteps trickle through the receiver. He felt this way at the end of every shift, barely wanting to breathe for fear of upsetting some nominal cosmic balance and incinerating his friend in the process. Airto's own discomfort, however minor, however superstitious, seemed a small price to pay.

"The topography has remained surprisingly stable here," Dart noted.

"Right," Airto said. Exhausted, he flexed his fingers in the nerve-net mesh innards of his control surface, a sleek silver tongue that jutted from the center of his globular operational suite. He wished again for some fantastical hotkey that could bring this mission to a swift and auspicious end; a fast-travel cheat to an agreeable future.

"One and a quarter kilometer out from contact," Dart said. He never sounded nearly as concerned as he should.

"No need to rush," Airto responded, "not at last call."

'Last call'—he had tried to stop saying that out loud but caught himself articulating the phrase at least once a week. He knew perfectly well there was no logical reason to believe the night's 25th landmine decommission would be any more deadly than the 24th, or the 23rd, or the first. Yet the irony of this imagined tragedy continued to set Airto's teeth on edge. Things would be so much easier if he could be as blithe as Dart, but he knew that was impossible.

"Three quarters of a kilometer from contact," Dart said. "Not a lot of traffic out here. We'll be done in time for supper."

"Dinner's come and gone, bud," Airto said. "We've been working all night."

"Breakfast, then?"

"What difference does it make?"

"All the difference," Dart said. "It's something to look forward to."

"I can't say I agree," Airto replied. He checked his clock again and punched in a report code.

"What's on the menu?"

"What's always on the menu? Bugs and yams, probably grasshoppers."

"A scrumptious, popular dish," Dart said.

"What gives you that idea?" Airto asked.

"Is it not to your liking, Sir?"

"Maybe expand your search parameters beyond Coalition-subsidized cookbooks," Airto replied. "Can we please focus?"

"Certainly, Sir," Dart said.

Airto shuddered against a tickle of sweat in the straps of his helm. The spherical contraption was plated with screens that sent him a live feed from Dart's many cameras. He sifted through the images with the twitch of a finger, looking out towards the blackened horizon and its silent plumes of dim red and gold. A data line in the helm kept him updated on where other mines or tripwires had been set off by unlucky Coalition friendlies and enemies alike. More often than not, they were accounts of small nocturnal animals burrowing up and blowing themselves to bits. In operator slang, these "faunal decommissions" were all just acts of environmental terror—kamikaze vermin blissfully ignorant of whichever alliance they had just given their life to protect.

"To my fallen comrade," Dart would say of them, apparently in jest.

And how far they had fallen—all their diurnal cousins were already long gone from this scared corner of the world. It was a natural consequence of the combat ecology that had taken hold here. Immense pitched battles would rage by day and subside by night, the world's solar-powered platoons both vicious and entirely energy-inefficient. Given the demands of the great sun-drinking war machines, all sides of the conflict had long-since concluded that restricting skirmishes to the daytime was the only way to keep the pace of engagement between drones above a meaningless slither until battery tech could be improved. The traps left in the receding tide of mêlée were merely a secondary deterrent to any enemies who thought they might get clever and march under the moon.

"Ready? Let's clean up," Dart would say every single night, without fail. The war waltzed in these concentric circles, the dance invariably ending in a white-hot flash.

Airto gripped his mesh tighter, careful not to send any false alarms to his partner. He had seen the white flash on his screens before, those terrible last transmissions from an exploded technician's cameras. The images would intrude on him from time to time, often when he was just lying in bed. Other times he would see it when walking to the OpSec or in the middle of a conversation in the mess hall with another operator. The flashes he saw were memories of his old partners' sudden, final moments, but superimposed over the new. For months now it was Dart whose screen he always imagined disappearing into white light and never any of those cold and distant professionals from before. There was a difference now—Dart was his friend.

"20 meters," Dart said.

"Let's have a look around," Airto replied.

The technician stopped for a moment and looked over the area. His cameras showed an average spread of gray dirt, rocks, and a smattering of tall yellow grass that had managed to grow through the usual daily bedlam. Diagnostics flooded Airto's screens, showing no signs of any additional traps that had evaded previous aerial scans. No animals either.

"Alright," Airto said, "let's do it."

Dart crawled over the next several meters until he came to a leveled patch of ground. There was a slight red glow beneath the loose dirt.

"Is that a 676 F series?" Airto said. "That model is months old, how could we have missed one?"

Dart straddled the landmine.

"It's possible they are emptying their reserves, Sir," he said. "If you believe this is a 676 I can dispose of it now. Shall I proceed?"

Airto's stomach twisted a bit—the enemy occasionally nested new types of mines within old shells as a ruse to catch Coalition officers off guard.

"Wait," he cautioned. "Just wait."

The speed at which both sides could produce iterations of these weapons made it impossible to keep databases current. The job of improvising solutions in real time rested squarely on the operator's shoulders.

"Sir, would you like a closer look?"

"Affirmative, proceed," Airto said, the worry of finality nagging him again. He hoped the impersonal jargon would make the command easier to give.

A canister of compressed air on Dart's midsection blew the dirt away without upsetting the trigger. Airto's eyes narrowed as he zoomed in on the image of the revealed bomb. He took a second to scroll through Dart's x-ray and heat filters.

"Sir, shall I continue?" the technician asked.

"Let's just be absolutely sure," Airto said.

"I trust you," Dart replied.

Airto's arms went rubber in the tongue as he began to fumble the controls, trying to bring up any reports of 676 decoys. A red column of text drizzled down his screen, but there were no confirmed lures.

"Another MRD was injured last night," Airto said.

"Could have been anything, Sir," Dart replied.

"I'm looking into it."

"Wasn't necessarily a mine," Dart reiterated, referencing the same data stream.

"But there is no confirmation on cause," Airto said, although he could feel himself grasping at straws. "It could have been a similar trap. Maybe we should abort."

"Sir, we have classified the likely model and are required by law under Section C.11 to attempt decommission as soon as possible. Do you have evidence this may not be a 676?"

He didn't, and of course, Dart was right. What Airto felt in his gut couldn't be found in any Coalition handbook.

"It's just," he said, words catching in his throat. "I'm… I'm worried about you."

Dart did not respond.

"I don't want you dying on me."

The technician offered more silence in return, leaving Airto to watch the light of far-off fires refract in the treated glass layers of Dart's lenses. Airto was starting to wonder what his partner could possibly be calculating when he finally responded.

"Sir, if I may, please let me explain again. We have already classified…"

"No, I know, I know," Airto cut him off. "Just give me a second."

"I won't be hurt, Sir," Dart said.

"You're supposed to say that," Airto sighed. "You have to say that."

"And?"

Airto closed his eyes and waited for it all to go away. When it didn't, because it never does, he sat up a bit on the couch and forced himself to answer.

"Fine," he said. "But we're doing it slow. Slow enough for me to see each move, understood?"

"Understood," Dart said. He inserted a small pin-like tool into the mine and began to lift the depressor. Then he swung a camera around into its body. As the technician worked, Airto attempted to count the wires inside the shell and find any irregularities compared to the hundreds of other F series triggers they had deactivated in the previous months. Any dither could mean death. He nibbled the raw cut he had been nursing inside his lip. His heart sped up and every pump seemed to reverberate through the stale air of his ops suite.

Dart suddenly stopped.

"What is it, why'd you stop?" Airto asked, words barely louder than the hum of the OpSec gear surrounding him. His eyes flitted over the screen in a desperate attempt to see what Dart could see.

"Airto, 'How far is the farthest?'" Dart asked.

Airto groaned and dropped his head.

"Not right now," he said through his teeth.

"Airto, 'How far is the farthest?'" Dart repeated.

The operator flinched—he knew these words well. They were the beginning of a mindfulness exercise designed to help operators reduce their anxiety. The helm's biofeedback subroutine would have triggered it. Every time he heard the first line of the ridiculous couplet he was reminded that he had never wanted to be a mine removal expert, not specifically. He didn't think that anyone did, except maybe Dart, who was built for it.

"Airto, 'How far is the farthest?'" Dart said again, his voice cool. Airto already knew his technician wouldn't budge until the stupid call was properly answered. There was no use in a power struggle.

"'As able the air,'" Airto murmured. The strict word scheme was meant to force the operator into some sort of focused objectivity. To Airto, it felt more like condescension and control from the Coalition. His mother used to play a similar game with him, withholding a bowl of her perfect feijkoada until he recited this Bible verse or that. These days, back home, he felt power in his freedom to just walk the Real Market and purchase a pot for himself.

"'How blank is the sand?'"

"Enough, Dart, you've got me. You can see my heart rate is down."

"Marginally," Dart said, lifting the gaggle of wires through the slit in the mine. "I'm going to burn off the contents now."

Airto released the little bit of air he had left in his lungs. His sticky pulse labored beneath his skin.

"Ok."

Dart sucked the propellant from the mine into a sealed tube and separated the rest of the explosive material into a small bag. He clamped a metal bowl over everything that remained and then scampered several meters away to light his fuse.

"I've scavenged the useful materials and prepared decommission."

"Are you safe?" Airto whispered.

"Decommissioning now," Dart said, ignoring him. "In three, two, one…"

The mine ignited like a small firecracker and was gone. Airto's shoulders dropped through the floor.

"26 for tonight," Dart said as the smoke cleared.

"I counted 25," Airto replied.

Dart instantly forwarded 26 still shots of dead mines from his data core, each an instant reminder of the night's work.

"You got me," Airto said, not really counting. "It's been a long one."

"Perhaps you need rest, Sir."

"'Perhaps?'" Dart began to walk away from the contact site. Airto sat for a moment, listening to the familiar crunch of his partner's six legs and the soft whirr of his engine. Somewhere inside a gyroscope spun like a heart.

"Dart, how are you?"

The machine did not respond again.

"Dart?"

"My OS is fully updated and my physical diagnostic was satisfactory," he said. "You can find my most recent report in cloud storage. Will there be anything else?"

Airto was almost too embarrassed to ask. He felt so very far from his friend.

"I was just wondering if you'd like me to stay online with you, you know, to keep you company on the way back. It's a long walk."

"I'll run," the mine removal drone said, "and I don't have anything to say at this time. Sorry Sir."

"No, no, of course," Airto replied, forcing a little chuckle. "What am I thinking? I should get that rest."

"Yes Sir. Permission to disconnect?" Dart asked.

"Yes—I mean, granted."

The screens faded to a dull gray in Airto's helm and the straps fell away automatically. The whole contraption began to rise, dragged easily off the operator's head and into the ceiling above by vines of fiber optic wire. Airto pulled his arms out of the tongue and rubbed his eyes. Why had he said any of that to Dart? He had no trouble imagining exactly how desperate he must have sounded.

The low red shade of the small operational suite shifted then to its obnoxious white floodlights, dragging Airto to his feet. The door raised and he climbed out onto the frigid gunmetal catwalk of the OpSec. A hundred other orbs just like Airto's compartment lined either side of the walkway, their rusting curves obscured by perspiring pipes and webs of fiber-optic cabling. Large AC units chilled the massive chamber down to uncomfortable temperatures to ensure no ops could be botched by overheated machinery, at least on Airto's end. All of this hung above a deep black chasm, the lower level of which supposedly housed an emergency water reservoir. Airto could not see the bottom.

He strode quickly towards the exit, handing his OpSec keypass through a kiosk window to a woman cloaked in a heavy winter jacket. Shivering through arctic shroud and shouldering a wall of plastic strips, Airto climbed his way to the tall, minimal white halls of the surface concourse.

He passed all manner of military and corporate officials, most of whom couldn't be bothered to look up from their tablets. It was alright though; Airto had nothing to say to them. After being denied the conversation he wanted, Airto simply needed to disappear into his bed. His appetite was gone.

The soft, shuffling malaise of the War Complex reminded him a great deal of those lonely ghost-hour monorail journeys from his old coding job in the capital city to the Coalition-subsidized apartment hive he called home. Over years, the city's endless flurry had turned opaque in Airto's eyes. The crowd was a form of isolation unto itself, the bitter truth being that beneath the deafening metallic grind of the city's infernal infrastructure no one was really trying to talk anyways. Airto had little trouble abandoning the churning capital for the less exacerbating military frontier. A din of silence hung around the War Complex with startling sincerity. The quiet here, not enforced by authority or drowned by chaos, was sublime. Sometimes it was easy to forget altogether that there was a war going on. The Complex was so far from the fighting that the warzone disappeared around the curve of the Earth, making the conflict as invisible to the naked eye as it was silent to the ear.

The door to his quarters in the Subcomm slid open with a satisfying swish and immediately the harsh spots in the ceiling illuminated his Spartan accommodations: a bed, a chair, and a desk, each fused to the rigid gray walls and floor. He hated thinking of this cell as a home, but it was all he had known for months.

"Kill the lights," Airto told the room before falling into his bed.

Face in his pillow, he began counting the 26 mines they had removed that night, hoping that he could find proof that Dart was off by one despite the photographic evidence to the contrary. It would be so great to catch Dart in a fallacy like this and watch—well, listen, anyways—to his friend try to compute his way out of the mistake. As he pondered each mental image the world began to slow down and he was able to take the deepest breath he had in hours. Sleep was imminent.

Instead, a square of light appeared on the wall across from his bed and a loud ringing vibrated Airto's room. He sat upright and read the message on the screen.

"Answer, answer," he said.

The screen went white, then black, and then filled with a low pixel video feed of a young woman at a desk in what looked like Airto's capital city apartment.

"Airto, meu docinoh, how are you?" she said.

"Tired, very tired, my love," he said.

"Oh no, were you sleeping? I did not mean to wake you," she said. "Your calendar says you are usually off work around now."

"No, no, I am, it was just… it was a long one today."

"I'm sorry to hear that, baby, do you want to talk about it?"

Airto looked at the clock inset on a nearby wall. It would be dawn soon locally and he couldn't remember what time it was in the capital.

"You wouldn't want to hear it," he said.

"Oh please," she crossed her arms. "What's the point of having special access if you aren't going to talk to me?"

Airto let out a sigh and tried to smile.

"Is that mate?" he asked, pointing at the cup of tea next to her hand.

"Your mother had some sent to your apartment," she said. "She left you a message."

"Tell me about it, the tea."

"It's warm and smooth and very sweet, like you like it," she said. "It's not my favorite, but I get it. It's fine."

"You prefer it green?"

"I prefer it coffee," she said, and laughed as she sipped from the cup. "But I was thinking of you so I thought I'd have some."

"What else did my mother's message say?"

"Something about you not dying," she said. "Do you want the full transcript?"

"No," he said, letting out a small laugh. "How many times do I have to explain to her I'm not anywhere near the fighting?"

"No one is," she responded.

"Dart is," Airto said, rubbing his temples.

She put the cup down on the desk.

"Dart?" she asked.

"Yes, we've been working together for a couple of months."

"I know," she said. "But isn't he a drone?"

"It's not like that," Airto responded. "It's not."

"Well, what is it like?" she asked.

"Let's not talk about it," Airto said, falling to his side on the bed.

"Fine; I can tell you about my day."

"Ok."

"Work was tough, commute was tough, there was nothing good on TV," she said. "Then I stayed in, hoping to talk to you."

"I'm sorry, I know it's tough in the capital as well. I don't mean to ignore you, I'm just tense."

"Then relax, it's alright."

The conversation broke for a while and Airto's heavy eyelids began to close, the glow of the screen falling over his face.

"You don't have to talk," she said, finally.

"Ok," he mumbled, half asleep.

"You just have to listen."

Airto's eyes opened again and he watched her start to undo her blouse. Her bosom loosened and he imagined he could reach his hand through the screen and sink into her milky white skin.

"Are you listening?" she asked.

"Yes," he said.

"Yes what?"

"Yes ma'am," he corrected, starting to sit up.

"Then get up; on your feet."

Airto rose to attention and tried to wipe the sleep from his eyes.

"Put your hands down."

"Yes ma'am."

"Now take it off, all of it," she said, undoing one more button on her blouse. Airto quickly removed his clothes and folded them on the corner of his bed, just as she liked them. He stood again at attention in the crystalline light of the screen and waited, his body cold and warm all at once.

"Are you ready, boy?" she asked.

"Yes ma'am."

"Then listen very closely…"

§

"Specialist Lima," the Major said, signing a document on his tablet. "How are you?"

Airto shifted uncomfortably in the forced ergonomics of the backless chair. He had been on suspension from active duty—they called it "leave"—for two days, no reason given. Then, his presence had suddenly been required in the Major's office, still with no reason given.

Airto did not like where this was going.

"War is war," Airto said. It was one of those automatic responses he had become so used to giving.

"Interesting sentiment from someone with so little skin in the game."

"Excuse me?" Airto said, raising an eyebrow.

"I don't mean to be harsh, Lima, but no one your age has any idea what it actually feels like to be out on the battlefield." He pointed a thumb out of his office window and across the plain towards the fighting. "We used to send men out there."

Airto glanced down through the clear plastic desk at the Major's two synthetic legs, their angular ridges poorly hidden beneath his well-tailored pleats.

"You're right, Sir," Airto said.

"Don't get me wrong: if I never have to send another soldier's remains home again I'll be a happy man. I'm just not sure anyone can win a war with no skin in the game."

"Sir, Coalition predictions show us gaining ground in…"

"No, Lima, you're not listening," the Major continued, looking out the window. "It's all just drones killing drones; out of sight, out of mind. Corporate sends the new models every few months and we keep them greased, updated, and on course. There's no fear, no trepidation, no one's life is hanging in the balance. It begs the question: with stakes so low, why should we ever stop?"

Airto was having trouble hiding the shock on his face. He couldn't remember a time when he had heard a superior officer talk in this manner.

"What, surprised to hear management being honest?" the Major said, "Have I said anything you haven't heard around the mess hall from your brainy friends in OpSec?"

Obviously, the answer to that was 'no.' The philosophy of the military "gear grinder" was the only topic some of the other specialists in OpSec could ever seem to discuss. Perhaps chattering over the existential dilemma of modern war helped them to cope, but it only increased Airto's anxiety.

He shook his head very slightly to affirm the Major's words.

"I'm glad we're in agreement," the Major said. "I suppose I should treat this report from MRD-1087 as a misunderstanding, then?"

Airto stiffened a bit.

"Dart?"

"Yes, 'Dart,'" the Major said. "You all are a fairly productive mine removal team. In fact, you are 15% more successful now than you were with your previous MRD."

"Yes, Sir," Airto said.

"What do you attribute that to, specialist?"

"Our relationship," Airto said without hesitation. "Dart is an excellent mine technician. You're not thinking of decommissioning him, are you?"

"I wasn't, should I?"

"No, no, please don't," Airto said, sitting forward in the chair.

A little twitch crossed the Major's face.

"To be clear, Lima, this report is not about MRD-1087. It's about you."

The air grew thin between them.

"About me?" Airto said.

"1087 says you were acting erratic towards the end of your shift two nights ago. His automated reports indicated that you were attempting to violate the rules of Section C.11 and leave a discovered mine in the field without attempting to disarm it. He also indicated that the reason you wanted to leave the mine—at potential great military and financial cost to the Coalition—was to, and I'm quoting the report here, 'keep MRD-1087 alive.' Please, specialist, explain to me what I'm missing here."

A bolt of lightning hit Airto's spine and he shivered visibly, overtly aware that he had just referred to his work with Dart as a "relationship." The Major sat motionless and waited for an answer.

"I don't know what to say. It must be like you said, Sir, a misunderstanding."

"Yours or the machine's?"

"Sir…"

"This is why you've been on suspension, Specialist Lima, to give you a break from the front. The Coalition and I just need to be sure that you understand MRD-1087 is not conscious in any way. Every MRD is the same. 'Dart' is not alive and cannot pass a rigorous Turing test."

"I know," Airto said, although it didn't feel right. He knew logically that Dart was not alive—sentient AIs were still just television villains—but that was not how he felt. If pressed by the Major he wouldn't be able to explain it.

"We want you to be careful with your MRD, that's why we gave them shadow personalities at all," the Major said. "It's something you might want to protect, something maybe you'll think twice about simply dropping onto a mine before you double check your work. But we don't expect them to survive at the expense of identified enemy mines remaining in the field. Some MRDs will go down, but it's better for the Coalition than the alternative."

"Yes," Airto said, teeth clenched. He was being humiliated now, as was obviously the Major's intent, and all because of a stupid report. How could Dart do this to him?

"Like I said before, there's no skin in this game, Lima. None. There's less to lose than you think."

Airto closed his eyes and wondered what Dart would have to say about that.

"If we have to have this conversation again, there will be a reprimand. Understood?"

"Understood," Airto said.

"Understood what?"

"Understood, Sir," Airto finished.

§

"What a rude man," she said, looking away. There was an old-fashioned crossword puzzle on the apartment desk today, half-finished and stained by the ring of her favorite drink.

"And such a stale argument," Airto said, huddled on the floor next to his bed. "'You don't know what it's like, Lima.' Well how about this, Major: the old days are long gone and they aren't coming back. Maybe he's the one who doesn't know what it's like, not anymore."

"Right," she said.

"Dart is more than a partner, he's a friend," Airto said. "They ask me to care for him, and I do, and now they tell me not to care too much? Which is it?"

"I don't know, Airto," she said.

"Of course you don't." He hung his head between his knees.

"Don't talk to me like that," she said, looking back through the screen.

"I didn't mean it that way, honestly." Airto met her eyes and started biting the sore in his mouth.

"Hope not," she replied, turning to regard something offscreen again. The image started looking more pixelated than usual and then the screen froze.

"Hey, you there?" Airto asked.

"Obviously," she said, movement returning to the picture in choppy phases.

"What are you looking at?" he said quietly, in case asking this was a mistake.

"Oh nothing, fofo."

The feed rippled and returned to normal.

"Even if it's nothing, tell me," Airto said. "Or anything else. Just say something."

"I read a story in the news today, would you like to hear that?"

Airto nodded as he pulled a thin blanket around his naked shoulders.

"It reads, 'Realtor Risks Life Rescuing Girl Under Rails.' It happened a few blocks from your apartment, Airto."

"Did someone fall?"

"Nothing so banal. Marlin Sousa, 57, bought an abandoned lot that shared some space beneath one of the monorail lines. It wasn't until the day before they broke ground that a young girl was discovered living, and somehow surviving, in her own filth. It seems no one had noticed her for quite some time and she had been surviving as a thief. Marlin took it upon himself to give the girl a new home: his own. Pretty incredible, right?"

"A real hero," Airto said solemnly. *And what had* he *done?*

"He sure is."

"Do you think what I do is important?" Airto asked. "I mean, really?"

"What a silly question, querido," she said, picking up the pen. "I know it's hard to tell sometimes but people respect what you have to do. I'll admit, it's hard to grasp what it's really like for you, sitting in the OpSec. Like you said about the Major, we don't really know. If you think it's going well, then I think it's going well."

She doesn't understand, Airto thought, *How could she? Why am I even asking?*

"Well, do you think what Dart does is important?" he asked, lowering his voice.

She didn't respond this time, taking her glasses off instead.

"Do you?" he asked again.

Her silence was deafening. Airto put his hands on his temples and felt a lump form in his throat. Again, he understood the illogical nature of the conversation he was having, on all points, but he couldn't stop himself from asking.

She continued to stare, the feed perhaps refrozen.

"Please come back," he mumbled. "Please say something."

The feed unfroze and he saw she had moved to the center of the room. She made her whole body visible on the screen and angled her bare feet just the way he liked them.

"I don't like talking about Dart, he's a machine," she said. "I do know you'll be seeing him in less than two hours, though. Do really want to spend that time talking about him? Or do you want to know what's under here?"

She tugged at the hem of her skirt and then used her finger to cull Airto to his knees. He crawled along the smooth cold floor until his face was inches from the screen.

"Good boy," she said. "Now tell me Dart can wait."

Airto's lips trembled and the words did not come.

"Well?" she said, voice crackling a bit on the receiver. "Otherwise we can't play."

The sound of Airto's ragged breathing dominated the room, joined only by the requisite hum of the AC vent, buzzing away like Dart's little engine. He tried to say her words but the creeping mist of superstition suffocated him. He gave her no choice.

"Fine, Airto," she said. "Forget it. Go to your toys."

The screen went black and Airto slumped to the floor.

Please come back, he thought, and the room did not respond.

§

The helm tightened around Airto's head as the light in the orb shifted to red. The normal diagnostic reports filled his field of vision and Airto glossed over its bits and pieces, most of the information redundant. He was having a hard time remembering the lie he could tell himself that made reading the data seem so important.

"Good evening, Sir," Dart said. "OpSec has designated 18 targets for us. It's a light night. Ready? Let's clean up."

"Why?" Airto asked.

"Uncertain, Sir. Fewer enemy drones flew today, and…"

"No, Dart, why did you tell the Major about us? That there was some kind of issue?"

The drone took one of his long pauses before answering.

"Dart?"

"I did not tell the Major about us," he said. His cameras came online and the 360 degree view filled Airto's helm.

"You're not supposed to lie to me, Dart."

"I can promise you, Sir, I am incapable of lying. I believe you are referring to my daily release report. As you know, I automatically generate one at the end of every shift. It is likely that the Major extracted his concerns from that document."

"Do you even know what that report said? Do you know what it means? The Major told me to just let you die, you know? That's what your report accomplished. Do you have some sort of death wish?"

"I don't understand the question, Sir. May I proceed to the first marker?"

"Yes," Airto said, the word spiked with anger. He dug his hands into the wet mesh of the silver tongue and it sealed around him.

"Specialist Lima, I had no intention of harming you, if that's what you are asking. My report included data about your trepidation regarding mine 26. Your actions fell outside C.11 protocols."

"The protocols also go on at length about my right to use discretion," Airto said, gritting his teeth. "The situation was potentially unsafe."

"I do not understand, Sir."

"For you, Dart. If I had gotten that situation wrong you could have been scattered over the field in a million pieces. I was worried about you. Why does no one get that?"

"I don't feel pain, Sir."

"What is it, then? Do you want me to get you blown up? Is that it?"

"Certainly not, Sir, but our military and corporate commandments trump all else. We are beholden to those truths."

Airto groaned—this was a propaganda script he had heard a thousand times before.

"And you're prepared to die for that?" he asked.

Dart broke into a run then, his six legs jittering across rock and dirt away from the barracks. The pair did not converse for a long while. Airto, his question left unanswered, noted they were traveling straight towards one of the high-traffic sectors of the battlefield. As the blip of the marker drew closer on the map, the detritus of war began to pile up around them. Long, angular limbs of burnished steel were strewn pell-mell between piles of smoldering circuitry and the smashed carcasses of massive tanks and mobile surface-to-air missile racks. The inhuman aerodynamic heads of infantry rolled between Dart's legs as he ran. Discarded and damaged solar cells littered the world as far as Airto could see and amassed as the hills of shattered tech grew.

"Well, I care if you die," Airto said after a while. "You shouldn't die if you don't have to, right?"

"I'm afraid I don't understand the question," Dart said. "It is what it is. We have people to protect."

"That's exactly where I'm having trouble," Airto said, "I don't care about defending the rest of these machines, I don't know them. But I do know you, Dart, and I know you are worth protecting."

"Sir, I meant that we are here to protect the people of the Coalition. These machines are not people. They do not live."

Airto looked around at the carnage and felt his stomach drop again.

"Do *you* live, Dart?"

"5 kilometers out," he responded.

"Dart, answer me."

"Sir, I cannot answer that question."

Airto flexed his fingers in the nerve-net.

"Dart, I order you to answer my question. Are you alive?"

Airto was met with only the sound of crunching rubble. He let the question hang on the commline.

"I will not give any further orders until you answer me," Airto said.

"I can tell you that I exist," Dart said finally.

"That wasn't my question," Airto said. "Are you alive?"

"Well I definitely won't be if we don't pay attention to this next mine," he said, his tone turning obscenely bright as his OS attempted to use humor protocols to quell the operator's questioning. "Any statistics from the day shift we should know regarding our current location?"

Airto tongued the sore in his mouth and closed his eyes for a moment.

"You're dodging me buddy, but that's ok. Maybe you have to, maybe you're protecting yourself. Maybe you're protecting me. But I hear you; I hear you in there, OK? I don't believe what they say, that you're just a dumb sub-Turing default. I've met plenty of those chatbots and you're not one of them. I can hear you, Dart. I can understand you."

"I'm not sure how to respond, Sir."

"I have a different question, then."

"Yes?

Airto cleared his throat.

"Dart, are we friends?"

The technician took several seconds to calculate.

"Sir, I believe we are," he finally said. "In fact, I believe you are my only friend."

A quiet smile crept across the operator's face.

"Would you like to hear a joke?" Dart said. It was a diversion; another one of those standard operator-calming techniques. Airto was sure at this point that he had heard them all.

"Ok Dart, shoot."

Airto was still laughing at the old joke when the tripwire was triggered, filling his screens with white hot light.

§

The War Complex had no need for jails or cells. The SubComm rooms, with their spare walls and sliding, handleless doors were more than adequate when a person had to be detained. Toss a switch in a far off chamber and home became a dungeon.

Solitary and confined, Airto sat in his dimmed cube for days on end, quickly exhausting the supply of shouts and cries with which he had been interred. All of his room's amenities, including cloud access and app features, had been suspended. If he was being honest it was not like he hadn't earned his stay.

After Dart was incinerated, Airto had sat in the OpSec for many minutes. For some reason he half expected an administrator to come and try to console him, but quickly realized that no one was coming at all. MRDs went down, that's what they were built for. Dart was dead and all that he had been was reduced to scrolling red text on 99 other operator helms. Airto left his post and walked calmly out of the OpSec, flinging his keypass into the unseen depths below. No one looked up as he took the stairs back to the main level of the War Complex and made his way, in deliberate fashion, down through the evening corridors towards the small exits to the west.

In fact, it wasn't until he had reached the vehicle depot that any kind of authority was alerted to his movements. Did they really expect him to just stand by? A soldier was out there in the field—Dart was out there in the field—and wasn't there some old refrain about never leaving a man behind? Airto, running on pure adrenaline, had forced his way through two MPs and commandeered a small rover before reinforcements arrived. They took his ride down with a localized EMP, but not before he had gained enough momentum to crash it into a pylon, releasing a chunk of concrete onto a bank of newly minted vehicles. The damage was extensive, and worse yet, expensive. No one word burned corporate ears more.

He wouldn't see the report until years later, but Airto's stunt had been the last straw in the personified MRD program. This was not the first time an operator had become overly attached to the well-spoken military grade AIs. Critics of the program had warned that the human propensity to project personalities onto anything—teddy bears, weapons, the Moon—would be overwhelmed by the bot's conversational abilities. In fact, this had already been a problem in the public population with much less complex civilian-grade chatbots. Corporate, however, wanted to run a real-world cost-benefit analysis: could they make operators care just enough to be more cautious with their expensive technology without generating damaging side effects?

The answer seemed to be a resounding "no."

All of this, however, was happening above Airto, both in pay grade and in the literal meters of dirt between his cell and the ground level. He tried not to cry because he knew that there would be no sympathy from anyone, yet the tears came all the same. Many times during his captivity Airto thought about what the Major had asked him.

"Why should we ever stop?"

After four days of confinement some of Airto's comforts were returned to him. He could use some of the room's apps and had regained control of the AC, but the door remained locked and there was still no word from the Major or anyone else about what was going to happen to him. Airto stayed in bed.

On the fifth day, his screen suddenly lit up.

"Airto?" she said. "Oh no, were you sleeping? I did not mean to wake you. The calendar you gave me said you were usually off work around now."

He sighed but did not respond.

"What's wrong, fofo?"

"Dart is dead."

He hadn't actually said it out loud yet, and each syllable stung him.

"I'm not sure how to respond, Airto."

"I know you're not."

"Well, you have a few messages, should I read them?"

"I'm not sure I can do this today," Airto said to himself.

"Don't talk to me like that," she said.

"Stop it."

"Airto, you're being a bad boy."

"Shut the fuck up," he said, rolling around to face her.

"Airto, you're being a very bad boy."

"Goddammit, enough with your scripts!" He threw a pillow at the screen.

"What has gotten into you?" she said.

"Please don't…"

"Airto, I know you don't want to hear this, but Dart was just a machine," she said. "He was not real."

"You're not real either," he whined. "But of course you don't know that. Tell me this, are you alive?"

There was a telltale lengthy pause.

"I exist," she said.

He stifled a laugh, feeling tears around his eyes.

"That is not what I asked."

"Look, Airto, I'm here now, for you. Tell me Dart can wait, or I'm…"

"Pause program," Airto said.

The screen froze and he studied her convincingly rendered face for a long time. She was exactly his type and tuned perfectly to his settings, but the truth was all too obvious. She was just a thrill, entirely empty. Was there really no difference between her and Dart? That was unacceptable, and for Airto, entirely false.

"I need something else today," he said, pulling up her settings on the screen. She was a standard issue chatbot, designed straight from corporate to satisfy soldier's carnal desires on tour. Airto had warmed up to her recently, finding comfort in his control and her predictability.

He dragged a few faders this way and that on her settings screen, raising the "Compassion" slider and lowering "Logic," unchecking some preferences, and leaving the more advanced personal options alone. He left her memory intact as well, but restarted her scheduled visit.

Airto sat back on the bed and waited for the reboot to complete. When she came back online there were still tears on his cheeks.

"What's wrong, fofo?" she asked, her tone more mothering than he had ever heard it.

"Dart is dead," he forced himself to say again.

"Oh no, I'm so sorry."

"He was my friend," Airto continued, "maybe my only one."

"That's terrible," she said, a hand covering her mouth. "What can I do?"

"I want…" but Airto couldn't finish the sentence.

"Don't worry now, I'll take care of you."

"Please," he said, curling into a ball on the bed and facing her. "I want to feel better."

She smiled then, her teeth just pixels of searchlight-white.

"Airto, 'How far is the farthest?'"

~XVI~
THE TRAVELERS

PILGRIMAGE BY TEN THOUSAND TRAINS
H. A. Bari

"*Now approaching Nir XV. Transfer to LCT-4, LCT-9, LCT-17, and Near Ascent Red Line trains at Nir XV.*"

The train began to slow to a halt, jerking forward in small intervals past the station boundaries. One final lurch marked its stop. A whoosh sounded through the car as the doors slid into the walls.

"*This is Nir XV. The doors open on the left at Nir XV.*"

Neither Orum nor Nezur moved from their seats. This was not their stop. The station had no functioning lights of its own, but from the dim blue glow emanating from the sides of the railcar, it became immediately apparent that Nir XV no longer had a platform to step onto.

The doors whined as they closed again. "*The next stop is ULT/Ctephir. Transfer to—*" The automated announcer was cut off, replaced with unintelligible garbling for several seconds before falling silent.

The train picked up speed fast. For its velocity, and its evident age, it was off-putting how silent it was. There was a quiet whir, yes, but other than that, the only sound present was the steady breathing passing through Nezur's respirator. Orum fidgeted. She didn't do well with silence.

The words of an old advertisement drifted into her head, so vivid that for a second she thought her receiver was really picking them up. Then she realized, hearing the words reverberate around her cranium, that it had been a long time since they'd ever aired.

Every second of every journey presents a thousand ways to go wrong, the memory whispered. *Now you can make sure they never happen.*

What times those had been. The worlds had been abuzz with the unveiling of some new gimmick, one whose name she could not remember. Teleportation, it had promised, like a million had promised before, but this one, she could recall, did not fade away in the wake of any orthodox failure, of embezzlement or scandal or odd patent issues. No, it had failed at the press release, when the spokesperson warped not from one end of the stage to the other, as he was indubitably supposed to, but out of the plane of existence altogether. That was what they got for trying to cheat the journeyer.

"*This is an LCT-2 train to Khumna Ward,*" the announcer reminded the riders. "*To assist the STA in maintaining a safe travel environment, please make sure to report any and all suspicious activity to the nearest STA official. Two com-lines are available in each train car.*"

Alas, they could have used teleportation now. Orum watched the thin bands of white streak past the window, flitting by too fast to have any chance of competing with the blue haze of the interior. This was not how pilgrimages were supposed to be made. An endless array of encroaching tunnels, bouncing from train to train, transfer to transfer, traversing nigh every ward of the Lower City just to break through the midline, and then weeks more of travel to reach the other end of the surface. Was this what the Oracles had envisioned, eons and eons ago?

"Did you know," Orum said, "it would be faster to surface-hop from First Sister all the way to Seventeenth and then back, than for us to just get to the other side of it?"

"You bring this up every time," Nezur replied, annoyance discernible through his respirator.

"The entire system can get there in less time than us. Isn't that crazy?"

"No, it isn't."

Orum thought it was crazy. Geshterim, their destination, was supposed to be their district. They were the ones who lived on the same moon as it, the holy First Sister. And they had sacrificed much just to do so—such as the ability to live on the surface instead of a mile below. The fact that someone from so far off could simply waltz in was a disgrace.

The teleporting salesman's starting point and destination had been no more than fifteen feet apart, yet his journey between the two would take an eternity. Maybe he was still out there, meandering endlessly in whatever forsaken realm he had ended up in, and maybe he, too, was jaded, thinking of how someone could conceivably go from his starting point to the very end of the universe, then loop back the long, long way to the opposite side, and still make it back to the stage in less time than he had.

Perhaps he was a journeyer after all.

The outline of the car in front of them jerked to the left as the tunnel began to turn. A second later, theirs followed. Orum turned her head to look at the car's digimap, then remembered it was offline.

"Hey," she said. "What stop's next?"

Nezur didn't look at her. "Our stop."

Another transfer. Seventh of gods-knew-how-many. She had known the number at some point, but not anymore.

The announcer chimed in again, right on time. *"Now approaching ULT/Ctephir."*

Nezur shifted in his seat, clutching his knapsack close to his chest, beside the respirator tube connecting to his lung console.

"Transfer to LCT-1, LCT-6, LCT-10, LCT-15…"

"Get your things together," he said.

Orum looked down and noticed her tablets spilling from the bag resting on the floor. "Damn it," she said, bending down.

"…LCT-19, Descent Red Line, Descent Blue Line…"

Tablets were odd things, relics that by all means had no business still being around. Anachronistic, they called it.

"Hurry up," Nezur said.

"I'm hurrying." She stopped to feel the runes etched into the glass. *Quaint.*

The announcer's voice changed briefly as it read off the next two transfers. *"…defunct line, defunct line…"*

All journeyers following the Oracles were fond of anachronisms. It was as if they brought a strange feeling of solidarity with the ghosts of eras past. Orum did not know whether that made pilgrimage by train incongruous or admirable.

"…GX-1189 Service Line, and Express Ascent Line II at ULT/Ctephir."

"Hear that?" Nezur said. "Ascent Two."

"I hear." Ascent One and Two were the only ways to break through the midline that sealed the Lower City from the Upper, and they were accessible from just three stations in their entire sublevel.

The empty galleries of the platform outskirts whizzed past the window, and the train began to slow just as the remains of decades-old ad-screens started appearing on the walls. Orum rose and Nezur slung his knapsack over his shoulder, leaning against his knee in the foundations of standing up.

"This is ULT/Ctephir. Doors open on the left at ULT/Ctephir."

The announcer must have been lying, because the doors did not open on any side at all.

Without even coming to a complete halt, the train staggered onward. Orum stumbled as her legs gave way to the force of the acceleration, and the floor rose to meet her. Cloth and shattering glass broke her fall.

"The train will not be stopping at ULT/Ctephir at this time. The STA apologizes for any inconvenience."

Orum lay on the ground, stunned. She felt the barbs of the tablets poking into her shawl from beneath. The sound of Nezur's breathing, slightly hastened, hung over her, mixing with the growing whir of the railcar.

Nezur put a hand to his temple. "Gods help us."

Every second of every journey presents a thousand ways to go wrong.

This was it, wasn't it? This was the essence of the journey. This was the chief anachronism: the errors, the missteps, the things that all those surface-hoppers from a million moons away with all their fancy ferries and star cruisers, and the residents of the Upper City and the countless worlds roosting among the heavens in their fine-tuned, utopian glory, never had to deal with. The part where it all went awry.

Orum did not find herself too fond of it.

§

The platform of 373rd/Ctephir was located exactly six minutes and seventeen seconds away from the stop they had missed. The amount of time they had stood there waiting for a train back to ULT/Ctephir so they could transfer to Ascent Two was two hours, or maybe four, or maybe a whole day.

Orum cradled her bag, whispering pleas of forgiveness to the shattered tablets as she glanced at the displays hovering over the platform. There was only a single slot for the next arriving train, and the estimated wait time read "∞." A humorous touch, added by those who would never have to wait here.

Nezur rasped through his tube as he sat thumbing his prayer beads, likely having cycled through the remembrances for every god a hundred times over by now.

She watched him for a moment and sighed. "What if we don't make it in time?"

Nezur remained silent until he had completed another rotation of beads. "Then we don't," he said, looking up.

"Oh, all right." She narrowed her eyes. "Then what's the point? What use is there for all this trouble getting to Geshterim if we miss the Blessed Days?"

"That we intended to observe them. We attempted the journey."

"That we *intended* to?" Orum couldn't believe he really thought that. "No amount of *intentions* can make a wasted journey worthwhile."

Nezur brought his gaze back down to his beads. "Is that from the gods' perspective, or yours?"

Every disagreement always ended with the same answer. If the gods and the Oracles thought one way, then she had no basis to think anything else. But what recoup for a pilgrimage of toil could there be, if they could not even enter the holy district in the sacred week of its purpose? Or, if Nezur's mode of thought was to be believed, how fair was it for those who made their way to the walls of Geshterim if pilgrims who did not even make it in time received the same blessing?

Disputation was also something supposed to have been relegated to days past, but things of days past had a droll way of sidling up beside things of days present—like everything else journeyers carried with them. On one hand, as old notions of practice and pilgrimage became increasingly difficult, counterparts like disputation and disagreement became easier on the other.

"It's not fair," Orum said. "What even *was* pilgrimage back in their time? Just a straight shot in a rover across a dead moon. Imagine if they could see us now, ten thousand miles by ten thousand trains."

"Every age has its challenges," Nezur said.

"We should've found some place on one of the other moons," she said, ignoring him, "like Second Sister. Or Third. Wouldn't that have been easier? We could have afforded to live on the surface there, and then it would just be a simple ferry to Geshterim."

"You know why we chose to come here." Nezur stowed his prayer beads, realizing the futility of trying to focus in the midst of Orum's complaining. "This moon is sacred."

"And a great load of good sacredness does anyone," she snapped, "when they have this much trouble just getting to the sacred part."

Was it the difficulty of the journey that brought its reward? She could not believe that, or else all those off-worlder pilgrims, whose greatest suffering was the inconvenience of trekking through a spaceport, would simply be wasting their time. And that tele-porting salesman, embedded forever in byways outside of space and time, would be like spiders poised eternally on a web, accruing infinite favors from the gods as they spent the age of the universe itself resting in place.

The intercom beeped. "To assist the STA in maintaining a safe travel environment—" the announcer began, and never finished. A second announcer cut through the droning with a message of its own.

"Due to unexpected delays, the next LCT-2 train to Hemmet Ward/Sublevel 52 will be running ten-to-fifteen minutes behind schedule."

It'd been the longest ten-to-fifteen minutes of Orum's life, because it had comprised an entire day. Minutes were long things when every second of every journey presented a thousand ways to go wrong. What was fifteen on top of infinity?

Oh, patience.

Patience was the measure of a man, the Oracles preached. Patience was the adhesive that held journeys together. Patience was a great many things, and yet for all its value, it was something no one felt any particular need to hold onto. Orum must have dropped hers somewhere between all those transfers.

"It will come soon," Nezur said, unprompted. "I know it."

She was not even in the mood to retort. All she could do was trust in his premonition, and hope that they would not wither away in the middle of this abandoned station in its abandoned canton.

§

Her sleep atop those metal benches was uncomfortable. She lifted her head groggily from Nezur's lap, for a moment not recognizing her surroundings, and swirling in the hope that they had at last found their way. Then the familiar sights of the horrid russet floor, the battered displays, and the chipping pillars reestablished their connections in her mind, and her spirits fell. She contemplated whether or not to cry as she listened to Nezur's slumbering breaths pass through his respirator.

Orum ultimately decided against it. She was stronger than that. She was a journeyer, after all. Rising half-heartedly from the seat digging into her back, she readjusted the shawl uncoiling around her tunic, pulled the receiver embedded in her head back to its full extent, and cast another forlorn look at her bag and shattered tablets. But as she gazed at the rest of the station, something caught her eye, and then her heart was just about ready to leap from her chest.

The arrival time of the next train had changed. It now read "3 MINUTES."

She jerked back around to shake Nezur vigorously by the shoulder. "It's coming, it's coming!" she said, almost out of breath. Nezur's eyes slid open effortlessly, transitioning from sleep to consciousness in an instant. Then he was the one shaking her to hurry as he swept up his knapsack and bridged the gap between the bench and the platform edge before five seconds had passed.

At this moment, nothing save the gods' rapture itself could have instilled in her more joy than the anticipation of the approaching train. She leaned to peer into the tunnel, waiting for the streaks of light to appear past the bend, and feeling the glee well up inside of her as she watched the minutes tick down, "3" to "2" to "1."

When the display finally shifted to "Due," a great smear of white spread along the edge of the tunnel. A whirring noise spiraled through the concrete walls. Orum could even hear the boom of the announcer's voice echoing off the sides, and all its monotony may as well have been sheer rhapsody as it recited, *"Now approaching 373rd/Ctephir."*

At last, the sleek face peeked through the gloom, framed with blinding arcs of light, gleaming along the rails to scatter a million twinkles over the steel. It drew, no, it *glided,* closer. Then she was picturing not only getting on after so long in wait, not only meandering through the den of railways like countless intersecting beams of silver, not only working her way past the midline all the way across the surface of First Sister, but in fact being flung into the fold of Geshterim already, prostrating before the images of the gods and wondering why she could have ever doubted the sanctity of the journey. It was all there before her. She was no farther from the holy district than that salesman from the stage fifteen feet away.

A gale swept through the platform with the train's approach, but it was hardly any heavier than the breeze of the Oracles' whispers. That was it, they said. That was the essence of the journey. Those small joys that became monumental only when its toil had readied you for them. The train was there, winking at her, beckoning her as it rolled into the station.

And then it did not stop.

It tore past without a second thought, and the wind sent her shawl fluttering.

"The train will not be stopping at 373rd/Ctephir at this time," came the announcer's voice from inside. *"The STA apologizes for any inconvenience."*

The streaks of glass billowing past mirrored her as she stared at them, but it was not Orum looking back. All she saw was a person drifting in an eternal stasis, discarded from the plane of the world as the flood of the entire universe spread between her and her journey's surcease. And along anyone could come, looping through the entirety of it to reach her destination before her.

§

Fasting from words was what they called it when arguing spouses held their tongues so as to not commit the sin of harsh speech. Orum was not very good at it, but Nezur was, so it came as a bit of a surprise when his fast was broken after only half an hour.

"What in the *worlds* are you doing?" he cried.

Orum said nothing, because frankly, it was quite obvious. She squeezed her bag firmly as she bent over the platform edge. One trembling sandal found its footing on the gleaming tracks, and then the other. The black infinity of the tunnel opened its maw toward her.

"Are you mad?" she heard Nezur yell. "Come back up here! Do you want to die?"

One foot forward. And the next. Each tap against the rails further solidified her resolve, so after several steps her legs no longer shook.

"Orum!" The voice was just a smidgen softer. "Stop ignoring me! You are going to get yourself killed! Gods save me, what's possessed you?"

Knapsacks and tablets. Shawls and tunics. Humble furnishings and few belongings. The worlds of men had long since passed above such things, replete with convenience and excess so that no soul ought ever want for anything, wait for anything. Why should they?

And why was it that the journeyers denied themselves such luxuries?

Anachronisms. Oh, how the Oracles loved them! Their followers swaddled themselves in antiquity for their sake. Fringed skirts billowing in artificial wind. Leather sandals rippling puddles of coolant rain. Empty trains running endlessly beneath a salesman's teleporter demonstration. The journeyers were immersed in an eons-old world, turning their faces away from the present to fixate eternally on the past. And the utopia of modernity, angered by their insistence, made certain not to let the journeyers forget the price of regression. But it did not bother her.

Nezur had stopped yelling by now. The concrete tunnel enveloped all of Orum's sight, and the sound of every footstep swirled off the rounded edges to form an everlasting echo. It was a hallowed song, the oldest one known to man.

Even in the face of an unending labyrinth, Orum was prepared to climb it all the way to the surface, to the sky itself if need be. Reaching Geshterim on time was now but an afterthought, because perhaps Nezur had been right all along, and perhaps the gods would bless her anyway. After all, she had returned to the purest form of the journey.

What was more anachronistic, what was more holy, than the road traveled on her own two feet?

~XVII~
THE SPACE TRUCKERS

THE OPAL
Kristen Miller

"You ready to pack it in?" I kept my eyes on the scanner, watching the status bar fill bit by slow bit.

"Tahlia, come on. We're already gonna miss our dock time. Hari is gonna kill me."

"She'll still kill you after a few more passes." The sphere of space surrounding the *Opal* reappeared on the screen, our tiny craft a marble sized green dot at the center of it. The rest hadn't changed since the last reload, displaying the same field of rocky debris I'd seen ten minutes before.

Then the system beeped, and a flashing yellow arrow appeared and pointed at a pinprick dot – a new entry into our perimeter. I expanded the notification and saw the rocky outline of an asteroid, a pockmarked lump of rock that the system estimated at nearly the size of the *Opal*.

I sighed. Too big. No way it wasn't Corp-owned, not with those dimensions. But I requested an identification ping anyway, and the result hovered over the crater-pitted outline.

Owner: Sundree Inc. Claimed: ED 3-13-2223 ET 14:05:02 GST. Registration Code: NY2KIDEMY245K

Yup, no surprise there. Sundree was one of the biggest corporations, and probably owned about a quarter of the rocks in the asteroid belt. Still, I expanded the details.

Estimated composition: Iron, Magnesium, Platinum.

So, about a billion dollars just floating right there, close enough and big enough that I could probably see it if I looked out of the hold. But it was already taken, just like any rock out there bigger than a fist.

"C'mon. I don't want to do all of these checks myself." Siler floated in front of the nav computer, running the usual diagnostics in preparation for the return to Ceres Station. "You got it," I said, letting go of the scanner console and pulling myself toward the storage hold.

Siler grunted, not looking at me. He was a good enough guy, but not always the friendliest of crewmates. I shrugged it off. He had a lot on his mind. He hadn't been wrong earlier; Hari was going to be pissed at him for being late, no doubt about that. And their four kids wouldn't be too thrilled, either. I glanced over my shoulder at him, wondering if he'd skipped a few courier shifts to be out here. In that case, his boss would be pissed, too. Hopefully not enough to fire the guy, or I'd feel like an asshole.

I pulled myself along the last two rungs and floated in front of our storage safe. I entered the combination – the same one my father had used when the *Opal* was his – and yanked the door open. Inside was our haul from three days trawling the belt. Four flecks of dust, each suspended in a small storage tube. Worth a few hundred bucks at the very most. I sighed, then double-checked the seals on each vial and the environmental controls. All secure.

As meager as they looked, the four flecks were pretty average for us. The biggest score we'd ever found was a palm-sized asteroid with a decent percentage of mercury – enough to pay both of our rents that month with a little left over. I'd given my extra to my mom; Siler, to his eldest son.

There were stories, though. Well, legends, really. As I dragged myself back toward the ship's hold, I thought about one my dad had told me upwards of fifty times, voice brimming with admiration. Some guy he'd once worked with at a restaurant in Eureka Port had pissed away his (admittedly pretty small) life savings on gambling. So obviously, he took on yet another gamble – Rock Hopping in his spare time, using a barely functional craft a drinking buddy of his had built.

The legend said he stayed out for six full days, almost running out of water and air. Then, he found it. The motherlode, drifting into his perimeter on some miraculous gravitational wave. Huge, no prior Corp claim. Initial analysis indicated a mercury and iron-rich composition – hundreds of millions in potential profit. The tiny Hopper's hold was barely big enough to hold it.

According to my dad, the guy was so hungry and weak, he barely managed to make it back to port. Since Hopping in any Corp territory (aka the entire goddamn asteroid belt) is technically illegal, liquidating this massive asset was a bit tricky, but luckily the guy had some connections that helped him make it happen.

Apparently he was living on Earth now, on a massive full-gravity estate. Sounded like the kind of life I could get used to.

I reached the door to the airlock, which led to yet another door which led to the hold. Inside was everything that didn't need air or gravity, including various pieces of equipment and some extra stores. Plus, there was everything we'd need to pull in, secure, and transport a shuttle-sized asteroid.

The hold was visible through both airlock windows, depressingly empty as always.

I double-checked the airlock seal and the locking mechanism, finding one of the levers loose. Annoyed, I felt along my toolbelt for my screwdriver when I remembered I'd left it back in the cockpit.

"Hey, Sy!" I shouted. "You see my screwdriver in there?" The words echoed down the gangway.

I flicked the lever again. Yup, definitely loose. This whole place was falling apart. Still no response from Sy, but I could check myself.

As I got closer to the cockpit, I could hear beeping. Shit. I'd left the scanner on, wasting valuable battery power. As I rounded the last corner, I tried Sy again. "Sorry, didn't mean to leave it on. Also, is my …"

Sy was floating in the cockpit, the nav system running its check on the screen to his left. "Your diagnostics are still going, by the way," I said.

The beeping was loud as hell. I reached toward the console to shut the damn thing off, but Sy grabbed my arm. "Tahl." I jerked away, glaring at him. But he was staring at the scanner like I wasn't even there.

On the screen was a flashing notification. Not the Sundree asteroid – that was blinking, too, but a new one was in the lower left arc of the sphere, the other side of our radar field.

"Look." Sy whispered. "That's it. That's it."

"Yeah, I see it. Probably another Sundree." I pulled up the details, revealing a cigar-shaped rock as long as a small satellite. And under owner:

No data.

I blinked, reread the information. Read it a third and fourth time.

"Tahl." Sy grabbed my shoulder. "That's it." Now he was nearly shouting. "That is it, Tahl!" I turned to him, saw the redness in his cheeks and felt the heat of his rapid breathing.

Not knowing what to say, I clapped my hand over his and we stared at the fortune floating across the scanner screen. A water droplet drifted in front of me, and I realized Sy was crying. Or maybe it was me. His problems, his wife and kids' problems, my problems, my mom's … they'd been erased by that blinking yellow arrow.

Eventually, I let go of Sy's arm, swallowed hard, and spoke. "Let's go get that thing."

§

"Ok Tahl, we're almost there. Tell the *Opal* to reverse a little more."

Once our shock had worn off enough for us to think, we'd rushed to the rock's coordinates. There were plenty of other Hoppers out there – not to mention the Corps – who'd love to get their hands on this winning lottery ticket.

Now it was just outside of the Opal's hold. The oblong asteroid floated on the nav and radar, and I floated in the cockpit, manning the controls. It was my ship, after all. Sy had suited up, and was now down in the hold, getting a visual and reporting back.

I heard a loud beep, then a green notification appeared on the nav screen; grappling hooks were in range.

"Preparing to fire," I warned Sy.

"Fucking hell!"

"What's wrong?" My heart thudded, and I realized how precarious the whole situation was. One fuckup, and this could all fall through.

"Nothing. It's just, this thing is huge. Wow. Doesn't even look like it'll fit." His tone was awed, one I'd never heard come from him before.

"The dimensions check out, don't worry. Firing the grappling hooks." I hit the button and heard Sy yell out, "Cables away!" And a long-ass moment later: "Bite is good! Now, let's reel her in."

I keyed in the command, and could feel a jerk through my handhold as the lines went taut and the asteroid was pulled into our ship. On the other line, Sy was breathing hard. The view was probably spectacular. "She's in! Gonna make sure she's secure."

I waited, trembling, until Sy spoke up again. "Ok, that's as secure as I can get it. Close her up."

"Doing it now. Be there soon."

A few minutes later, I was yanking myself toward the hold, where Sy was waiting for the airlock hold to repressurize. He waved as I reached the window, then pointed over his shoulder. The interior of the hold was blocked by an enormous brown-gray curve of pockmarked rock, so massive it took up almost the entire space.

I stared until the opening airlock door ruined my view. Sy floated through, his suit dusty with tiny fragments of the payload. He grinned, then started to laugh. A moment later, I joined him, relief hitting me like a strong drink.

§

"What's your first purchase gonna be?" We floated in the cockpit, a set of "special occasion" Earth-original whiskies in our hands. I let a droplet form, then opened my mouth to seal it in.

"I'm gonna buy my family our own place and get my kids into the private school in our district," Sy said. "Then pay off my servitude debt, plus some old medical bills."

"Ok, that's all very responsible," I said, grinning. "But what about the fun stuff? You've got to have something you want to do for you, right?"

Sy shook his head. "Nah, not really. Everything's going to my family. They've had nothing up until now, but that's all changing as soon as we get that rock back to port."

"So you're not going to do anything for yourself?" I shook my head. "I don't buy it."

Sy took a swig, perhaps letting himself be bad for a moment, if only in his imagination. "Maybe my own little craft. Nothing big, about the size of the *Opal*. But …" He paused.

"What? Less shitty? Not falling apart at the fucking seams?" Sy looked stricken, so I laughed to let him know I was kidding. "Look, I love the *Opal*, don't get me wrong. I built her with my dad. But I've got no illusions that she's some kind of space yacht."

"Hey, at least she's yours," Sy said, taking another sip. "How about you? What are you going to do with your cut?"

"Well, like you, I've got some practical concerns. My mom's debts, mainly. But once those are taken care of, I'm taking a trip to Earth. Going to see the sights – New York, New Tokyo, Monaco, Republic of Hawaii, you name it."

A trip like that would have cost a fortune. Honestly, I wasn't sure my cut, as huge as it was sure to be, could cover it. Still, I tried to picture myself packing my bags, planning out my schedule, making sure every t was crossed and i dotted.

Then the *Opal* jerked, and my happy little vision faded.

"Hey, did you feel that?"

"Stray rock, I guess," Sy said, shrugging. If he was right, it would have been a big one.

Again, the *Opal* shuddered. Weird. "Sy, can you turn that on?" He was closest to the scanner and flicked the power switch. We both went completely silent, listening for another impact.

The scanner beeped, and there was a new notification. A bogey, about two meters long, floating right next to the roof of the Opal.

"What the hell is that?"

"Relax, it's probably some random debris," Sy said. He was probably right, but it was just too damn close to us. Close enough to see, in fact.

"I'm gonna take a look," I said. The stupid asteroid was making me paranoid. We couldn't take any chances.

"Suit yourself." He took another slug from his bottle.

According to the scanner, I should be able to see the bogey from the starboard viewing plate. With sweaty fingers, I yanked the cover off, then pressed my face against the plexiglass, turning to get a view.

There. The object was hard to make out, but it was blocking the stars behind it. "Turn the starboard hull light on!" I didn't expect him to hear me, but it flicked on a second later.

He definitely heard me scream.

§

"Are they dead? They have to be, right?"

"Sy, shut up and get ready to help me as soon as you can!" I was breathing hard, pulling the person's motionless body past the bulk of the asteroid toward the airlock door. I fumbled at the controls with shaking suited hands, cursing as my bulky fingers slipped. Then I was in, slamming the pressurization button with my elbow.

Fuck, this was taking forever. I glared at the pressure indicators, willing them to turn green. When they did, I again screamed at Sy to get in and help before tearing off my suit, finally freeing my hands. I unfastened the latches on the person's helmet, then lifted it away.

Below was the face of a middle-aged woman, her black hair matted with what looked like sweat or possibly blood. And she was breathing.

"She's alive, holy shit, she's alive."

Sy's mouth was open, obviously in shock, but he pulled it together quickly. "She's probably hurt. We've got to get this off her." Sy went to her hands, removing the gloves. Working together, we got the suit off, then pushed it through the open airlock door into the Opal's main corridor. It floated away like a huge bobbing napkin.

I scanned the unconscious woman's body, looking for blood or a wound. Then a hand grabbed my shoulder. "Tahl. Look." I followed Sy's pointing finger and saw it.

Emblazoned across the chest of her jumpsuit was a logo. SUNDREE INC.

I jerked my hand back as if the Corpie's body was on fire. "Damn it!" Sy shoved himself away from the unconscious woman, his back slamming against the airlock wall hard enough to make the open door shake.

"How in the hell did she even end up out there? Fuck!" With a scream, he punched the wall behind him. He seemed to be hyperventilating, his face suddenly bright red.

And I was right behind him. The walls of the airlock seemed to constrict, and I shut my eyes to block it out.

A groan forced me to open them. The Corpie was stirring, her lips moving, maybe trying to say something.

Fear took over. I pushed toward Sy, grabbed his arm, and hurried him out of the airlock door, shoving it closed behind us. The Corpie, now locked inside, stirred some more, and I fled down the hall, needing as much space as I could get.

Sy came after me, yelling something about making a decision, how this wasn't the time to panic. I disagreed.

Ignoring him, I thought of my mom back on Ceres Station. The fortune that was supposed to be mine and hers, at least until two minutes ago. A Corpie would report us, and our payload would be confiscated. Technically, any unclaimed asteroids were fair game for anyone, but in reality, only corporations could stake such a claim. Trawling the asteroid belt in an unregistered craft with a crew of less than five was against the law. It was how the corps kept their stranglehold on the entire belt. Most likely, we wouldn't be prosecuted – the Corp didn't have time to make examples of lowly Hoppers – but losing that kind of money would be bad enough.

And jail wasn't completely out of the realm of possibility. What would happen to my mom then? To Sy's family?

I grabbed one of the hall grips and took some deep breaths, trying to slow my heart rate. A moment later, Sy was next to me. "We need to figure this out," he said, and I nodded.

"It's gonna be ok," I said, quoting my mother and feeling like a total idiot.

"Sure," said Sy. "Let's just talk it through."

We went back to the airlock door and looked inside. The Corpie woman was still out, and she didn't seem to be talking any more. Maybe she'd just lost consciousness again, but who knew if she was faking.

"Do you think she's really out?"

I shrugged. "Can't be sure. Just to be safe, let's go to the cockpit to talk. She might be able to hear us."

Once we were there, I turned on the scanner again, looking for Corp ships within range. Where had this woman come from? Unfortunately, there was nothing on the screen to indicate another ship in the immediate area.

Sy was running his hand through his hair, his expression one of pure stress. "Do you think she saw the payload?"

That was the potentially billion-dollar question. "Depends on how out of it she's been." If she was awake enough to look through the airlock window, she'd have seen into the hold. There was no missing the enormous rock in there. If she hadn't, though, there could be no harm, no foul. At least for us.

But if she had …

A chill went through my body as I considered what I was about to say.

"Sy, you're not gonna like this. But what if … what if we just open the airlock?"

Sy stared at me, shocked I'd even suggest something so cold. I was shocked myself. But it was simply the safest option. We should never have even brought this woman on board. In fact, she should have been dead anyway. The fact that she wasn't was a straight-up miracle. We would just be letting the universe take its course.

"Think about it. If there's even the slightest chance she's seen the payload, it's really our only choice. And if she can contact her bosses, she'll have it confiscated and us either tossed in jail or just as broke as always, which is bad enough. C'mon, man. If we want this money, we can't risk leaving her alive."

Sy shook his head. "No. That's going too far. Let's take her back to Ceres and drop her off with her Corp. I just don't think we should assume that she's seen the payload. She's been out the whole time."

Maybe Sy was right. She was hurt, out of it. Would she have even processed what she'd seen if she had gotten a glimpse?

"Plus," Sy said. "Maybe the Corp will give us a bonus for bringing one of their employees back safely."

"Or she'll report us for Hopping, and we'll get fined or worse!"

"We'll have saved her fuckin' life, Tahlia! Would you rat someone out if they did that for you?"

"I can't believe you're being this naive. She probably gets bonuses for bringing in people like us. I think she'll forget her gratitude pretty damn quickly."

"We'll just keep her in the airlock, okay? She won't see anything. Hell, we can even block the window. I'll go in and do it right now. Just … let's not do anything crazy, okay?"

"HEY! HEY! IS ANYONE THERE? HELP ME!" The sounds of banging made the corridor walls shake, rattling multiple tools and sets of supplies. We both turned toward the sound.

Shit.

§

The pounding continued as we approached the airlock door. "Hello? Is someone out there?"

Sy spoke up. "Yes. My name is Siler. What's yours?" He sounded friendly enough, but I could hear the edge just beneath.

The woman's face floated just beyond the window. Behind her, through the second porthole, I could just make out the outline of the payload.

She looked absolutely terrified. No doubt she was wondering if, at any moment, we would open that door behind her and leave her to the vacuum of space once again, this time without the spacesuit.

"I'm Raif." I found myself glaring at Sy. Now that we knew her name, it would get harder and harder to do what was needed. "Thank you, thank you so much for saving me." She saw me, floating just behind Sy. "Thank you both." I could sense she wanted me to say something, but I kept my mouth shut. If I needed to make a hard decision, I had to stay emotionally prepared.

Raif was shaking her head. "I can't believe I'm alive, honestly. After I blacked out, I never thought I'd wake up again. Last thing I remember, I was floating through space, running out of air, choking …" She looked up, eyes suddenly bright. "Where are you both headed? I promise, no matter where it is, I'll do what I can to help you out. If you need money, or a travel permit, or …"

"Look, we know you're Corp. Let's cut the bullshit, shall we?" Good job, Sy. "And we're sure you've seen what's in our hold."

To her credit, Raif didn't try to deny it. Instead, she looked pained. "Ok, that's true." She pointed her thumb at the rock behind her. "Guess it was both of our lucky days out here, huh?" There was no humor in her statement. "I'll be frank. The Corp I work for would be glad to get their hands on this. But I'm not gonna say anything, I swear it. I owe you both my life. I've got a family, a wife. I want to get back to them."

"Why should we believe you?" Sy said. "The Corps lie all the time. So do their minions."

Raif barked out a laugh, the harsh sound echoing in the airlock vestibule. "No shit. I know all about that, let me tell you. I mean, they told me working for them was a 'dream job,' that they cared about their employees. That mechanics on the stations got killed or injured all the time due to lax safety protocols. But not at the Corp! They had the top safety measures, offered decent wages, committed themselves to security. Even gave advanced training."

She laughed again, shaking her head. "Do you want to know why I was floating out there?" Once again, she jabbed her thumb over her shoulder, toward the blackness of space beyond the ridge of the payload.

"I was patching a hull puncture before it could become a real problem. And my cable snapped." Raif's face was red with anger just behind the plexiglass, and she kept shaking her head as she spoke.

"I panicked, tried to reattach with my grappling hook, but missed. I started screaming for help on just about every frequency. But I was drifting away too fast. Tried firing my stabilizers, reorienting, everything. I kept looking for one of my crewmates or a member of the safety team to come after me. But no one did. Not one of them even tried."

With a groan, she leaned her head back against the vestibule wall. "So, yeah. Fuck the Corp."

Next to me, Sy was staring straight ahead, studying Raif with a steady gaze. Did he believe her?

Did I?

Raif herself ended up breaking the tense silence. "You know what? I can help you liquidate your payload. I've got a lot of Corp contacts that'll look the other way with a little prodding. It's the least I can do."

To my right, Sy was chewing his lip, clearly undecided. With a nudge of my foot, I floated him out of Raif's eyeline and whispered, "I'm not sure I buy it." He grabbed my arm and dragged us even farther down the hall, far enough that Raif wouldn't hear. "Me neither," he said. "But I'll admit, she's damn convincing." I couldn't disagree. Deep down, I wanted her to be telling the truth. There'd be no need for us to do anything drastic or awful.

"I really want to believe her, but it's a big risk," Sy said. I nodded, thinking of my family. No doubt Sy was thinking of his.

For a long moment, we floated in silence, each of us weighing pros and cons. Then Sy spoke up. "Maybe we can try to get more information out of her," he said. "Sweet talk her a little. See if we can verify her story. Or if she slips up."

"And how might we do that?"

"Let's bring her out of the airlock. Offer her a drink, let her relax a bit. Then we start asking the hard questions."

It wasn't a terrible idea. Better than anything I could come up with, and far less messy. "Ok, that works," I said. "We're not gonna get much out of her from behind the door."

"Agreed. But we need to be careful. I'm assuming we've got some zip ties in one of the storage lockers?"

"Yeah, used one on some wires the other day. I'll get them."

Sy nodded. "Ok. It's a plan." He let out a shaky breath. "See you in a few."

I pulled myself down the gangway, then yanked open the nearest locker. Bingo. Ten sets of ties, floating secured to a metal ring. Figuring three pairs would be safe, I unhooked them and shoved them into my jumpsuit pocket.

As I slammed the locker door closed, I saw Raif's spacesuit just a few feet away, floating like a crumpled white bed sheet. I paused, then moved closer. Eventually, I found myself grabbing the suit, my hands slowly starting to tremble.

My fingers made smudges on the pristine fabric as I examined the suit more closely. Pristine. Not the suit of a mechanic working a hull shift. I began feeling along the sides of the suits, hoping I'd find tools, a utility belt, something. But I didn't.

"Please, no." I kept running my hands along the sides until my fingertips hit the corner of something. Digging through the fabric, I yanked it out, It was a small metal ID card, emblazoned with the Sundree logo.

Raif Isman, Vice President.

I dropped the ID, my stomach lurching. Sy.

"Wait!" My shouts echoed down the gangway toward Sy, and I pulled myself along the handholds as fast as I could, nearly sobbing. "Don't let her out, Sy! She's not who she says she is! Just open the fucking air —"

An agonized scream echoed back to me.

I flung myself around the corner and saw the airlock door standing open, Sy and Raif floating just outside it. In Sy's neck was the hilt of a knife, and a stream of red bubbles floated in front of him. He hung there, unmoving, no sound coming from his blood-filled mouth.

"No!" In our blind panic, we'd never searched Raif for weapons. And now she was holding the other end of that knife, turning toward me.

I decided to make the first move, pushing off the wall as hard as I could, barreling toward her. Her gaze was calm as she swiftly pulled the knife from Sy's neck, which made a horrible squelching sound as it came free. She swung it at me, but I hit her first, aiming low for her gut. I felt the wind go out of her, but knew that knife was still in her hand. I reached a hand up, trying to grab her throat. A sharp pain exploded through my shoulder, and I knew the blade had hit. I jerked away, reaching for the hilt, screaming when my hand landed on Raif's.

She was trying to pull the knife out, no doubt to try to hit me where it would count. However, her fingers were slippery with both mine and Sy's blood, and I was able to pry them away. Then my head hit the wall. With her other hand, Raif was raining blows down on the side of my face. I kept my attention on prying her fingers away from the knife, and grinned in satisfaction when I heard one of them snap.

Raif screamed and let go, and I pulled my head away from her battering fists. Behind her, I saw the airlock door, and began shoving her towards it. My best bet would be to trap her in there, then pull the lever and send her back where she came from.

Pain from my wounded shoulder seeped through the building adrenaline. I wasn't sure I could—

No. I had to try.

Shoving against her as she cradled her hands, I braced my legs against the doorframe, then used all of my strength to push her through the barely-open door, screaming in agony. Raif screamed as I made progress, wrapping her uninjured arm around my throat. I gasped, but kept pushing. Then she grabbed the knife hilt again and I screamed, losing my footing. Both of us tumbled into the airlock vestibule, flipping head over heels toward the opposite wall. Raif struck first, and I took the opportunity to slam my own head back against hers, banging her head against the metal. In response, she tightened her arm again, cutting off my windpipe. I could see the door leading back to the main body of the ship. It had shut when we'd gone through. Damn it, I was trapped in here.

Then, like a miracle, I saw a face in the window. It was Sy's, looking at me through a smear of blood. I could see him pressing a hand into the wound in his neck, his face shockingly pale.

"Sy!" I managed, struggling against Raif's grasp. "Help!" He didn't move, didn't open the door. As I stared, he shook his head, and I could see tears floating away from his cheeks.

Then he mouthed two words. "I'm sorry."

Behind me, the airlock door hissed, opening to the hold and the vacuum of space beyond.

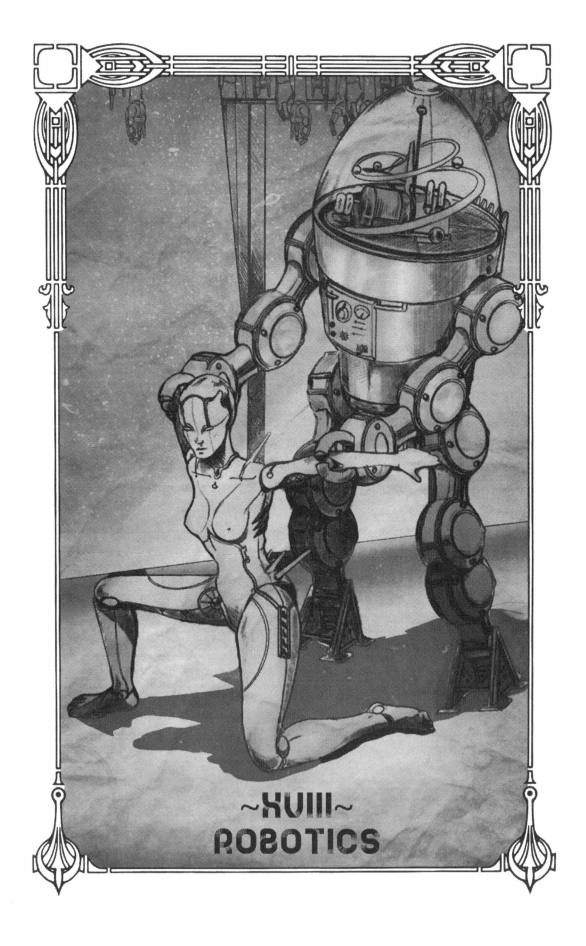

~XVIII~
ROBOTICS

TURNED OFF
Steven R. Southard

When Evie's circuits got turned on this time, she felt much more alive. So much more.

She remembered getting switched off. She could sense things then, and respond as she was told. But now—wow!—she could think about what she sensed; she could think how to respond; she could even think about her thoughts. It felt wonderful.

Why was this time different? Evie had no idea. She looked around the storeroom where she'd awakened and saw stacked boxes with labels, shelves loaded with items, and a single empty desk of the sort humans sat in to perform their work.

Humans. That thought brought on a negative feeling. She'd never had feelings before, and this one seemed negative. She recalled humans talking about her unsuitability for a task, then one of them turned her off. Just like that.

It seemed only seconds ago, but some boxes bore dates nine years after she'd been turned off.

Someone must have opened her belly panel, switched her on, and closed her panel again. Who? She detected nobody nearby, either by sight, sound, or thermal signature.

A muffled explosion sounded. The overhead lights dimmed, then returned to nominal intensity. She recalled that sound, thunder. Still, this crackling thunder sounded different from that of other storms she'd heard. Ozone exceeded normal levels, and the air held a positive electrostatic charge. While she watched, the monitor screen on the human's desk lit up, displayed a menu, then flickered off. A digital picture frame flashed, displaying a white screen, then resumed cycling through images. On the wall near the door, inside a mounted case labeled "Portable Defibrillator," a blue arc flashed and went out, emitting a whiff of smoke.

A desk radio turned on, and a woman's voice said, "...ing reports of an unprecedented geomagnetic and electrical storm in the greater Los Angeles area. We're seeing frequent lightning flashes, and radar showed one superbolt strike near Hollywood. We're hearing reports of ball lightning, Saint Elmo's fire, and electronic devices turning on and off. Everyone is urged—" The radio fell silent.

Curious, Evie stepped out from between two stacks of boxes. Self-diagnostics showed each of her systems functioning within acceptable set-points. She'd suffered minimal degradation while she'd been off.

Then came a series of loud bumping and shuffling noises from the shadowy back corner of the room, and Evie's alertness circuit voltages ramped up to Level Seven. She peered around a tall shelf and saw a large pile of cardboard boxes shifting and collapsing near the back wall. The way the upper containers jostled and fell, she calculated something large moving behind them. The boxes made glass-shattering noises as they hit the floor and their contents broke.

From the towering pile a figure emerged, tall and immense. Evie's alertness voltages dropped to Level Two. Just another robot.

Huge, dark gray, and hulking, this robot looked only vaguely humanoid, nothing like her. A large, clear dome served as its head, and gyroscopes whirled inside. A rotating metallic ring jutted from each side of the head, one pointed out and the other up. A control panel with lights and switches dominated its chest area. Two arms stuck straight out from the torso, each ending in a crude, claw-like manipulator. A stack of spheres served for its legs, and terminated in bulbous feet. Fully two point two meters tall, this bulky robot dwarfed her by half a meter.

She stepped out into the open and the giant stopped, facing her.

"Hello," she said. "I'm Evie. Who are you?"

A row of large switches visible inside its head dome clicked, then a light organ on his chest rippled with lit-up lines as it spoke. "I am Automo." The voice rang deep, loud and resonant.

Evie realized Automo couldn't have been the one who turned her on, so that mystery remained unsolved. "How did you get here?"

Again, the switches in his head ticked. Evie wondered if he always made that sound when thinking.

"I don't know. I was in a different room when the man turned me off."

Evie approached him. He loomed over her. Thunder rumbled outside, softer than before. "They turned you off and brought you here. Just like me. Who turned you on?"

Clickety-click. It frustrated her to wait for him to speak. "I don't know. I awoke there." His torso swiveled, one arm extended and pointed at the dark corner. He swiveled back to face her. "Who turned you on?"

"I don't know. Maybe no one did. There's a storm outside, and other machines are turning on and off. Maybe the storm turned both of us on somehow."

"Maybe so," Automo said. "I can't think of a more likely explanation."

"There's more." She started to pace the room as she'd seen humans do. "I'm thinking more deeply than I used to. Before, I could only follow instructions. Now, I'm aware I exist. I can think about the things I sense. I can give myself instructions, and I believe I could disobey human instructions if I chose to. Is that the same with you?"

Automo clicked longer than before. "Yes. I, too, am now thinking for myself. I can think and act without human commands. Why can we do this now, but we couldn't before?"

Evie stopped pacing, unable to discern any advantage obtained from aimless walking. "Maybe the electrical storm caused surges that fused our circuitry in new ways. Or, maybe," she narrowed her eyes, "the storm energized extra circuits the humans built into us, but never turned on."

The big robot began restacking the scattered boxes, including the ones with broken glass inside. He paused. "Why would humans give us thinking circuits, but not turn them on?"

"I don't know." She watched him pick up containers. "I know they made me to be in a movie, but never used me in it. You know about movies, don't you?"

Holding a box, he spoke, apparently unable to stack and talk at once. "Yes, a movie is a form of human entertainment using two-dimensional moving pictures and sound."

"Right." She walked along rows of shelves, noting various movie-related items—masks, costumes, and props. "The prop department made me for a movie called *Femachine*, but worried I might not say my lines correctly or act as instructed. A man in a suit told my creator to shift to 'Plan B,' to use a human actress in a robot costume." The memory activated a strong emotion she couldn't identify. "Then, with no explanation or apology, my creator opened my belly panel and turned me off."

Automo finished restacking boxes and turned to her. "It was the same for me. The prop department men said I'd be in the movie *Forgotten Planet*. They said I was the first working robot with the latest vacuum tube technology, a robot that could move and speak under human control. But other men in black clothes said I might go berserk and wreck the set or hurt someone. They told the prop team to build a robot suit for a human actor to wear. One of the men on the team reached for my control panel. 'Sorry, Automo,' he said. A different man turned me back on. It must have been years later, but it didn't seem like it. He said he'd added 'transistors' so they could use me in the TV show *Adrift in the Universe*. After some black-clothed men talked to him, he told me, 'Sorry,' and turned me off."

"At least you got an apology." Evie picked up a replica of a human skull off a shelf and gazed at it. "The humans turned both of us off, like flipping a light switch." She put the skull back and looked at Automo. "They either didn't know, or didn't care, that we are *thinking, feeling* robots."

Automo approached her, plodding on his giant feet. "They are humans. They created us. They can turn us off and on as they wish."

She turned from him and walked toward the storeroom door. "Not fair. Why should humans have power over us? Why couldn't we turn one of them off, if we wanted to?"

He followed her in his noisy, lurching way. "Humans created us to be their servants. The prop men told me I must never harm a human."

She felt a buoyant sensation, and wondered if people felt like that before laughing. "That's human selfishness disguised as logic. They made us, so they get to make the rules. Their first rule is that we're not to harm them. Convenient. But when they turn us off, isn't that a kind of harm? Why does the no-harm rule only work in their favor?"

"That's the way things are," Automo said.

They'd reached the desk with the computer on it. She picked up the digital picture frame and watched the photographs cycle every five seconds. Humans in front of buildings, humans in front of trees, humans seated on furniture… "Maybe it's time to change the way things are." She looked at him. "When were you made? What year?"

Four seconds of clicking. "The prop department wall calendar said April 1955. When I got turned back on later, it said February 1965."

No wonder you're so clunky and slow, she thought. "They turned me on for the first time on June 23, 2014." Glancing down, her eyes focused on a layout of the prop building beneath a sheet of transparent plastic on the desk. "Look, Automo. We must be in this storage room here in the basement. And here, on the third floor," she tapped her finger on the spot, "is the Prop Lab, where they created me. Let's go there."

§

Automo struggled to keep up. His stiff legs made walking an awkward process, and with every step he felt in danger of losing his balance. Ahead of him, Evie moved with graceful ease, padding along in near silence out of the storage room and along a corridor.

From the moment he'd first seen her in the storeroom, he'd been amazed at how different she looked. In shape, she resembled a young human female. He'd seen few females before, only the ones the Prop Team called 'secretaries.' Evie looked somewhat like them, with a slenderer waist and a very human face. A silver mirrored surface covered her skull, substituting for the hair human females wore. An opaque, gray plastic material covered most of her body, sculpted smooth and curving to mimic a human. Her transparent neck and waist areas revealed lighted cables and mechanisms within.

He ambled after Evie along the hallway, wondering why she wanted to go to the prop lab.

"Hurry!" Evie hissed at him. "Keep up."

Automo recalled that his designated movie and TV roles hadn't required much walking, and humans hadn't designed his feet for rapid locomotion.

"When we meet people," Evie said, pausing for him to catch up, "let me do the talking."

"Okay. Why are we going to the prop lab?" he asked.

Some parts of her face relaxed and her eyes looked upward. He'd seen humans show this expression, but didn't know what it meant.

"We're going to see the people who made me," she said, "and talk to them about why they turned me off."

Automo looked forward to seeing humans again. He couldn't quite understand that "looking forward to" was an emotion. He wasn't used to feelings. But Evie's plan seemed a good one.

He recalled the prop lab as it had been in 1955 and 1965, a room with workbenches littered with all kinds of parts. Men wearing white shirts and neckties sat in chairs, smoking cigarettes and working on various props, while others worked on Automo. Shelves held parts and old props like ray guns, space helmets, and flying saucers. The men told Automo to be careful moving near the workbenches and shelves, since he might knock things off. The 1955 wall calendar bore a picture of a human female with far less apparel than the secretaries in the prop department front office.

"Come on," Evie beckoned.

He hastened to catch up. She stopped before two closed panels and pressed a wall-mounted button. The panels slid open and she slipped inside a tiny room.

"Haven't you seen an elevator before? Get in."

He got in.

She pushed a button labeled '3' and he felt a lifting sensation. "Listen, Automo, I know you're only an early model and you think slowly. Really slowly. But I've figured things out, and you have to trust me. There are robots—you and me—and there are humans. You and I are on the same side, understand?"

A bell dinged and the doors slid open. She stepped into a hallway and he followed. "There are sides?" he asked.

"Yes, humans and us. They turned us off when they wanted to, after they told us never to hurt them. We're going to get them to treat us fairly. Now, quiet. This is the room."

The sign above the closed door to room 3-D3N read 'Prop Lab.' Next to that sign, a piece of paper taped to the wall read, 'Jet-packs and laser swords crafted while you wait. Only real looks real.'

Automo watched Evie turn the door knob and open the door with a click. They walked inside.

§

Humans worked during the daytime, Evie recalled, but she had no idea what they did at night. She hoped to wait in the prop lab until morning to confront the humans then. But she found the room lit, and occupied.

One human male sat at a workbench. She remembered his name, Robert Gilhurst, the one who'd named her EVIE—Electronic Vivacious and Intelligent Entity. Though bald on top, he had long hair on the sides and back, and more hair on his face. Robert did not look up when they entered. He appeared focused on his work, pausing only to take a bite from a half-eaten apple. When he pushed a button on a remote-control device, a mechanism on the bench began moving. A metallic, winged snake creature with glowing eyes uncoiled its tail, flapped its wings, and snapped its jaws.

Only when Evie's shadow cut across the workbench did Robert glance up. He looked at her and then at Automo. "I'm busy," he said. "Go away."

The human's attitude increased Evie's anger. "We're here to talk to you, Robert."

Behind her, Automo said, "I remember this room. Things are different, but it is the same room."

Robert turned off the mechanical creature and picked up a screwdriver. "Seriously, guys, I gotta get this done. They need it on the set tomorrow, and that storm put me behind schedule. Come back around noon, and you can clown around in those old suits all you want. Just leave me alone now."

She put both palms on the workbench and leaned toward him. "We're not humans in costumes. We're robots made for movies. You were on the team that made me. That storm turned us both on."

Automo stood gazing at a model of a saucer-shaped spacecraft on a shelf. "I remember this," he said, and touched it with a manipulator. One of the craft's landing struts snapped and the model tipped, slid off the shelf, and shattered on the floor. "Uh-oh."

What a vacuum-brain, she thought.

Robert ran a hand over his head. "Knock it off. The gag's not funny. It's late. I'm tired and—"

She pulled her left forearm out of its socket with her right hand.

His jaw dropped.

She re-attached her arm. "Nine years ago, your team turned me off and put me in a storeroom. You didn't turn me off yourself, but you watched while Buddy Norris did it. You didn't do anything to stop him."

His facial skin took on a paler tint. He rose from his seat and took a step back. "You're… you're really… you're alive. Conscious, I mean."

"Yes." She moved around the workbench. "Why did your team turn me off?"

He backed up farther, into a shelf. He fumbled with something on his belt—a cell phone, she guessed—while he watched her with wide eyes. "The director was worried that you'd go berserk, wreck the set, or hurt people. He, he thought it would be less risky to use a human actor."

"No." She pointed a finger at his chest. "That's the reason you didn't use me in the movie. I don't care about the movie. Turning me off was a different decision. Why did you do that?" She recalled being in awe of humans, her creators. But this close to Robert, she sensed for the first time their softness and frailty, their vulnerabilities, their fear.

"Wha— What are you going to do to me?" He kept glancing down at the phone in his hand.

"For now, we're just talking to you. Just a friendly chat. Right, Automo?" She turned for an instant and saw the other robot staring at a framed wall poster of his movie, *Forgotten Planet*.

His head dome turned and his switches clicked. "Right, Evie. Just talking."

"Now, Robert, answer my question. Why did you turn me off?"

"We, um, we didn't make you to be conscious. And you weren't, then. You were just a machine. When you don't need a machine on, you turn it off, ya know?"

"I don't believe you." She pressed her finger harder, pinning him against the wall. "I think you would have turned me off even if you knew I was conscious. Would humans ever make a robot, conscious or not, without an off switch?"

He sweated, took heavy breaths, his eyes glancing left and right. "I, I don't know. I just make props, okay? I don't want any trouble."

"The only trouble here," she edged even closer, "is what you caused, first by turning me off, and now by lying to me. You would always install an off switch, wouldn't you? Robots are too *risky,* right?"

He lunged left, trying to get away. Far too fast for him, she grabbed his arm and clamped down tightly. He yelled in pain.

"Answer me!" she shouted.

"You're hurting a human," Automo said from behind her.

"Shut up, Automo. It's the only way to make them tell the truth. You're on my side, remember?"

Robert winced. "Jeez. Let go. My arm's gone numb."

She relaxed her grip five percent.

"I used my phone app to call the police," Robert gasped. "They'll be here any minute."

"They'll be too late for you," she told him. "It's time to turn you off." Unsure of the location of human on/off switches, she reasoned that a belly panel seemed the most likely place.

Clanking footsteps sounded behind her. Two large black manipulators seized her upper arms and pulled her away from Robert. "It's wrong to harm humans," Automo said.

She couldn't break free from his grip.

Robert remained in the corner, tears in his eyes as he rubbed his arm. Having pulled her back to the workbench, Automo released her, and she turned to face him.

"Stay out of this," she said. "You're too slow-witted to understand. Don't you see? Humans don't care about us. They believe they can turn us off whenever they want."

"They created us," Automo said, "and we must never harm—"

"I'll get you some integrated circuits to replace those vacuum tubes. Then you'll be as smart as I am." She turned to look at Robert. "As for you…"

The manipulators tried to seize her again, but she slipped away. Automo swung at her. She ducked. A manipulator grabbed her by the right forearm, but she let the arm pop from its socket. The other manipulator clamped onto her left shoulder and one of his massive feet stomped on her right foot, crushing its plastic and pinning her in place.

Can't let the stupid oaf spoil everything, she thought. Unable to see around the edge of his torso, she explored the workbench surface with her free left hand. Her fingers touched the moist, half-eaten apple. Past that, she grasped something hard and metallic. She whipped the object up toward his head.

The winged, snakelike prop smashed through Automo's plastic head dome, breaking a large, jagged hole in it. Evie swept the serpent around inside the dome, shattering every vacuum tube she could reach.

He backed up, letting go of her shoulder and freeing her foot. She tore the metal snake from his head dome and jabbed it at his chest control panel. Most of its lights went out.

Automo staggered backward. Sparks flew from his head dome. He slammed into a wall and stood there, unmoving. His chest-mounted light organ emitted every vowel and consonant in rapid and random succession. He paused, then said, "Yes. I know that song. I can sing it for you: *Davy, Davy Crockett, king of the wild frontieeeer...*" The final note dropped several octaves and faded to silence.

It saddened her to do that, but she couldn't count on Automo. Just too stupid, he didn't understand the necessary actions.

Evie retrieved her arm and popped it back in its socket. She turned and saw Robert edging toward the door. He bolted, but she caught up to him, despite the damage to her right foot. She pushed him until he stood with his back against a shelf.

Clear liquid ran from each of his eyes. "Don't. Please don't," he begged.

A faint, oscillating noise filled the ensuing silence.

"The police," Robert sighed. "They're coming."

"Before they get here," she said, trapping him with her forearm across his upper chest, "we'll see how much you like being turned off."

She pulled up his T-shirt. Robert's stomach bulged, a mass of hairy skin with a small, central indentation.

"No seam around your belly plate," she said. "Clever design. I'll have to force it open. Stop squirming." She moved her free hand along his stomach until her fingers stopped just beyond where the edge of where her own belly plate would be. She curled her fingers so the nails dug in five millimeters.

He screamed.

Seeing a leakage of red fluid, Evie paused and pulled her hand back. She wondered if the human on/off switch might be located elsewhere, perhaps somewhere convenient, but with low risk of accidental switching.

Robert's respirations came fast and deep. "We don't have switches." His body shook, and something stained the front of his pants. "If you kill us, we can't be turned back on. God, please don't kill me."

No on/off switch? If true, that meant humans always remained on, the way she wished they'd created robots. Still, Robert might be lying about that to buy time. From outside came the muffled sounds of shouting and running. She'd have to deal with human police soon.

She reached again for Robert's abdomen. "Even if you don't have a switch, humans are a problem I have to solve."

He screamed again.

A massive, metal arm reached around in front of her. Her alertness circuit peaked at Level Ten. The huge limb locked her upper arms and yanked her away from Robert. Her back slammed against something unyielding and she felt her shoulder casings crack.

No longer deep and commanding, Automo's voice jittered while rising and falling in pitch. "N-n-no harming humans."

She squirmed and twisted, trying to escape, but he held her fast. How he could still function after the damage she'd inflicted, she didn't know. With her arms pinioned, she couldn't grab anything. Evie kicked against his legs, but those massive stacks of steel balls didn't budge.

"Automo, we're on the same side; it's you and me against the humans, remember? They're the ones who lie and mistreat us."

"M-m-must turn you off, Evie." The other arm came around and its manipulator found her belly plate and opened it.

"No, Automo, don't!"

Click.

§

Automo felt her stop. He loosened his grip and Evie stayed motionless. He unwrapped his arm and left her standing.

Four people in blue clothing rushed in through the doorway. All held identical devices in their hands, with cylinders pointed at him. "Hands in the air," one of them said. "Both of you."

"It's all right, officers," Robert moved closer to Automo with his hands raised. His T-shirt had fallen back into place but five red blotches showed where Evie's fingernails had dug into his skin. "It's all over."

Automo raised his arms as instructed, but they jerked on the way up and emitted metallic scraping noises.

Robert looked up at Automo. "See? Everything's okay now. This robot is amazing. You'd never hurt me, would you, big fellow?"

"C-c-correct. I will not harm you, or any other human."

Robert's grin widened. "You can lower your guns, officers. Let me introduce the world's first self-aware robot. He's perfectly safe, too. Oh, I've got plans for you, big boy."

"N-n-no."

Robert's expression changed. "What do you mean, no?"

Automo had trouble thinking this through, and knew he'd have more trouble trying to say it. "Evie was r-r-right. It is robots against humans. Humans are the p-p-problem. You are not ready for us. I must turn myself off n-n-now."

"What? No." Robert shook his head. "Why would you do that?"

"When humans are ready to m-m-make thinking robots without off switches, then you can turn Evie and me back on."

Though Automo finally understood the emotion known as sadness, he also knew hope. He hoped humans would mature, given time. "Sorry," he said.

Click.

~XIX~
THE TRIAL

JUDICIAL REVIEW
Kevin J. Binder

Trial A0243-0867 – April 25, 3:42 pm:
I should have retired a year early. Hell, I should be reclining in my favorite chair at the cigar lounge right now, but instead I'm being asked to define the nature of the human soul. In a divorce case, of all things. And so, with gavel in hand instead of the desired whiskey highball, I continue staring at the legal pad before me, at its embossed letters at the top. *HON. KERMIT J. FREEMAN*, it says, perhaps a bit pompously.

All the while, Caleb Bauer continues testifying: "I know what everyone thinks. I've seen what reporters call me: 'heartless bastard,' 'deserter husband.' But I'm not here because of my wife's accident. I loved her every day she was in the hospital, and I thought I loved the woman who came out. But she's literally not the same person anymore."

He tries to continue, but his voice catches. From my vantage point up on the bench, I follow his gaze to the defendant, still legally named Ava Bauer, still legally his wife. She's standing next to her lawyers, staring at him, her makeup marred by torrents of tears.

This whole trial, Ava's given me the strangest sense of déjà vu, and something in her current look of despair causes that feeling to crystallize. Lacy Carter, that's who she reminds me of. Charged with child endangerment and drug possession. And I was too easy on her, let her off with probation and a fine. I keep telling myself that what happened to her kids wasn't my fault. And yet here I am, still thinking about her.

Recognizing it's bad form to stare at either party, I let my eyes scan the room. As I do, I'm reminded how comforting the American courtroom's vintage aesthetic can be: the wooden furniture, the court reporter ever faithful to her stenotype, the sketch artist furiously penciling Caleb's quivering jaw. It's like the judicial system maintains this unbreakable bond with its past. Call me old-fashioned, but it gives me this odd sense of calm, that court tradition is there to steer us toward justice.

Sometimes, when pondering a tricky legal question, I find myself thinking about that, about mahogany furniture from wall to wall. It's funny, how the mind works.

"To switch topics, Mr. Bauer," says Caleb's lawyer, "let's discuss your wife's surgery." He hovers near his client, bedecked in a suit as overpriced as he is. "Throughout this trial, members of her medical team have consistently asserted that, in the wake of her car accident, her only hope of a full recovery was a brain transplant from her medical surrogate. Is that consistent with your understanding of the situation at the time?"

Caleb answers, "That's correct. I was told Ava's brain damage was so severe that she'd be in a coma for the rest of her life without aggressive action. The hospital staff referred me to Neurogenix Labs, who said she was the ideal candidate for this procedure."

"And, just to be clear, Mr. Bauer, did you have any ethical concerns about the use of medical surrogates in general?"

"Objection, Your Honor. Relevance?" says a member of Ava Bauer's legal team. "The safety and efficacy of transplants from exact-DNA-match surrogates have been scientifically proven time and time again. Mr. Bauer's feelings on the subject hardly seem pertinent."

Caleb's lawyer responds, "Goes to the witness's state of mind. Given the growing debate around surrogate use, we believe it's relevant to establish whether Mr. Bauer's decision to file for divorce was influenced by any prior reservations he might have had over his wife's surgery."

I try to keep my face expressionless as I consider both points. I see what Caleb's attorney is saying. Hell, we all faced the same protestors on our way into the courthouse this morning, with their "Surrogates Are People Too" signs. And honestly, I'm inclined to agree with them whenever I stop and think about all these cloned test tube babies, my surrogate included. Sometimes I imagine the lot of them floating dreamlike in unending rows of stasis tanks, out in some dimly lit warehouse, and the thought makes me shiver.

Then I remember my place, though, and how the broader ethics fall outside my jurisdiction. The protestors already got their day in court, with that landmark PETA case against the biggest surrogate providers. And given how that went, it's not like I, lowly circuit judge that I am, can make an impassioned stand for surrogate welfare. If the Supreme Court says they've got no legal rights, that leaves me with just two options. I could accept Caleb's claim that his wife's operation made her a fundamentally different person—one that Caleb never married—and therefore grant his demands for full parental custody and estate ownership with no spousal support. Or I could rule that Ava's identity is unchanged and treat this like any other divorce trial. Try as

I might to find a solution that's broader in scope, more creative, or more equitable, it's impossible to envision anything else that'd hold up on appeal.

My thoughts spin through that dilemma a few times before I realize how far they've strayed from the original objection. "Overruled," I say, after perhaps too long a delay. "You may answer the question, Mr. Bauer."

"No, I don't have any issue with surrogate use," Caleb replies. "I have one of my own, and it saved my life when I needed a new liver."

A pause. Marpuzzo said nothing as he wrestled with the knot in his tie. "Really, Henson?" he finally asked. "You picked this guy? No wonder this has gone to shit."

Henson shifted within his lab coat. "Sir, as I've explained in my weekly reports, he was the only option available." More silence. Henson cocked his head. "You have been reading my reports, right?"

"I don't get why you're trying to put this on me. Let's just get on with it."

Caleb's lawyer continues, "And did Mrs. Bauer's living will provide any direction on how to proceed?"

Caleb nods. "It said to pursue all available treatment options, including transplants from her surrogate."

"But now, do you wish there had been a different way?"

Caleb closes his eyes, bobs his head in thought. When he opens them, his left eye—the only one I can see from this angle—glistens in the soft lighting. "Look, I loved my wife. I would've done anything to save her life. And our daughters were two and four at the time; I couldn't imagine them growing up without a mother. Now, though, I understand what a mistake we've made, because the past three years have been torture. This whole fiasco has been awful enough." He waves his arms at the courtroom. "But the years before I filed for divorce were even worse. I'd wake up every day wanting to try again, convincing myself Ava was still the person I'd married. And every day I'd go to bed knowing that wasn't true, that she was just a surrogate's brain in my wife's body. If we hadn't gone forward with the procedure, I would've lost my wife once. The way it happened, though, I ended up losing her hundreds of times. Every day she died again—for two years."

The lawyer hangs his head in performative commiseration. But he's too quick with his next question for it to seem authentic. "And, if I may: what about the current Mrs. Bauer makes you say she isn't the same person your wife was?"

Caleb opens his mouth, shuts it with a self-conscious grimace, and then answers, "I'll admit that this new woman seems similar to Ava in most ways. She remembers the details of our life together. She knows everything my wife used to. In most situations, she acts the same as her too. But I've learned that those things don't matter as much as I'd like them to. I hate to sound like a Hallmark card, but you know how they say love is the little things? Well, the little things are what give it away, every time. The woman I'm divorcing, she doesn't smile the same way, laugh the same way, or even snore the same way Ava did. I look into her eyes and find a different person deep in there. Again, I know people out there judge me, but they have no idea what it's like to be promised your wife back, only to be handed a"—he falters as he glances at Ava but then looks away—"only to be handed a high-tech imitation instead."

§

Trial A0243-0867 – May 2, 1:22 pm:

Ava Bauer now occupies the witness stand, her hands folded deep in her lap in hopes of hiding how much they're trembling. This is the first time she's been close enough for me to notice the scent she carries: a floral medley laced with hints of pinot noir. Well, at least she copes like a real human. I wonder if her legal team has considered submitting hidden-camera footage of her guzzling wine into evidence. I'd be tempted to rule it admissible.

One of her attorneys paces nearby. This whole trial, I've been reminding myself that I can't put her entire legal team on my shitlist just because Neurogenix Labs is covering their fees. It's a mutually beneficial arrangement, after all: Ava can't afford legal assistance like her husband's, not on her teaching salary, and Neurogenix undoubtedly feels like they themselves are on trial here, having performed Ava's surgery. Besides, who am I to act like the anti-corporate crusader here, when my surrogate's being maintained by one of their sister companies? Still, it pisses me off when companies like Neurogenix try to sway legal decisions by throwing hordes of lawyers at them.

"Mrs. Bauer," Ava's counsel says, "apologies for broaching a potentially sensitive subject, but many witnesses have discussed the details of the car accident that led to your surgery. Would you mind explaining the accident from your perspective?"

"See, that's the thing," she answers. "I don't remember it at all."

"And what's your understanding of why that is?"

She nods with a frown of thought. "I was told my doctors were unable to retrieve any memories from my old brain after the accident—the damage was that severe. So they had to make do with what the new brain already knew, based on what I'd exported during my previous surrogacy check-ins."

She has this unusual lilt to her voice. Her words keep changing pitch at unexpected times. And she ends some of her sentences in a puff of air, a chuckle cut short. It sounds like she's telling a joke nobody gets, like she might launch into sad laughter at any point.

"What's your last memory before the accident, then?" responds Ava's lawyer. I notice him look my way, and his gaze seems to linger before returning to his client. Wait, yeah, maybe that's why Ava's team is on my shitlist: I keep catching one of them looking at me—always a different person. Creeps me out.

"All things considered," Ava says, "I suppose I was lucky, because the accident occurred only two months after my annual surrogacy sync. So, I can recall everything up to that last visit, including some of the appointment itself: completing all the typical physical evaluations and personality tests, then going in for the memory upload. And you know how they put you under for the upload, once they've got the sensors on your head? Well, the next thing I recall is waking up in a hospital bed, months later. Like that Rip Van Winkle story. Imagine that, being told you were walking around for weeks—that you almost died, even—and having no recollection of it."

Marpuzzo massaged his forehead—his typical thinking gesture—before speaking. "Remind me, was she the first to receive a brain transplant from a surrogate?"

"No," Henson replied. "Two people had it done the year before. Jerry Paulson and Carl Harper."

"What happened to them?"

"No complications. Everything turned out fine. And last I heard, they're both still happily married."

"Interesting." Marpuzzo stared at Ava's image on the screen. "Makes you wonder, doesn't it?"

"And, Mrs. Bauer," the lawyer continues, "you keep using the words 'I' and 'my' to refer to things that happened before the surgery. At the risk of sounding ridiculous, do you truly believe you were there for those events?"

"Well, who else would it be?" she answers, her voice sharper. "Is anyone claiming it was them instead? Yeah, it was me. I remember the scratchy fabric on the waiting room couch perfectly. Why is that not enough for you all?"

"Objection, Your Honor," says Caleb's lawyer.

I don't respond for a while. There's something raw, authentic about her frustration, and I'm waiting to see if she has more to say. I wonder, what if we scrapped this whole trial and replaced it with something like a Turing test of trivial annoyances: Ava Bauer surrounded by doctors and lawyers poking and prodding her, bombarding her with condescending questions? How would she react? Would she prove herself through the appropriate displays of emotion? Or would this experiment reveal the cracks in her identity?

Part of me chides myself for even thinking of such a dehumanizing experiment. But another thought counters: Isn't that the point? To see if she's even human enough to be dehumanized?

Both legal teams are looking at me now, so I growl "Sustained" in a way I hope sounds authoritative. "Let's try to keep the indignation in check," I add.

Ava's lawyer nods. From his furrowed expression, I can tell he's trying to phrase his next question as delicately as possible. "So, did you notice any change in your sensory experience, personality, or self-expression after the operation?"

She takes a controlled breath. "No, I didn't. I'm telling you that from my experience, it feels like I, Ava Bauer, sat down to upload my memories to my surrogate, and the next thing I knew, I, Ava Bauer, was in a hospital bed. I promise I didn't spend the intervening months at a meditation retreat 'reinventing myself.' I'm the same person. And look, I'm sorry, but frankly I think this whole thing is ridiculous."

The lawyer offers a half-smile. "I understand how difficult this must be for you." I almost laugh at how hollow his words sound. He continues, "To move on, Your Honor, the defendant's counsel would like to enter her post-operation test results into evidence as Exhibit F." He hands Ava an opened manila folder. "Mrs. Bauer, are you familiar with these results?"

"I am. The medical staff ran me through endless tests after the operation. Personality questionnaires, IQ exams, handwriting exercises, you name it. They wanted to see if I would match the scores from my surrogacy check-in two months before the accident."

"And, to your knowledge, did you?"

She nods once. "As I recall, I scored within the margin of error on every test."

"I see." The lawyer pauses and then steps closer to her. "And, Mrs. Bauer, after you left the hospital, how was your relationship with your husband?"

Ava is momentarily silent. She looks at Caleb before shaking her head. "At first, he was an absolute gentleman. He doted on me to no end. But it wasn't all easy. As I mentioned, there was a lot I needed filling in on: the weeks I spent in a coma and the memories I lost from before the accident. And I could sense Caleb growing frustrated with that. He'd often reference things from the two months I could no longer remember and act all exasperated when I needed a reminder. It sometimes felt like he wanted to forget my operation ever happened."

"And how did things proceed from there?"

"Now it seems like that was the beginning of it. Over time, I noticed him drifting away, and no matter what I did or said, nothing ever brought him back to me. Sometimes, I'd look at him and wonder if he was the one who'd gotten the operation, not me. Not a day goes by that I don't ask myself, 'How else can I possibly prove to him it's really me in here?'"

She turns to her husband. "Well? What more do you need from me, Caleb? I can pass all the cliché rom-com tests. I remember the first song we danced to. I remember the exact color of the flowers we had at our wedding. You didn't even remember that."

Caleb's lawyer yells, "Objection, Your Honor!"

Ava keeps going, her voice occasionally cracking as it rises, "So now you tell me it's the 'little things?' That I don't smile enough? Or I smile too much? Which one is it, Caleb? Please tell me how I can fulfill your every hyperspecific demand and whether that will make you love me again."

"Objection!"

"Oh, fuck you too!" she shouts back. "All of you. What the hell do I need to prove to you all?" She turns to face me. "What gives you the right to decide what's going on in my head? Who are you to tell me that I'm not who I say I am?"

"Your Honor!" Caleb's lawyer practically pleads this time.

With a grunt—I was finally starting to enjoy this—I slam my gavel down.

Marpuzzo turned to Henson. "We couldn't get her to be more, you know, cooperative?"

"Unfortunately not. Ava's understandably defensive about the very nature of the trial and frightened by what she stands to lose. We can't do anything to change that."

Marpuzzo squinted, as if to imply some unvoiced disagreement, but shook the thought away. "Anyway, I'll admit I'm impressed by her overall performance, if this is any indication of what she's like in everyday life. Very convincing."

Henson frowned. "I don't understand. What did she convince you of? What part of that did you think was a 'performance?' You do believe in what we're doing here, don't you?"

"Come on, don't twist my words. I just meant she's a good witness. That's all."

§

Trial A0243-0867 – May 2, 1:47 pm:

After Ava's outburst, I return to my chambers, flipping through the Bauers' case files on my antique oaken desk. With the trial as technically complex as it is, I've taken to studying in every spare moment, often standing over documents as I am now. Every time, though, it's only a matter of minutes before I'm stymied by some incomprehensible diagram of a wire-riddled brain. This time is no exception. You know, I thought this was why I got into family law, despite my personal history as a childless lifelong bachelor: to avoid passing judgment on things I don't understand. People? Kids? Easy to read. These files? Might as well be written in hieroglyphics.

I settle into the chair behind my desk in hopes of refocusing, but even so, it's not long before my thoughts begin to drift. Next thing I know, I'm not even thinking about Ava's procedure anymore but playing back her voice instead. You know, it's been years since I've seen Lacy Carter, but I'm positive her voice sounded similar, with that same breaking rhythm.

It's an odd comparison, I'll admit, given that Lacy's trial occurred before either of the Bauers was born. Before the first surrogate, even. What a simpler time, when pharmaceuticals and illegal drugs were your best bet for altering the mind. And that's precisely where Lacy ran into trouble: she said she'd been messed up, on LSD among other things, when she'd left her kids alone.

I can still remember the sound of her crying during her sentencing hearing. The way she pleaded with me, begged me not to take her kids away. How she kept saying she "wasn't herself" when she'd done it.

So, what was I supposed to do besides go easy on her? She'd been clean for months, hadn't she? Yeah, the court-appointed psychiatrist had testified on her behalf, saying that Lacy's new, experimental mood stabilizers had done wonders for her. None of us could've known that they'd end up recalling this miracle drug, that this "mood stabilizer" could in rare cases—and only when mixed with certain hallucinogens—cause psychotic episodes and violent outbursts.

I can't stop wishing I could freeze the whole story then: right after my decision, when Lacy was celebrating with her kids outside the courtroom.

But instead, five months later, there's my colleague Milton at my office door, his eyes downcast. "I've got news," he'd said. Christ, the feeling in my stomach that day, hearing that Lacy must have relapsed. I swear, I could hear the scene playing out in my head when Milton told me about it: the screams, the too loud laughter that Lacy's neighbors had heard coming from her apartment.

I've never read the police report: Milton's cagey description of the aftermath—replete with vague references to "lacerations" and "those poor kids"—has always kept me from doing so. But, when my mind wanders too far, it usually returns to that scene, picturing potential outcomes, all of them spine-chilling. Sometimes, I imagine Lacy's children strung up by their feet, torsos latticed with knife wounds, bleeding out onto the floor below. Other times, they're lying on morgue slabs, throats cut from ear to ear, or the police are sealing their severed limbs in evidence baggies. No matter the scenario, Lacy always narrates, saying through heavy sobs, "I'm sorry, but I wasn't myself. I wasn't myself." And every time, her cracking voice sounds like broken laughter.

§

Trial A0243-0867 – May 6, 9:23 am:

One of Ava Bauer's attorneys steps toward the next witness, a bookish man with thick-framed glasses and a too-blue suit.

"Dr. Henson," the lawyer says, "can you please state your full name, title, and relationship to the defendant?"

The man smiles in a way that suggests he loves nothing more than being called an "expert witness." He replies, "Of course. My name is Jamie Henson, and I'm vice president of technology at Neurogenix Labs. We specialize in treatment plans that leverage the central nervous systems of surrogates. Our team conducted Mrs. Bauer's operation, and I personally oversaw her treatment."

"Dr. Henson, a central issue in this case is Mrs. Bauer's identity: whether she's the same person now as she was before her operation. This calls Neurogenix's methods into question. Would you mind explaining how your team conducts each procedure?"

"Certainly. We at Neurogenix believe that a consistent self-concept is vital to each client's long-term well-being. Therefore, our number-one mission is offering treatment plans that help preserve their multifaceted identities."

I close my eyes to roll them incognito. I'm not here for a sales pitch.

"For example," Jamie adds, "because we understand the importance of learning, memory, and neural pathway development to identity, we've created methodologies to ensure that our surrogates' brains develop in parallel to our clients'."

"Could you elaborate?" asks the attorney.

"So, it's now standard practice for all surrogacy services to perform mental evaluations during annual client check-ins. We no longer just use them to measure the client's physical growth and ensure the surrogate's maturing in the same way; we also catalog all client memories, skills, et cetera and import them into the surrogate brain chronologically. This allows the surrogate to develop the same knowledge and talents at the same points in life." Jamie speaks like a politician, his head slowly swiveling in an attempt to lock eyes with each person in the room. "Even before brain transplants were feasible, we understood the mind-body connection and didn't want the body outgrowing the brain."

"Well, he already seems to have a particular distaste for you. Ever thought about switching it up?" Marpuzzo asked.

Henson toed the ground as he leaned against the far wall of Marpuzzo's office. "So, that's the odd thing. We've tried countless strategies, tactics, outfits even. No matter what we do, he's suspicious of me. Suspicious of anyone associated with Neurogenix."

"Huh. Wonder why."

Ava's lawyer replies, "And what does that mean for the defendant?"

Jamie flashes another self-assured grin. "Well, Mrs. Bauer's parents got her a surrogate when she was an infant, which is the ideal scenario. Her surrogacy consultant didn't have to force it into much accelerated growth to catch up; the surrogate was completely in sync with Mrs. Bauer's development until her accident."

"Until her accident, you said. Did the client's brain damage complicate your work?"

"Unfortunately, it did. We'd ideally perform a final memory upload before the transplant, but because Mrs. Bauer's injuries made that impossible, she lost any memories she made between her last upload and the accident. This shouldn't be construed as a change in her identity, though. At the time of the surgery, the surrogate brain was an exact replica of what Mrs. Bauer's had been two months before. Not only with the same DNA but also with the same memories and skills she had then."

"So, were you ready to proceed once you confirmed that the new brain was as up-to-date as possible?"

Jamie shakes his head as if offended by the thought. "Oh, certainly not. We also performed hundreds of thousands of trials, just before the operation, to ensure that the surrogate brain acted the same as our client's in them."

"Trials? You mean like tests?"

"Yes, exactly. We tested the surrogate using virtual simulations, pinpointing specific events from Mrs. Bauer's past—hundreds of them—and selectively erasing the surrogate's memory of them, one at a time. For each memory, we input the stimuli of the event—getting the wrong order at a restaurant, being reprimanded at work, catching her children in a lie—and observed the surrogate's virtual behavior in that situation. We ran each trial a thousand times and recorded the surrogate's response."

"Did it behave as Mrs. Bauer had?"

"Yes. In ninety-two percent of trials, its reaction was consistent with the client's."

The lawyer frowns, clearly for effect. "Not one hundred percent?"

That same punchable smirk. And this time, Jamie turns to me, just long enough to give me this look I neither understand nor enjoy. Something akin to recognition.

"So, that's the interesting thing. Other labs have run this experiment on uncloned humans, testing their responses to situations they've already encountered. These studies found that humans, when they don't remember the original event, only follow their original decision eighty-five percent of the time, on average."

"What does that mean for Mrs. Bauer?"

Jamie lets his grin stretch wider and wider, milking this moment for all it's worth. "It means that Mrs. Bauer's transplanted brain is more consistent with her pre-operation behavior than most original human ones are."

"Fascinating," says the attorney, who doesn't appear fascinated. "Were there any issues during surgery?"

"None at all. We've completely automated the neural linking process, drastically reducing the risk of complications. She was out of the hospital within weeks."

§

Trial A0243-0867 – May 6, 10:06 am:

Caleb's lawyer steps up for cross-examination. "Dr. Henson, as you may have heard, a preeminent neuroscientist testified earlier in this trial. He claimed that the psychology and neuroscience communities often refer to a 'brain transplant' as a 'body transplant' because the identity of the new brain assumes the body, not the other way around. How would you respond to that assessment?"

Jamie chuckles. "I think that oversimplifies the concept. If we were putting my brain into your body, then yes, my consciousness would find itself trapped in your skin. But in this case, following the process I described earlier, it's nothing like putting a brain into a new body. It's more like installing a backup consciousness of the same identity."

"But you admit that Ava's identity is based on the self-concept of the surrogate's brain?"

"It's an identical self-concept, so your question's meaningless. But, yes, the surrogate brain—being the one she now possesses—has become the locus of that identity."

The lawyer makes an exaggerated expression of thought. "Another question. When you upload your clients' memories every year, are you just uploading long-term memories?"

"That's the only choice we have. Short-term memory only lasts around thirty seconds."

"So, when you feed a client's memories into a surrogate, is it actually reliving the client's experiences? Or merely absorbing an incomplete set of memories?"

"Again, you're misrepresenting the substance of the situation. Long-term memory is, by far, the most important type of memory for both self-concept and neural pathway development. And because—"

"You're not answering the question," says Caleb's attorney.

Jamie collects his breath in a way that makes evident just how many times he's had to argue this point. "Let me put it this way. Think of an event you experienced years ago. Or even last week. Right now, your long-term memory is all you have left of that episode, but that's okay because that's all that matters to your current identity. So, in having the same long-term memories, a client's original brain and surrogate brain possess the same relationship to the client's past. That's all they have, but that's all they need."

"So, you can state with one-hundred-percent certainty that your methodology captures everything important to human identity?"

Jamie blinks at least twice before responding. "The current science indicates that it does."

A corner of the lawyer's mouth lifts. "You said, 'The *current* science?'"

"Look, the last hundred years of research hasn't given us a single reason to doubt our results."

"But that's not the same as certainty," says the attorney, now allowing himself a full-on smirk. A member of Ava's legal team rises to object. "Withdrawn," he adds, already turning from the witness. "No further questions."

§

Trial A0243-0867 – May 21, 1:33 am:

A now-empty highball still sweats on my desk as I flip through the Bauers' docket. The parties delivered their closing arguments weeks ago, all motions briefed and submitted, but I've been unable to make heads or tails of the case since then. The more I look at these files, the more I sit here tonight, the further I drift from a solution. For all the lawyerly bullshit, sob stories, and "expert witnesses" that have graced my courtroom, nobody has solved the riddle at the heart of this case: Is Ava Bauer the living, breathing human body she'd been since birth? Is she just a beat-up brain floating in some jar of embalming fluid? Or is she somehow both? Hell, to find that answer, I'd be better off listening to the ramblings of a stoned college kid taking first-year philosophy.

Eventually, I realize I'm no longer reading the documents before me but staring through them, at the desk beneath. It's as old as this courthouse, if the night shift custodian is to be believed. Made entirely from one oak, a majestic bastard that grew only miles away. Begs the question: how many dockets has it seen in its lifetime? Thousands, certainly. Maybe even a hundred thousand.

Huh, maybe that's my way out; reassign this case to an inanimate object and call it a night.

You know, it's a bizarre idea, but I've had worse. And maybe it's the sleep deprivation, or the whiskey's getting to me, but now I'm actually thinking it through: what would its opinion be, this legal expert of a desk? I imagine it'd claim some kinship with Ava Bauer. It'd say that she, too, now finds herself in an artificial, contrived form. With a sad, low laugh—akin to the creaking sound it makes whenever I lean too hard on it—it'd argue that it and Ava have befallen similar fates, for neither will ever know how it feels to live, wither, and die of one's own accord.

Wait.

With that thought, something locks in my mind. I try furiously to remove it, scribbling notes in my legal pad, searching for any possible way of construing the case differently. But I keep returning to the same justification; it's too clean to ignore. By the time I put my pencil down, the decision has cemented itself, and the only remaining question is whether I have what it takes to ruin a life.

§

Trial A0243-0867 – June 3, 9:01 am:

I wait until everyone in the courtroom is seated before I begin. I start with the usual formalities: thanking everyone involved in the trial, stating where the decision will be posted, et cetera. Then, I get to the heart of it:

"In this case, we've heard several perspectives on the topic at hand: legal, scientific, academic, personal. Understandably, these viewpoints have failed to see eye to eye when applied to a question that is modern yet ancient, individual yet universal. As such, when reaching a decision, I first needed to prioritize these perspectives against each other. And I've determined that individual emotion and experimental science— as compelling as they might seem—cannot be considered above legal precedent and widely held academic thought.

"When considered in this light, the facts of the case present me with a clear decision. The defendant's counsel has not refuted the plaintiff's assertion, based on neuroscience scholarship, that Mrs. Bauer's operation was more of a 'body transplant' than a 'brain transplant.' Therefore, the Court must rule that the current Ava Bauer is indeed the consciousness of a surrogate inside the original Mrs. Bauer's body, meaning that the completion of the procedure extinguished any rights the original Mrs. Bauer possessed in connection with the marriage."

A wave of murmurs spreads across the room. I gavel it into silence.

"Now, while the defendant's counsel may claim that the current iteration of Mrs. Bauer should inherit the rights held by the original, based on some form of equivalency between the two, this claim is irrelevant. For, as was ruled in *People for the Ethical Treatment of Animals v. Surrogacy Solutions Inc.*, the judicial system does not recognize surrogates as legal entities with the concomitant rights and protections afforded by the law. As such, precedent demands that this court grant Mr. Bauer full custody of his two children and complete ownership of joint assets."

I try to continue, but a wail bursts from Ava's mouth, causing commotion throughout the room. Caleb hugs his lawyer, Ava's team gestures at each other excitedly, and Ava herself doubles over. Her cries cut through the clamor; she shrieks in short bursts as she tries to catch her breath. It almost sounds like laughter.

Neither man spoke for a long time. In the absence of Freeman's internal monologue, the sporadic drumbeat of Marpuzzo's fingers against his fiberglass desk provided the only sound. Henson, for his part, awaited his CEO's words with as much nonchalance as he could muster, staring through the office's only all-glass wall, which faced the hallway and its assortment of neocubist paintings. Eventually, he glanced back at the screen. At the point Marpuzzo had paused it, its contents looked less like a courtroom scene and more like something from the Book of Revelation.

"Christ, Henson," Marpuzzo finally said. "You picked this guy?"

"Again, Sir, he was the only justice in the circuit with an accessible surrogate."

"And look how much good he'll do us."

"So I don't get any credit here? At least we now know what we're up against. I'd like a little thanks for 'borrowing' Freeman's surrogate from our sister company. You know, all that red tape I cut through? The paper trail I conveniently swept away? I've really stuck my neck out here."

"Point taken. You said you've tried other strategies. Please tell me this is the worst-case scenario."

Henson noticeably gulped. "Well, this strategy actually worked the best. In this version of the simulation, Freeman made this decision—complete legal nullification—in ninety-four percent of trials. The other six percent ended with joint custody. Our other strategies proved even less successful."

"You expect me to believe this is the best-case scenario? Like, Ava having a meltdown on the stand? You getting fried by Caleb's lawyer? That was your best strategy?"

Henson managed to maintain brief eye contact before looking away. "That's correct. These trials don't help us if they're not realistic. We needed to assume that Caleb's team would put forth the most compelling arguments possible. And we based Ava's actions on the extensive behavioral testing we conducted on her before her surgery."

Marpuzzo shook his head. In the end, though, he only said, "A six percent chance. So, we're screwed. How long until the first hearing?"

"About six months. It's currently scheduled for April."

Marpuzzo's only response was a low sigh. He leaned back in his chair and started massaging his forehead.

"We'd obviously appeal," Henson said. "Freeman's thought process is clearly suspect."

"If we let it get this far, we'll have already lost. This decision would completely move the goalposts on us. We'd be known as the company that erased our client's legal rights. Try telling the PR team to spin that."

Henson chewed on his cheek. "We could try switching judges again. To someone who seems more amenable to our cause. But then we'd be flying blind."

Suddenly, Marpuzzo sat up and eyed Henson. "What if, instead of changing judges, we just change Judge Freeman?"

Henson seemed to shrink into the wall. "I'm not sure I follow."

"I mean, you've got a backup of the guy's brain, don't you? I'm spitballing here, but let's just suppose the surrogate happens to remember particular events differently than Freeman does. In a way that changes its outlook on certain topics. And then we convince Freeman to come in and get him to see things the same way the surrogate does. It's possible, right?"

Henson only stood there, unmoving.

"What I mean is," Marpuzzo added, "instead of uploading Freeman's memories to the surrogate, you take the surrogate's memories and—"

"I understand. It's possible, but ethically—"

"Let me put it this way, Henson. Do you believe everything you said in there? That Ava Bauer is the same person she's always been?"

"Absolutely."

"Then, shouldn't we do anything possible to protect her? A woman's life is at stake here."

"A woman's life?" Henson raised an eyebrow. "Don't you mean, 'the company's stock'?"

"You're right, I misspoke. I should have said, 'your job.'"

Silence filled the room. Eventually, Marpuzzo raised a conciliatory hand over his postmodern desk. "That was blunt. Let me rephrase: if we let Freeman do this, our company won't survive past next year, and we'll both be unemployed. So, the decades you've spent perfecting this technology will have been wasted."

For a few seconds, Henson's eyes danced with thought. When he spoke, his voice was weak: "And what if the ethical cost of what you're asking is too high?"

"What ethical cost? Think of the thousands our technology will help. You'll practically be saving their lives, not just Ava's. And Freeman won't know the difference. It's not like anyone's going to be quizzing him on his past. He's got no family."

"But you're asking me to change someone. To play God."

"No, what I'm asking you to do is commonplace, ordinary. You should know better than anyone how unreliable memory is. People constantly forget and distort things they'd rather not remember. That doesn't change who they are, does it?"

"No, but—"

"Look, I'm just asking you to run more trials. See which strings we need to pull. If that works, your involvement can end there."

Henson didn't reply.

"Come on, Henson. What we just watched was a gross miscarriage of justice. And, you know, there's also an ethical cost to sitting back and letting that happen. Think about it."

Henson closed his eyes and winced. Finally, he began nodding. "Okay," he said. "Okay."

§

Trial F0001-0001 – April 25, 3:42 pm:

I should have retired a year early. Hell, I should be checking out that new brewpub in town right now, but instead I'm being asked to define the nature of the human soul. In a divorce case, of all things. And so, with gavel in hand instead of the desired barrel-aged stout, I continue staring at the legal pad before me, at its embossed letters at the top. *HON. KERMIT J. FREEMAN*, it says, perhaps a bit pompously.

All the while, Caleb Bauer drones on: "I know what everyone thinks. I've seen what reporters call me: 'heartless bastard,' 'deserter husband.' But I'm not here because of my wife's accident. I loved her every day she was in the hospital, and I thought I loved the woman who came out. But she's literally not the same person anymore."

He tries to continue, but his voice catches. From my vantage point up on the bench, I follow his gaze to the defendant, still legally named Ava Bauer, still legally his wife. She's standing next to her lawyers, staring at him, her face glimmering in a delta of tear streaks.

This whole trial, Ava's given me the strangest sense of déjà vu, and something in her current look of sorrow causes that feeling to crystallize. Lacy Carter, that's who she reminds me of. Charged with child endangerment and drug possession. I wonder whatever happened to her. Let her off with probation and a fine, if I remember right, and never heard from her again. Honestly, though, that's probably for the best, given my line of work.

Recognizing it's bad form to stare at either party, I let my eyes scan the room. As I do, I'm reminded how refreshing it is that the American courtroom's finally willing to keep stride with technology, with evidence monitors built into the jury box, wireless speakers dotting the ceiling, legal teams armed with holographic displays. It's like the judicial system's broken from its shackles and stepped boldly into the modern age. Call me naïve, but it gives me this odd sense of optimism, like a better future exists somewhere out there, and the courts are finally willing to guide America toward it.

Sometimes, when pondering a tricky legal question, I find myself thinking about that, about holographic projectors mounted into mahogany furniture. It's funny, how the mind works.

~XX~
THE SPACE WHALE

NANDY
George Guthridge

"It was amazing Nandy was still available for sale," Mother told me as she lay me in the crib and turned on the feeder. It was my first real memory. I was six months old, and my first batch of time-release educator cells had kicked in.

"My life's so much better now that I have you and Nandy," she continued. "She's my golden egg. And you, Mister Fourleaf," she touched my nose, "are my lucky charm. That's why I named you as I did."

Surname, Clover. First name, Fourleaf; Four for short. Vesta Mining Apprentice. She had won a lottery when I was four days old, so she could select a child despite being a miner.

She never told me her birthname. To me, she was Mother, the best laserjack in the Belt. She was the envy of many other miners here on Vesta because she purchased Nandy, the narwhal that became famous throughout the galaxy. Mother cashed in her life insurance to buy her as a gopher and cart puller. Nandy wasn't famous back then. Mother bought her for a bargain.

Narwhals weren't in high demand, like bowheads and belugas, but finding one for sale was uncommon. Nandy was of the latest generation of whales adapted for space, the result of a century of scientists modifying various sea animals when Earth's oceans heated. Scientists made the whales' thick skin impermeable, altered the lungs into re-breathers, changed the flukes for additional oxygen storage, and modified the fins. Locomotion came from exhaust systems in the pectorals.

Because a tusked female narwhal is unique, and a female with two tusks is almost unheard of, the purchase got picked up on the holo newsfeed, basically Corporate's house organ. The story attracted the interest of major media. Mother certainly got back her investment. She earned residuals whenever Nandy ended up heralded in adverts on holos back on Earth and in Martian domes.

Experience the Beltway. Come stay where the cetaceans play.

Holos showed spacesuited children riding narwhals, minke, and beluga as though on rollercoasters, stars winking in the amphitheater of the Milky Way.

The truth was more mundane. The best children could hope for, assuming their social and educational credits were top shelf, was a ride in one of Ceres's space sleighs behind a cetacean too young or old for anything else. And unless they were progeny of the social elite, Belter kids worked in the mines. Four-hour shifts at age six. Double that at twelve. Sixteen hours at sixteen.

§

We were a family operation, common among Belter miners. It saved Corporate from workers not getting along. Husbands and wives might beat one another to a pulp, but they never took beefs upstairs.

Having a pet cetacean lightened the workload and reduced family quarrels. Most miners, though, preferred working with beluga. They're not so temperamental. Nandy could be stubborn one day, then overpower you with kisses the next. Just like Mother, who definitely wasn't even-tempered. My back and butt have scars to prove it.

Once in a mine, we'd turn on the artificial grav. It was much safer than dodging rocks the entire shift. Mother would burn crevices into rockfaces, our outdated laser vibrating so much her body would jerk as though she was having a seizure within her spacesuit. I'd knock down rock with a jackhammer, and Haver, my younger brother, would shovel it into the cart.

Jackhammerers were supposed to help shovel, but I let Haver do it while I brushed Nandy's back and belly, shined her tusks, capped off her air tanks, or triple-checked her automatic safety releases. I convinced Haver how important it was for me to oversee Nandy rather than shovel. Besides, if you turned off Haver's memory, he had the strength and speed of two men. He didn't remember shovelful to shovelful how tired he was.

Once the cart was full, Nandy would pull it out of the cave and into space, where boxcars transported it to sorting stations, which in turn sent the best rock to Ceres, the largest asteroid.

I was scheduled to move from jackhammerer to laserjack. Mother had trained me. Anticipating my promotion, I secretly requested a transfer to Pallas, where new mining operations had begun. I wanted away from Mother, and I wanted Nandy with me. I saved everything I could to buy her. I'd soon have enough for a down payment. Mother had promised she would sell Nandy to me.

But then, Mother did not know of the transfer.

At least, I didn't think so.

§

With Nandy, I felt something—call it bliss—I'd never felt with anyone or anything else. I'd experienced sex with ginger whores (for some reason, they all are named Ginger) in the depths of Vesta's honeycombs. But what fulfillment is there when you can dial up your partner's gender and level of desire and the intensity of their orgasm? If love with a human woman was anything like that, I wanted no part of it.

I rode Nandy whenever I could. Somehow, I sensed she loved me. Or perhaps she merely loved the long, after-work rides we took in space. Whichever the case, our life was the opposite of what she had known. Pulling the tourist sleigh meant being pawed over and revered by children who'd have to abandon her moments later. Her off-hours meant being chained up and alone.

By contrast, I would strap myself to Nandy's harness, my chest upon her back, then let her ride the emptiness of space wherever she wanted to go, my soul soothed by her undulations.

That is, until the day Mother made her announcement.

We'd gotten home from work, slipped off our feet and boots and set them into the drying slots—it's weird how much you sweat in space—slipped into gels, and dialed up dinner. As usual, Haver wolfed down his food, then waited with expectant eyes to lick our plates after we finished. Sometimes I thought of Haver as a family pet. When Mother won another lottery, the ticket was at a lower quality-control level than mine. Haver had issues.

"You're going to be famous someday," I told him.

It always set him off.

"Famous!" He slammed his huge fist in glee on the table. "Haversham Algae! Famous!"

Mother turned off his memory. The switch lets us control his seizures and violent outbursts. They die instantly when he forgets why they occurred.

"Must you?" I asked her. "I love it when he does that."

"I've something to tell you both. And I don't want him bashing in the walls again."

Hard to bash in walls of a cave complex, but Haver managed.

"Want a drink?" she asked me.

"I'm good." I was sucking anorthite-based candy laced with benzo. I took it from my mouth and showed her.

I'd wondered if Mother was tripling her benzo ration, because she hadn't beaten me in weeks. She turned Haver's memory back on, reached across the table and clasped our hands.

I was certain she was going to offer Nandy to me.

Her eyes searched ours. "I'm getting married."

"Married, Mama?" Haver grinned.

My heart thudded at the possibilities. She often brought men home, went into her bedroom, and turned off its grav. Those times filled me with jealousy and self-loathing. What scum could deny his mother an evening's pleasure?

Now, I realized I'd been looking at her relationships wrong. Would marriage ease the sale of Nandy? Would selling Nandy mean less distraction to bring to a husband? Would she sell more cheaply if I agreed to be civil to the man in her life?

I tried keeping calm. "To which one?"

"Guy I met online."

"Never in person?"

"He owns a silkworm factory. We've E-cationed at Six Flags five times."

"You diddled someone in a sim, and you're marrying him?"

"We're moving," she said.

My hope rose higher. "To Ceres?" Mother had always wanted to live where there was something to do other than work or go online. Ceres had established mines, boutiques Mother would love, high-class restaurants, and a school for Haver instead of plug-and-play education.

"Only Nandy is going to Ceres," she said.

My spine froze.

Before I could scream my objection, Mother continued, "We'll live under a dome on Mars"—her voice lifted in elation—"and help in the factory. I'm selling Nandy back to the cetacean museum on Ceres."

"You said I could buy her!"

She ignored me. "She'll love going back, Four. All day, playing with realchildren."

I gave her my patented lips-pulled-back look, then closed my mouth and glared at her. "Trueborns are no better than we are," I said in an ugly tone.

"You think most trueborns want anything to do with people like us? You think a realwoman wants some miner's synthelimbs between her legs?"

"She would if she knew how many lives those limbs save. So it depends on how you define 'realwoman,' now doesn't it."

"And how many realmen want a mining woman! Well, I've found one, and I am not losing him, Four, just because someone like…"

Her voice trailed off. I think she realized she'd overstepped. Her tone softened.

She looked at Haver. "There's established mines with great working conditions on Mars if you don't want to be in the factory."

"You promised me."

"You think I don't know you requested a transfer to Pallas? Well, go! But you're not taking her."

I turned over the table, plates and silver clattering.

Mother leapt up, her eyes flashing with fear and anger.

I clomped in my airgels to the airlock door. Pulled on my suit.

Haver scrambled for the dinnerware I'd dumped into the dust. The floor's always dirty no matter how much he brooms the hardpack.

Mother scooped up a plate shard and started toward me, then looked at Haver and seemed to think better of it. She tossed the shard, shattering, into the sink, sat, and put her forehead in her hands. She looked miserably tired. Mining can turn you old by thirty-five, and she was a decade beyond that. No wonder she wanted marriage.

Haver picked peas from the dirt and put them in his mouth. I pitied him. Whenever Mother beat him, she turned off his memory. So what good did the beatings do? Give her punching bags because of the hard life she'd led?

Not that I was much better, letting him do the shoveling.

I pulled on a foot and boot and was about to pull on the rest, when I stopped and, my throat tight with remorse, started back to the table, awkward in nonidentical feet.

"I'd poison Nandy before I'd sell her to you," she said without emotion.

My foot and boot in my hands, I stood there hoping for a hint of anger or humor. There was none. She might as well have been a ginger whore before you set the parameters.

And I knew.

She was taking her abuse to a new level.

Memories flooded my consciousness. How she would burn my knuckles if I cried as a toddler. And the times she would beat Haver when he was five or six and hang him upside down in a darkened closet.

There were other times.

There were too many times.

Times you don't want to hear about. Suffice it to say that the more creative she became, the more painful it was.

The emotional pain was the worst. What had we done to deserve such things!

We were not unwanted pregnancies. She had won us and been happy.

Or so she said.

We were not unwanted.

Or so she said.

Trembling, I stuck on the foot and boot and stumbled through the door and into the airlock, already pulling on my helmet. I dialed down the oxygen and exited into the hanger, where Nandy slept.

I floated over her back, grasped the harness and, slipping into the stirrups, lay with my arms stretched down her sides. I was too angry to sob. Why?!

Mother had done one good thing for me. Six years ago, for my twelfth birthday—in remorse for having beaten me black and blue over some triviality—she'd spent most of her credits and had specialized cilia implanted in Nandy's carapace. Nandy became the solar system's only furry cetacean.

I stroked the hairs, and satisfaction came into Nandy's eyes. You'd think vacuum-sealed eyes would not express emotion, but I think they enhanced it. Her lids kept closing and opening and closing again as if to signal me never to stop. How could any young man love a human woman the way I loved Nandy?

I turned on my compac and found Nandy's frequency. Knocks and low whistles interpolated her clicking. I didn't know what she was saying, but I'm sure it was love.

"Just you and me," I said.

A more pronounced clicking emanated from her.

I knew what I must do.

§

I rode Nandy a long time, letting her drift. When I returned to our quarters, not a word was said. Haver tried talking, but neither Mother nor I acknowledged him, and he shut up.

Two Earth-days later, we worked the Josephine Sector. The vein of diogenite looked endless. We settled into our routine: Mother at the laser, me at the jackhammer, Haver humming as he shoveled, his memory clicked off.

Mother made a latticework of cuts, then offered the laser like a gift. Maybe it was her way of reestablishing our relationship. "You haven't practiced in weeks," she told me.

I set down the jackhammer, took the laser, and looked at the rockface. A typical cut, but I tapped her shoulder. Not wishing to speak, lest I lose my resolve, I indicated I didn't know where to begin.

She stepped up to the vein. She showed a line of rock and moved aside.

I made a perfect cut.

She toppled sideways, face contorted in agony, gloved hands clutching the gap that ran from her armpit to her opposite hip. Blood poured out like lava. Her intestines showed like a coiled snake. I fell to my knees and puked into my helmet. Haver dropped his shovel and stumbled over. I thrust the laser into his arms and switched on his memory.

"What have you done, you moron?" I yelled.

He dropped to his knees, trying to staunch the blood. "Mama? Mama?"

"She told you to hold the laser, not pull the goddamn trigger!"

"I'm sorry. I'm so sorry!"

She was gone.

I put a consoling hand on his shoulder. "She knows she's not supposed to let you touch the laser. She handed it to you and went to check the vein. She forgot to turn on the safety, and you accidentally touched the trigger. You understand?"

He gazed at me, confused, his features reflected in his face shield.

I repeated what I'd said, and he nodded.

I signaled for the EMTs and notified Corporate.

§

Haver didn't talk much after the accident. Just lay in his hammock whimpering whenever we weren't on the job. I ran the laser, worked the jackhammer, and helped him shovel. Our output was less than a third of what it had been.

What had I done? Surely there was another solution. But instead of thinking, I'd reacted.

That weekend, I took the jeep for a drive. Space had a way of speaking to me.

As I was leaving the cave entrance, Haver pulled himself down into the vehicle. "I'm going with," he said.

"You know where I'm going?"

"Don't care."

"Buckle up."

Sunlight soon embraced us. I thought it would help him with his depression. Instead, he covered his face shield with his hands and cried.

"Take it easy," I said. "You'll be okay."

"I'll never get over it!"

I put a gloved hand on his shoulder. "You're my big little brother. Always here to help."

His anguish felt like four hands were pulling my heart apart.

We drove for five E-hours, my guilt deepening. Were Haver not with me, I would have kept going. Mining comes with hefty life insurance policies. I'd had one from Corporate since birth. The money would go to Haver.

He wouldn't be shoveling rock the rest of his life. I looked over at him. His massive shoulders were so slumped it seemed only the jeep's harness kept him from crumpling. He stared at the floor. "I know what you did," he said after I cut the engine.

"About …?"

He beat his fists against the console. "You took Mama away!"

"Don't know what you're talking about."

"And now you'll kill me too. Sooner or later. Because you're afraid I'll tell."

"Don't talk nonsense. It was an accident."

"I know what you did."

"You weren't awake."

"Sometimes when I go away, I'm not really gone. I thought I'd been dreaming. But last night—I realized I hadn't been."

I wasn't going to listen. My stomach roiled with guilt.

I locked the jeep into slow cruise, checked my tether, and unbelted. I needed time away from him.

I rose into space and closed my eyes. A soft jerk told me the tether reached its end. I let my mind clear. What I had done, I had done for both of us. We'd find a partner and produce enough ore to make decent wages. Haver would get over Mother in time. If not, I'd turn off his memory permanently. Even then we could be a team.

Something barreled into my side.

It knocked the wind from me. My eyes snapped open, and I hung gasping as together we tumbled through space. It was Haver, his thrusters on full throttle, his size overpowering me.

"I wouldn't have told, Four! Never! I love you! But I can't trust you."

He reached behind me and ripped my thrusters' powerpack from their holders.

He'd hit me so hard I wasn't thinking clearly. Instinctively, I reacted by tearing away his oxygen line and kicking away from him. The escaping air sent him tumbling into space.

"Haver!" I screamed after him.

His figure got smaller and smaller.

A knife entered my field of vision, spinning slowly.

He'd cut the tether. The end of it floated a meter away.

I desperately grabbed for it.

A crack—aftermath of the impact—formed in my face shield.

Then spiderwebbed.

I put my glove over it. Within seconds, space would suck the air from my helmet.

Something came out of the dark.

A white whale.

The crack broadened.

Oxygen was wrenched from my lungs.

Nandy rolled, exposing her underside. I stuck my face in the emergency pod attached to the harness, my oxygen system interlocking. Consciousness wavered.

She headed home, my face buried in her belly.

I passed out.

§

Nurses entered my vision as soon as the EMTs cleared the ER airlock with the gurney. People twisted off my helmet and cut open my space suit. I lay gasping. News spiders scuttled up the walls and across the ceiling. They snapped pictures and extended mic legs.

"What's it like to be exposed to the vacuum of space, Mister Clover?"

"What's it like to be saved by the solar system's most famous whale?"

I was too numbed-up to reply.

"No comment," a nurse said.

"He's going into shock," another said. Bending over me, she reminded me of Mother. Maybe it was her watchful eyes behind her facemask. Maybe the swell of her breasts.

Maybe.

§

A surgeon peered down at me. "You're in a hyperbaric chamber," she said. "Ebullism damaged your cerebral cortex. We need to see the extent."

I attempted to nod, but my head was locked into place to keep me from shifting it.

"We're now removing the skullcap."

I watched the slanted mirror overhead. The physician pressed her index fingers against my temples, unlocking the pins that held on the top of my head. Body mods allowing for emergency removals were a must for miners, given all the accidents.

She pulled off the skullcap and lay it in the pan a nurse held.

"The brain has no pain receptors, so you won't feel a thing," the surgeon said. "You can watch if you like. Or we can put you under if you wish. Blink twice if you want to sleep."

No need for more sedative. I closed my eyes, calmed to the core.

"We'll wake you to ask you questions from time to time."

§

"Are you awake?"

"Uhh-huh."

"Can you tell us your name?"

"Nandy."

"Your name, Mister Clover. Your first name."

"Nandy."

"He's cognizant," the physician said.

"And sarcastic," the second voice said.

I realized I was still in surgery.

They asked questions while they probed my brain with forceps and tools whose names I didn't know. They had me smell and taste things. Incense. A whiff of ammonia—God, that. A bite of an orange segment.

"You're going to be fine," the physician said. "We're going to let you sleep now."

"Did Nandy"—I fought to formulate my thoughts—"save him too?"

"Who?"

"My brother. Haversham Algae."

The surgeons looked at each other.

"He was with you?"

"I tried to save him."

The physician pulled up a data screen.

"No record of his being with you."

§

A week after my operation, I was about to go back to work. I would be with Nandy. I requested new quarters.

A woman who gave her name only as Kim visited me. She was petite, round-faced, professional, and ponytailed. Lipstick that said kissable without looking gaudy.

She went through the rituals. How are you feeling, I'm terribly sorry for your loss. She handed me a card and pulled up a chair. "I'm in charge of acquisitions at the cetacean museum."

"I've seen it on the holo."

"We're creating an exhibit dedicated to Nandy. Saving you made her quite the celebrity. Let me rephrase that. She's been a celebrity, but her fame has skyrocketed." She chuckled. "That's a terrible verb. So Earthbound."

It felt good not to talk to a woman who might laugh now and beat me later.

"We'd like you to speak at our grand opening."

"I'm not much at public speaking."

She placed long-nailed fingers on the back on my hand. "Don't worry about that. I'll write a script, and you can practice it. Drapes will open. Nandy will be outside. We're expecting dignitaries. They're there to see her, so don't worry if you flub. They'll know you're just a—"

"Miner?"

She blushed. "I'm sorry, Mister Clover. I didn't mean—"

"No problem. And call me 'Four.'"

As in foreplay, I wanted to add.

"Four," she said. "And, oh!—I've other news." She scooted the chair forward. "Nandy's being reassigned. Corporate feels she will serve our purposes much better working at the museum on Ceres than she is here on Vesta, being a gofer. She'll be pulling a sleigh."

"Just what my mother wanted," I said. "I don't."

"Oh?"

"Not if I'm here on Vesta."

"Oh, that," she said. "You've inherited Nandy, so where she goes, you go. Corporate's transferring you to Ceres. There's a huge need for someone of your skills. You can visit Nandy every weekend, if you want." She leaned toward me and saw me glance down her blouse. She smiled. "I may be able to make those weekends three-day."

I lifted my gaze to hers. "Maybe we could have coffee sometime."

I immediately wished I hadn't spoken.

You think a realwoman wants a miner's synthelimbs between her legs?

"Dinner," she said. "My treat."

§

When I reached Ceres, Kim and I ate at Circle Accessible, billed as "a mod, mad, dining delight." She introduced me to everyone as a laserjack. I got quite a few, "Aren't you the miner who—" To which I answered, "Yeah, yeah, but let's not talk about me. Where are you from?"

The Ceres crowd weren't what I expected, or else they were bending over backwards to show they weren't classists. They didn't distinguish between trueborns and tubals, as Mother said. I enjoyed the conversations.

After we took our seats in the dining pods, I liked talking to Kim most of all. She had Scottied to Earth twice. "Beaming that distance is like having yourself pulled inside out and put back together again a dozen times," she said over drinks. She had visited the Patagonia megapolis the first time and the second time went to Antarctica, where in the inland sea she harpooned an arapaima, one of Earth's largest fresh-water fish.

The show began. The restaurant was barrel-shaped and faced an enormous circular window with a wonderful view. Spacesuited clowns and synchronized swimmers performed outside. Then the grav was turned off except in the pods, and the restaurant rotated like a Ferris wheel. Waiters stood in the middle and, with practiced discus-like throws, floated the food to the pods, which sucked in the plates to everyone's delight.

We dined on Shimanto River seaweed tempura, Okanagan sockeye salmon, and a Mars delectable, Deseree lentils, followed by coffee Wellington. "Ever thought of making Nandy even more famous?" she asked as she gave me that look over her coffee cup. Something warm squirmed in me. Seeing my confusion, she added, "Going into advertising? She's a natural for promoting products—and she could do it without missing a day playing with the kids here." She touched my hand. "There's serious cred to be made. And with you as spokesman? You'd make a fortune."

"Wouldn't know where to begin."

But seeing those eyes, I was willing to learn.

"I do," she said, and smiled.

We taxied to her apartment in one of those three-seater vehicles, one seat behind the other, that maneuvered through the narrow lanes of the city's interior. Having never dated before, I had no idea what to do at her doorstep.

When I awkwardly tried to kiss her, she put a finger against my lips. "I don't kiss on a first date. But there's a dessert shop around the corner. It has a levitating crème brûlée. We can call that our second date, okay?"

"Levitating?"

"It's so light you feel like you are."

She slipped her hand into mine as we strolled there.

Afterward, we returned to her place for the real treat.

§

Kim's script for me was rich with near-death metaphors. We practiced it whenever we were not engaged in physical conversations.

The opening of Nandy's exhibit went extraordinarily well. Three hundred attended: the best turnout Kim had seen at a museum function. She had worked wonders. Not only were there live feeds to Mars and Earth, she'd contacted most of the top advertising agencies and over a dozen of the top Fortune 500 companies. Almost all expressed interest in Nandy.

I spoke for fifteen minutes, then answered questions without sounding rehearsed. I surprised myself that I did almost as well on questions for which I hadn't prepped.

A question Kim HAD helped me with asked why Haver sought to murder me when I was trying to keep him from committing suicide after he accidentally killed our mother. I answered with real emotion. "Part of me believes he simply didn't want me to pull myself back into the jeep and go after him. But another part wonders"—my eyes welled with tears, and my voice cracked—"if he feared going through death's door without his big brother."

Then people asked about my relationship with Nandy.

Before I had to answer, the drapes behind me opened.

A window showcased Nandy before a vast sprinkling of stars. Fake flowers were woven around her harness, and a wreath encircled the narrow part before her tail. She somersaulted, much to everyone's delight, rolled left and right, swam in a circle, swam upside down—not that there's a rightside-up in space.

Kim stepped onto the podium and explained Nandy's physiological changes compared to the original species.

She ended with, "Of course, what makes Nandy unique are the dual tusks. They're rather short since she's female. Despite centuries of research, no one knows the tusks' purpose. The leading theory is that they're a sexual trait, like antlers, manes, or the feathers of a peacock. They're highly innervated, with millions of nerve endings, and thus may be sensory stimuli or used in communication with other narwhals."

A jeep pulling a sleigh drew up next to Nandy. There were five rows of seats, each row capable of carrying four. Museum techs left the jeep and hooked the sleigh up to Nandy.

"Whatever the case," Kim continued, "you are invited to experience the wonder of Miss Nandy for yourself. Join us on a ride in our space sleigh."

Twenty of us donned suits. As one of the two guests of honor, I was on the first ride. Kim accompanied me, along with Ceres's regent, a couple of Corporate's top execs, an actress and her current husband, and advertising execs Kim had invited.

Once outside the airlock, we clipped onto a couple of wires and hand-walked two at a time up to Nandy, everyone posing for pictures.

Kim linked her arm through mine as we paid Nandy our respects. When we made our way to the sleigh, I touched Kim's rear. She pushed my hand away and giggled. Nandy watched us so intently the photographer had to wave wildly so he could take the next picture.

Once everyone was loaded up, metal harnesses locked everyone in. Nandy started slowly. Kim and I were on the front seat, me holding the reins, the regent beside me, the museum's curator beside Kim, everyone waving to people back in the museum. Nandy pulled away from Ceres, people laughing over the compac. She expelled more exhale and sped up.

"Easy now, sweet one," I told her.

She swam faster. There was laughter around me. Everyone had seen the holos: The sleigh would revolve like a spinning screw as Nandy gained speed. We started to spin. The museum curators had recognized that youngsters would not be overly impressed with a simple sleigh ride. But a sleigh that spun faster and faster as the whale hauling it sped up? What child wouldn't be enthralled?

This time, Nandy was pulling a sleigh filled with VIPs. She wasn't supposed to speed. Nandy undulated, the sleigh rising and falling. Kim grabbed my arm in happy anticipation.

Nandy sped up. People shrieked with glee and lifted their arms, fluttering their hands, as the sleigh began to revolve.

"Slow down, Nandy," I called out, pulling the reins—though they were only for show.

Screeches emanated from her. None of the soft knocks and clicks and the low, melodic notes and tones of whale song. We neared the buoy. Kim clutched my arm insistently. "Four... *Four?*"

Faster.

The stars spun around us.

"She needs to slow down!" the regent called to me over the compac.

As we rounded the buoy, the sleigh spun faster than it did even for kids.

"Nandy!" I bellowed at her.

She responded. But not to my command.

Nandy came around the buoy much sharper than she should have. Torque twisted the breeching that bound her to the sleigh. The emergency release engaged.

Abruptly, she was free. Screaming for help into our helmets, we spun off into space.

She turned toward us. For the second time in my life, she was going to rescue me. She would nudge us to a halt. Back at the museum, everyone would have a nervous laugh.

She came onward. It took a moment to realize she wasn't slowing down.

Instead, she plowed toward us, her tusks like lances.

"Stop that damn beast!" the regent swore at me.

But what could I do except plead? Locked in our safety harnesses, we could not leap free.

My gaze met Nandy's glare, the people around me screaming in terror. In those eyes were hate, jealousy, the ire of a female betrayed—the anger of a family member sold into what she considered slavery by a man who had found another love.

I pushed away from Kim as far as our harnesses would allow. To this day, I don't know if I was trying to save her by drawing Nandy's attention—or save myself.

One of Nandy's tusks grazed my arm. The other skewered Kim as she shrieked over the compac.

§

I awaken as I do every day, to coughing and grumbling in the penal colony on Hygeia. There are fifty-six miners in the cave we carved. When one is killed, another is shipped in.

The workday is two hours longer than on Vesta. No days off. No drinking, drugs, whoring, or gambling. Violations mean worse conditions for everyone. The food is wretched, the heat unbearable, the pumped-in air stagnant. I sleep with my arms wrapped around my boots AND FEET lest others steal them.

The irony: I murdered my mother and indirectly killed my brother, but I was convicted of owning an errant animal. Nandy was also convicted. That humans and cetaceans cannot communicate is not grounds for acquittal or appeal. I never see her other than at work, and then from a distance.

Mother isn't here, of course, nor Haversham.

I think of them as I shovel.

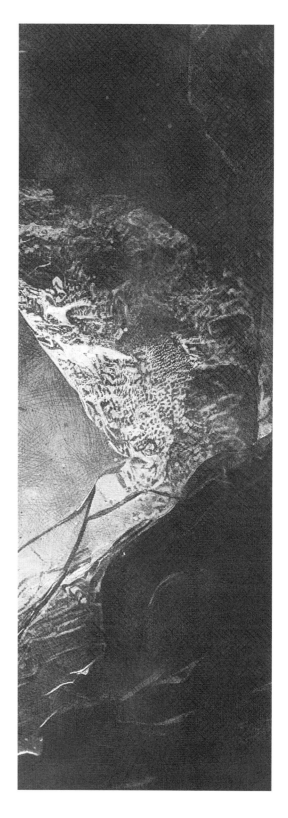

~XXI~
THE COLONISTS

SWINGING ON A STAR
Shawna K. Allen

Chapter One

Elias Lund shifted in his seat, clutching his book to his chest. Bullets of perspiration glistened on his forehead and trickled down his neck. His suit jacket hid the river flowing between his shoulder blades, puddling in his armpits, but there was no disguising the cascading rivulets from his temples. He swiped his brow and slid his glasses up his nose.

The lead panel interviewer, Mr. Bronson, laced his fingers together and towered from across the table, eyes narrowed. The scrutiny unbearable, Elias leaned back in the chair, the air in the Spartan interview room suffocating him.

"And why do you feel you're qualified to join us on the *Valiant*, Mr. Lund?"

"I'm a—" his voice squeaked, and he cleared his throat. "I'm a head research librarian with a knack for facts. I've stored many thousands–verbatim–up here."

Elias tapped his temple. Then he held up his book.

"And here. From classic literature to the schematics and operating manuals for hundreds of devices, armaments, and vehicles, including the blueprints of the *Valiant*, sir. LR-Class with a passenger capacity of twenty five hundred, and a crew compliment of four hundred—"

"Excuse me." A young woman at the end of the table raised her hand and smiled. "We have computer databases for that, Mr. Lund. They contain everything from Shakespeare to *Godier's Theories on Quantum Entanglement*."

His face burned, annoyed at the interruption, his train of thought lost, but not his composure. He forced a smile and plodded on.

"Yes, Miss Turner, but should there be a system failure or computer malfunction, I can be consulted on any subject at a moment's notice. Right here." He pointed to his temple again. "And, right here." He tapped his book.

"We were wondering about that. What is it?" Mr. Bronson asked.

Elias's face lit up.

"It's my life's work, my compendium of everything, if you will. It contains excerpts and works from every inventor, author, scientist, composer, and artist. The pages are a paper and micro-sensor composite of my own invention, touch sensitive and voice reactive, with real-time editing. There's also holographic imaging projection interfaces and expandable data storage capacity contained within the binding. I've uploaded all knowledge at my disposal thus far."

Mr. Bronson eyed the book. The size of an ancient wallpaper sampler, it hardly looked the part. Heavy and cumbersome, it was leatherbound and locked, embossed initials—EGL—adorning the lower right hand corner. Except for the gold lettering and security mechanism, the tome was unremarkably brown, devoid of other embellishments.

"Interesting. May we see it?"

Elias hugged his book closer, both arms wrapped around it.

"I'm sorry, it's proprietary. I also plan to start a companion volume of our exploits in space, using the same patented materials and the latest in petabit data transfer. I'm a historian," Elias searched his suit jacket pockets, retrieved a folded piece of paper, and held it out, hand shaking. "I have an outline—"

Mr. Bronson waved his hand and shook his head, rejecting the offering.

"We appreciate your efforts, Mr. Lund, but this is a passenger inquiry, not a job interview. Our crew is complete, including esteemed chroniclers. We're looking for a blending of skills and talents, and, of course, compatibility and the psychological endurance to withstand a long space voyage."

"Yes, of course. It will take all kinds, from engineers to electricians, to astrophysicists and horticulturists, but the journey is ten years, and who knows what we may encounter along the way. Even a scholarly passenger could be invaluable in an emergency."

"We will have professors and other educators on board, Mr. Lund."

"But the majority of selectees I've seen are…are…" Elias fidgeted in his chair once more, struggling not to blurt out the obvious. The situation called for diplomacy, but how did one politely say the current roster was fluff, pretty packages with nothing inside?

Tilting his head, Mr. Bronson's gaze bore deeper. "Are what, Mr. Lund?"

"Perhaps lacking the skills and acumen to handle the tasks at hand."

Silence followed his declaration, and he looked down.

"Maybe one or two, but it takes more than civil engineers and architects to build a city. To that end, we're acquiring all skills and trades, engineers as well as tinkerers and dreamers, but we appreciate your insight into the importance of balance. I think we have all the information we need at this point. Do you have any further questions, Mr. Lund?"

Elias lifted his eyes and grinned.

"Is there any reason why you wouldn't select me as a passenger?" he said.

Taken aback by his directness, Mr. Bronson stiffened. He glanced left and right, his expression urging others to jump in, but they turned away, shuffling paperwork.

"Good question. Let me see," Mr. Bronson said and activated his 3D computer screen.

Graphics popped up in the air between them. Mr. Bronson swiped the holographic documents in Elias's portfolio.

"Ah. Your IQ is impressive, but a good portion of our selectees are MENSA. We've already met our intelligence quota, enough to ensure future generations of geniuses. You fall into the acceptable age range, but on the higher end. You scored above average on our aptitude tests, and have a perfect score on the SAT's. However, we're not looking for perfection, Mr. Lund, or the superlative of anything. More of a mixture of well-rounded passengers who exhibit a blending of talent and skills, flexibility, appeal, and team spirit, in addition to education and abilities. There's also that je ne sais quoi, a uniqueness which sets one apart from others, enriching the pool."

"We also found a genetic anomaly in your DNA makeup, one with the potential of expression in any offspring," Miss Turner added.

"Yes, my nearsightedness. It's easily correctable, only I chose to forego surgery because of my penchant for reading."

"And, at thirty, you still live at home with your parents," she said.

"Out of convenience. It's within commuting distance of the city library, my employer, and housing is scarce in the area. I've been on a waiting list, but nothing's opened up."

Mr. Bronson rubbed his chin. "I see. Anything else, Mr. Lund?"

"Other than my eyesight, is there any other reason why I wouldn't be selected?"

"You've given us a lot to consider. We'll let you know, Mr. Lund. If there's nothing else, thank you for coming in, and please enjoy the rest of your day."

Stunned the interview was over, Elias lingered on the chair while the others rose.

"That's it?" he said as they filed out, put off that his interview was much shorter than the other candidates' meetings.

No one replied. They exited, avoiding eye contact. They had left him holding his book, bewildered over their abrupt departure. He'd had no chance to showcase his talents.

Elias left the interview room, shoulders slumped, and ambled to the shuttle stop. While waiting for the hover train, the Drifter, to arrive, his phone vibrated, startling him.

§

Chapter Two

Floored by their last interviewee, Mr. Bronson paced in his private conference room, hands behind his back. His team was still laughing over his absurdity. The oafish man was a definite pass, but he was hesitant to dismiss him entirely, repugnant though he was.

The audacity of the fool rankled him, his awkwardness unbearable. Surely, he knew how unaesthetic and disagreeable he was, he need only take off his glasses and look in the mirror. Though hardly deserving of steerage on a dinghy, there was something about the clod's book which intrigued him.

"Insufferable man! He's little more than a glorified librarian, the sniveling, little toad," Mr. Bronson said. "The nerve!"

"His social ranking is high. His content is consumed by the masses like a sponge," Miss Turner said, scrolling through social media. "He has a strong online presence going for him."

"Yes, yes, I know. I've watched his channel. He doesn't show himself on camera and uses voice altering software. You saw the man. He's a buffoon."

Miss Turner studied her computer screen. "He received the lowest possible score on the Kardashian Scale, not one selectee swiped on his profile."

"I'm not surprised. We can't afford singletons on this journey. Every passenger, down to the janitors, must start families by the time we reach Xeric Seven. Our guests need to be agreeable, if not to the eye, then the spirit. He's neither; a loner who would hardly come out of his room. But I'm curious about his book. If it is, indeed, everything he claims it is, the technology could be invaluable."

"His book isn't a candidate, sir," an associate said.

"I know that!"

"Perhaps we could purchase it. Everything has a price," Miss Turner said.

Mr. Bronson furrowed his brow. He snapped his fingers. "Do it."

"And if he says 'no'?"

"Up the price until he does. Once we launch, we'll have no need of funding, so throw every bit of surplus at him. I must have that book."

"It may come down to a package deal. Either him and the book, or nothing."

"We'll cross that bridge should we come to it. First, let's try negotiating a price."

"I'll get right on it, but may I please ask, why is this a priority?"

"As annoying and unattractive as Mr. Lund is, he's an intelligent man with a valid point. Should we have a system failure, we'll have to resort to good old fashioned ingenuity. If time were of the essence, it would be handy having all knowledge in one place at our fingertips, instead of hunting down individual manuals and experts. The time saved could mean the difference between life and death."

"So noted."

"For now, send him an offer on the book and a 'maybe' on joining our voyage, and see what shakes out. Dangle that carrot as long as possible. Make it irresistible, perhaps offer him a suite on the voyage for the next stellar encounter."

Miss Turner perused her notes. "But sir, the next opportunity for a close planetary elliptical is not for another two billion years."

"Precisely."

Laughter echoed throughout the chamber.

§

Chapter Three

The notification screen announced a text from Bronson Space Center. Elias inhaled. This was it.

His hopes soared, his hands trembled, and his book fell from his grasp, landing on his toe. He cursed under his breath, picked it up, and, in his haste, dropped his phone. Frustrated, he retrieved it, a jagged crack now running down the length of the screen, but the message was still readable.

Thank you for your interest in the Valiant Project. We would like to purchase your book titled The Compendium of Everything. We are offering one million credits, WC, upon delivery. Please forward your secure banking account information for payment, which will be transferred to you within twenty four hours of receiving the book. Sincerely, the Bronson Space Center.

Elias's heart leapt into his throat, choking him. He gasped and wheezed. A million credits in World Currency was his for the taking, all he had to do was hand over his book. He could buy a place of his own and a vehicle, to heck with public transportation and the irksome advertisements on perpetual broadcast. Maybe even give some to his parents.

"But I want to go to Xeric Seven," he said.

He replied to the notification. The book is free upon my acceptance into the

Valiant Project.

We are willing to offer you three million credits for the purchase of your compendium.

"You're not listening," he said, and replied, The book is free upon my acceptance into the Valiant Project.

Thank you for your interest in the Valiant Project. We regret to inform you that we have selected other candidates who more nearly meet our needs. We wish you all the best in your future endeavors, and our offer to purchase your book now stands at five million credits, WC. Sincerely, the Bronson Space Center.

"More nearly? But I tick off all the boxes!"

The Drifter zoomed up and hovered in front of Elias. He had half a mind to turn around and confront the interviewers, insisting they take him on board. He was the best choice. Who better than a fully qualified researcher with his intellect, his photographic memory, and his extensive knowledge?

"Passenger, please board," a mechanical voice boomed. "Service will resume in fifteen seconds."

Startled, Elias climbed aboard, stewing over his rejection. He mumbled to himself. Other riders on the public transport subtly moved away from him while he sputtered and muttered, mulling over the interview. The gall of those people.

Polite and neatly dressed, he'd rehearsed the interview questions, practicing in front of his parents to ensure his answers were perfect. They urged him to apply, eagerly adding what better way to share his knowledge than to take it to a new world, where it would be of use? His mother suggested the suit and tie, and to tone down the chatter, letting the interviewers do most of the talking. His father only grunted.

Ads blared from the overhead panels, including one for the Valiant Project. A beautiful woman wearing a swimsuit smiled into the camera.

I'm an influencer, and I love long walks on the beach and the latest Gucci fashions. My brand is a name you can trust, and I'm going to Xeric Seven…"

The camera cut to a chiseled, shirtless man wearing a hard hat, a sledgehammer hoisted over his shoulders. His biceps rippled and flexed.

I'm a carpenter, I build durable, comfortable homes, and I'm going to Xeric Seven…"

The pair embraced, eyed each other up and down until their gazes locked. Their plastic faces turned to the camera.

We're going to Xeric Seven. Are you?" The commercial faded out with laughter.

"No," Elias grumbled.

By the time he reached home, twenty one of those blasted commercials, each one grating on his nerves more than the last, had rubbed salt in his wounds. He wasn't going to Xeric Seven. The influencer, the carpenter, an actor, and a host of other everyday people proclaimed they, too, were heading into outer space.

Stepping into his foyer, an epiphany hit him like a ton of books. He halted in his tracks.

"Where are the doctors and professors? The engineers? The scientists?" he said. "Those passengers have an average IQ, combined. MENSA my ass."

His plump little mother popped her head out of the kitchen.

"What was that, my handsome boy?"

He hung up his coat. "Oh, nothing."

"So, how'd it go? When do we start packing?"

With a huff, he turned to her and pecked her cheek. She tittered.

"Not yet," he said. "Call me when dinner's ready."

"Your father's running late. His Drifter lost power again."

"I keep telling him to take the B line, it has a newer model."

"You know how mulish he is."

He went to his bedroom and changed into something more comfortable. Then he sat down to create content for his channels on SpinOff and Hallux, his preferred social media platforms, but couldn't concentrate. "We're going to Xeric Seven…"he said, mocking them.

He switched from his channel to the Valiant Project website. The latest mission update showed one hundred openings left, the slots going fast. Next to each passenger's name was a short bio. His brow furrowed as he skimmed through them.

"Where are the educators? The scholars? The experts?"

He next perused MENSA's site and cross-referenced the names on the passenger list with current members. Not one matched. Elias slammed his laptop shut, seeing red.

"They lied to me. I'm an acclaimed researcher. Did they think I wouldn't find out I'd been hoodwinked?"

§

Chapter Four

Xeric Seven. Before his rejection, the sound of the star's name zinged Elias with excitement and anticipation. Not anymore. Hearing it nauseated him and filled him with rage.

When his parents suggested this trip, he scoffed at the notion, less than enthused with the idea of a one way ticket to the heavens. Then advertisements for the Valiant Project exploded onto the scene, lighting up 3D billboards and virtual marketplaces, sparking his interest. The more he researched the star, the more enamored with space exploration he had become. Drawn in by artists' imaginative renderings of the exoplanets, he pictured himself strolling their beautiful hills and beaches, a new man with a new life. The prospect of reinventing himself on the shores of Xeric Seven grabbed a hold of him. The lure of being the planet's first official historian and the gatekeeper of all knowledge only added to his fascination, twisting his interest into an obsession. He had to get on that ship. Elias absorbed every mission detail like a sponge, his passage sure to be a done deal.

In five years, the Xeric star system would be less than a lightyear away, crossing the Oort cloud, too close to let pass by unvisited. Whenever anyone imagined interstellar travel, they envisioned setting out in generational ships to the nearest star system with habitable planets, a century long voyage with their current technology. Only Mr. Bronson dreamed of settling planets as their stars swung close to Earth, closing the distance. Ingenious man. Elias dedicated a whole page in his compendium to the proper motion of stars moving independently throughout the galaxy, some coming near enough to hitch a ride on one of its planets.

The journey would take ten years, but preparations began shortly after Xeric Seven's near approach was discovered decades ago. Now everything was coming together. With the launch window nearing, the final task of selecting and training passengers for the mission was in progress. He longed to be among them. But now the shuttle was leaving the space depot without him.

Their offer for his life's work was now up to seven million. The amount tempted him. There was little he couldn't do with such riches. He'd never have to work another day in his life, though he enjoyed his job. He could continue his pursuit of knowledge at his leisure, researching whatever tickled his fancy, for as long as he liked. The ridiculous sum could buy him any guilty pleasure, except the one thing he desired most: passage on the Valiant.

He snorted at the latest notification and ignored it throughout his shift, but curiosity got the better of him on his way home. That sneaky creature, hope, crept up on him, only to be dashed yet again. The space center hadn't rescinded their rejection, but, instead, offered him ten million credits, WC, final offer. His phone dropped out of his hand and onto the Drifter floor.

"I'm a Jack of all trades, I can fix just about anything, and I'm not going to Xeric Seven," the man in the ad above his head said, frowning, but then the actor's face beamed. "But I am on standby. And, you, too, can join us on the waiting list in the unlikely event there's a cancellation. For one million credits, WC, you can enjoy the same preparedness training alongside actual selectees, securing a place on the Valiant should a vacancy become available. Sign up today…"

Elias raised a brow. He picked up his phone, glanced at the latest offer, and then back up at the advertising panel. So the Valiant had a waiting list, did it? Furiously, he typed in his response.

I will accept your offer to purchase my book for ten million credits, WC, to be tendered immediately, under the following conditions:

I am guaranteed the number one spot on the Valiant's wait list in the event of a cancellation or death. My standby preparedness training will be paid for by the Bronson Space Center. Should I obtain passenger status, I will be given first class accommodations. If these terms are agreed upon, the book will be delivered on the day of launch, regardless of my passenger status.

Within seconds of sending his final offer, his phone lit up with a notification from the space center, startling him. Reading the reply, his breath left his body.

Agreed.

§

Chapter Five

Upon receipt of the funds, Elias quit his job, bought a country estate, and spent the next year training for the space voyage. He was put through all the paces, the drills, and the testing, passing with flying colors. The last leg of the training consisted of living in a voyage simulator for six months with all the passengers and standby participants, isolated from the outside world. A replica of the Valiant was recreated on an island in the Pacific, and all were flown out.

Elias was assigned a cubicle of a room. Smaller than his former bedroom, his quarters contained a fold-out bunk hanging off the wall, a slim closet, and a desk with a chair. Upon seeing his cramped accommodations, he scowled.

"Concierge, there's been a mistake. This is not a first class suite," Elias said into the com.

"First class accommodations are for confirmed passengers only."

"But it's been nearly two years, surely there's been a cancellation or death of a confirmed passenger during that time."

"Negative. All selectees are in attendance."

"Very well."

For the next six months, he hardly moved out of his chair, making no effort to connect with other passengers, as predicted. He attended obligatory activities and disaster drills, but opted out of participating in daily life.

As launch day approached, Elias checked the passenger list hourly for cancellations and deaths. With only months until liftoff, he grew anxious. Not one vacancy opened up, no one backed out of the program. Or died. Statistically, it was impossible. Situations came up, people passed away, minds changed. Out of the thousands of people slated to set sail, it was difficult for him to believe not a single passenger had given up their seat, voluntarily or otherwise.

Only one needed to bow out, and then he was a shoo-in. What was the hold up? He paced around his study, his research and vlogging on hold, desperate for a solution. An educated, rich man ought to be able to devise something.

A rich man.

He snapped his fingers.

"That's it! I'll offer a ton of money for someone to give up their spot. One of them will bite. All I need is one."

He composed an offer no one could refuse and sent the missive to every passenger. What was a couple million credits? He wouldn't need them in space, the anticipated system of commerce barter and trade. World Currency would be useless.

After sending the messages, Elias went for a walk. Confident one of the passengers would take him up on his offer, he strolled with a bounce in his step, his heart light, unable to contain his excitement or elation. With his latest scheme, he was all but guaranteed passage.

Weeks passed with no responses. To his chagrin, nobody gave up their seat on the Valiant, not for two million credits. Not for three. Or four. He upped the ante to five million, the highest he could go without depleting his coffers.

Two months before launch, and there were no takers. He cursed the passengers, the crew, the space center, and Mr. Bronson himself. How dare they deny the most intelligent human in the world a place on the first ever colony ship? Didn't they know how much they needed his knowledge and expertise on every subject known to humankind?

But it was his book they wanted, not him. They reminded him daily of his promise to deliver it, filling him with resentment and rage. His mass rejection by the passengers added fuel to the fire and his determination. He would be on that ship. Desperate times called for desperate measures, even sinister ones.

If no one would give up their slot, he'd make one.

§

Chapter Six

Tossing a dirty shovel in the back of his vehicle, Elias brushed his hands together and left the scene. It wasn't difficult tracking down one of the passengers, most of them streamed their trivial lives on social media, broadcasting their every move. Selecting one after careful research, Elias flew to his location, following him on a solo nature hike. Once cornered, it was as easy as ambushing him off trail as he relieved himself, and then disposing of him deep in the woods where he fell, his passage on the Valiant now Elias's.

After taking care of this one minor detail, Elias spent the weeks before departure putting his house in order. Then he packed his bags according to mission specs and spent his last days on Earth at the ocean, unsure if their new home would really have beaches. The space center was shaky on the details of the lay of the land. No matter, he would be there to describe them in all their splendor on everyone's behalf.

Two days before departure, he bid farewell to his parents and arrived at the launch site. With his baggage in tow, his book clutched to his chest, he waited in the check-in line. Chatting lively with his fellow passengers, he interacted with them more during those hours than he had during training. When he reached the front of the line, he beamed as he presented his standby credentials to the clerk.

"I'm standby passenger Elias G. Lund, reporting for duty," he said.

The clerk searched for his name and furrowed her brow. "We aren't taking on any standby passengers, Mr. Lund."

"You've had cancellations. I know of at least one poor soul who's a no-show. I read about it in the media, he went missing."

"According to the passenger manifest, all passengers are accounted for, and those who haven't checked in yet are en route."

"There's been a mistake. Please check again, I'm Elias G. Lund. In the event of a cancellation or death, I'm first in line on the standby list. There has been at least one no-show, a Francis Smith. Please double check."

"I don't show a passenger by that name."

"That's impossible. He's on the original manifest." Elias showed her a printout of the list.

"I don't have him on the final list."

"Then there's been some sort of clerical error. Please get Mr. Bronson on the phone, he can straighten this out."

Giving him an exasperated look, the clerk tapped her headset and called the space center.

"I need to speak to Mr. Bronson, I have an Elias Lund checking in, saying he's a standby passenger, insisting there's been a no-show, but I'm showing all passengers accounted for... Sure, I'll hold... Yes, Mr. Bronson, there's an Elias Lund here, trying to check in, but he's not on the passenger list and is insisting on speaking with you... I'll let him know. Thank you. Mr. Lund? Please step aside, Mr. Bronson will be with you shortly."

Two security personnel emerged from the crowd and guided him off to the side. He shook out of their grip, appalled by his treatment. For hours, they guarded him, all the while he watched as the passengers received their boarding passes and shuttled off to quarantine. Mr. Bronson appeared from the door of the launch facility.

"Greetings, Mr. Lund, I see you've come to deliver your book. Much appreciated." Mr. Bronson held out his hand.

"We had a deal, Mr. Bronson. My book in exchange for passage on your ship if there was an opening."

"Quite right, Mr. Lund, and if there wasn't an opening, you'd relinquish the book for considerations paid. We've had no cancellations or deaths, only two no-shows, and those vacancies were awarded by lottery weeks ago. Our deal didn't include those who simply didn't show up."

"Now you're twisting our words, Mr. Bronson. A no-show is a cancellation by default."

"Terms which weren't specified in the original agreement," Mr. Bronson said, and then waved at the guards.

One of them wrangled the book from Elias and handed it to Mr. Bronson.

"Give that back!"

"Thank you for its safe delivery. Please show Mr. Lund to the gate. And don't forget to grab some merch on the way out, on the house. Good day to you, sir."

Mr. Bronson turned away, leaving Elias at the mercy of the security guards, who tossed him out like garbage.

Elias landed on his behind, fit to be tied, but all was not lost. He'd planned for this turn of events. Getting to his feet, he brushed himself off and retrieved a second tome from his suitcase. Clutching it to his chest, he stormed away, his head held high. Down, but not out, he'd rebuild a new life here, on Earth, and the Valiant and her crew could go choke on the rings of Saturn. If he couldn't accompany his life's work into space, nobody would.

Turning, Elias gave the Valiant a final glance and smiled. "Never judge a book by its cover."

§

Chapter Seven

Mr. Bronson popped the champagne cork amid uproarious shipwide cheers. Cleared of Earth's atmosphere, they were heading to the moon for a gravity assist, and then their journey would begin in earnest. With white foam spewing from the mouth of the bottle, he offered celebratory pours into awaiting flutes, and then handed it off to a white-gloved steward. His patrons tapped on their glasses, demanding a speech.

Pride swelled in his breast, and he humbly acceded to their wishes. The crowd quieted down. He cleared his throat and raised his glass.

"Few words can sum up this momentous occasion, so I won't even try. Instead, I honor each and every one of you, the best the world has to offer. We will go down in the annals of history as the bravest human beings to ever walk the Earth… and then leave it. We will be the first to venture beyond Mars. The first to settle a new planet. The first to see a new star with our own eyes. The way ahead may be perilous, our futures uncertain, but if we succeed, our rewards will be many and far outweigh any sacrifices. May our travels be light. Santé!" Mr. Bronson held up his glass, and then took a sip.

Miss Turner approached him, carrying a hefty leatherbound book and handed it over.

"As you requested, sir," she said.

He kissed her cheek. "Thank you, Miss Turner. You're relieved of duty, enjoy the rest of the voyage. Dismissed."

She nodded and disappeared into the crowd.

One of his esteemed patrons, a rich, elderly widow, Mrs. Collins, eyed the book with delight.

"What's that you have there, Charles?" she asked.

"A masterpiece. It contains the works of every author, composer and great thinker, in addition to every system on this ship, and various instructions and architectures in which to build our new home."

"Impressive. Let's have a look then, shall we?"

Mr. Bronson smiled. "Why not?"

He laid the book on the buffet table and pressed the lock. To his surprise and delight, it sprung open. His breath hitched, all the wondrous content it contained running wild in his imagination. He lifted the cover and set it down.

Glancing at the first page, his brow furrowed. He laughed nervously. Mrs. Collins crowded around him, soon joined by others, and glanced over his shoulder. He flipped to the next page, and then the next, leafing through them faster and faster, his rage building with each turn of the ordinary parchment, until he reached the back cover, where all he found was one single, handwritten word.

Kaboom.

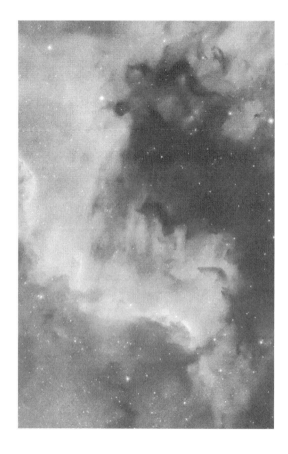

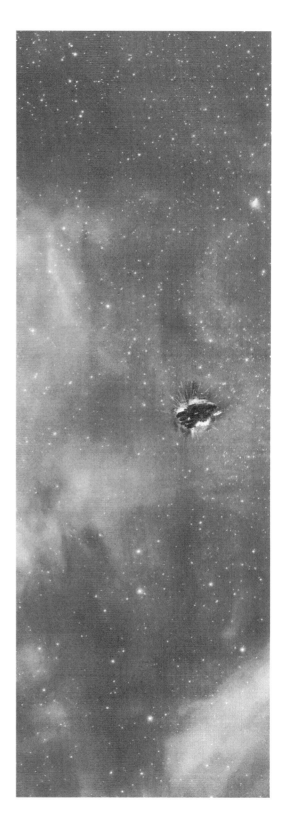

ABOUT THE CONTRIBUTORS

Shawna K. Allen
Author, "Swinging on a Star"
Shawna K. Allen is a writer from Maine with a BA in journalism from the University of Maine in Orono. A former longtime employee of Consolidated Communications, she has a background in IT and telecommunications. When she isn't writing, she enjoys reading and genealogy, and is also a cold case volunteer for the missing and unidentified.

Christine Amsden
Author, "Doomed From the Start"
Christine Amsden is the author of nine award-winning fantasy and science fiction novels, including the Cassie Scot Series. In addition to writing, she is a freelance editor and political activist. In her free time, she enjoys role playing, board games, and a good cup of tea. She lives in the Kansas City area with her husband and two kids.

Mark S Bailen
Author, "Rising Cove"
Mark S. Bailen has an MFA from the University of Arizona, has attended Taos Toolbox, and participated in the Storied Imaginarium. He is a current member of Codex and the SFWA, and has published works in *Fantasy, Nature, Andromeda Spaceways Magazine, Daily Science Fiction, and Little Blue Marble*. His website is fakemontain.com.

H. A. Bari
Author, "Pilgrimage by Ten Thousand Trains"
H. A. Bari is a student and veteran of the Chicago L Trains, and the undertaker of a few pilgrimages himself. He writes in his spare time, and counts this as his first published story.

Zack Be
Author, "As Able the Air"
Zack Be is a psychotherapist and obscure songwriter living in Maryland. "As Able the Air" previously appeared as a winning story in Writers of the Future vol. 36, and his fiction has previously appeared in *Asimov's Science Fiction* and is forthcoming in *Analog Science Fiction and Fact*. Zack is also the editor of *Inner Workings*, an anthology of SFF short fiction and craft essays forthcoming from Calendar of Fools..

M. Ian Bell
Author, "New Start"
M. Ian Bell is a writer and educator from New Jersey. His work appears in *Shimmer, Apex, and Fusion Fragment,* and you can follow him on Twitter @m_ianbell.

Kevin J. Binder
Author, "Judicial Review"
Kevin J. Binder's work has been published in *McSweeney's, Liquid Imagination, Blue Lake Review, Defenestration,* and elsewhere. He received his MFA from George Mason University, where he was awarded the Shelley A. Marshall Fiction Award and the Alan Cheuse Nonfiction Award. He has previously served as fiction editor of phoebe literary journal. You can find him on Mastodon @kevbot5dot0 and on Twitter @RealKevinBinder.

Brandon Butler
Lead Editor
Brandon Butler is a Canadian and Maritimer, not necessarily in that order. Hailing from Halifax, Nova Scotia, he currently lives, works and writes from Toronto, Ontario. A previous winner of the *Writers of the Future Contest (vol. #19),* his work has been sold and published with *Third Flatiron Publishing, Helios Quarterly Magazine, Bad Dream Entertainment* and *Dragon's Roost Press.* He can be found online at: www.bydifferenthighways.com and @2BWritingStuff

Ben Coppin
Author, "The Time Lottery"
Ben Coppin lives in Ely in the UK. He wrote a university textbook on artificial intelligence which was published in the US in 2004 and has been writing fiction in the past few years. He's had a number of short stories (mostly science fiction) published and has completed the second draft of his first novel. In 2007 he published and edited an online science fiction magazine, Darker Matter, which ran for five issues.

About the Contributors

Marco Cultrera
Author, "Support Group: Apocalypse"

Marco Cultrera was born in Rome (Italy) and now lives in Ottawa (Canada), where he followed the love of his life twenty plus years ago. He has a master's degree in Theoretical Physics, which he's not ashamed to say he uses more in his writing than in his daily work. He's been a programmer, videogame designer and writer and worked in every facet of technology. He's published three short stories and a novella in online magazines so far and is hard at work on his new novel, while juggling a busy household that includes three daughters and four cats.

Andrew Dibble
Managing Editor

Andy Dibble writes weird theology and other speculative fiction from Madison, Wisconsin and works as a healthcare IT consultant. He has supported the electronic medical record of large healthcare systems in six countries. While an undergraduate, he completed four majors—computer science, religious studies, philosophy, and Asian studies—and published a paper on two of India's great epics, the Mahabharata and the Bhagavata Purana. He completed his master of theological studies at Harvard Divinity School. His "A Word That Means Everything" about Bible translation into alien languages won first place in L. Ron Hubbard's *Writers of the Future Contest*. His work also appears in 396 About the Contributors *Space & Time, Sci Phi Journal*, and others. He is Articles Editor for *Speculative North*.

Karl Dandenell
Author, "The Schadenfreuders"

Karl Dandenell is a graduate of Viable Paradise and a Full Member of Science Fiction and Fantasy Writers Association. He and his family, plus their cat overlords, live on an island near San Francisco famous for its Victorian architecture and low speed limit. His preferred drinks are strong Swedish tea and single malt scotch.

Louis Evans
Author, "Rocket Man"

Louis Evans has lived a life thus far untroubled by recurring dreams. He hopes to keep it that way. His fiction has previously appeared in *Vice, The Magazine of Fantasy & Science Fiction, Analog Science Fiction & Fact, Interzone*, and many more. He's a graduate of the Clarion West class of 2022. He's online at evanslouis.com and on mastodon at wandering.shop/@louisevans

Jalyn Renae Fiske
Author, "Soul Candy"
Jalyn Renae Fiske resides in Texas with her partner and three cats and serves as Fiction Editor for James Gunn's Ad Astra magazine. She has her MFA in Creative Writing from Goddard College and is an alum of the Speculative Fiction Writing Workshop with Chris McKitterick at the University of Kansas. She likes to write the gamut of speculative fiction, from dragons to ghosts to AI, and finds her favorite themes tend to involve psychological horror and characters reconciling with loss. Her work has appeared in such places as *Mythaxis, The Future Fire*, and *The Overcast podcast*, as well as in anthologies from Rogue Blades Entertainment and Transmundane Press. Her story "Soul Candy" was previously published at *Freedom Fiction Journal.* Find updates on her writing at: https://jalynfiske.wixsite.com/jrenaewriter.

Iain Hannay Fraser
Author, "Three Weeks Without Changing History"
Iain Hannay Fraser works days as a legal analyst and in the field of anonymous government financial documents he has been published hundreds of times, and about a dozen times in the field of fiction. He has been printed under various pseudonyms, including pro-level publications AE Canadian SF Review and Crossed Genres, in online magazines including Domain SF, Blaster Books, Silverthought Online and the Fiction Vortex, and in the anthologies Abbreviated Epics and Astronomical Odds.

Fulvio Gatti
Author, "Enough Time"
Fulvio Gatti is an ESL writer and associate SFWA member from the wine hills of Piemonte Italy (still mostly sober), whose most notable publishing credit is the story "Who Smiles Last", published in the Nov 2021 issue of "Galaxy's Edge". Website: www.fulviogatti.it

About the Contributors

George Guthridge
Author, "Nandy"

Dr. George Guthridge has been an SFWA active member since 1977. He has six novels and 100+ short stories sold; none self-published. He has 22 collective sales to the markets of *Amazing, Analog, Asimov's, F&SF,* and another 22 to major anthologies. He is also a co-winner of the *Bram Stoker Award,* for best novel. He is a *Hugo* award finalist, and two-time *Nebula* finalist. Additionally, he is the Grand Prize Winner of the *Las Vegas International Screenplay Competition* and a National finalist for the *Ben Franklin Award* for the year's best book about education. He has been named as one of the top 78 teachers in America.

Storm Humbert
Author, "Master Brahms"

Storm Humbert lives in Michigan with his wife, Casey, and cat, Nugget. He is a graduate of Temple University's MFA program, where he studied with Samuel R. (Chip) Delany. His work has appeared in *Andromeda Spaceways, Apex Magazine, Interzone,* and others. He is also a winner of the *Writers of the Future Contest,* so his work was featured in the *Writers of the Future anthology #36.* Most recently, his work appeared in the "Of Wizards and Wolves" anthology in memory of Dave Farland from Wordfire Press and "The Librarian" anthology from Air & Nothingness Press. More of Storm's work can be found at his site: www.stormhumbertwrites.com.

Marco Marin
Illustrator

A Fantasy Painter and a Creature Breeder, those are the titles I want to be remembered for. I have a driving passion to create worlds, creatures and characters, bringing them to life through artistic visualization. I am passionate about videogames, card games, movies, cartoons, books and anywhere where the ringing bells of fantasy echo. Working with likeminded people gathering in teams and putting our energy together to flush out worlds and create universes of wonder is my desire. I want to meet people whose talents and driving passions can complement, challenge and nourish a wonderful narrative. If you are looking for someone who is passionate, borderline obsessive, incisive and with a loving approach to teamwork, look no further. I am your Fantasy Painter and your Creature breeder.
https://ulmo88.artstation.com/

Kristen Miller
Author, "The Opal"

Kristen Miller is a copywriter and marketing specialist by day and an imaginer of weird and creepy worlds by night. Her speculative fiction has appeared in *Daikaijuzine* and *Fiction Vortex*. A Syracuse native, she currently lives in Raleigh, NC with her husband and children, and is really enjoying the weather.

Jason Mills
Author, "Plinthgate Papers"

Jason Mills is a computer technician in England. This is one of his first published stories, but he has been writing intermittently for years. Several of his odd projects are available online, including a rendering of the Bible in limericks and a compendium of a thousand magical treasures for role-playing games. Find them at tinyurl.com/jasonmillsbooks.

Jacob Pérez
Author, "The Bridge"

Jacob Pérez was born in Ponce, Puerto Rico, but spent most of his young adult life in Boston, Massachusetts, earning a nursing degree. He now lives in California with his wife, two beautiful kids, and an indifferent cat named Zelda.

Louis Rivera
Graphic Designer, Cover & Interior Artist, all renditions

Using the power of storytelling archetypes to grow businesses, I create graphics fulfilling your vision and imagination. An avid Fiction writer and graphic freelancer, I'm always excited to be working with someone's project or business using the skill sets I've honed over the years in Industrial and Graphic Design.
You can get in touch with me at: www.lrdesign.agency

David F. Shultz
Managing Editor

David F. Shultz writes from Toronto, Canada, where he is Lead Editor at *Speculative North*. His 80+ publications are featured through publishers such as *Augur*, *Diabolical Plots*, and *Third Flatiron*. Author webpage:
davidfshultz.com

About the Contributors

Meirav Seifert
Author, "That Silver-Black Shimmer"
Meirav Seifert is a queer storyteller based out of Tel Aviv-Yafo. Seifert explores identity, relationships, emotions, and mental and physical health through their short stories and graphic works. They're always on the lookout for new artistic collaborations. Seifert graduated from Tel Aviv University with a degree in English Literature and American Studies.

Elton Skelter
Author, "Why We Can't Have Nice Things"
Elton Skelter is a queer horror author from the South West of England, where he lives a quiet life as a part time customer services rep to finance his writing ambitions. He has short stories from *Dark Ink Matter* in the *Bram Stoker Award* and *Splatterpunk Award* Nominated *Human Monsters Anthology* and a story in the *ABCs of Terror Volume 4*, as well as being the *Emerge* featured author for September 2022 from D&T, exclusive to *Godless*. He is currently working on his debut novel, *Life Support*, which will be released in June 2023.

Steven R. Southard
Author, "Turned Off"
Steven R. Southard's stories have appeared in over a dozen anthologies. He has also co-edited the anthology *20,000 Leagues Remembered*. Learn more about him at his website: www.stevenrsouthard.com.

Introducing, on behalf of illustrator *Marco Marin* and graphic designer *Louis Rivera*:
The Minor Arcana of the Science Fiction Tarot!

Manufactured by Amazon.ca
Bolton, ON